KISS AND DON'T TELL

USA TODAY BESTSELLING AUTHOR

MEGHAN QUINN

Prologue

PACEY

Man, I'm a fucking idiot.

Bet you haven't heard that from a man before . . .

Yeah, every man on the face of this earth has uttered those sacred words at least a dozen times.

I've been a fucking idiot so many times, I've lost count.

But this . . .

This is by far the biggest screwup I've ever made.

Oh, you're intrigued? You want to know what qualifies this particular situation as my biggest screwup?

Easy.

One word . . . love.

Okay, okay, I know I'm not the only guy who's fucked up when it comes to love. Frankly, I believe it's human nature to fuck up with matters of the heart. But it's my first time. That's what makes this so special.

Yup, first-timer.

A virgin . . . well, not a sexual virgin, a love virgin. I've had plenty of sex. Not that we need to get into that, but I'm not a virgin.

See, this is the problem. This right here. The rambling, the not using my brain. I would like to blame my almost season-ending injury, but that would be a scapegoat. I'm just a dumbass.

Getting sick of me beating around the bush? If you were in my bed you wouldn't.

I know, I'm annoyed with me too.

Okay, so I fucked up. How? Well, I'll keep it short and simple . . .

Rainstorm.

Random girl shows up at cabin.

Random girl stays with us . . . don't worry, we will get into that.

Random girl turns out to be my half-brother's ex-girlfriend.

She doesn't know.

But I know.

Do you think I tell her?

Nah, why would I do that? That's the intelligent thing to do and as we established, I am a dumbass.

Does she find out? Yup.

Does she get mad? Ohhh yeah.

Does she leave me . . . sad, alone, and love deprived?

One hundred percent.

Do I deserve it?

More than you know.

But more importantly, do you think I should have a chance at winning her heart back?

NO?

What?

Before you decide, just listen to the story. I'm pretty sure you will have a change of heart.

Chapter One

PACEY

"Dude, you're killing the vibe," Hornsby says from the pool. "Don't make me be the dad and make me turn off the Wi-Fi."

Ignoring him, I watch the highlight clip on my phone one more time. Body fake to the left, deke right, crossover, shoots to upper left pocket . . . and he fucking scores.

It was simple.

Any teenager could pull off that move. Hell, I wouldn't even call it a move, I would call it basic hockey skills.

And yet, I didn't stop it.

"Watch it all you want. It's not going to change anything," Taters, our right wing, says.

"But how, *how* did we miss this block?" I toss my phone on my large pool lounger and lean back, pushing my hand through my hair. "It was fucking rudimentary, and I let it go right between my legs."

"That one shot didn't cost us the playoffs," Taters answers. "Everyone had a part in that massive failure of a game."

Yeah, but that one shot was the winning goal, which means the blame still falls on me.

"Nothing you can do about it now, though," says Eli Hornsby, the prettiest fucking defenseman in the game. He places his hands behind his head and lounges back, accepting the loss and allowing himself to relax. Not sure how he can. I'm still reeling from our loss and drop out of the playoffs. "And what's rule number one when we get to the cabin?" he continues.

"No fucking hockey," Posey says before he runs, jumps, and cannonballs into the pool.

Every summer, after the season, me and my boys head up to Banff, Canada, to Silas Taters's cabin—well, mansion, but he calls it a cabin—and we de-stress. We forget about the season, soak up the sun and picturesque mountains, and just . . . fuck around.

The cabin is the perfect place to do that, with views of the Canadian Rocky Mountains, the small-town feel of Banff, being away from Vancouver city life, and far from any sort of training facility—besides the million-dollar gym in the "basement" of the "cabin."

But this year, I'm not quite in the mood to relax. Not when we were so close. So fucking close for our third championship win. I wanted that win. I'm not sure how much time I have left in front of the net, and after we were so close to making it to the finals, for a chance to hold the Stanley Cup over my head again and skate around the ice, knowing that my team, the Vancouver Agitators, are number one—fuck, it burns my soul.

I thought we had it this year. We were the sure win.

A stacked team.

The favorite.

And we fucking blew it.

How can they be so accepting with how the season ended?

"You're scowling," Taters says, splashing water in my direction.

Silas Taters, the fast-as-fuck right wing, currently has a chip on his shoulder for other reasons we won't get into, and he's known for using snarky quips to provoke the people around him, and doing it well. He signed the same year as I did, and I know he wanted this win just as much as I did. So, he's either in denial, or he has a hell of a way of compartmentalizing.

I stand from the lounger and say, "I'm going to grab a drink."

"If you're going to do that, be a gentleman and grab everyone a goddamn drink," Hornsby says.

Eli Hornsby, our team pretty boy. Hell, our league pretty boy. Perfect teeth, perfect nose, perfect face. He's strong as shit, thighs for days, and the horniest motherfucker I've ever met. I think he's slept with every single woman in Vancouver, plus or minus a few. He trains like a badass, parties as though it's his job, eats as if food won't be here tomorrow, and then does it all over again the next day. His lifestyle gives me anxiety, and he's the one always trying to get me to "loosen up."

"You want a chocolate milk?" I ask him.

He rubs his hand over his thick chest. "Milk does do the body good, as you can tell, but bring me a brewski."

Rolling my eyes, I head into the house proper from the indoor pool. Taters says the space is called a natatorium, but that's just a fancy word for a patio enclosed with sliding glass doors. It is nice, though, because you feel like you're outside when the doors are open, but when it's cold, you can turn up the pool heater, close the doors, and still swim.

I enter the kitchen just as Posey closes the fridge. Caught red-handed, he has a piece of bologna hanging out of his mouth and a beer in each hand.

Levi Posey, the dedicated bruiser of our group, and an absolute beast. Known as a teddy bear on the inside but a brutal devil on the ice, you don't want to be smashed into the boards by this guy because it'll feel as though a freight train just took you out.

"Why do you eat that shit?" I ask him.

He takes the bologna out of his mouth and says, "Honestly, I think I have a problem, and I don't even think I want help with it."

Posey is the king of bologna. Before every game he scarfs down a bologna sandwich with mustard. It's vile, and how he can skate the way he does with that churning in his stomach makes me queasy just thinking about it.

"Is one of those beers for sharing?"

He glances down at the drinks and then back at me. "Uh, no. They were both for me."

"Do me a favor and bring Horny and Taters one as well." I move past him and open the fridge. Every shelf is stacked with beer, even the deli drawer where Posey keeps his bologna. We always have a chef come stay with us while we're here. He's really chill and ends up hanging out with us in the evenings. But he's supposed to show up tonight, therefore, the fridge is currently stocked only with beer.

Loads and loads of beer.

So much beer that someone might walk in and think there's a problem in this household. But taking down one can at a time is how we decompress from a long-ass season.

How we relax.

And how we forget.

I grab myself a can and then shut the door. I glance around the living room of the open-concept floor plan and ask, "Where's Holmes?"

"I think on the balcony, that's where I saw him last," Posey answers.

"He have a drink?"

"Nah, not yet."

I reach back into the fridge, grab a beer for Holmes as well, and head upstairs to the balcony, because if I know anything to be true, misery loves company.

"I think he wants to be left alone," Posey calls out to me.

"When does he not want to be left alone?"

I take the steps to the second floor two at a time.

As the only single guys on the team, we, the guys here in the cabin, made a pact to come here during the off-season while our other teammates are off with their families and girlfriends. It works for us.

Especially for Holmes, who prefers to be alone.

I spot him on the balcony, just like Posey said, leaning back in a rocking chair, shoulders slumped, his eyes trained on his lap rather than the majestic view of the mountains in front of him.

Halsey Holmes, center, the best hands on the ice, can snap a puck off the stick so fast you don't even realize he attempted to score until the buzzer is sounding off. He holds the record for most goals and assists. He's the glue that holds the team together on the ice, even though he's falling apart off the ice. Two years ago, he lost his twin brother, Holden, in a car accident. Being one of three Holmes boys playing hockey professionally, Halsey has completely separated himself from his family, ignored life, and has focused on hockey and nothing else. He comes to Banff because we force him. When we leave, we all trade off on helping him through the off-season.

I open the screen door to the balcony. He doesn't even bother to look to see who joined him. I hand him a beer, and he takes it.

"Care if I join?"

"Nope," he says while cracking his beer open.

"I can't be down there right now, with them acting as though we didn't just blow the fucking playoffs." When Holmes doesn't say anything, I continue, "It's been a week and I'm still rethinking that last goal, over and over again."

"You froze," he says, lifting the beer to his lips.

"What?" I ask.

"I saw it happen. The minute Frederic planted his foot to shoot, your body stiffened and you froze."

"I didn't—"

"You still have fear," Holmes continues, not making eye contact with me. "As the goalie, you need to be fearless. Your body isn't yours in the game, your body belongs to the team. You act as if it's still yours, and that's why you missed that block." When I don't say anything, he says, "Prove me wrong."

And that's the shit part, I can't.

It was one fucking hit. One shot . . . and I blacked out.

As a goalie, that's not supposed to bother me. But when I realized there were specific problems, that's when shit got real.

I bring my beer to my mouth and say, "I can't prove you wrong."

And it's true, I can't.

He's fucking right.

If I think about it, I did freeze.

In that moment, when I saw Frederic plant his foot, fear crept up the back of my neck, just like every other time I anticipated a slap shot. But this time, I wasn't quick enough. I let the fear consume me.

Off in the distance, a crack of thunder echoes through the mountains. The once blue sky quickly shifts to gray, the clouds moving a mile a minute.

A storm is coming.

Feels about right.

Because a storm is brewing inside me as well.

"I DON'T THINK Stephan is making it up here tonight," Posey says as he sits at the bar of the kitchen, another piece of bologna in his hand.

"He has to," Hornsby says, looking in the fridge. "We don't have anything to eat besides Chips Ahoy cookies and Cheez-Its."

"Don't forget my bologna," Posey chimes in. "I can make bologna sandwiches for everyone."

"No one wants your goddamn bologna," I say as my stomach rumbles just as loud as the thunder.

The storm picked up quickly. The cell service is spotty at best, the Internet is out, and the windows are being pelted by rain while lightning lights up the dark night sky. It's a rough storm; with every crash of thunder, you can feel the house shake beneath your feet.

Stephan is our chef—the best there is—and unfortunately, I think Posey is right. There's no way he's making it up here. The house is at the top of a steep dirt hill. When it rains like this, that hill turns into a muddy slip and slide. Even Stephan's truck doesn't stand a chance.

"I can live off cookies until morning," Hornsby says while picking up the package. His eyes narrow, he pulls out the plastic sleeve, which he discovers is empty, and turns a furious glare at Posey, who steadfastly refuses to meet his eye.

"What the actual fuck, Posey? You ate all the cookies?"

"How do you know it was me?" He tosses his hand to the side. "It very well could've been Holmes for all we know."

"Wasn't me," Holmes says from the couch where he's reading a book.

Posey could've picked on someone more believable. Holmes is a hermit; he's not going to spend his time in the kitchen scarfing down cookies.

"You're the only one who's been hanging out in the kitchen all day," Taters says, snagging the package from Hornsby. "And who the hell puts the package back like this? That's just a dick move."

"How was I supposed to know there was going to be a storm? If anyone is to blame, it's YOU, Taters. You're the host, you were supposed to provide us with food." Posey has a very valid point.

"I did. I provided you Stephan."

Posey folds his arms over his chest. "I think we know how well that went, you fuck."

Thunder crashes around us, causing us all to sink into our shoulders from the forceful booming sound.

"Think it's too bad to drive into town?" I ask.

Taters laughs. "Unless you're excited about sliding down a dirt road, I'm pretty sure you're going to want to stay put."

It was worth a shot.

"My bologna sandwich is looking more and more delicious, isn't it?" Posey asks with a grin.

Just then, there's a knock at the door.

We all look at each other in surprise.

"Holy shit, Stephan made it?" Taters jogs to the entryway. When he opens the door, he reveals a short, drenched figure. Raincoat on, hood over their head, they stand there shivering as lightning shoots off in the distance. The scene could be picked straight from a horror film, and yet, we all look closer.

"I don't think that's Stephan," Hornsby whispers.

At that moment, lightning strikes what sounds like the roof. There's a brilliant flash of blinding light and a deafening crash, and the stranger's head jerks up, the lightning illuminating the lower half of their rain-soaked face while leaving the rest in hollowed shadows. The velocity of the storm, along with that sudden movement, startles us all backwards. And I can probably vouch for every man in this house when I say our balls just curdled from the horror.

"Jesus, fuck," Posey says, falling out of his chair. "Satan." He points toward the door.

Satan is right. What the actual fuck is this? Why is Taters still holding the door open? Does he not watch horror films at all? This is how people receive an axe to the skull, because they don't slam the door.

The person flips their hood down and collectively we hold our breath while a timid voice says, "No, I swear I'm not a murderer."

That's a girl's voice.

"Turn on the outside light, for fuck's sake," I say.

Taters flips on the light, and the girl's face comes into view, but this is no girl.

Nope, our visitor is a woman with drenched blonde hair, scared eyes, and a perfectly heart-shaped face.

Shivering, she says, "I'm s-sorry to bother you, but my car got stuck in the mud. I saw the lights from the pool and followed them. Do you have any cell service?" The storm booms behind her, causing her to shrink even smaller.

"We don't. Sorry." Taters goes to shut the door, but Hornsby quickly stops him.

"What the hell are you doing?"

Confused, Taters says, "Our phones aren't working, and that's what she's looking for. Clearly, we don't make a match."

"Ask her if she wants to come inside, you idiot."

Taters looks from the girl to Hornsby, and back again. "She could be a murderer." He doesn't bother keeping his voice down.

"She said she wasn't," Posey says while picking at the crumbs in the Chips Ahoy sleeve.

"So we're just going to take her word for it?" Taters asks.

We all turn to the girl for confirmation. When she realizes we're waiting, she stumbles out, "I'm not. I don't do the murdering things. Hell, I don't even know how to murder."

Taters rolls his eyes. "Everyone knows how to murder."

"I don't know how to murder and get away with it," she corrects herself.

Once again, Taters scoffs. "Please, everyone knows a wood-chipper is a solid bet."

"Jesus Christ," I say. "Just let her in."

"What if she's a psycho?" Taters asks. "You want a psycho in here?"

Chiming in, the girl says, "I promise I'm not a psycho. I was just hoping I could use your phone."

"And like I said"—Taters does a dramatic pause as he turns to her again—"they aren't working. So, sorry for the inconvenience, but you should be on your way."

"Holy shit, dude, where the hell is your chivalry?" Hornsby asks, pushing Taters out of the way and holding the door open wider. "Excuse our friend. He's an enneagram six. A stranger in his house is his worst nightmare."

With understanding in her voice, she says, "My best friend is a six. I totally get it. I got her a Ring camera for her birthday and she told me it was the best gift she ever received."

"Was it the Ring Doorbell Pro?" Taters asks, perking up. "Did you get her a spotlight as well? You know you can link them together."

"Ignore him. Come in," Hornsby says.

The girl doesn't move. Instead, she scans the space. "I don't want to bother you. Your phones aren't working, so there really is no reason for me to be here."

"Where are you going to go?" Hornsby asks.

"I don't know, back to my car, I guess, to wait out the storm."

"You'll be waiting for a while." Hornsby nods inside. "Seriously, we don't mind."

She glances around again, and when her eyes land on me, taking me in, I have a moment of déjà vu. She looks . . . familiar. "Not to sound rude or anything, but it seems as if you're a bunch of big guys. I have nothing with me but my backpack, which despite my best friend begging me to fill it with self-defense items, is instead stuffed with snacks. I'm not sure I could trust *you* not to murder *me*."

"You have snacks?" Taters asks, sounding more welcoming.

"I do," she says skeptically, backing up.

"He's not going to take them." Hornsby pushes Taters completely away. "Ignore him. His blood sugar is low. And yes, we might be big and intimidating, but we aren't murderers. We're Agitators."

She backs away again. "That doesn't sound reassuring."

"Vancouver," Hornsby clarifies.

But not an ounce of comprehension crosses her face, just nerves and uncertainty.

"We play professional hockey," I say, clarifying, because who really understands someone just saying the word Vancouver? Her eyes land on me, dark lashes highlighting concerned pupils, and I swear they feel like heat rays, zooming in on me.

I know her. I swear I fucking do. But from where?

Turning away from me, she says, "I don't watch hockey."

All the guys groan together as Taters quickly goes on the defensive. Every time someone says they don't watch hockey—which isn't too often, given we all live in Canada—Taters makes it his mission to find out why.

"You don't watch hockey? Is there a reason for that?" His body language reads that he's ready to fight.

"Uh, better things to do?" she asks as the wind picks up, shooting some of the rain into the house.

"Better things to do?" Taters asks in disbelief. He shakes his head and thumbs toward her. "I was right about this one, she needs to move on."

"Cut the shit," Hornsby says. "Not everyone watches hockey. Are they making poor decisions in their life? Yes, but we're not here to judge. We're here to help." He turns back to the girl. "Seriously, we're not going to hurt you. It would be stupid on our end. Bad publicity. We're good guys. I promise."

"How do I know you're telling the truth? That you're hockey players?"

Hornsby pulls out his phone. "You can look us up."

"Internet is out," I say.

"Fuck." He sticks his phone back in his pocket and then thinks for a second.

"I know." He pulls out the umbrellas from the umbrella stand and tosses one to Posey and one to Taters. He doesn't bother with Holmes, because we all know he hasn't even lifted his head since our visitor knocked on the door. Then he snags a coaster off the coffee table and says, "Let's show her. Lawes, set up a goal."

"Seriously?" I ask.

His eyes land on me. "Yes, I'm fucking serious."

Sighing, I push two bar stools to the side in front of the island, using the counter as the top of the goal and the chairs as the side. I stand in front of the goal and get in position.

"Now, watch carefully as we display our extreme athleticism." Hornsby, our defenseman, drops the coaster on the floor and moves it back and forth with the tip of the umbrella. It's comical that he's attempting to have some semblance of coordination like Holmes. "This isn't ideal, especially being guarded by two players. Holmes, I could use your help."

"Nope," he says.

With a sigh, Hornsby says, "Taters, you're out. Make this two on one."

"Fine by me." Taters takes a seat and uses the umbrella as a mic. "I'll announce."

Hating every second of this, I watch as Hornsby gets in position, Posey defending him. Together, they tap the ground and then each other's umbrellas. They do this three times, and then Hornsby snags the coaster and spins toward me. Look at Horny, making the moves—most likely trying to impress the girl since he's not playing his actual position right now. Posey is right on his ass, though, using his shoulder like he does best as he reaches for the coaster.

"Welcome to an impromptu exhibition of umbrella coaster athleticism," Taters says. "Guarding the goal tonight, we have Pacey Lawes. Quick on his feet, he's a menace in front of the net. They're going to have to work hard to squeak something by him. Socking across the hardwood floor, we have Eli Hornsby with the green umbrella, struggling to keep the coaster close to him, or to even slide across the floor. I believe he's regretting his choice of puck at the moment."

"Accurate," Hornsby says, his voice tight.

"And with the yellow umbrella, we have one of the best defensemen in the league. Unafraid to throw a punch and then end the night with a bologna sandwich, Levi Posey sticks to Horny like glue."

"Don't call me that in front of company," Hornsby says as he spins toward me. I keep my eye on the coaster, ready to make a grab for whatever shot he attempts.

"Horny is zeroing in on his target, but will he be able to get by the Chips Ahoy annihilator? Or will an entire pack of cookies affect Posey's ability to move quickly enough to steal the coaster away?"

"Really feeling those cookies?" I ask.

"Light as a feather over here," Posey says, grappling for the coaster.

"Knock it off with your goddamn elbows," Hornsby says as he takes the coaster the other way, then switches back.

"He's closing in. This goal will be his. I can feel it," Taters says. "Signature move. Deke to the left, spins and . . ."

Hornsby flicks the umbrella, shooting the coaster to the upper left side of the "goal." Without even a second thought, I reach up and block the coaster. Hornsby had no chance.

"And the coaster is stopped by Lawes, a block he could've easily done in his sleep. That must sting for our dear friend Horny."

"Uh, what about my superior defense?" Posey asks.

"I think it was the take down of the Chips Ahoy package that helped you. You were unmovable."

Done with this, I toss the coaster on the counter and take a seat at the island again while Hornsby shoves his umbrella in the stand. He pushes his hair back and asks, "So, does that help?"

The girl stands there, holding the straps of the backpack resting on her shoulders, taking in the scene. I don't blame the absolute confused look on her face right now. Hell, I'd pay good money to know exactly what she must be thinking at this moment.

"Uh, no, just made you more insane. And the nickname 'Horny' doesn't help either."

"They're idiots," Hornsby says.

"Here," Holmes says from the couch, handing over his phone.

Taters walks over to him and takes his phone in his hand. "You have the team photo on your phone?"

Holmes doesn't say anything. Instead, he goes back to his book.

Hornsby snags the phone and shows it to the girl, who examines the photo intently. Smirking, she asks, "Why aren't you all smiling? It's a team photo, after all."

"Athletes aren't supposed to smile in photos," Taters says. "We're supposed to be intimidating."

"Oh, was that the look you were going for? You look more constipated than anything."

We all bust out in laughter as Taters snatches the phone from her. "You realize this is my house you're trying to gain access to, right? Referring to me as constipated isn't going to grant you access, but rather punch your ticket out of here."

"Settle the fuck down," Hornsby says. "Come on, at least dry off for a bit. We have Cheez-Its and bologna sandwiches and plenty of beer. Maybe we can find some cell service while waiting it out."

She still seems suspicious but instead of backing away this time, she steps into the entryway.

"Let me take that for you," Hornsby says as he reaches for her backpack.

She sheds her backpack and then takes off her raincoat as well, revealing an hourglass figure in a pair of black leggings and a tight red top that shows off her cleavage.

Damn.

I think I know what's going through every guy's mind in this house—besides Holmes, who hasn't lifted his head from his book—this girl is hot.

But the question is, are they having déjà vu thoughts like I am? Because I swear I've seen her face before.

Chapter Two

WINNIE

Oh God, they're all looking at me.

I've never in my life been in a room with this many solidly attractive men.

I'm pretty sure the one they keep calling Horny is a Disney prince reincarnated. Solid jawline and just a beautiful face. Frankly, he's too pretty.

Potato, I think that's his name, the one who owns the house, he's got that whole "I don't care about my appearance" look, when we all know he does, which of course makes him even hotter.

The cookie monster has sincerely one of the best smiles I think I've ever seen. Full of boyish charm, it makes me want to smile just looking at him.

I can't see much of the book guy other than his hands, and wow, those are big.

And then there's the goalie. I can't quite recall his name. Lawes, maybe? I was too distracted by his glacial-blue eyes and his dark blond hair. It's longer than I prefer on a guy, hitting him just below his chin, but it's incredibly sexy on him. Not sure it's his eyes or the beachy waves in his hair, but he intimidates me, more so than the pretty boy.

But the thing that bothers me the most about the goalie is there's something vaguely familiar about him. As if I've seen him before.

I really shouldn't be here. Katherine, my best friend and personal bodyguard, would have a heart attack if she knew I just walked into a strange house full of burly men I've never met before, men who could easily capture me and hide me in their basement—her words most likely. Every situation I'm in always ends with me held in a basement by my captor, according to her. It took lots of convincing and leaving WITHOUT her blessing in order for me to go on this trip. And I had to promise that if I did wind up in a captor's basement, that if I called her for help, she gets to tell me "I told you so" first.

I hope stepping into this house isn't going to prove her right.

But what other options do I really have? I don't think I would be able to find my car in this storm. I almost slipped and fell multiple times just trying to make it to this house. I can't imagine going back out there, looking for another safe haven.

When my car got stuck, I realized that I had one option, fill my backpack with as much from my suitcase as I could, along with food and water, and hope for the best.

I'm standing in my only option.

Hand to his chest, the nice one says, "I'm Eli Hornsby. That's Silas Taters, the owner of the house and your gracious host. On the couch is Halsey Holmes. I doubt you'll have any interaction with him at all. He keeps to himself. Over there with the big smile, that's Levi Posey. He likes bologna sandwiches. And then at the kitchen bar is Pacey Lawes. His first name has nothing to do with the show *Dawson's Creek*. Just a coincidence. He likes to let everyone know this."

Pacey.

I love that name. Matches his looks totally.

"And you are . . ."

"Winnie," I answer. "No correlation to Winnie the Pooh, just a coincidence." I smirk, and when I glance over at Pacey, I get a smile from him as well.

"What about Winnie from *The Wonder Years*?" Levi asks.

I point at him. "Now that I can't be too sure of. Given my mom was a huge fan of Fred Savage, I could see the correlation."

"My dad was obsessed with her," Levi says. "I remember watching reruns with him and him telling me over and over about how much he thought he was going to marry Winnie Cooper when he got older. Spoiler alert—he didn't marry Winnie Cooper, but rather got a lady named Yessica pregnant. A classic drunken night. They didn't get married, my dad claimed custody, and here I am, a product of whiskey. I think that's why I like it so much. Whiskey, that is. Fucking good."

Eli clears his throat. "Posey is a talker."

"Do you call each other by your last names?" I ask. "Because I'm barely hanging on to who everyone is." I point to the homeowner. "I know I heard your name, but all I can think of is potato. And I know that's not your name, but that's what I want to call you. And Eli, right? I'm having a hard time discerning if you're Eli or Horny."

"Both," Levi says. "And you can call us whatever you'd prefer. Personally, I think I might start calling Taters 'Potato'. Has a nice ring to it."

"Don't even fucking think about it," Potato says, walking past me with a huff.

I can sense we're not going to be friends.

"Are you hungry?" Eli asks. "We don't have a lot of food, but we can offer you a beer and a bologna sandwich. Our chef was supposed to come up tonight and make us some food, but because of the storm, we're pretty sure he won't be making his way up here tonight. Hopefully tomorrow."

"Well, I don't want to eat what little you have. I can dig into my backpack for something."

"What, uh, what do you have?" Levi asks while motioning with his finger at my backpack. That smile of his is totally disarming.

I walk over to where Eli set down my backpack and unzip it. After moving my clothes to the side and digging to the bottom, I take out a bunch of protein bars, some applesauce pouches, and quite a few trail mix packages.

"Whoa, we hit the jackpot," Eli says and then turns to Potato. "Aren't you glad we invited her in? She has your favorite kind of Quest Bar. Birthday cake."

"Is that, uh, is that the flavor?" Potato says, stretching his neck to get a better look.

I pick up a birthday cake Quest Bar and chuck it over at Potato, who catches it with one hand.

"Whoa, nice toss, Winnie," Eli says.

"Thanks, I used to play softball. Played in college too." I hold up a Clif Bar and say, "Peanut butter up for grabs."

"I'll take that one," Eli says. He snags a blueberry muffin, too, and tosses it toward the guy with the book. Halsey, I think they said his name is. "Heads up, Holmes. Blueberry, your favorite."

Halsey turns from his book for a split second to catch the bar and then buries himself in the pages again.

"Don't worry about me, I'm going to have a bologna sandwich," Levi says. "Want me to make one for you?"

"You know, a bologna sandwich sounds pretty good, actually," I answer.

Levi perks up. "I think I just found my newest best friend." He lifts off his chair and goes to the fridge.

"Under one condition," I say, and he pauses. "I watch you make it right in front of me. I need to make sure no drugs are slipped in there. You know, just making sure when I do get in touch with my friend that I can tell her I checked all the boxes in safety . . . besides the whole eating a meal in a stranger's house thing."

The guys laugh and Eli says, "You knocked on the wrong door. We're not in the business of drugging women, capturing them, or keeping them as our prey. We're just trying to relax after a long-ass season."

"Sounds a little like me," I answer honestly. "Besides the playing hockey thing." Turning toward Pacey and trying not to get lost in his eyes or stutter while I speak to him, I ask, "Would you like a protein bar?"

He eyes the pile of protein bars on the floor and his lips twist to the side as he decides. I find the little quirk of his lips endearing.

"I'll take the apple pie and a pack of trail mix . . . that's if it's okay."

"Of course," I say. My hand feels shaky as I pick up his order and toss it to him. He catches with ease and then smiles at me.

"Thanks."

"Yeah, sure," I answer shyly.

"I have the ingredients prepped," Levi says. "Ready to watch?"

Looking away from Pacey, I say, "Yup, ready." I walk over to the kitchen counter, on the opposite side of Pacey, and consider just how insane this entire situation is.

I know any other intelligent human being would not have come into this house. Especially any other single girl alone with no cell service.

But here I am, about to eat a bologna sandwich, sharing my snacks, and getting wrapped up into this once-in-a-lifetime situation where I'm trapped in a cabin with a bunch of professional hockey players.

You can't make this up. They played a game of "hockey" with coasters and umbrellas to prove who they were. That is—grown-up boys.

I'm just grateful to be out of the rain. If I'm taken into the basement later, then so be it.

But . . . please, Jesus, don't let this be a basement abduction.

———

"ADMIT IT," Levi says while elbowing me.

We're sitting at the dining room table meant for twelve, but we only take up half of the table. I'm sitting at the head of the table, between Eli and Levi, the two friendliest out of the bunch, and we're finishing up our "dinner."

"It's good. Tell the boys just how good that sandwich was."

I swallow and wipe my mouth with my napkin. "Besides the bread sticking to the roof of my mouth, it was pretty darn good."

"The bread sticking to the roof of your mouth is all part of the bologna and Wonder Bread experience."

"If that's the case, then ten out of ten."

Levi smacks the table and points to all the guys. "Told you, fuckers. Regretting it now, aren't you?"

"Not even a little," Potato says, leaning back in his chair and bringing a bottle of water to his lips.

"You know, we never asked, what brought you up here? Where were you headed?" Eli asks.

"Coming from Seattle," I say, keeping things vague. Yes, they seem nice, but they also don't need to know my life story. "Decided to head up here, take some time off. Never been and Banff has been on my bucket list, so I hopped in my car and started driving."

"From Seattle?" Levi asks. "That's almost twelve hours."

I shrug. "Put on one of my favorite podcasts. I left around seven this morning. Hasn't been terrible."

"Are you staying in town?" Eli asks.

"Uh, not sure. Haven't thought that far."

The boys all exchange looks and the silence between them starts to make me nervous.

"What's going on?" I ask.

"You don't have reservations or anything?" Levi asks.

"No, I figured I'd find something when I got up here."

Eli cringes and says, "I would be impressed if you found vacancy anywhere. Banff is really popular this time of the year, especially for the views. I'm not sure you're going to find anything open."

My hope falls. "Really? Here I was, trying to be spontaneous. I didn't even consider lodging." I think about my car stuck in the mud. If I can get it unstuck, there's enough room in the back seat. "Looks as if I might be crashing in my car, then." I try to laugh it off but none of the guys laugh.

"If you're worried about being abducted, sleeping in your car is a surefire way to make that happen," Pacey says, keeping his eyes trained on his water bottle. He hasn't said much this entire "dinner" but when he does talk, for some reason it feels as if I hang on his every word.

I don't know what it is about him, he's not really elusive or broody like the men are in all those books I read. He's just . . . uninterested?

Wow, that says a lot about me.

Get it together, Winnie.

"Why are you up here, again?" Eli asks.

"Adventure," I say, swallowing down the real truth. "So, you know, I can just travel back. No biggie." I shrug and pass it off as nothing, even though in the back of my head I'm panicking.

This is exactly what Katherine didn't want to happen. She didn't want me traveling alone, getting lost, and then, once again, abducted and with no cell service, of course. And apparently now, half the food I arrived with.

Not smart, Winnie, not smart at all.

Seeing that the rain has let up, I know I've probably overstayed my welcome, so I stand from the table and say, "Well, thank you for the company and the opportunity to get dry, but I don't want to keep you guys any longer from enjoying your time off together."

"Great," Potato says, standing as well. "It was nice of you to stop by."

"What the actual fuck, Silas?" Eli says. "You're not kicking her out."

"I'm not." He motions to me. "She's on her way out. I was being polite and saying thank you for stopping by."

"And where the fuck do you think she's going to go?" Eli asks.

"Uh, back to her car?"

"I'm uncomfortable when Mom and Dad fight," Levi says, pulling at a cloth napkin.

Leaning in close, Pacey asks, "Which one is Mom?"

With that signature smile, Levi says, "Taters, of course. Easily the bottom."

"Fuck you, I'm not the mom." Turning back to Eli, he says, "If she wants to leave, let her leave."

"I really don't want to cause any trouble," I say, taking a step back. "I was just hoping you guys had a phone I could use. I really appreciate you letting me stay for a little bit. It's been quite kind." I turn and head toward the door. Behind me, Eli and Potato argue while I gather my things.

It's obvious Potato doesn't want me here, and I'm not about to make someone uncomfortable in their own house. I take my jacket off the coat rack and notice that it's still wet. That's fine, it's drizzling out anyway, and if I find my car—that's a big if—I have more clothes in there.

God, this is idiotic.

I shouldn't have left the car in the first place. But fear took over, I saw some lights in the distance, and I followed them. Which brought me here. Much good that did.

I start to put my jacket on when a strong hand lands on my shoulder.

I turn to find Pacey staring down at me.

"You're not going anywhere," he says quietly while taking my jacket. Eli and Potato are still arguing. Halsey is back on the couch, reading, and Levi is watching "Mom and Dad" while nervously fidgeting in his chair.

"That's o-okay," I stutter, feeling incredibly intimidated by his intense blue eyes. "I really don't want to impose anymore."

Still talking quietly, he asks, "And where are you going to go?"

"Back to my car."

"And where is that?"

I swallow hard and wave my hand toward the door. "You know, that way."

"I see."

Just then Eli comes up to us as Potato storms off. "Sorry about that." Eli looks behind him and then back at me. "It's nothing against you. Taters is working through a bad breakup with a girl he's been with since high school. As you can see, he's not handling it well."

"Oh, that's awful." I look off toward the hallway he just stormed down. "I'm sorry to hear that."

"It seems any female will piss him off at the moment, so it's nothing against you, just your sex."

I nod. "Well, I don't want to make him even more mad while he's on vacation." I reach for my jacket but Pacey doesn't allow me to take it. "If you don't mind."

With concerned eyes, Eli says, "It's eleven at night, you have no clue where your car is, it's still drizzling out, and the roads are mud. You're not going to do anything but get into more trouble if you leave now. There are plenty of bedrooms here. Please just stay the night, and in the morning, we can help you find your car." When I don't say anything, Eli adds, "My parents would fucking murder me if they knew I let you leave here."

"I can show you to your room," Pacey says, picking up my backpack and hoisting it over his shoulder.

I look between the two men who I just met, and even though I still feel as if this isn't a good idea, I don't think my other option is better. Warm bed, or cold, frigid night trying to find my car while sinking into the mud. One comes with possible abduction—although, I think we might have established these guys are okay—the other comes with possible broken bones.

Succumbing, I say, "Okay."

"Good." Eli looks behind him again. "I'm going to go check on Taters. Lawes, you don't mind showing her to her room?"

"Nah, I got it," Pacey says casually. He nods toward a hallway in the opposite direction Potato went. "Come this way."

As I start to walk away, Levi holds up his hand in a wave while he picks at the trail mix Potato didn't finish. "Have a good night. See you in the morning."

He's funny.

"Good night," I call out, and then I follow Pacey down the hallway. He turns on lights as we walk, and I can't help but notice the way the lights shine down on his back muscles and how they pull against the fabric of his light blue T-shirt. It's unmistakable the man is an athlete with his broad, thick shoulders and his narrow waist and . . . oh God, he has a nice butt.

A really nice butt.

All bubbly and tight—

"This okay?" he asks as we stop. My eyes quickly retreat from staring at his ass and up to his face. God, did he catch me?

Do not stare at the man's ass, Winnie. Honestly, what is wrong with you?

"Oh yeah, this is—" I finally look at the bedroom, and oh my God, it's gorgeous. Just like the rest of the house, which is styled with gray-washed woods, the ceiling is vaulted with wooden beams, accentuating its height, and a gorgeous clear chandelier dangles from above. The black, wrought-iron canopy bed is impeccably made with white and light blue linens, and makes the entire room seem like a dream. And right across from the bed is a fireplace with a comfortable-looking rug placed in front with an accompanying sitting chair.

Uh, yeah, this is looking much better than my car right now.

"This is more than I could ask for. Honestly, I could just sleep on the couch."

Pacey walks into the room. "You're not sleeping on the couch when there are plenty of empty rooms for you to stay in." He sets my backpack in front of the fireplace and then reaches around to the side and flips on a switch. The fire roars to life.

Wow.

Just wow.

"That was fancy."

He looks up at me, a smirk on his face. "If you found that impressive, wait until you try out the heated towel rack."

What is this life? Did I stumble into an alternate reality where I get to stay at a five-star resort with a bunch of hunky hockey players? Pretty sure I'm maxing out my luck right about now.

"Bathroom is in there." Pacey points to a closed door. "Everything is stocked that you might need. I'm pretty sure there are some spare clothes in the closet for men and women. Taters likes to be that kind of host, even though it might not seem like it, and if you need anything, I'm two doors down on the right."

"Okay. Um, thank you. This was very kind of you."

He moves toward the door and I quickly step out of his way. He stops at the door and looks over his shoulder. The scruff on his jaw is accentuated by the light of the fire. "If you're still worried about abduction, then I suggest locking the door and shimmying that chair over there under the handle." With that, he winks—my bosom heaves—and then he takes off, quietly closing the door behind him.

I inwardly squeal and thank my lucky stars that this night didn't end up worse than it could've been.

Maybe Mom really is helping me on this trip. I take a seat

on the bed and lie back on the plush comforter so I'm staring up at the vaulted ceiling.

Squeezing my eyes shut, I allow myself to be thankful.

Very, very grateful.

I'll enjoy this comfortable bed and warm fire tonight, and tomorrow morning, I'll make a plan. I'll find a place to stay, and I'll get my car out of the mud.

I came up here for a reason, and now that I'm here, I need to figure out how to follow through.

Chapter Three

PACEY

"Mornin'," I say as I walk past Holmes, who's reading at the kitchen bar.

"Morning," he says, his head stuck in his book.

It's five thirty in the morning, and despite wanting to sleep in, it was next to impossible after all the "excitement" last night. Holmes is always an early riser, doesn't care to sleep in much. But I also think that's because he wrestles his demons when he's asleep. I also think it's why he gets lost in his books, so he doesn't have to face reality.

"You know, it wouldn't kill you to make coffee for us if you're up this early," I tease him.

"Why make it if I don't drink it?"

"You drink it."

"On occasion." He closes his book and lays it face down.

I scoop coffee into the filter. "What are you reading?"

"Some fucked-up thriller." He places his hand behind his head and stretches. "Think you should wear a shirt."

I glance down at my bare chest and then back up at Holmes. "Am I turning you on?"

His face remains stoic. "There's a girl in the house."

"Think she's never seen a bare chest before?"

"It's respectful."

I shrug. "She probably won't be up for a while. She seems really happy with the guest room." I start the coffee and then lift myself up on the counter. "Kind of crazy that she stumbled over here, right?"

Holmes nods. "Yeah. Better us than someone else."

I scratch the side of my cheek, still trying to wake up. "Taters was a dick about it."

"He wanted a guys' trip. Having her here fucks that up."

"It's one night." I roll my eyes. "There's no way in hell we would've turned her out."

"Yeah, that wouldn't have happened." Holmes stares at me for a few seconds and then says, "You seemed to like her."

My brow creases. "How would you even know? You were buried in your book most of the night."

He shrugs. "I see things."

"You're delusional."

He shrugs again and opens up his book again.

"I mean, yeah, she's good-looking."

He nods but doesn't look up at me.

"And, sure, I think her curves are nice."

I see him lift his brow, but he still stares down at his book.

"And am I a little curious why she's in Banff with no reservations . . . and alone? Sure, but anyone would be."

He makes a sound under his breath.

"And does she remind me of someone?"

Holmes lifts a brow. *Again.*

"Maybe she does, but I'm having a hard time putting my finger on it. But that's beside the point. I wasn't expecting a girl to come tumbling in here last night. Just shocked. Surprised, is all."

Holmes leans back in his chair and lifts his book up.

"And call me crazy, but I think there's something she's not telling us. Like, some mystery she's trying to solve. I mean, who comes up here without a reservation? Especially in today's age when technology sits in the palm of your hand? Seems weird, doesn't it?"

My coffee starts brewing, the bubbling sweetness of caffeine almost ready.

"But we don't need to worry about it because she'll be out of here today. Just going to be one of those stories we talk about when we're older." In an old man voice, I say, "Remember the time that girl came to the cabin in the middle of a thunderstorm and she gave us Quest Bars as a peace offering? That's quite the story our grandchildren would get a kick out of."

Holmes continues to be silent so I drop it at that and jump down from the counter to get a coffee cup.

"Oh, I didn't think anyone would be up," a shocked feminine voice says from the living room.

I turn to find Winnie standing there in a pair of leggings and a tight-fitting green shirt, different from the red she wore yesterday, but still the same shape. Meaning, once again, she's showing off those curves that I seem to enjoy.

But when I look at her face, I not only notice she took a shower, but I see the way her eyes are scanning my chest.

My bare chest.

Hell, Holmes was right, I should've worn a shirt.

For some reason, I feel like picking up two coffee mugs so I can hold them in front of my nipples to cover up.

"Early birds," I say awkwardly. "I thought, uh, that you'd sleep longer. I can go put on a shirt."

"Oh, don't worry about that. I mean, if you want to put a shirt on, please put one on, but don't put one on because of me. I've seen a man's chest before. I mean, not quite as fit and muscular as yours, but, I mean . . . not that I was looking. Obviously I looked, but I wasn't staring. I just noticed, is all. But, sure, if you want to put a shirt on, go ahead, but not on my account. I'm fine. Not offended by your nakedness." She takes a deep breath. "You're not naked. That's normal for a man, to not wear a shirt." She thumbs toward the door. "Well, this has been embarrassing, I'm going to go now. Can you thank the guys for me?"

"Wait. You're leaving?" I ask.

She nods. "Yeah, figured I should go find my car; I took up enough of your vacation time."

For some reason, I don't feel comfortable with her going out there alone, especially since all the woods and roads are new to her. So instead of letting her leave, I say, "I'll go with you."

I catch a smirk from Holmes, but choose to ignore it.

"Oh no, that's not necessary at all."

Forgetting the coffee, I ask, "Do you know your way around these roads?"

"I mean, it can't be too hard, right? I have a general idea. Nothing a little poking around won't solve."

"You have no idea where you are." I move past her and down the hall. "Be right back." I jog toward my room, past hers. I glance in to see her bed made and as if nothing was touched. I make it to my room, snag a shirt from my dresser, and slip on my socks and running shoes. I throw my hair up into a man bun and then jog back down the hallway, where I see Winnie putting on her shoes.

When she spots me, she says, "Seriously, you don't need to help me."

"And there's no way I'm going to let you go out there alone. Not only do you not know where you're going, but it's probably slippery, and you might need help getting around."

She stands tall after tying her shoes and puts her hands on her hips. "You think I'm going to fall on my ass?" There's a sassy tone in her voice that makes me smirk.

"With that kind of attitude, I very well might be wrong."

"You are." She lifts her backpack, but I snag it from her hand and slip it over my shoulder. "I can carry that." Her protest falls flat.

"I know you can. So can I." I walk to the front door and open it for her, but she just stands in the living room, staring at me. "Are you staying now?" I ask.

"No, but I don't like to be bossed around."

A snort comes from Holmes at the kitchen table. He's getting way too much joy out of this.

"I can see that, but remember, I'm doing this out of the kindness of my own heart, so maybe you just follow along."

"I didn't ask for your help."

"Trust me, you need it." I head out the door and hope that she follows behind me. When I hear her irritated footsteps pound behind me, I smile to myself. The door shuts and I turn to find her standing with her arms crossed, her jacket clutched in one arm.

The sun is already rising, making it much easier to see than last night, and I notice the moment she takes in the sights for the first time. Her eyes widen in awe and her mouth pops open slightly. The tension in her shoulders from our small dispute eases.

The sun peeks through the tall, whispering pines, which stretch what seems like a mile high. Moss blankets the ground and in the far distance, the beautiful Rocky Mountains in all their glory, stretching across the landscape, majestic and the perfect backdrop for a peaceful vacation.

"Told you it was different in the daylight."

"Wow." Her eyes travel up the height of the trees. "It's gorgeous here. No wonder why you like to come here for relaxation." She's silent for a second and then says, "Listen to that, just the sounds of the birds chirping, a creek bubbling in the background, nature surrounding you. It's incredibly peaceful."

I nod toward the back of the house. "You should see the backyard. Taters set it up so there's an outdoor kitchen and patio, but in the far back, past the lawn games, there are different seating areas. There's an egg chair—that's what he calls it—and from where I've positioned it, you get the perfect view of Cascade Mountain. Breathtaking."

"I can imagine."

She seems to have calmed down now so I take advantage of that. "Come on, I'll help you find your car. I run these roads all the time. Give me a direction and I think I could find your car."

She sighs and walks up to me, succumbing to my offer. "You run while on vacation?"

"Yeah. I like exercising. Helps me clear my head."

"Maybe I should have that kind of attitude. Help me shed down these thighs of mine."

That would be a detriment. I like thick thighs.

"Nah, you're good," I say casually, and to change the subject so I don't say something stupid—like, I like thick thighs—I ask, "Do you remember what direction you came from?"

She pauses and takes in the driveway of the cabin and then points at the mailbox.

"I remember almost running into that mailbox and I was walking downhill, so I came from the left."

I nod. "That would've been my guess, but I wanted to make sure. Did you stay on the road?"

"Yes," she answers. "I know that for sure—at least, I thought I was staying on the road." She winces.

"If you weren't on the road, you'd have tripped over logs and fallen trees. Did you trip?"

She shakes her head. "No, just slid around in mud."

"Then we're good." We head up the slight incline, and because my legs are much longer than hers, I take it slow.

"You really don't have to do this, you know," she says softly. "But I do appreciate the help."

"Not as if I have any plans for the day. You could've stayed for breakfast, though, you know. It would've been a breakfast of Cheez-Its and black coffee, but at least it's something."

She chuckles. "Although the fine dining at your place is nice, I didn't want to impose any more than I did. I know Potato, uh, I mean . . . uh, God, I don't even know his name."

"Potato?" I laugh hard. "Oh shit. You mean Taters?"

"Yes, him. What's his name?"

"Silas Taters."

"That's right. It's so confusing with you guys using last names and first names, I can't remember everybody."

"Do you remember my name?" I ask, eyebrow raised.

"Yes." Her cheeks turn red.

"And what is it?"

"Pacey."

"Then you know the most important name in the house. But Potato, that's one I'm going to keep in the back of my head."

"Oh God, don't tell him I said it. He already hates me."

I scoff. "Taters doesn't hate you. He's just in a bad head-space right now. I'm sure he'll feel like a dick at some point for the way he acted. He always does, then he goes on the tour of apologies."

"Well, either way, I think it was best that I was out of the house before he woke up, just in case."

"Hornsby will probably be heartbroken that he didn't get to say goodbye."

"That's Eli, right?"

"Yeah."

"He was so nice. A real champion for women."

I laugh. "Yeah, and the biggest player you'll ever meet."

"Really?" she asks, seeming completely surprised.

"Oh yeah. Well, to be fair, he always lets the girls he's with know his intentions from the very beginning. He's not looking for a relationship, just a good time. He's *not into breaking hearts*, is what he tells us. But I know, one day, when he's least expecting it, some girl is going to come spinning into his life and flip his world upside down. Offer him a real challenge, and that's the girl he'll end up falling for."

"That's so shocking. That is not how I saw it." She shakes her head.

"Oh yeah? How did you see it?"

She glances at me quickly and then looks away. "You don't want to know."

"Wouldn't ask if I didn't." She's quiet, so I bump my shoulder against hers. "Come on, give me your first impressions."

"Are you sure you want to hear this?"

"Obviously."

"Okay, I warned you, though." She clears her throat. "Well, Halsey—that's his name, right?"

"Yup."

"He's an easy one. Damaged and working through demons. He hangs out so he's not alone, but likes to be alone. If that makes sense."

"Very accurate," I answer just as she slips on some mud. I reach out and catch her arm before she falls forward.

"Whoa, close one." She laughs nervously. "Thank you." She slowly lets go of my hand as she straightens out. "Uh, Silas—"

"Aka, Potato."

She chuckles. "Yes, Potato—I pegged as just a general asshole because of the way he treated me. A rich guy who has better things to do than hand out charity."

"Eh, he can be an asshole, but also really generous. I think you caught him on a bad night. Like we said last night, he's fresh from a breakup and not taking it well."

"I can understand that, which is why I'm not fully pegging him as an asshole. That title is pending. Now, Levi—he was my favorite last night."

"Posey was your favorite?" My brows lift in surprise. "How the hell did he win that title?"

She shrugs. "He was funny and kind of a ditz. Was concerned about filling his stomach more than anything, didn't have a care in the world when it came to a stranger in the house, and then waved goodnight to me like a little boy. I don't know, he just made my heart happy. And he has a great smile."

"The son of a bitch does have a great smile. I thought you were going to say Hornsby was your favorite, since he was a champion for women."

The sun beats down on us, even this early in the morning. She wraps her jacket around her waist and ties it securely. "Eli was incredibly sweet and I was very grateful to him. But not my favorite. I also thought that maybe he was . . . gay."

I pause and then full-on belly laugh. "Gay? You thought Hornsby was gay?"

"He's too pretty," she says. "He was so clean-cut and perfect. No offense, but I've never seen a man that well put together who wasn't gay. This coming from a girl whose best friend is gay. I've seen many gay men."

"I thought your best friend is a girl."

"A girl can have more than one best friend. Katherine is my overbearing, overprotective friend who would rather hide behind a spray of disinfectant than go see a movie, and then Max is my other best friend. The one who said to live my best life and come up here. And Eli reminded me of him. Just . . . beautiful to look at."

I scratch the side of my face. "Hornsby is a pretty boy, that's for damn sure, but he's also very much into women. Unless he's trying to overcompensate for something I don't know about. The man is as straight as they come. I do have a gay teammate, though. He came out last year. Proud of the guy."

"Really? Who?"

"Ian Rivers."

"Hmm, that name is familiar. Maybe I read it in the news." She slips again, but this time catches herself before I have to help.

"His coming out was all over the news. Pretty badass, actually." I nudge her shoulder again. "What about me? What was your first impression?"

"Now, this . . . I don't think you want to hear."

"Ooh, must be good, then. Go ahead, give it to me."

She lets out a long breath. "You asked for it." She pushes her hair behind her ear and says, "I thought you were the player, not Eli."

"Me?" I point to my chest. "Why me?"

"I never met a man who looked like you, with the topknot, who wasn't a player. Plus, you just have this whole . . . I don't know, tempting look about you. And whereas Eli was very welcoming, you were kind of indifferent, so I figured you were the one who played around."

I drag my hand over my jaw. "Or maybe I'm just shy. Ever think about that?"

"You're not shy right now."

"Because I'm in my element and I don't have to look you in the eyes. Trust me, if we were face to face, this would be a different interaction."

She pauses in the road, and I stop as well. I lift my eyes to her deep blue ones and I feel a bolt of electricity zap between us. Fuck, I know this girl from somewhere, I really do, but just from our brief conversation, I'm getting the feeling that she doesn't know me at all. There's not even an ounce of recognition in her eyes. So, am I fucking crazy? Am I losing my mind? I'm not one of those people who believes in multiple lives, but . . . did I know her in another life?

Humor in her eyes, she asks, "Are you implying that I intimidate you?"

I grip the back of my neck. "You know, just never been too good with girls, is all, let alone pretty ones." It's not a line; there's no humor in my voice. It's just plain facts. I've never been the guy who prowls around with girls fainting at his feet.

Her cheeks blush.

Hell, my cheeks blush.

And then she starts walking forward again. "You know, I was right."

"About what?" I ask.

"You are a player, and you just don't know it."

Chapter Four

WINNIE

Three things.

One—Katherine would be LIVID if she knew I was walking into the woods with a stranger right now. A stranger who insisted on carrying my only source of protection, my backpack. I can practically hear her nagging voice in the back of my head, voicing her opinion on what an absolute careless idiot I'm being.

Two—Max would be squealing his handsome head off, telling me to "get it" and "make your move" if he knew I was on a morning jaunt through the woods with a hunky man. He'd absolutely die if he knew I was hanging out with a bunch of professional hockey players, let alone allowing one to join me on a walk and carry my backpack for me.

Three—Pacey Lawes thinks I'm pretty. Not that I know what kind of weight his name carries, because I know nothing about hockey, but nonetheless, this attractive and mysterious but kind man with eyes that intimidate me thinks I'm pretty.

Vain? Maybe.

But it's never a bad thing when someone calls you pretty. Nothing like a boost to the ego to make you feel better. Confident. Makes a girl shake her hips a little harder, puff out her chest, and lift that chin.

"So, are you from Seattle?" Pacey asks.

And then there's that—his memory. For a guy who didn't seem as if he was paying much attention to the events last night, he sure does seem to remember a lot. And in my experience, that doesn't happen very often. Being that I was ignored heavily in my last relationship, being noticed now feels like a world of difference.

"Yeah. Born and raised. Right in the city, too. Love it there. What about you?"

"Small town in Minnesota," he answers.

I nod. "That makes sense, since you play hockey. But you don't have an accent."

He chuckles and it's a deep, hearty sound. It's nice. "Yeah, it comes out every once in a while. But in Minnesota where I'm from, you either play hockey or you drink beer. When you're old enough, you do both."

"Drunken hockey—that must be fun."

"Yeah, I've received a few good shots to the moneymaker from some drunken hockey games."

"You mean punches?" I ask.

"Yup." He scrubs his hand over his jaw, and I notice how the scruff that lines his handsome face is just a little thicker than last night—not that I was paying close attention or anything.

"Oh God, but aren't you a goalie? I don't know much about hockey, but I wouldn't think goalies get in many fights."

"We don't normally get in fights, but on occasion, we get in the mix. But when I'm playing with the boys back home, there aren't any goalies, which means everyone is fair game."

I shake my head. "I could never imagine getting punched in the face. Does it hurt?"

He laughs. "Well, it doesn't feel good. But I guess in the moment, you don't really think about it. Especially in a game, when the adrenaline is pumping, you kind of go numb and nothing fazes you. And then of course when you're drunk, you're not really feeling anything in that moment either."

"Other than good, right?"

"Right."

Looking up ahead, Pacey says, "Okay, we're going to come to an intersection. Were you coming from the highway?"

"Yes, but then I took a wrong turn somewhere and thought I would find a way to turn around, but never did with all the rain."

He nods and chuckles. "I was going to ask, how the hell did you get up here if you were planning on heading into town?"

"I hate to admit it, but driving and directions aren't my strong suit."

"Got it. If you were coming from the highway, that means you came from the west. This way." He nods and I fall behind him for a few steps. And that's when I catch sight of his solid calves. Holy cow, those are muscular. As a matter of fact, his entire leg looks as though it's made from stone. Solid, rippling with strength. My oh my. I guess that's what happens when you skate on ice for a living.

"So, you really didn't go into detail about why you're here. You said adventure, but a part of me doesn't quite believe that."

Feeling comfortable with Pacey, I say, "Yeah, I've never been too good at hiding my facial expressions."

"I could tell this morning when you caught me in the kitchen with my shirt off."

Oh, dear Jesus.

Yeah, I'm sure he understood exactly what I was thinking when I saw him with his shirt off.

Could he tell I wanted to motorboat his pecs? That I was tempted to run my fingers through his short-clipped chest hair? Could he see how enticing I found the idea of walking up to him, placing my palms on his chest, and then running the flat part of my tongue over his nipples?

Christ, I hope not.

My face heats up again and he smiles at me. *The tease.*

"You said you were shy," I point out. "You're a liar. No shy boy would ever say something like that to a girl."

"Maybe I'm comfortable now. Comfortable with you. Doesn't take that long for me to warm up to someone."

"Good to know. I shall prepare myself for more bold statements." We keep walking along together in the shade from the canopy of the tall trees. It blessedly blocks the sun, but the wind stirs the trees on occasion and sends light droplets of last night's rain showering down on us.

"So . . . your adventure?" he prods.

"What about it?" I ask, trying to act casual.

"Care to elaborate?"

I shake my head with a smile. "Not really. I'm good. Thanks."

"Uh-huh. I see. That's fair, but tell me this—what are you going to do about lodging?"

"Well, I thought I'd focus on finding my car first. Without a car, there's no adventure."

"Makes sense, and once we locate your car, because we will, what are you going to do after that?"

"Oh, you know, the regular stuff—stroll into town, see if anyone wants to shelter a girl who's on an adventure. Classic adventure-type behavior. Spontaneity is the key."

"You think it's going to be that easy?"

We ascend a small hill, taking one step at a time. I forgot how muddy these roads were when I was driving last night. No wonder I got stuck. "I mean, I can be pretty convincing," I say.

"And when you don't find a place to stay because everything is occupied?"

"Pitch a tent. Nothing says adventure like living in a tent."

"Do you have a tent?" he asks.

"No, but I've been watching *Naked and Afraid*, so I've learned some basic survival skills from that show. Minus the whole 'losing your car in the woods' thing."

He taps his chin. "I thought your friend didn't want you to be abducted."

Hands on my hips as we make our way up the hill, I say, "You know, I think we're being too harsh on the human population. Not everyone is out to be a creep. Not everyone is looking to abduct humans. There are some good people out there."

"Yeah, like me and the boys." That's very true. "But you got lucky last night. You never know who you'll run into. And, yes, Canadians are well-known for their politeness and hospitality, but there are still creeps out there. Anything could happen, especially when you least expect it."

"Aren't you a ray of sunshine."

He laughs. "Just trying to give you some perspective."

We make it to the top of the hill and, lo and behold, there's my car.

Oh, look at her, her poor little wheels all stuck.

"Please don't tell me that's your car," Pacey says in disbelief.

"Yup, that's my car. Isn't she beautiful?"

"You thought driving a Mini Cooper through the Canadian Rocky Mountains was a smart idea? In a torrential downpour nonetheless?"

"I didn't think it was going to rain," I say as we walk up to Minnie. "Oh, Minnie, what happened to you?" I ask, patting her hood.

"Minnie? You named your Mini Cooper Minnie?"

I nod. "Minnie and Winnie, two girls on an adventure."

Pacey drags his hand over his face. "Jesus. You're lucky you didn't get stuck anywhere else and that you made it this far." He steps down into the small ditch to assess where my wheel is stuck. He shakes his head. "Not sure you're getting out of this hole."

"What do you mean?" I ask, walking over to where he's

standing. My feet slide down the ditch and right before I lose my balance, Pacey grabs my elbow and holds me up.

"Careful. It's really muddy."

"I see that now. Sorry you have to keep catching me. That must be annoying."

His eyes meet mine, sincerity ringing true. "Nah, it's good."

Those eyes, they will be my undoing, I'm sure of it. I know I'm going to do something really stupid because of those eyes.

"Um, so, the hole?" I ask. *Focus, Winnie, not on his eyes, but at the problem at hand.*

"Yeah, look at your tire. It's at least five inches deep into this hole and the back tire is just as bad." Pacey points to the back so I crane my neck around him to take a look.

Hmm, he is in fact correct—Minnie has some pretty deep holes she's dealing with.

"Well, can't we just, you know"—I make a motion with my hand—"push Minnie out?"

His brow raises. "Do you have Herculean powers I don't know about?"

"I can bench the bar. I found that out when I attempted to work out at the gym a few months ago. Does that mean anything?"

His brows flatten. "That's forty-five pounds."

"Really?" I ask with pride. "Huh, I thought it was lighter than that. Look at me. How much can you bench?"

"Three hundred."

Oh wow.

"Okay, yeah, so, uh . . . you're strong." I clear my throat, trying not to remember what he looks like with his shirt off, but my mind fails me, and all of a sudden, I visualize those thick pecs. God, he really is strong. "So, with your three hundred and my forty-five, that means together we can push three hundred and fifty pounds. Rounded up to make it easier. So that's about the same as pushing a car, right?"

He leans against Minnie's door and laughs. "I would love to

live in the world you seem to live in, where a car weighs three hundred and fifty pounds."

"That's not accurate?"

"Not even close. Sorry."

"Well, maybe our adrenaline will kick in and, you know, leverage and all. The wheels should help us. Why don't we give it a shot? Never know until you try."

He shakes his head but then lifts off the car and holds out his hand. "Keys."

"Oh, I left them in the car."

"You left your keys in the car?"

"I mean, I didn't think anyone would take it."

"Unbelievable," he mutters and opens the car door. He reaches in, turns on the car, and then puts it in neutral. "Okay. Given that we're on a hill, it would be best if you push from the car door, in case, for some miraculous reason, we're able to get these wheels out of the holes. Then you can at least stop the car before it rolls down the hill."

"Oh, smart." I tap the side of my head. "Looks as though I snagged the hockey player with the brains."

"There aren't many of us," he says with such a cute smile that I can feel my insides churn with butterflies.

God, he really is cute. Well, not just cute, he's completely and utterly the most handsome man I've ever seen. But when he smirks like that, ooh, it's adorable. Can make anyone weak in the knees.

Not to mention the affinity I seem to have with him. It feels as if I've known him in a previous life. I'm so into that. Maybe he was a barkeep and I was the piano-playing whore in an old western town. Best of friends. He keeps telling me I need to get out of the business of spreading my legs, and I keep telling him the bills aren't going to pay themselves. He wants to take care of me, but he's barely scraping by with his low wages. That is, until he's presented with an opportunity of a lifetime when a huge poker tournament comes into town—

"I'm going to push. Hello, are you listening?"

"Huh? What?" I ask, blinking a few times. "Are you good at poker?"

"What?" he asks, completely confused.

"Huh?"

"Are you okay?" The dazed look on his face almost makes me laugh out loud, but I keep it together because I'm not looking too sane at the moment.

"Sorry, got confused."

"What does poker—you know what, never mind." Probably for the best. "As I was saying, I'm going to push from the hood. I'm hoping pushing down rather than up will give me more leverage."

"Love that idea. Absolutely brilliant, Pacey."

He gives me some serious side-eye and then says, "Careful though, it's slippery over here. With your track record, I don't see a high success rate of you staying on your feet."

I start to move past him. "What little faith—whoa." I slip and he catches me again. I steady myself and let out a deep breath. "That was a horrible coincidence."

"Okay, keep telling yourself that." He then slips his hand in mine and I can't help but give myself a second to memorize what it feels like to have such a large hand in mine, helping me. Guiding me. "Grab the door right here." He places my hand where he wants it. "That's it. And try to find some footing in this mess." We both look down at our shoes. They're covered in mud.

"Oh gosh, your shoes are so gross. I'm sorry."

"No biggie. I can hose them off when I get back to the cabin. Just please concentrate on staying on your feet. I would hate for you to fall face first in the mud."

Yeah, that would not bode well for me.

"I got this. Don't worry."

"Okay."

He moves around me and then heads to the hood, where he

gets in place. "On three, we're going to push. Remember, you're in charge of hopping into the car to stop it if it rolls down."

"Yup. Got it. Now bring your best muscles, Lawes. I know you have them."

"Thanks to the shakedown you gave me with your eyes earlier."

"No need to embarrass a girl," I say, trying to play it cool even though I want to bury my head in the mud from humiliation.

"Don't worry, I gave you the same shakedown last night when you came into the cabin."

Okay, yup, cue the red cheeks again.

But can we reflect for a moment—he gave me a shakedown? I wish I'd seen it. I wish I'd been able to capture the look on his face, what it looked like to have him take me in. Did he like everything he saw? His statement leads me to believe he did.

"On three, Winnie, we push. One. Two. Three."

Together we push Minnie.

My feet slide in the mud.

He grunts.

I grunt.

The car doesn't move.

I pull up and so does he.

"Would you look at that. Didn't move an inch," Pacey says in a sarcastic tone.

I turn to look at him. "You know, I don't think you were trying your hardest. Do you really bench three hundred? Or are you a bar presser like me?"

His brows shoot to his hairline and it makes me chuckle. "I bench three hundred, and one time I hit three thirty-five."

I fold my arms over my chest. "Prove it."

He waggles his finger at me. "You sure know how to get under an athlete's skin, don't you?"

"Possibly. Come on. On three, we can do this. Ready?"

He nods and gets into position.

"One. Two . . . three."

We both push at the same time and the car budges.

"Gah . . . keep . . . going. Dig, Pacey. Dig."

We push and it moves some more.

"Harder, Pacey. Harder."

"Don't . . . say . . . it . . . like . . . that," he grunts out as the car moves some more.

"We're doing it. Harder. Just like that."

"Fucking hell."

Another budge.

"Oh my God, yes. Pacey, yes."

"Stop sounding like you're . . . orgasming," he yells just as the car slips out of the holes.

"Gah, yes," I scream as the car careens out of my hands.

Entirely too thrilled, I clap my hands together and cheer for our valiant efforts, but those cheers are overshadowed by Pacey yelling at me. "The brakes. Winnie, the brakes."

"Oh shit!" I lunge forward and would you believe it . . .

I slip in the mud, and instead of catching my car as it rolls backward, I fall face first into the mud and my car careens into a ditch.

Plop.

Splat.

"Motherfucker," Pacey says as he squats next to me and helps me to my knees. Luckily, I spared my face from the mud, but the front of me is covered. I look down at poor Minnie.

I clear my throat. "Uh, any chance you think we can push Minnie out of that ditch?"

"No," Pacey says, exasperated.

"Yeah, I didn't think so. But you know, there is one thing to be said about all of this."

"What? That I said you weren't going to be able to stay on your feet?"

"Well, that, but also . . ." I poke his chest, his rock-hard

50

chest. "Mr. Doubtful, we were able to get out of the holes. That's something to be proud of."

"Yeah, pushed the car right into a ditch that's now going to require a tow."

"But don't you feel that you accomplished something?"

With a laugh, he helps me to my feet and asks, "What do you need from your car? I'll help you carry it back to the cabin."

Keeping my arms out to my sides since they're covered in mud, I ask, "Would you mind grabbing my suitcase from the trunk? And maybe we should bring the keys this time."

"Yeah, might be a good idea."

Like the good man he is, he scrambles down into the ditch, grabs my things, and then takes me by the hand to help me to a more solid piece of the road. "Come on, let's get you back to the cabin and cleaned up."

Chapter Five

PACEY

"I can carry my suitcase now. You really don't have to," Winnie says.

I glance over at her and can't help but smile. She's completely caked in mud except for her face. How she was able to avoid that, I've no clue, but every other bit of her front side is dripping.

"I told you, I can handle it. You have other things to worry about, like staying on your feet."

She's slipped two more times on our way back to the cabin. Either she's incredibly clumsy or this is her first time walking.

"You know, I think it's my shoes. They're old, and there isn't much tread left on them. Can't avoid slipping when you have no gription." *Gription?* Cute.

"These are my shit shoes and I've been fine."

"Well, aren't you a god of walking?" she says with humor.

"Never been called that before. I think I like it." The cabin comes into view and so does a large red truck. "Thank fuck, Stephan is here."

"Stephan? Wait, isn't he the chef?"

"Yes. Which means he probably has something cooking for breakfast." I sniff the air. "Yup, I think I smell bacon. Do you smell that?"

"I'm trying not to smell anything right now for fear that I'll get a whiff of any animal feces that I might have lain in."

I chuckle. "Smart. Just one more descent. Think you can handle it?"

"Maybe it's smarter if I treat my body like a sled and this hill as a slide—you know, just glide right on down."

"Nah, the mud is too sticky at this point." I grip the suitcase in one hand and then take her hand in my other. "I got you."

Together we make it down the hill and to the driveway of the cabin. Yup, that's bacon.

"Might be best if we leave our shoes out here. Taters will freak the fuck out if we get mud all over his floor."

"Oh God, I forgot about his dislike for me."

"I'll take care of him. Don't worry about it."

We strip out of our shoes. I open the door and set down her mud-free suitcase and backpack.

The boys are all at the dining room table, enjoying a meal. They turn to look at us.

"Holy shit, what happened?" Hornsby asks, coming out of his chair.

I thumb toward Winnie and say, "This smart one thought we could get her car out of the mud."

"And we did," Winnie defends.

"Yes, we did, and then we sent it right into another ditch."

Posey snorts and brings his napkin up to his nose.

"Winnie fell into the mud, and now here we are. She needs to get cleaned up and then we're going to call a tow to get the car out of the ditch."

"Jesus. Okay. Stephan made egg skillets. I can have him make two more."

"That would be awesome," I say.

"Uh, I have an allergy to eggs," Winnie says, wincing. "Don't worry about me. I can have a protein bar. Just require a shower." She pops the handle to her suitcase. "Mind if I head back to the guest room? The mud is starting to crust."

"Go ahead," I say, and she quickly wheels away. I head into the kitchen, where I give Stephan a fist pump. "Hey, man. Smells amazing."

"Sorry about last night," he says. "Didn't think it would be safe to try to get up here."

"No worries. Do you have some extra bacon?"

"Yeah, I can whip up a skillet for you. And your girlfriend?"

I choke on my own saliva. "She's not my girlfriend. Just an, uh, unexpected guest."

"Ahh, I get it." He winks at me.

"No, not like that. Literally, she came out of nowhere last night. Her car got stuck and she stumbled upon our cabin."

"Damn, lucky girl. She want a skillet?"

"She's allergic to eggs, apparently. Anything else you can whip up?"

"Got her covered." Stephan gets to work and I take a seat at the kitchen island, letting myself relax into a deep breath. I work out for a living, skate with two-hundred-pound men on a daily basis, but walking up and down those hills in mud . . . shit, my legs are burning. Talk about a new torture device for Coach. Just send us out in the mud, we'll get all the workout we need. Add some suitcases, a backpack, and a girl who walks like a newborn fawn, and we're toast.

"So, riding your white steed this morning?" Taters asks, taking a seat next to me after dropping his empty plate in the sink.

"What?" I ask. Hornsby joins us as well. Posey and Holmes remain at the table, talking about the book Holmes is reading.

"You know, knight in shining armor."

"Fuck off," I say, passing my hand over my face. "She was going to leave the house without help, in search of her car that she didn't remember where exactly she left. I couldn't let her just get lost out there." Whispering, I say, "If you haven't noticed, she's a bit of a hot mess. She can't stand on her own two feet, she thinks she can just adventure with no plan, and she leaves the keys to her car . . . inside her car. I honestly don't know how she's survived this long. Sheer luck, if you ask me."

Hornsby and Taters are both silent as they stare at me, arms crossed, observing.

"What?" I ask.

"Do you see it?" Taters asks.

"See what?" I ask.

"Oh yeah, I thought I was the only one," Hornsby says. "But you see it too?"

"Oh yeah," Taters says with a smirk. "He's crushing on this girl."

"What?" I ask in shock. "You two are totally off-base."

"Denial. Classic," Hornsby says.

"Never seen a more classic move," Taters adds.

"It's almost embarrassing watching him in denial," Hornsby says.

"Who's in denial?" Stephan asks.

Taters, or maybe I'll start calling him Potato now, leans forward. "Lawes. He doesn't think he's crushing on the girl, but we all see it."

With his back to us, Stephan says, "Oh yeah, I could see it the minute he told me about her food allergy."

"I'm being fucking nice. Want me to be a dick to her? I can act like Taters did last night."

"Mmm, I wouldn't say I was being a dick last night, more annoyed."

"You practically kicked her out in a torrential downpour," I say. "That's not annoyed, that's being a dick."

"I couldn't have kicked her out if I tried with you two asshats leaping at her beck and call."

Leveling with Taters, I say, "Hey, dude, just because your girl was a bitch to you doesn't mean every girl is a bitch."

"I choose to be proven wrong," Taters says, leaning against the counter and crossing his arms.

I roll my eyes and turn to Hornsby, the reasonable one in the group. "Her car is in a ditch; not sure she's going to be able to get it out anytime soon. Remember when Posey's car needed to be jumpstarted? The tow truck wouldn't come up here until the roads were completely dry, right?"

"Yeah, the guy doesn't risk it."

"That's what I thought," I say. "I'm pretty sure she's fucked for a bit, especially since the forecast is calling for more rain tonight."

"Yeah, I thought about that." Hornsby looks off to the side. "And when the Internet came back on, I checked on a few reasonable places around town, and they're all booked."

"Uh, what's happening here?" Taters asks, cutting in. "What I think is happening, better not be happening."

"Come on, Taters," I say. "She's in a foreign country—"

"It's Canada. It's not as if she was dropped off in Dubai without a wallet."

"It's still a foreign country. She seems to be on a mission. I don't know for what, but she doesn't seem to be smart about it. What are you going to do? Force her into town and hope she finds a place to stay, even though she won't have a car?"

"She was asking for adventure . . ."

"You're such an asshole," Hornsby says. "Jesus, dude, it's not going to kill you to have her around for a few days."

"Yes, it will, it'll kill my vibe."

"And what vibe is that?" I ask. "Sulking in the corner, pissing people off, and then later on apologizing as you rest a beer on your stomach?"

"As a matter of fact, that's the exact vibe I was going for."

"You can still be like that, but with her here." I didn't think I was going to have to push Taters on this so much. On the walk back, I considered the idea of asking him if she could stay, not for my benefit—because I'm really not getting anything out of this—but because Winnie doesn't seem to know what she's doing. She seems lost . . . alone. I think she needs help, she just doesn't quite know how to ask for it.

"No, I can't rock out with my vibe with her here. What if I want to fart? I'm going to have to excuse myself so I can fart in my own house."

"Seriously?" Hornsby asks. "That's what you're worried about? Farting?"

"And other things. What if I bring a girl back here?"

I scoff. "When have you ever brought a girl back to the cabin?"

"Never, but it's nice to know I have the option."

"You can still bring a girl back to the cabin. Jesus. She's on the opposite end of the cabin and since she's already terrified of you, I'm sure she's going to do everything possible to stay out of your hair."

Taters straightens up. "She said that? She's terrified of me?"

"Yeah, you fuck," I say. "You made quite the impression on her last night. And it wasn't a good one."

You can see the moment his conscience kicks in because the dent between his eyes eases and his shoulders slump. "Fuck, you know I don't like being known as the bad guy."

"Then don't act like one. Extend an olive branch. It seems as if she needs one right now."

He looks between us and then asks, "You don't think this is all a little odd? I mean, what woman in her right mind comes to a random house, full of five huge hockey players, stays the night, and acts as if everything is okay?"

I stare down the hallway and say, "I think someone who might be lost, that's who."

"Order up, man," Stephan says, sliding a steaming skillet on a trivet across the kitchen island. He tosses me a fork and I catch it with one hand.

"Maybe it'll give you some good karma," I add. "Opening up your home, that shit comes back around. Who knows, maybe you two might hit it off?"

Taters laughs. "Yeah, I'm sure you wouldn't even let any of us get close enough to her to let that happen."

I hold up my hands. "I lay no claim."

"That's why you were up this morning and out of the house before any of us were allowed to say good morning," Taters taunts.

"Not true," I say, scooping up a pile of scrambled eggs mixed with cheese, peppers, and hash browns. "Holmes was up this morning before me. He was probably waiting to make his move."

Hornsby laughs under his breath. "That would be the fucking day. The man barely talks to us. Pretty sure he's not going to be talking to a random girl who came crashing into our house late at night."

"And even if he did, it's not as if you gave him a chance. Holmes told us he told you to put a shirt on but you refused to."

"Oh, fuck off, that's what he told you guys?" I shake my head and take another bite. "I told him I didn't think she was going to be awake that early. I wasn't intentionally trying to be bare-chested in front of her."

"Uh-huh," Hornsby says, taking off for his room, down the hallway on the opposite side of the house from where Holmes, Winnie, and I are rooming.

"So, are you going to let her stay?" I ask, exhausted over this conversation.

"Is that what you want Daddy to do?" Taters grins.

"Do not call yourself that."

Stephan laughs from across the island as he whips something in a bowl. "I kind of like the sound of it. I mean, he's my sugar daddy, giving me the money I need."

"Daddy pays you well," Taters says with a wink.

"That he does."

"This is so fucking disturbing."

Taters puts his hand on my shoulder and says, "If you want your girlfriend to stay, then Daddy says it's okay." He leans in and presses a kiss to the top of my head. "Daddy will do anything for his precious baby."

I push at his chest. "Fuck off."

Taters laughs as he takes off toward his room, as well.

"Assholes," I mutter under my breath.

"Want something to drink?" Stephan asks.

"I can grab some water," I say, starting to get up.

"I got it, man. When I said Daddy pays me well, he pays me very well."

I chuckle. "God, he must love that you called him that."

"I think he was tickled, for sure." Stephan hands me a glass with ice and water. Then he leans forward and asks, "So . . . do you like her?" He wiggles his brows and I shake my head.

"Jesus, not you too, man."

"It'll be just our secret."

"I haven't spent enough time with her to even make that kind of assessment. I'm just being a nice guy." To a hot-as-fuck girl, but I won't mention that. And I wasn't kidding when I said I can be shy around girls. I've always been protective of my sister, but around her friends, I've been . . . standoffish. Besides, Winnie's probably out of my league.

Just then, Stephan lifts up and looks over my shoulder. "I didn't catch your name. Seems as though the boys are lacking in manners."

From behind me, I hear Winnie say, "Ah, what they're lacking in manners, they make up for in chivalry." She comes up to the island and takes a seat next to me. The aroma of fresh soap and lavender hits me as I turn to look at her.

And . . . *fuck.*

She's wearing a low-cut tank top that leaves little to the

imagination. She's fresh-faced, all dewy from her shower, and her wet hair is pulled up into a tight bun on the top of her head, showing off the stunning angles of her face.

Yup, *hot-as-fuck* was right.

"My name's Winnie, and you're Stephan, from what I've heard. The man with the food."

"That's right." Stephan offers his hand and they shake. "Can you believe these idiots traveled up here with no food?"

"Seems pretty unintelligent to me."

I turn to her. "As unintelligent as driving a Mini Cooper up a dirt road in the Rocky Mountains?"

"That's just living life. At least I packed food." She chuckles.

Stephan lifts away from the island and says, "I hope you like pancakes. I made some vegan blueberry pancakes. That okay?"

"Are you serious?" Winnie asks in surprise. "I told you, you didn't have to make me anything."

"I'm a chef. It's my responsibility to make sure everyone is fed." He places a plate in front of Winnie, and hell, those look good.

"Why the hell did I get scrambled eggs and she gets pancakes?" I ask in a teasing tone.

"Because you little bitches complain about packing on the carbs, even when on vacation."

Winnie laughs next to me, but it's true. We do complain about the carbs.

"But we never bitch about the dessert."

"Which is why you get eggs in the morning, so you can enjoy those desserts later."

"Oh my gosh, these are delicious," Winnie moans in appreciation. "Thank you so much, Stephan."

"You're welcome." He winks and then makes the rest of his batch. "I'll put these in the fridge so you can pull them out and toast some when you want more."

"Oh, thank you, but I won't be staying."

"Not what I hear," Stephan says in a sing-song voice before going back into the pantry.

Winnie turns toward me. "What did he mean by that?"

I shovel the rest of my skillet in my mouth and then wash it down with some water before addressing Winnie. "The guys and I were talking, and we don't think you have any other option but to stay with us. Hornsby—"

"Eli?"

"Yes, Eli—was looking at lodgings this morning and everything so far has been booked. And as far as your car, we know the tow man, and he won't come up here unless the ground is dry. It's supposed to rain the next couple of days."

"Oh." Her shoulders slump. "Well, that doesn't seem promising for me."

"Yeah, not so much. But we spoke to Tat—uh, Potato."

She grins.

"And he said that you're more than welcome to stay here for as long as you need."

She gives me a *get real* look. "He did not say that."

"Something like that," I say. "But seriously, this is going to be your best bet. Any lodging that might have occupancy is going to be sketchy or astronomically priced. At least here, you have company, or you can be left alone, you'll be fed, and we can help you get back down the mountain when it dries out."

She nibbles on her bottom lip and looks down at her plate. "But it feels as though I'm taking advantage of the situation, and I'm not that kind of person."

"You're not taking advantage of the situation if we invited you. Seriously, we have the space, we have the food, and it's no problem. And, hey, whatever you really are here for, you can focus on it in peace, or we can help you. We're just hanging out here."

"I don't want to be in your way."

"You won't be. And if you feel like you are, then just retreat to your room."

"It doesn't feel right." She picks at her pancake. "I didn't come here for charity."

"Then make it up to us," I say. I want her to stay. I want to find out what this adventure is all about. I want to try to figure out how I know this girl. And . . . yeah, maybe I just want to get to know her better. She's interesting. A little quirky, very stubborn, but incredibly independent. She fascinates me.

Plus, she's someone else to talk to besides my boys. Don't get me wrong. I would fight to the death for them, but I've also spent an entire season with them. Some female companionship wouldn't kill me.

"I don't have a lot of money," she says, looking embarrassed.

"Good, because we wouldn't want your money. Make it up to us in different ways."

She lifts a questioning brow. "Excuse me, sir, but I don't do that kind of stuff. Well, I do perform those kinds of things, but in a consensual relationship, not as favors . . . if you know what I mean."

"Jesus, not like that." I chuckle. "I didn't even think about how that sounds. I mean, like . . . help us in other ways."

"And how would that be?" She gestures to Stephan. "It's not as though I can make you dinner. And for being five men in one house, you're all really clean." She looks around the house. "I honestly don't know what I could do to pay you back."

"Then don't. Why don't you just let us be nice?"

"Because I'm used to doing everything myself," she answers briskly while looking away. "I—" She lets out a deep breath. "I don't usually look for help. Coming here last night, staying here, that was hard. Accepting help has never come easily to me, so staying here for longer, I just don't think I can do it."

"Well, I hate to break it down like this for you, but you're in a tough spot." I force her to look at me by reaching out and placing two fingers on her chin until her eyes meet mine. There they are, those deep blue eyes, a color I've never seen in person before. "Your car isn't getting out of that ditch at least for a few days. There's no hotel available in town and, unfortunately don't have any other options. It's either us or staying in your car in a ditch until help comes, and frankly, that would be insulting to us if you chose your car over this nice cabin."

She worries her lips and then exhales softly. Her shoulders slump and I see when she capitulates. "Unfortunately, I think you're right."

"I know I am." I stand from my chair and stretch my hands over my head. "Make yourself comfortable, Winnie. Looks as if this is your new home for a few days."

And then I take off toward my room for a much-needed shower.

I TOWEL off my head just as my phone rings on my nightstand. I quickly throw on a pair of boxer briefs and then jog over to the nightstand where I spot my dad's name across the screen.

"Hey, Dad," I answer while taking a seat on the bed. "How are you?"

"Doing pretty good," Dad says, his gruff voice sounding clear over the phone. Retired now from teaching for over thirty years, he's spending his days with my mom in Minnesota enjoying a calm, peaceful life. "Are you and the boys in Banff?"

"Yeah, got here yesterday."

"Your mom and I really need to get up there soon. We enjoyed our trip two years ago, and I'm thinking of a repeat."

"Just let me know when and I'll be sure to be here as well. There is room here at the house, we could even put you in a spot here."

"No, no," Dad scoffs. "You know I don't want to bother you boys, especially when you're trying to unwind. The last thing you need is for a couple of old people cramping your style."

"Not sure what you think we do here, Dad, but until yesterday, we've never had a girl here . . . if that's what you're implying."

"You mean Silas never had his girl up to the cabin?"

"Well, she was different, but we don't bring girls back to the place."

"Uh-huh, so then why did that change yesterday? Who brought someone? Wait, let me guess, Horny did."

I chuckle. "No, surprisingly. The girl is actually someone who dropped by yesterday. Bad storms led to her car getting stuck in the road, which led her to the cabin for help. She stayed the night because there was nowhere to go. Taters is mad about it but we couldn't turn the girl away."

"I would hope not. Good on you guys for making sure she was going to be okay."

"Yeah, you know . . . she looks really familiar. Can't quite put my finger on it."

"Maybe you knew her in another life," Dad says, causing me to roll my eyes.

"You know I don't believe in that shit."

He laughs. "That's why I said it."

"Was there a point to this phone call?" I ask, teasing him.

"Just checking on my boy, seeing if you've heard from anyone."

"That's ominous," I say. "Am I supposed to be hearing from someone?"

"Maybe," he says.

"Care to elaborate?"

He clears his throat, so I know he's about to get serious. "I had a call from Josh."

Huh, wasn't expecting that.

"He actually called you?"

"Yeah, to say I was caught off guard is an understatement."

"Was he just checking in?"

Dad pauses and then says, "No, he was actually apologizing."

"Seriously?" I ask, not quite believing that. "What brought about an apology? I mean long overdue given how he's treated you and me, but out of the blue he decides to apologize?"

"He did. He said he wanted to apologize to you as well. He needs to explain himself."

Josh can apologize all he wants, I don't think that's going to change shit for me.

Josh is my half-brother. He's been a dick ever since I've known him and has rejected the idea of ever getting to know me. So why the hell do I want to offer him the chance to apologize?

And why now?

"From your silence, I'm guessing you're not open to a conversation with Josh right now," Dad says.

"Not quite. He was a dick to you, Dad. You just accepted his apology and everything is fine now?"

"He's my son."

"He's an asshole," I shoot back.

Dad sighs. "I know this isn't easy for you to understand, but when he does reach out to you, and he will, please, Pacey, please have an open heart."

Yeah . . . okay.

"Sure, Dad," I say to appease him, even though I know damn well there is no way I'll be answering that phone call.

"Thank you." Although Dad's relief does make me feel slightly guilty. "Okay, well I should be going. Your mom made a play date for me on the golf course."

I chuckle. "She's a good woman."

"That she is. I love you, kid."

"Love you, too, Dad."

Once I hang up, I toss the phone on the bed. That wasn't a phone call I was mentally prepared for.

But knowing Josh and his track record, nothing will come of it.

At least, that's what I hope.

Chapter Six

WINNIE

I nervously bounce my leg as I wait for my friends to answer the FaceTime call. I have no idea what Katherine is going to say, but I'm really not looking forward to the lecture.

"Hello?" Max says as his face comes onscreen. "Fucking hell, it's Winnie. Katherine, get your ass over here. It's your friend who's made us sick with worry."

Oh man, it's already not starting off well.

Katherine snatches the phone from Max and her bloodshot eyes come into view. She has a scarf tied around her head, masking what I know is hair made insane from her pulling on it, and she looks as though she hasn't slept in two days. Not to mention, the vein between her eyes is twitching.

Yup, this isn't going to be a fun conversation.

"What in the fresh hell have you been doing? You were supposed to call us and tell us you arrived." She points to her eyes. "Do you see this? See these bloodshot, horrendously ugly eyes? That's from you. I thought you were run off the side of the road, pulled from Minnie, and then thrust into a cage until they could start making a profile of you for the black market. With those eyes and those tits, you'd sell for a pretty price."

"Oh my God, Katherine, you need to stop it with those crime shows you watch all the time."

"Oh . . . you think that's fictitious? Ohhhhhh no, that's real life, sweetheart. And what I described is the nicer version, because you're a prime candidate. Hot and clueless. They'd snatch you so fast."

Max tears the phone away from Katherine and says, "Dude, she was showing me some articles about captors and their captives. She had me up all night worrying about it. Then I made her buy me a cronut this morning because I couldn't sleep last night. And you know what—that cronut, although tasty, didn't help me forget the traumatic mark Katherine left on me last night. I'm scarred. This is your fault."

"I'm sorry," I say, finally able to get a word in. "Trust me, I didn't avoid you two on purpose. There was a horrible thunderstorm last night. Rain was pelting poor Minnie, making driving visibility incredibly poor. The Canadian Rockies don't offer much in the way of phone reception, and to add to that, the Internet wasn't working. But the Internet finally came back this morning, so I was able to FaceTime."

Katherine snakes the phone from Max and peers into the screen closely, her face a psychotic display as she attempts to observe my surroundings. At least, that's what it seems like she's doing.

"Where are you?"

And here's the question I didn't want to answer, because she's going to freak out. There's no doubt in my mind that there's going to be a massive loss of minds, and not only do I have to deal with the lecture, but I'm also going to have to deal with the bitching from Max. Because when I get off the phone, Katherine is going to fly off the deep end and Max will be the recipient of her crazy, and then I'll have to listen to Max complain about Katherine. It's what happens when your friend is so distraught and obsessed with personal safety.

"Well, before we talk about where I am, I need you to take a deep breath first."

"Winnie," she says, her throbbing vein intensifying. "If you say you're in some sort of brothel, I'm going to lose my shit."

"Good news, then. I'm not in a brothel, therefore there should be no losing of shit. Glad we got that out of the way. Phew. Now we can just relax and have a conversation like normal friends."

Katherine shakes her head. "As if I work that way. You should know better by now. Where are you?"

It was worth giving the blasé attitude a shot.

"Let me preface this story by saying this is a tough trip for me, so if you could not lecture me on my choices, I would appreciate it."

"Ooh, she's pulling the *I lost my mom* card, and early on too," Max says. "Wherever our dear friend is residing, there's no way you're going to approve, not when she has to preface her story."

He's right.

"Just tell me where you are," Katherine says. When I don't say anything, she rolls her eyes and says, "Okay, I'll take it easy on you."

"Promise?"

"Promise," she says through her clenched jaw.

Here goes nothing.

"Okay, so I got to Banff last night. I tried texting you guys, but the text wouldn't go through. The storm was really bad and as I was heading into town, I couldn't see that well and ended up making a wrong turn."

"The first mistake of being kidnapped."

"Katherine, for the love of fuck," Max says. "Chill with the abduction shit. You have me looking over my shoulder every goddamn second."

"We need to be aware."

"Trust me, we're all aware." Max shifts the phone so they're both in view. "Go on."

"Thank you." I clear my throat, getting ready for the tough part. "Well, the wrong turn kind of took me into the mountains." I can see Katherine go to say something but then she keeps her mouth shut as Max shoots her a look. "The road turned into a dirt road."

"Dear Jesus," Katherine says, pinching her nose.

"And because it was raining so much, the road turned into mud, which Minnie didn't handle very well, and she ended up getting stuck. Nothing I did could get her out. I didn't have much of a choice but to try to get help because my phone wasn't working."

Katherine starts to rock back and forth.

"I packed some things and then ventured out into the storm. I saw some lights in the distance so I headed in that direction. Trust me when I say, it was scary. The storm was so bad that I thought I was going to be swept away in the mud and rain. Luckily, I made it to the lights, which turned out to be a house, so I knocked on the door, hoping to use a phone."

"Blink twice if you're captured right now. Let me know if you need help." She whacks Max in the arm. "I told you we should've put that GPS tracker on her."

"I'm not captured. The guys were very kind last night."

"Guys?" Katherine shouts.

"Guys, huh?" Max leans forward. "What kind of guys?"

I bite my bottom lip and then I lean forward and whisper, "Professional hockey players."

"What?" Max stands from the couch they're sitting on, taking the phone with him. "Hold the fuck on. You're telling me that you took a wrong turn in the middle of a thunderstorm and just so happened to stumble upon a house full of professional hockey players?"

I nod. "Yeah. I didn't have any idea who they were. They had to prove it to me that they were who they said they were, and this morning I did some recon when the Internet came back."

"And who are they, exactly?"

"Master manipulators who are going to take advantage of her when she's least expecting it," Katherine shouts in the background.

Katherine needs a tranquilizer.

"Uh, they're on the Vancouver Agi—"

"Agitators," Max says before I can finish. "Holy fuck. If you tell me Ian Rivers is there, I'm going to fucking flip out. Is he there?" Max grips his forehead. "Wait, don't tell me. I don't want to know." He gets close to the phone so I can only see half of his face, and he whispers, "Is he there?"

"Ian Rivers—he's the one who came out, isn't he?"

"Yes. And fuck, Winnie, not only is he a beast on the ice, but he's hot. Really fucking hot. Is he there? If he is, I'm coming. Tell me where you are and I'll be there."

I chuckle. "He's not here."

"Damn it. Who is there?"

"Um, let me see if I can get this right. They all call each other by their last names but introduced themselves with their first names. It's so confusing. Uh, the house belongs to Taters, uh . . ."

"Silas Taters," Max says. "Oh hell. Is Eli Hornsby there?"

"Yes," I say with enthusiasm. "He is. And oh my God, is he pretty. Like . . . wow. I don't think I've ever seen anyone as pretty as him. It's hard to look at him because the beauty of that man's face is almost too much to handle."

"You have issues then, because I have no problem looking at pictures of him. I could look at him for days. Who else is there?"

"Levi Posey."

"Hmm, don't know much about him."

"He's funny. I like him," I say as I catch Katherine pacing in the background. I smile inwardly. This must be killing her. "And then Halsey Holmes."

"Ooh, he's a scoring god. He handles the puck better than anyone on the ice."

"Yeah, he's pretty quiet," I say. "He doesn't say much, just reads. And then the last guy is Pacey Lawes."

Max's jaw drops and then he blinks a few times. "Pacey Lawes, as in, the Agitators goalie? He's pure magic. He has the most saves in the league. The most fucking saves, Winnie."

My cheeks heat up.

The man with the most saves in the league said I was pretty.

He also offered me a place to stay—despite it not being his house.

He also kindly helped me push my car into a ditch.

Max sighs. "You literally walked into my wet dream, you lucky shit."

I laugh while Katherine walks up to the phone and asks, "Okay, wonderful. You met some celebrities, but what happened after you met them? Did they let you use their phone? Did they attempt to touch you in your no-go areas?"

"No, Katherine," I say in an exhausted voice. "And, well, that's the thing." I start squirming again. "It was such a bad storm that the phones weren't working and I really didn't have any options other than to take them up on their offer."

Katherine's eyes narrow. "What offer?"

"To stay the night." I swallow hard and cringe.

"For sexual favors?" Katherine shouts.

I quickly turn the volume on my phone down, hoping no one heard that. "No," I shoot back. "God, Katherine. They were just being nice. They offered me a guest room for the night. I considered going back to my car to sleep but they wouldn't let me. They said if I really wanted to be abducted, that would be the way to do it."

"So you stayed the night at their place?"

I nod and then turn the camera around on the phone to show off the room. "That's where I am now. At the house, in the room I stayed in last night."

"Uh, it looks as though you're at some luxury resort," Max says. "Not someone's house. Is that a vaulted ceiling?"

I point the phone up to the ceiling. "Yup. With exposed beams. And look at the chandelier."

"Oh my God, no one cares about the chandelier," Katherine shouts. "You need to leave right now. Are you insane? Hockey players are huge, and there's five of them in the house with you? I can smell a circle jerk, your back being the landing zone."

"Jesus Christ, Katherine," Max shouts. "Fuck, what's wrong with you?" He points his finger at her. "You need psychological help."

"Technically, there are six guys," I say. "There's a beefy chef named Stephan. He makes delicious vegan pancakes."

"Homemade syrup?" Max asks.

"I think so. It was in one of those creamer things, and it was infused with huckleberry."

"Ooh, that's fancy."

"Are you two kidding me right now?" Katherine asks. "Winnie is facing death and all you can talk about are chandeliers and huckleberry-infused syrup?"

"I'm not facing death. They actually really saved me."

Katherine folds her arms over her chest. "Uh-huh, is that why you're still there? Because you think they saved you? You know that's how they get you, right? Build trust first and then swoop in for the kill."

"Katherine." I grow serious. "I'm still here because I have nowhere else to go."

"What do you mean?" Katherine asks. I'm actually nervous for her blood pressure. I've never seen the vein so . . . prominent before, and FaceTime doesn't usually provide a crystal-clear image, but man, can I see the pulse of her anger vein.

"Well, Pacey tried to help me push my car out of the holes this morning."

"Ooh, was his shirt off while he was doing that?" Max asks.

"No." I smirk. "But it was off this morning when I went out to the kitchen, and oh my God, Max, I've never seen that many muscles before."

"God, I hate you."

"Please, back to the story about your car," Katherine says.

"Yes, well, we pushed it out of the holes, but then I forgot to stop it and it rolled back into a ditch."

Katherine tosses her hands up in the air and walks away while Max snorts.

"If it makes you feel better, I fell face first into the mud and embarrassed myself. But, yeah, Minnie is in a ditch now and needs to be towed out. And because we're on back roads, a tow truck won't come up here until the roads are dry. It's supposed to rain the next couple of days so I'm without a car."

"Dear Jesus, I think . . . yes, I think I'm having a heart attack." Katherine takes a seat on the couch and clutches her chest.

"You are not having a heart attack." Max rolls his eyes.

"Um, if you didn't like that part, you might not like this next part, either." I wince.

Katherine's head snaps toward the phone. "What now?"

"Well, do you remember when I was leaving, you asked where I was staying in Banff?"

"Yessss," Katherine drags out.

"Well, I told you that fancy place where all of the celebrities stay."

"Uh-huh."

"So, that was a lie."

Katherine's eyes turn murderous.

"I thought I would show up and just grab a room at that hotel. Turns out, when I was on a lunch break from driving, I looked it up and the prices were astronomical. It's a popular time to be in Banff right now. One of the boys told me it's because the lakes are the most beautiful this time of the year. Something about glacial melting, I don't know. Anyway, I thought I'd find a place to stay when I got here, and then the boys informed me everything is booked."

"If you tell me you're going to camp, I will disown you."

I perk up. "No, I'm not camping. The boys offered me the guest room for as long as I want it."

"That's even worse," Katherine shouts.

"How is that worse? They're really nice."

"Of course they're nice. They're trying to gain your trust so when they turn you into their sex slave, you start to think that's your new normal."

"Okay, you need to go take a nap," Max says, taking Katherine by the arm and ushering her down the hall toward her bedroom. "I'll bring you a cold compress in a few. Just chill." When she's out of earshot, Max says, "You realize you just made my life exponentially harder."

I cringe. "I know, I'm sorry."

"Do you know how you can make it up to me?"

"How?" I ask.

"Try to get Ian Rivers's phone number for me."

I chuckle. "I'll do my best."

"And do you know what else you can do for me?"

"Score you a date?" I ask.

"Well, that, but also . . . live your best life, Winnie." His eyes turn soft as he smirks at me. "Katherine loves you, that's why she's so insane, but we know you need to do this, so do it the way you need to, and if that means spending a week in a vaulted-ceiling cabin with five hunky hockey players, then do it. Take this time for you."

The tension in my shoulders eases as I lie back on the comfortable, plush bed. "That means a lot to me, Max."

"But please just be careful, okay? I think you and I both know these guys are probably down-to-earth and nice. They're not stupid enough to do something, you know, illegal, but just be careful. That heart in your chest, it's fragile right now. It's been through enough to last a lifetime. Take good care of it."

I press my hand against my chest. "I will." I smile at Max. "Thank you. I needed to hear this. I was really worried. I don't want Katherine to be mad at me."

"You know Katherine, her bark is bigger than her bite. Don't worry about her. I'll give her some sedatives here on the home front. Just take care of you and take care of your business. We need you back here, refreshed, and with a clear mind. Okay?"

"Okay."

"And for the love of God, check in often. Even if it's a text."

I chuckle. "I will. Don't worry. But if you don't hear from me in a while, look up the weather forecast for Banff before you freak out. When it storms, correspondence can be low, so keep that in mind as well."

"Got it." He winks. "Now go have fun with some hockey players."

"I will."

"Before you hang up, tell me . . . do you have your eyes on Eli Hornsby?"

I burst out laughing. "He's far too pretty. I don't think I could ever go for a guy like him."

"But . . ."

I shy away, putting my hand over my face as I feel it heat up. "But Pacey is . . . God, there's something about him that I'm completely drawn to. He's so handsome."

"Ooh yes, Winnie. Pacey is a certain kind of man. He wears his hair well, ties it up in a knot when he wants to, those thighs of his could crush a watermelon, and his eyes."

"Yes," I whisper into the phone. "His eyes sear me."

"You need to go for it."

I snort. "You're insane. There's no way someone like Pacey Lawes would ever go for someone like me. Not to mention, I'm just passing through."

"Uh, have you looked in the mirror? You're gorgeous. You also have that special zip about you."

"Special zip?" I laugh. "What the hell is that?"

"You know." He rubs his fingers together. "This bubbly, infectious personality that people like to be around." Whispering, he says, "The opposite of psychotic Katherine."

I snort so hard I have to wipe my nose. "Well, thank you for the vote of confidence, but I don't plan on making any moves on anyone. Doesn't mean I won't take advantage of the views, though."

"That's my girl. And trying to get that phone number, right?"

"Ah, yes, Ian Rivers's phone number. I'll ask around."

"It's the least you can do, since when I hang up the phone, I'm going to have to probably slip Katherine a crushed-up sedative in some applesauce just to make it through the day. I don't prefer to drug my friends, Winnie."

"I know, but sometimes it has to be done."

"Yeah, this is a must." He chuckles and says, "You know, though she talks about personal safety, little does she know her best friend is ready to slip her a Xanax."

"What she doesn't know won't hurt her. Love you, Max."

"Love you. Have fun."

We hang up and I toss my phone to the side as I stare up at the ceiling. So, this is it. This is where I'm staying for a few days.

Could be way worse.

Not sure it could be any better.

I'll take it and I'll be grateful, because it's been tough of late.

And like Max said, I need to get back to them whole and with a clear mind.

Ready to get back on the merry-go-round that is my life.

Chapter Seven

PACEY

"Where's your friend?" Taters asks, taking a seat on the lounger next to mine.

"She's not my friend, she's just . . . a guest."

"Whatever you want to call her, where is she?"

"Not sure." I take my hat off my head and place it over my face, blocking the peekaboo sun. It was sunny this morning, but clouds for the storm we're expecting later have been steadily gathering. But even though there's some cloud coverage, it's still nice out, and I'm trying to soak up as much sun as I can get when it comes out from behind the clouds.

"You don't know where she is? I thought you were her gatekeeper."

"Can you not be a dick?" I ask. "I offered your house as a place to stay because she had nowhere else to go. If you didn't have your head so far up your ass, you probably would've done the same thing."

"My head is not up my ass," Taters defends.

"Dude, you know I care about you and I always tell it to you like it is because that's what brothers do, so I'm going to tell it to you like it is. You've been an ass ever since Sarah broke up with you. And I get it, you've been together since high school, and that's hard, but you're not letting us help you. You're bottling it up and then taking it out on everyone."

"Maybe because I don't want to talk about it. Ever think about that?" He drops his sunglasses over his eyes and leans back in the lounger.

"Yeah, I didn't want to talk about my injury, but you still made me."

"Because I needed your head in the game. The way you played affected my game. Can't have my goalie afraid of a damn puck."

"I'm not afraid of the puck," I shout, and then realizing how worked up I am, I calm myself. More quietly, I repeat, "I'm not afraid of the puck, and if you don't think your breakup with Sarah affected the team, then you're in denial."

"Fuck you. You know I leave that shit off the ice. When I step onto the rink, nothing else passes through my mind but hockey."

"You made mistakes this postseason that you never would've made before. You let players get by you, you missed shots. You let guys take you out that never even would've had a chance before."

Taters lifts up and says, "Are you blaming the loss on me? Is that what you're trying to say?"

"No," I huff out. "We all had a part in losing. But what I'm saying is you're not addressing what happened, and without addressing it, you're never going to get over it."

"The only way I'm going to get over it is by getting under someone else."

"You know you don't want to do that," I say. Taters might put on a show, but he's as loyal as they come. He loved Sarah. Fucking infatuated with the girl. They grew up through the system together. They'd been each other's backbones. Taters is the man he is today because of her. He's not the type of guy who can write off one girl with another. He doesn't work that way. Not sure any of us do. Hornsby maybe, but I think that's because he's emotionless inside. He's a solid dude, but when it comes to actual feelings, his own feelings, I'm not sure he's in tune with those.

"I'm a new man," he says. "I can do whatever the fuck I want."

"Yeah, and I'm guessing what you really want is to not be here with us but to be back in Vancouver trying to make up with Sarah."

Taters shakes his head. "She made it known she doesn't want me anymore. So, I'm going to respect her wishes. Why go after someone who doesn't want me?"

"And why doesn't she want you?"

"Not talking about it," he says. "That's not why I came out here."

"Okay, then why did you come out here?"

"Your friend—"

"Winnie. She has a name."

"Well, Winnie hasn't said 'thank you' to me yet."

Jesus Christ.

"Probably because she's terrified of you. Ever think of that? Also, I don't think she's left her room all day because she doesn't want to be a nuisance. She doesn't want to bother us."

"It bothers me more knowing she's here but not here."

"You're impossible, you realize that?" I stand from my lounger because I'm not lying here anymore. "Do you know if dinner is done?"

"Do I look like a triangular bell that announces dinner? I have no fucking clue what Stephan is doing in there."

Not in the mood to argue with Taters, I pick up my water bottle and head for the house. I push the sliding glass door open and am immediately assaulted with a mouth-watering aroma.

Stephan has a bunch of steaks on a plate, lightly seasoned. Roasted potatoes are fresh from the oven, I can still see the steam coming off them, and there's a large salad brimming with vegetables in a bowl on the island.

Taters can really be a dick, but he also takes care of us, and one of the ways he does that is making sure we're well fed. I am worried about him, though. I have no clue what it's like to lose someone you love who's been in your life for so many years. You don't just *get over it.* But he needs to find a way to move forward and not stay . . . ruined. And I have no idea how to help him with that.

"Hey, just the guy I was looking for. Do you know how Winnie takes her steak?" Stephan asks.

"Uh, no."

"Do you know if she eats steak?"

"No."

"Do you think you can find out?" Stephan laughs.

I pull on the back of my neck. "Sure."

I set my water bottle down on the counter and head toward her room, wondering when I became her handler. Hornsby was the one who was adamant about her staying first. I just got sucked into it.

When I make it to her room, I lightly knock on her door. When I don't hear anything, I knock again.

Nothing.

Did she . . . leave?

I glance down the hallway to the entryway and spot her shoes. I don't think she'd leave without those, so I knock again. When I still don't hear anything, I wonder if she's asleep.

I guess only one way to find out.

I test the doorknob gingerly. It gives under my hand, unlocked, and I slowly, and I mean *slowly*, open the door.

"Winnie?" I call.

No response.

I crack the door open farther and stick my head inside, just enough to see her bed. She's not in there.

Huh.

I push the door open farther and scan the room, and catch a glimpse of movement off to the right.

"Oh my God," Winnie squeals. I turn just in time to catch her clutching a towel around her body.

"Oh shit . . . oh shit, I'm sorry." I turn away and place my hand over my eyes.

"What are you doing?" she frantically asks.

"I'm sorry," I say again, feeling my entire face turn red. "I'm not some Peeping Tom, if that's what you're wondering. I didn't even see anything. And I'm not just saying that to make you feel better. I swear, I didn't see anything, just your towel around your torso. I swear, my eyes are virginal when it comes to your body."

That's not true, you stared at her cleavage this morning.

But not going to mention that tidbit.

"Okay," she says, a little calmer. "I believe you, but what are you doing in here?"

Keeping my back to her, I say, "I was knocking on your door and you didn't answer. I thought maybe you left or something."

"I was in the bathroom. I didn't hear you. Maybe you need to learn to knock louder."

"I'll pound on the door next time. Maybe shout your name a few times, as well."

She chuckles and then says, "I'm all covered up. You can look now."

I straighten up and then casually turn around as if everything is normal.

But hell, nothing is normal when it comes to seeing Winnie in a towel. Her hair is piled high on the top of her head and her face is completely devoid of makeup like this morning, showing off a light spattering of freckles. And even though my eyes desperately want to scan her in that towel, I keep them north.

Very far north. No sense in making this situation more uncomfortable by checking her out.

But hell, do I want to take in every last inch of her in that towel.

I stick my hands in my pockets and ask, "So, uh . . . enjoying another shower?"

She smirks. "No, a bath this time. I had to try out that jacuzzi tub."

"Yeah, sure. Cool."

She tilts her head to the side. "Was there a reason you came in here?"

"Oh yeah. Stephan wants to know if you eat steak."

"I do. I love meat."

I swallow hard. "Okay, so do I."

Her smile grows, and I know it's because she can sense how awkward I feel right now.

"Anyway, how do you take your steak? The guys all like it medium rare."

"Me too. That would be perfect."

"Cool. I'll let Stephan know."

I turn to leave when she calls out, "Hey, I was thinking—what if I pay you guys for the food I eat? I can tally it up or something like that."

"You know Taters isn't going to take your money. I already told you that."

"But can't he take something from me?"

I shrug. "I mean, I can ask him, but I'm pretty sure I know what the answer is going to be. He doesn't even let us pay for anything."

"Okay." Her lips twist to the side and then her eyes light up. "What if I did the dishes? That would help Stephan, right?"

"Why don't you get dressed and we can talk about it later?" With that, I leave her to get dressed and head back into the main living space, where the boys are gathering.

"Finish your book?" I ask Holmes as he pulls a beer from the fridge.

"Yeah."

"That was fast."

"It wasn't too long and I read fast."

"Does that mean you're going to hang out with us now?"

"No, he started another one," Posey says, grabbing a couple beers from the fridge. He tosses one my way and pops open the other for himself. The crack of beers opening signals Taters to come inside, as well.

"Stephan said steaks are almost done. He made one for Winnie. Know how she takes it?"

Know how she takes it?

"Shit, yeah. Sorry, I was meant to pass that one. Medium rare," I say. "Can you apologize to Stephan?"

Oddly caring, he nods his head and goes back outside to tell Stephan.

"He's in a mood," Posey says. "I was playing chess with him earlier and he acted like a little bitch every time I took one of his pieces. The game ended with him flipping the board over and stomping away."

"Wish I'd seen that bitch fit," Hornsby says as he grabs a beer for himself. We all gather around the kitchen island.

"Right." Posey picks up a chunk of roasted potato and pops it into his mouth. "Took me ten minutes to find all the pieces. I ended up playing a game against myself after that just to settle my nerves."

I take a pull from my beer and say, "The breakup is really getting to him. Anyone know why Sarah broke up with him?"

All the guys shake their heads.

"No fucking clue," Hornsby says. "That's something he'd normally confide in me but he's said nothing, just that they broke up and it's over."

"Did he do something?" I ask. "Something stupid?"

"Maybe," Holmes says, leaning against the counter.

We all turn toward him. "What do you mean?" Posey asks.

"Just that he could've done something stupid. The fame was getting to him."

Whispering, I ask, "You think he cheated?"

Holmes shrugs just as Taters comes back in the house.

Unfortunately, as a collective group, we're no good at being coy, so we all turn to look at him at the same time.

"What?" he asks, stopping right in front of the sliding glass door.

"Uhh, just wondering if you cheated on Sarah," Hornsby says, not even pretending to hide the conversation.

"Dude." I push at his shoulder.

"What? No use in hiding it. He either did or he didn't."

Taters's eyes narrow as he says, "I would never fucking cheat on her and you four should know that."

Stephan walks up behind Taters and says, "Steaks are ready."

Irritated, Taters storms off, leaving us—well, at least me—feeling like an asshole.

"Why the hell did you have to say that?" Posey asks. "Now he's going to be in an even worse mood."

"Got to break him at some point," Hornsby says while taking a sip of his beer. "Where's—ah, there she is. I wasn't sure you were actually still here because we didn't see you all day."

I glance over my shoulder to catch Winnie wearing a simple white tank top and a pair of sweatpants with the legs pushed up to her calves.

"Oh, I didn't want to bother anyone."

"You're not bothering us," Hornsby says. "You don't have to stay in your room. There's plenty to do around here. There's a movie theater and golf simulator in the basement. Ping-pong. Arcade games. We have some outdoor games in the backyard. Any good at horseshoes?"

She shakes her head.

"Well, we can teach you. There's also a library in the loft

with tons of books. Holmes has been taking advantage of that. Uh, there are trails that you can hike as well if you're looking to check out some nature, but I would take one of us with you; we know these woods better. No need to stay in your room."

"Well, thank you, I appreciate it."

"Dinner's ready, boys," Stephan says.

Hornsby gestures to the plates. "Ladies first."

Winnie holds up her hands. "Oh no, you guys go. I don't feel right going first. And don't press the point. No one is going to eat if you wait for me to go first."

"Fair enough," Posey says, grabbing a plate and jumping in. No shock there. Holmes goes second, then Hornsby, followed by Stephan, who announces he's going to make a plate for Taters and take it to him.

Probably smart. Not sure Taters wants to be around us right now.

"Everything looks amazing," I say as I pile some roasted potatoes onto my plate.

"Thanks. Hopefully the steaks are cooked to your liking."

"They always are," Posey says from the table.

"Hey, Winnie, help yourself to a beer or soda from the fridge," Hornsby says.

"Oh, I have a water bottle, and that should be fine. Thank you anyway."

She's acting incredibly polite right now, almost demure. Not the same girl I saw this morning, and I think it's because she's intimidated around the guys. I know she doesn't want to—as she puts it—bother us, but the guys really aren't fazed. So far, she's been easy to be around, funny. It's not as if we don't spend time with our teammates' wives and girlfriends. Especially when we travel. None of us are really into the "ravenous" fans like some players are, so I doubt any of the guys feel uncomfortable. Do we give off that vibe, though? *Do we intimidate her?*

Once we gather our plates, we take a seat at the dining room table, and I carefully watch as Winnie piles little scoops of food on her plate. And the steak Stephan made, she takes a half of it. When I catch a glimpse of her dinner, I realize just how small it is.

And then when she starts walking toward her bedroom, bypassing the table altogether, I ask, "Where are you going?"

She stops and glances at the table. "Oh, I don't want to impose. You guys do your thing. I'm going to eat real quick and then I'll be back to do the dishes."

"I got the dishes," Stephan says from the kitchen.

"No, it's the least that I can do. And thank you for dinner, it looks great." She heads toward her bedroom again so I hop out of my chair and jog after her. I catch her right before she enters her room.

I put my hand against the doorframe and say, "Hey, have dinner with us."

She shakes her head. "Seriously, Pacey, I don't want to interrupt your guys' trip. I'm okay with eating in here and trying to not rattle the boat . . . or however they say it."

"You're not . . . rocking the boat. It's going to be awkward knowing you're in your room, eating your dinner by yourself. You could've hung out with us today, too. You don't have to hide away. You know, we're pretty fun guys."

"I don't doubt that you are. I just feel . . . weird."

"Why?"

She looks behind her and then whispers, "Given the circumstances, I'm not sure many people crash the houses of famous hockey players."

"Ahh, let me guess." I lean forward. "Did you look us up today once you got Internet access?"

"Maybe," she says, looking away.

"Maybe tell a friend or two and they freaked out?"

"Maybe . . ."

"And now you're freaked out because we're no longer normal people in your eyes."

"Possibly." She nibbles on the corner of her lip.

I lift her chin with my index finger and say, "Well, sorry to be the bearer of bad news, but we're normal people. We're just idolized because we know how to play a sport on ice. But outside of that, we're normal."

"You don't look normal." She scans my chest and then lifts her eyes to mine.

"Can't do much about the looks department, unless—" I snap my fingers. "Want us all to wear bags on our heads?"

"Oh my God, stop." She pushes at my chest. It feels like a flirty move, and I like it.

I reach out and take her plate in my hand. "Seriously, come have dinner with us."

"Pacey."

"What?" I turn around and grin at her.

"I don't know what to say to them."

"Pretty sure they feel the same way. You're a girl, after all. Your female parts scare us." I pretend to shiver and she laughs even more.

"Stop being charming."

"Ahh, sorry, that's ingrained." I nod toward the main living space. "Let's go, Winnie. Hustle up."

"Your sports terms aren't going to make me move faster, just a heads-up on that."

She catches up with me and we walk to the dining table together. "The queen is going to grace us with her presence tonight," I say, setting her plate down next to mine.

"Is that how she wants us to refer to her?" Posey asks, his mouth full of potatoes.

"Queen Winnie, I believe," I answer.

"God, please don't." Her cheeks are pink from embarrassment, and I find it endearing, though I'm sure she doesn't at all. "Just Winnie and, Pacey, stop making this a big deal."

"But it is a big deal. You spent the whole day in your room, working on an equation that's going to help bring us closer to

Mars, and now we're having dinner with you. Please tell us more about your trans-planetary endeavors."

"Really?" Hornsby asks, and I hope to Jesus Winnie takes this moment to go along with it.

She glances at me and I grin while bringing a potato to my mouth.

With a flip of her napkin, she lays it across her lap and says, "Actually, it's not a very important equation, but important enough to help the Mars Lander make a better attempt at a 360 turn. More precise so when we detect other living forms, we can grab a snapshot of it within an instant."

"Holy shit," Posey says. "So, you're like a rocket scientist."

I pick up my beer and hide my smirk behind it.

"Technically just a project manager for NASA, but if you want to call me a rocket scientist, sure, I'll take it."

"Wait." Hornsby sets down his beer and asks, "So you know about Mars?"

"Sure do." Winnie cuts into her steak, totally playing along. I fucking love it. "Wow, this feels like cutting through butter."

"Do you think we'll ever land a person on Mars?" Posey asks.

"The question isn't if, but when," Winnie answers, and fuck, I'm enjoying this far too much. I have no idea what this woman does, but what I do know is that she's good at telling a story. "You see"—she points her fork at Hornsby—"we have the capability to be on Mars now, it's just all about the politics."

"What do you mean?" Posey asks. All the boys lean in, completely fascinated, even Holmes.

"Well, we're not going to go to Mars just for the hell of it, but if, let's say . . . Russia announces they're going to put a human on Mars, then we'd be there in six months because we have the capabilities to do so."

"Seriously? Holy shit," Hornsby says while popping a piece of steak in his mouth. "So basically, it's all about the politics now."

"Yup. Until then, I'm just going to work on my equation and be happy with that."

"So, you just work on the same thing over and over again?" Posey asks.

"I mean, isn't that what you do?" she asks. "You work on the same thing over and over again, perfecting what you do. How is that any different than what I do?"

"She has a point," I say.

"What happens when you solve the equation?" Posey asks.

"Then I work on another one. But let's be honest, the Mars Lander already has a pretty good spin radius. I'm just chilling until I feel pressure from the top. If you catch my drift." She winks and then takes a bite of steak.

Hornsby laughs. "I like your work ethic."

"I mean, I don't slack, I get stuff done. You know the whole 'potatoes on Mars' thing?" She points to her chest. "My idea. I tested some of the soil that we brought back to earth and saw that it has the perfect pH balance to grow potatoes. So, we tried it."

"No shit," Hornsby says, completely fascinated.

Oh hell, this is too fucking good.

"Who knew a rocket scientist was going to stumble into the cabin? Have you ever considered going to space?" Hornsby asks.

"I actually went to Texas for some training. I couldn't get past the zero-G training. Let's just say my stomach wasn't made of steel."

"Ooh, did you puke in those astronaut suits?"

She nods. "All over the face shield. Wasn't pretty."

"Is it true they pee in their astronaut suits?" Posey asks.

"Absolutely," Winnie says, and I really wonder how much knowledge she has on this topic. I'm not sure I could make up this much. "I've peed a few times in them just for the hell of it. It's weird, voluntarily peeing in your pants. But you get over it once you feel the sweet release for your bladder."

Holmes sits back in his chair and asks, "What's the name of

the Mars Lander that's working on Mars right now? I read an article that there are sixteen on Mars, but only one working."

Uh-oh. Looks as though she might be caught in her lie. Holmes is too damn smart.

"Falcon," Winnie says without tripping up. She picks up a potato and places it in her mouth.

Huh, maybe she does work within the space field, because that was a bullet answer. She seems to know—

"Funny, I thought it was Perseverance."

Winnie stops chewing as all the guys turn toward her. She smiles wide and I laugh out loud.

"Damn, girl, I'm impressed. I didn't think you were going to be able to take it that far. You know a lot about space," I say.

"What do you mean?" Hornsby asks. "Are you not a rocket scientist?"

Winnie swallows and starts laughing while shaking her head. "No, sorry. I heard Neil deGrasse Tyson on a podcast and found it fascinating. I have no idea what's going on in space or with Mars. And an equation for a radial turn—not even sure that's a thing, but thank you for thinking I'm smart."

"Man," Posey says, tossing his napkin. "I've never felt so duped. I really thought you knew what you were talking about. I had far too much excitement about picking your brain."

"I feel so let down right now," Hornsby says, and then he chuckles. "We need to watch out with this girl. She thinks she's the one who needs to be careful of being abducted. Did you see that on-the-spot lying? That's some crazy shit." He points his fork at Winnie. "She's going to murder us in our sleep. I mean, she answered 'Falcon' without even blinking. Falcon seemed like a legit name for a Mars Lander. I actually like Falcon better than Perseverance."

"I agree," Posey says. "If she'd said Perseverance, I don't think I would've believed her. But Falcon? That's a commanding name. A name that takes charge, that doesn't need an equation to spin properly."

"Maybe you should write NASA an email, tell them to switch it up. Offer them some suggestions," I say.

"Can we use your connections?" Hornsby asks Winnie sarcastically.

"Sure thing." Winnie winks and takes another bite of her steak.

"Well, since you don't work for NASA, what do you do?" Posey asks.

"Still trying to figure that out," she says quietly. "Kind of had a little break in life, and now I'm waking back up from that break. One of the reasons why I'm out here is to figure out what I want to do."

"Why Banff?" I ask, confused and also intrigued by her evasiveness.

"A few reasons," she answers, but keeps it at that.

"Doesn't look as though she's willing to share just yet," Posey says. "But I'm sure one of us will crack her by the time she leaves." Posey's eyes connect with mine and I look away, not liking his innuendo.

"I just appreciate the hospitality." She pats her stomach. "This food is amazing."

"Save some room," Stephan says from the kitchen. "I made some peanut butter fluff pie."

Leaning toward Winnie, I say, "You're really going to want to save some room. His PB fluff pie will be the best thing you ever put in your mouth."

Her eyes flit down to my mouth for a brief second before they're back up to my eyes. "I'm going to have to take your word for it," she says.

Chapter Eight

WINNIE

"You really don't have to do the dishes, you realize that, right? It's part of Stephan's job." Pacey presses his backside against the counter while speaking to me.

"The man cooked us a spectacular meal, and where I come from, someone cooks, the other person cleans."

Pacey leans in closer and whispers, "But it's his job. Hence why he's scowling at you from the corner."

I glance over to where Stephan is talking to Eli and there's not one ounce of scowling. He actually looks pretty happy. Relieved. Relaxed.

"He's not even looking over here," I say while I rinse off one of the pans used for roasting the potatoes.

"That's because he knows we're talking about him." Pacey snags a dish towel from the handle of the oven and picks up one of the pans I just cleaned.

"What are you doing?" I ask.

"What does it look like? I'm drying the dishes."

"I can do that."

"I realize you're more than capable, but I feel weird having you do our dishes, so I'm going to help."

"But that negates the purpose of me doing the dishes. I'm trying to earn my keep, but you're taking that joy away from me with your helpful hands." I take the dish towel from him but he snags it right back. "Pacey."

"I'm not sure if I'm supposed to apologize for helping or not. I'm going to go with no apology." He picks up another dish and starts drying it.

"Are you normally this kind?"

He chuckles. "I mean, I would say I'm not really doing anything out of the norm. Why do you ask?"

I want to hide the truth, which is instead of "working on an equation" all day, I was watching YouTube clips of the boys, and let me tell you, they didn't seem all that welcoming in their interviews. Very serious. Sometimes pissed off. Silas threw a water bottle in one, while Pacey knocked the microphone off the table in another. Not something I would expect from the man drying the dishes right now.

"Oh no, you're going to have to answer that question." He playfully nudges me with his shoulder. "Did you have some preconceived notions of what hockey players are really like in real life?"

"No . . ."

"Then what—wait." He turns toward me and I wince. "During your research, did you watch videos of us?"

"Would it be proper research without watching videos?" I ask.

"I see. And let me guess, the videos you watched must have been after games, right?"

"Possibly a press conference setup."

"And the most popular ones are the videos where we lose our cool, right?"

"They seem to float to the top," I answer.

"And a guy who loses his temper doesn't seem like one who would be so *kind*, now would he?"

I look him in the eyes, those glacial eyes. "Are you sure you're not some sort of detective? Your deductive reasoning is quite good."

"Are you sure you're not a rocket scientist? Your off-the-cuff knowledge about Mars was uncanny."

"Touché," I say. "Let's just call a spade a spade—we're good at all things."

"That's pretty fair. I'm pretty great at a lot of things other than hockey."

"Oh yeah? Name one." I hand him a bowl and he takes it from me.

"Hmm, one . . . it's so hard to narrow it down out of all the things I'm good at." He's really cute when he's joking around. So different than the menacing man in the videos, pissed off from a loss. I really like this side of him. Not that I've seen many sides of him at all, but I do appreciate his teasing. "I'm really good at finding four-leaf clovers."

"Really?" I ask. "I don't think I've ever met someone who's found one."

"That's upsetting. That must mean you haven't had a lot of luck in your life."

"Yeah, you can say that," I scoff.

"Care to elaborate on that?"

I glance at him. "Not really."

"Still a steel trap, got it. Also, I'm really good at reading the room and knowing when to back off or when to press. Can you tell?"

"I've noticed that about you. I've also noticed that you're cocky but not overtly cocky. You show it in small doses."

"No need to shove it down people's throats." He winks. "What about you? What's something you're really good at, besides being persistent about helping out and your Mars knowledge?"

I wet my lips as I rinse off another bowl. For some reason, my lips feel really dry up here. It's either the elevation, or my body telling me they need to be wet . . . by something other than my tongue. "Well, you already know too much about me. I can't give away all my secrets. How can I stay elusive if I do that?"

"Is that what you're trying to do?" he asks. "Trying to stay a mystery?"

I finish washing the last bowl and hand it over before rinsing the sink. "Isn't it more fun like that? You can always think back to the summer when the girl who pushed her car into a ditch stayed with you for a few days, but you never knew who she was, and she remained a mystery."

He sets the last bowl down and hangs the towel up to dry. "Or you can come have a beer with me outside and tell me one thing you're good at. Just one."

God, that's tempting.

So tempting.

It would be wonderful to have a moment with Pacey, to drink a beer with him and relax, but I fear if I allow myself more time with him, I'm going to grow attached, and that would be a bad idea.

Just from finding out more about him from my "research", I know he's not one of those guys you meet and quickly forget about. And from what I saw online today, he's not been seen with numerous leggy model-esque women on his arm either. *Not a one-and-done asshole.*

No, he's one that sticks around for a long time, maybe forever. A relationship guy.

Not sure I can handle that. Not right now.

"I'm actually getting—"

He shakes his head. "Nope. Remember when I said I'm good at reading the room? Also good at reading people, and that pause in your answer gave you away. You're coming up with an excuse to not hang out with me, and that bruises my soul." He clutches his chest playfully. "Want to make it up to me for staying here? Come have a beer with me out back."

Man, is he good.

I prop my hand on the counter and comment, "You really know how to hit people where it hurts, don't you?"

"Yup, and if you're wondering if I'm ashamed . . ." He leans in. "I'm not."

Gulp.

I just can't with him. With how handsome he is. With how perfect he looks even just in a simple T-shirt and athletic shorts. But it's the way the shirt clings to his arms and chest but is loose around his waist, it's the fit. And then, his ass . . . if I were a poet, I'd write sonnets about his ass.

Thou art the finest ass.

That's poetry, right?

"Do you, uh . . . do you have any hard cider? Or just beer?"

"We actually do have cider. Posey and I like it."

"You're a cider drinker?"

He nods. "Yeah, there's a local brewery here that Posey and I like to go to. We'll take you sometime this week—you know, once you figure out that equation." He winks and goes to the fridge to pull out two bottles. He pops open our ciders on a bottle opener on the side of the fridge, then gestures toward the sliding glass door and says, "There are some egg seats in the back."

"Egg seats?" I ask.

"That's what I call them." He leads the way to the back of the property, along the tree line. He ducks past a bush and holds the branches back for me. When we clear the bush, the stunning view of the Rocky Mountains steals breath from my lungs.

Just past the tops of the pine trees is a landscape view of blue mountains barely tipped with snow. Impressively stretching the length of the horizon, the mountains stand strong and proud, a view new to me, but a view that will last in my memory.

"Oh my God," I whisper. "This is . . . gorgeous."

He hands me my cider. "Aren't you glad you didn't retreat back to your room now?"

"I am," I say while taking it all in. The clouds are a heavy gray and I feel as if they'll open up with rain any second, but it doesn't tear me away from the picturesque combination of valley and mountains. Steep cliffs with arresting peaks, and vibrant green pine trees paint the mountainsides. It's probably one of the prettiest things I've ever seen.

And then my eyes land on the chairs, well—chair.

"I thought you said there were two chairs out here?"

He scratches the back of his head. "There were." He studies the large chair and then says, "It's big enough for two people, that's unless you're disgusted by me and can't have me that close."

Disgusted? More like dangerously attracted.

Nervous I might involuntarily lick his neck if he's too close.

Or try to lift up his shirt unknowingly.

Not saying anything, I walk over to the half-egg-shaped chair with navy-blue cushions and take a seat, giving him plenty of room to sit next to me so our legs won't touch. Not that I would mind if they did but, you know, just to stay safe . . . since apparently my brain is having all sorts of dirty thoughts.

As he takes a seat, he says, "So, not disgusted by me, then."

"Barely above repulsive. Consider yourself lucky."

He sips his cider and says, "I do."

I bring the cider to my lips to hide my grin, because when he makes little comments like that, it makes me think he's flirting. But there's no way someone like Pacey Lawes is flirting with me. He's just a nice guy. Someone who goes out of their way to make you feel good. He admitted it himself—he's good at reading people.

"So, you going to crack that door open a bit?" he asks as we both stare out at the mountains.

"What door?" I ask. "My bedroom door?"

"Nah, the door you're hiding behind. You know enough about me, thanks to the Internet, but I know nothing about you. Don't you think it's fair that you give me a little something?"

"I don't see how your celebrity status should hinder my ability to continue to be a mystery."

He nudges my foot. "Humor me."

"Why so interested, Pacey Lawes?"

He sighs and leans against his side of the chair. "Truth?"

"Always." I smirk.

"Besides the fact that I'm genuinely curious about your adventure and I think you're incredibly interesting, I just have this feeling I know you from somewhere and it's driving me crazy."

"You think you know me?" My hand falls to his leg as excitement bubbles up in me. "Oh my God, do you think we knew each other—"

"Please don't say in another life."

"—in another life," I say.

He groans and sucks down a large gulp of his cider. "No. I don't believe in that shit."

"Seriously? You don't think that we were secret agents in another life? Fighting crime and high-fiving once we solved the crime?"

He blinks a few times and then says, "Not even a little."

"That's upsetting." I sip my cider. "But I will say I felt you were familiar, as well."

"Really?"

I nod. "Yeah, your mannerisms seem familiar, but I can't place it."

He shifts in his seat. "Then, we should get to know each other. Maybe we can solve the mystery. Go ahead, tell me one thing you're good at."

"One thing?"

"Yeah, and then we'll go from there."

"Pushing your luck, Pacey."

"We have a mystery to solve, so I'll push as much as I find necessary. Now stop avoiding, and give me the goods."

I laugh. "Okay. Umm . . . one thing I'm good at . . . I would have to say I'm really good at Jenga." I hold my hand out to him. "Steady hand. See?"

"Oh yeah? What makes you think you're good at Jenga?"

"Umm, my winning record?"

"I see. Have you ever played a Jenga master?"

I turn toward him. "Are you calling yourself a Jenga master?"

"If the shoe fits." He sips his cider again.

"Oh wow, okay, this needs to be settled."

"One step ahead of you." He stands from the egg seat and says, "Be right back."

He sets his cider down and jogs back through the bushes. While I wait for him to come back, I pull my knees against my chest and stare out at the beautiful mountains. What is this insane life I'm living right now?

I'm sharing a moment with a complete stranger, and yet, it feels . . . right.

This all feels right, even though Katherine thinks I've lost my mind. None of this feels scary or as if something out of a horror film is going to happen.

Almost as if this was meant to be. All of this was meant to be. Now I just need to figure out why.

And Pacey is right—I think there is a connection between us, but we just can't seem to figure it out.

Pacey reappears with a table and a box of Jenga blocks.

"Should I be worried?" I ask.

"If I were you, I would be." He sets the table down and says, "I grabbed the box that has the questions on the blocks."

"Questions?"

"Yup." He preps the game. "On certain blocks, there are questions, and before you put it on top, you have to answer the question. If you choose not to answer, you have to repeat your turn."

"Ooh brutal." I get closer to the table and set my cider down in the grass. "I think I can handle it, though."

"Can you? You're going to have to crack that door open, you know?"

"For Jenga, for the title of Master Jenga-ist, I'll do it."

"Is that the proper term?" He chuckles. "Master Jenga-ist?"

"Yup," I answer with confidence. Anyone will believe you if you have enough confidence in your answers. Tonight was a prime example of that.

"Uh-huh, just like Falcon is the name of the Mars Lander?"

I pick up my cider and tilt it at him. "Precisely."

"Okay, Master Jenga-ist, you go first." He gestures toward the tower and I go for the kill, the bottom of the tower, and I pull out the left block.

"Savage." He shakes his head.

"I told you, I'm good." I scan the block and see there's a question. "Fuck, Chuck, Marry. Hornsby, Posey, Lawes." I scrunch my nose and look up at Pacey, who has a huge grin spread across his face. "What is this?"

"A question," he says. "And did I mention, the first question always has to be answered?"

"That's not the—"

He holds an index card up to me that states the rules of the game the boys obviously made up, and right there, the number one rule is the first question always has to be answered.

"Now, you can forfeit right now and I can claim the title, or you can answer—"

"Marry Posey." I tap my chin and think about the question. There's no way I'm going to let him win that easily. Knowing it will grate on Pacey's nerves, I finish, "Fuck Hornsby and chuck Lawes. Easy." I plop the brick on top and lean back in the chair while grinning at him.

He clutches his heart. "After everything we've been through,

you'd chuck me? That's brutal, Winnie. Really fucking brutal."
He reaches for a block as I try to hide my laugh. He pulls it out
with ease and then places it on top.

"Hey, don't you have to answer a question?"

"There wasn't a question on that block." He picks it up and
shows me. "Only some of them have questions."

"Oh, so I was the lucky one who pulled the 'fuck, chuck, or
marry' block?"

"Incredibly lucky . . . even though you didn't answer it truthfully." He smirks.

"And how do you think I should've answered it?"

He brings his drink to his lips and says, "We both know
you'd chuck Hornsby."

Yup.

We both know it.

"Isn't Horny the perfect guy to fuck, though?"

Pacey nearly spits out his drink when he laughs. "I guess so."

Pleased with myself, I grab another block, this one on the
bottom right so the tower is left teetering on one block. I like to
start the game off with a real challenge. I flip it over and find
writing. "Apparently, I only know how to pick blocks with
questions."

"Just the way I like it," Pacey says.

"Okay, what's your favorite . . ." I trail off and look up at
Pacey.

"What?" he asks, even though the humor in his eyes gives
him away.

"What's the theme of these blocks?"

"No theme, just questions the guys and I came up with."

"And you play this with each other?"

"Yup," he answers casually.

"So, you answer what your favorite body part is of the
person across from you?"

"Easily." He grins.

"I don't believe you."

He shifts in the chair and says, "Fuck, chuck, or marry—I would fuck myself, marry Posey, chuck Hornsby. Last time we played this, I sat across from Holmes. I told him my favorite body part of his were his thighs. Titans in jeans, thick as hell." He wiggles his brows and then leans back again. "No shame in playing with the boys. Now, do you have any other complaints?"

I pause and then ask, "You'd fuck yourself?"

"Usually the only kind of love I get, so yeah. Stick with what's working."

I snort and then cover my nose.

"What's so funny?" he asks.

"I'm sorry." I wipe at my nose. "I just wasn't expecting you to say that."

"What did you expect? Oh wait, that's right—you assumed I was the manwhore of the group." He picks a piece of lint off his shorts. "Can't always judge a book by its cover, Winnie."

"Apparently not. Well, that's, uh, interesting. I hope you're gentle with yourself. Kind."

He chuckles. "I'm always gentle, but commanding."

I laugh out loud. "Oh God, my mind is reeling right now and it shouldn't."

"Do tell what it's thinking." He takes another sip of his drink and leans against his side of the chair so he's facing me, and it's hard not to fall under his spell. His easygoing, open spell. It feels so normal talking to him. Simple. I don't have to try, it just flows, and all the credit goes to Pacey, because he makes me feel comfortable. Not sure I'd feel this way with any of the other guys in the house.

"No way. I'm not sharing the thoughts in my head."

"So, then they must be *really* good."

"It's humiliating." I clear my throat and then stare down at my block. "Okay, this game needs to move along. My, uh, favorite body part of yours?" I glance up at him, and it's a no-brainer for me. "Your eyes." I place the block on the top of the pile and wait for him to say something, to tease me over my answer, but he doesn't. Instead, he takes his turn and picks up a block.

He twirls it in front of me, showing it doesn't have a question on it, and then places it on top of the tower.

"How on earth are you doing that?"

"Luck."

Sighing, I reach for another block, wiggle it out, and then see once again there's writing. "Seriously? What's this one going to be?" I scan the text and cringe. "I think I'm skipping this one."

"Come on, what does it say?"

"It says to pick your favorite player and give them a hug. Is that something you guys really do?"

"Hell yeah. Never too cool to hug a bro." He spreads his arms wide. "Don't be shy. Come on in here."

Why is this so easy for him?

And why am I making a big deal about this?

You can hug Pacey Lawes.

Max would be climbing Pacey if he were in my position right now.

Why did I come on this trip? To let go, to be free. *To grow.*

Well, here's my moment. I can either hold back and hang on to that shy persona, or I can let go and just enjoy the ride.

I put the block on top of the tower and then lean in and wrap my arms around Pacey. The first thing I notice is just how much bigger he is than me. The second thing I notice is how rock-hard his back is. Strong, stiff—there's not one ounce of cushion. The third thing I notice is how freaking good he smells —all man, delicious.

And the fourth thing I notice—just how amazing it feels to have someone hug me like he is. Warm, consuming arms wrap around me. I feel protected, safe, cared for. And it's silly to say something like that—I've known the man for twenty-four hours —but the way Pacey is holding me feels just like that—protective. But that doesn't surprise me. His career is based on protection—protecting the goal, making sure he keeps his team on top —so why wouldn't his hugs have the same feeling?

When I release him and pull away, he says, "Damn, you give good hugs."

I place my hands in my lap and just smile.

"Not going to return the compliment?" he asks, picking up a block and showing me once again there's no question.

"You're good at hugging, too," I say as my cheeks light up.

And there I go, crawling back into the shy-girl persona again. *But who wouldn't?* I just hugged the most gorgeous man I've ever seen.

"YOU'RE SCREWED," Pacey says as I continue to wiggle a block from the tower. I'm pretty sure this is the tallest, longest game of Jenga I've ever played. And guess who has answered most of the questions? Me.

Luckily, they haven't been too terrible. I did stumble over what my ideal date with one of the players would be because playing with just Pacey made it all about him. I went with a stupid answer, saying Jenga in the backyard with cider, which then sparked Pacey to tease me about what we were doing right now and if it was a date. My cheeks didn't stand a chance.

"The commentary is not welcome," I say, the block held in by just the corner now.

"Whoa, whoaaaa."

I lift up and give him an evil glare that makes him laugh out loud.

"Seriously, you need to stop, you're wrecking my concentration." I hold my breath and then yank the last corner out. The tower wobbles for a few seconds and I wince, praying it stays up. When it doesn't fall over, I take a breath and then flip the block over.

Question.

Because why not?

"What does it say?" He has a huge grin on his face.

"Why are you smiling like that?"

"Like what?" he asks.

"Like you know what it says on this block."

"Because I do know what it says on that block. It's the only one left we haven't answered."

"Am I going to have to kiss you?" I ask, because we've had to hug and hold hands at this point, so kissing would obviously be the next step.

"Nah, there are no kissing blocks. Lips are sacred to us."

I laugh at that, thinking about how these men made these blocks but kept kissing off the table because "lips are sacred."

We're three ciders in at this point and I'm feeling a little funny, not drunk by any means, but good, and I think Pacey is feeling the same way. When we needed new drinks, we both had to go to the kitchen together to get them, because we didn't trust each other to not mess with the tower. Mainly, he didn't trust me since I kept getting frustrated about the questions.

"But kissing me wouldn't be a hardship, you know. I'm a pretty good kisser." Pacey motions to his lips. "I use lip balm daily. These puppies are soft."

"I use lip balm daily, too," I say with excitement, as if we just connected on a much deeper level.

"I could tell. Your lips look soft."

"You looked at my lips?" I ask, my nose scrunching up.

"They're on your face, aren't they?"

"Last time I checked," I answer.

"Then, yes, I looked at your lips."

I nod. "Checks out." I stare down at the block, but I can feel his eyes on me, so I glance in his direction and ask, "What?"

"You have a nice smile, too. Posey's is pretty damn good, but you give him a run for his money."

I tilt my head to the side and realize my lips are feeling really loose because I ask, "Are you flirting with me, Pacey?"

"Has it not been obvious?" He pushes his hand through his unruly hair. "I need to work on my game."

Oh God, he *is* flirting. Even with my brain feeling semi-foggy, I'm having a hard time believing it. I mean, I don't feel like I lack self-confidence. I think in a real-life situation—not in a got-lost-in-the-woods-and-stumbled-into-a-house-full-of-hockey-players situation—I'm a solid seven. I have a nice face. I like my hair. I could benefit from working out some, but I haven't had time the past two or so years. So, a seven seems like a good number. But insert me into the alternate reality I'm currently living in, a reality where I share a house with a bunch of men who don't even fit on the ten-out-of-ten scale—they're the men you make a new scale for—I'm easily a four.

I don't stand a chance. And that's not me being a Debbie Downer, that's me speaking the cold, honest truth.

So I can't imagine a time when someone like Pacey Lawes, a man with such corded forearms that it's my new favorite pastime to watch them fire off while he grips his drink, would even consider flirting with me.

"I doubt you have to work on your flirting, Pacey."

"Why?" he asks.

Is he really that oblivious?

"Uh, you know, because you're this hot hockey player and I'm just a plain Jane that stumbled temporarily into your life."

Pacey's eyes narrow and the side of his jaw ticks. "You think you're a plain Jane?"

I wave my hand at him. "Not looking for any half-hearted compliments, here. Just forget what I said. I have a question to answer." I look down at the question and read it out loud. "'Show your favorite sexual position with the person across from you . . .'" *Oh, Jesus, Mary, and Joseph.*

When I peek up at Pacey, he still has that disgruntled look on his face but he's setting down his almost empty bottle of cider.

"How do you want me?"

I hold the block up. "You think I'm going to do this?"

His eyes fall on the teetering tower and then back at me. "If you don't answer, you have to go again, which will most likely guarantee you the loss. Are you willing to lose over a question?"

I'm not.

If anything, I'm competitive and I like knowing that I could be the Jenga Master, especially after the game I've had. There has been taunting, roadblock questions, and doubting of my abilities. He's right, if I go again, there's a high chance I won't be able to make it through alive.

But perform my favorite sex position on Pacey? That takes the cake for embarrassing, because, well . . .

"I, uh, I only really know two," I admit, wanting to be swallowed whole from the confession.

"What do you mean, you know two?"

"Two sex positions," I say, and when my eyes meet his, I watch them turn soft with understanding.

Gently, he asks, "Well, then which was your favorite of the two?"

Confused, I ask, "You're not going to make fun of me?"

"Why would I make fun of you for that? Everyone has a favorite or two, hence the question. But from the way your shoulders turned in, I'm guessing it's a sensitive topic for you, so of course I won't make fun of you."

"I've only been with one guy," I say. The cider really has loosened up my lips. "He was my first true love, just like Silas and his girl. We were each other's firsts. I think he wasn't quite sure what to do with me, so we only stuck to two things that worked for him."

"Worked for him?" Pacey asks, brow lifted. "What do you mean *worked for him*?"

"That got him off."

"And what about you?"

I shrug. "It didn't matter. I just wanted to make sure he was happy."

Pacey sits straight up now. "It sure as fuck does matter." He must check himself because, he calms his voice and asks, "Have you ever had an orgasm?"

I think about it. "I mean . . . I think so."

"Winnie, you'd know if you orgasmed, if it actually happened."

"It didn't really matter, because we were in love, so I just loved being with him, you know?"

I can see his mind racing in the way his eyes connect with mine. I wouldn't say he's judging me, because he's proven to not be that kind of man, but I do believe he's confused and doesn't quite know what to say.

"Anyway," I set the block on the tower and say, "I'm just going to lie down and you can lie on top of me, for missionary."

I get down on the grass and lie stiff as a board, shocked that I'm actually doing this for the game. *Do the guys do this when they play? Surely not . . .* Pacey doesn't move. He's looking off into the woods, as if contemplating what he should do next.

"What are you doing?" I ask.

"Nothing." He shakes his head and then stands from the chair. Standing above me, he asks, "If missionary is your favorite, what was the other position you did?"

"Um, when I was on top. But I never liked that because I always felt silly. Josh never let me stay on top for long, so I thought that maybe he didn't like me up there, even though it felt better for me. I guess it made me feel self-conscious after a while."

Stunned, Pacey stares at me and blinks a few times. Almost as if he just realized something, as if a lightbulb went off in his head.

"Josh—that was your boyfriend?"

"Yeah."

He pauses again, his eyes diverted, as though he's trying to solve a math equation. When I'm about to ask him if everything is okay, Pacey mutters something under his breath and then gets down on the ground. He stares at me for a second before his hand slides up my thigh, and from that little touch, more excitement races through my veins than Josh ever gave me. With his eyes connected to mine, he spreads my leg open, causing me to catch my breath.

Oh God, what is happening?

"Do you, uh, do this with the guys?" I ask, trying to ease the heat that's building between us.

Pacey doesn't say anything, but instead pushes my other leg open so I'm completely spread for him.

A dull throb begins to pulse between my legs. I'm turned on.

Just like that.

Completely clothed.

Nothing but legs spread in the grass.

And I'm turned on more than I can ever remember being.

I swallow hard as he leans forward, placing his hands on either side of my shoulders, and then he lowers his pelvis to mine.

"This is how you liked it?" he whispers.

This wasn't how it was.

Not even close.

Josh wouldn't hover above me like this, but instead just bury his head on my shoulder and pulse in and out. He never intensely stared at me or even spoke to me.

Maybe that's what the problem was—we were missing the actual connection.

"Uh, it was a little different."

"How?" Pacey asks as his pelvis connects with me, and oh . . . my . . . God. That's his bulge.

That's a big bulge.

That's . . . wow. Josh was big, but this seems more intense.

"How is it different, Winnie?" he asks, his voice soft, ready to listen.

Everything is different.

His body is different. More commanding, more in charge.

His voice sends a wave of heat through my veins every time he speaks.

His eyes never leave mine, not even for a second.

He's in the moment with me, rather than acting as if it's some sort of chore. A box on a checklist.

"You're, uh, bigger than him," I answer.

"In what way?"

I should've seen that coming.

His pelvis slightly moves against mine. My limbs start to tingle and I realize, if he keeps doing this, if he keeps rocking gently, he could turn me into a puddle of desire. Right here, right now, I'm feeling so much more than I ever felt with Josh. It actually feels as if my insides are all pulling to the center of my body, wanting to feel what it's like to have him pulse inside me.

"Answer the question, Winnie."

I swallow hard. "Um, in every way."

"Lawes, you back here?"

Oh shit.

Pacey pushes off me just as Levi rounds the corner, catching us on the ground, fumbling to get away from each other. In the midst of our fumbling, my leg swings out, kicks the table, and the tower comes crashing down in a heap of wood.

Blocks tumble.

We scramble.

And the entire scene could not be more obvious.

"Uh, what's going on here?" Levi asks with that handsome smile of his. He's far too entertained by what he just walked in on.

Pacey stands from the ground and then offers his hand to me to help pull me up. I take it, because what's the point of not? We were obviously doing something we shouldn't have been doing. Or should we have been doing it? We're adults, but we're also adults who barely know each other.

"I don't know the etiquette," I say out of sheer defense.

Wait . . . did I say that out loud?

"The etiquette for what?" Levi asks.

"Uh, Jenga. He said I had to answer the questions." I point at Pacey.

"Oh, I see. Did you get the sex position block?" I nod and Levi continues, "I got that once. I had to do Hornsby doggy style. I think he enjoyed it way too much. And if you're worried about etiquette, then, yes, you're supposed to do what the block says unless you want another turn." He looks back at our tower. "But seems as if the game is over."

"Yeah, sure is." I take a step away. "Well, thanks for a great game, chum." I pat Pacey on the shoulder and grab the empty cider bottles. "I'll just take these to the kitchen and then hit the hay." I pretend to yawn, even though my body is wired. "Got to get that sleep. Never know what tomorrow will bring." I look up to the sky. "And hey, it never started raining—" A drop hits my head, and then another, and then it starts to come down. "Spoke too soon."

And then I take off toward the house, embarrassment consuming me.

No more cider for me. That's for sure. *And Jenga too.*

Chapter Nine

PACEY

"So, you're just going to ignore my questions?" Posey asks as we finally get inside the house after picking up the Jenga blocks.

"You didn't ask anything worth answering," I say. I take a dish towel from one of the drawers and lay it on the counter. I scatter the Jenga blocks over the towel and intently focus on making sure they're all dried off.

"Uh, I'm pretty sure I asked some damn good questions."

I turn toward him and gnaw on the inside of my cheek. "Dude, I think . . . I think I know her."

"What?" Posey asks, confused. "What do you mean you know her? Like from a previous life?"

"What the hell is wrong with everyone? No, not from a previous life. From this life."

"Where from?"

I scan down the hallway to make sure she's out of earshot. I grip the back of my neck when I say, "My brother."

"You have a brother?" Posey asks, his face scrunched up. "Since when?"

"Half-brother. Before my dad met my mom, he had a one-night stand with some girl. A year later, he got my mom pregnant and married her. They've been together since. But when I was fourteen, this kid comes out of the woodwork and says he's my dad's son. It rocked the family a bit. My dad tried to have a relationship with him, but it fizzled out after he moved to Seattle. He stayed in touch here and there, but I can't remember the last time I saw him. He wanted nothing to do with me."

"Okay, so why do you think you know Winnie through your brother? Oh shit, is she his sister?"

I shake my head and glance down the hallway again. "No, I think she dated my brother."

Posey blinks, his mind attempting to comprehend what I'm saying. "What? How do you know?"

"She looked familiar when she walked into the cabin, but I couldn't quite place her. But when we were playing Jenga, she said her ex-boyfriend's name is Josh and, it was as if it all hit me at once." I pull my phone from my pocket and open up my Facebook app. "My dad went to Seattle about six years ago to visit with Josh, and he posted pictures from his trip. I'd just finished college and had been drafted to the minors. But I remember the photos because Josh had a fine-as-hell girlfriend." I go to my dad's profile and start searching for his trip to Seattle, guessing he hasn't deleted any of his photos from years ago. *No one does.*

"So, you think Winnie is your brother's ex-girlfriend?"

"I don't think," I say as I find the pictures of Josh, my dad, and . . . Winnie, standing in front of the Space Needle. I flash the screen to Posey and say, "I know she was his girlfriend." *And that my half-brother wasn't only a dick to me and my dad but also a dick in bed to Winnie. Selfish.*

Posey takes the phone from me and pushes his hand through his hair in shock. "Holy shit, man. Does she know?"

I shake my head. "Nah, I wasn't even positive until just now."

"What a fucking small world." Posey hands me back my phone. "Are you going to say something?"

"I don't know." I scratch the side of my jaw.

Posey smirks. "Because you want a shot at her and if you tell her, she might not give you that shot."

"Not true," I answer, even though I'm pretty sure that is true. Winnie doesn't seem to be the kind of person who would float between brothers, even if they're half-brothers who are estranged.

"How's your relationship with Josh?"

"Non-existent. Dude hates me." My mind falls to the conversation with my dad. What the hell would he want to talk to me about? "Typical I-got-the-childhood-he-didn't situation. I've tried reaching out, but he wants nothing to do with me. Even tried giving him tickets to a game. He's pretty much set in stone when it comes to me. Therefore, so am I. He was an asshole to me and to my father, so he's pretty much dead to me now."

"So I'm guessing he wouldn't like to know that you're falling for his ex-girlfriend."

"Falling for her? Have you lost your mind? I've known her for a day. Falling for people doesn't work like that."

"You have experience on the subject?"

"Are you asking if I've ever fallen in love with anyone?" I lean against the counter.

"Yeah. You're closed off when it comes to your love life. Don't know much about it."

"As a matter of fact, I have fallen for someone."

"Really?" Posey asks, surprised.

"Yup." I push off the counter and walk up to him. I lift my hand and stroke his cheek. "It's about time I tell you how I feel."

He pushes at my chest and laughs. "Get the fuck out of here. I'm being serious, dude."

"Have I ever been in love? No." I shake my head. "Have I been infatuated? Yeah. But not in love. I've never connected with someone on a deep enough level to fall in love."

"And where are you with Winnie?" Posey asks.

"Uh . . . nowhere," I answer. "Dude, seriously, we just met—"

"Maybe, but I saw the way you two were looking at each other back there." He nods to the backyard. "That wasn't nothing."

"Well, it's nothing that needs to be talked about." I push off the counter and say discreetly, "Don't say anything about Josh. I don't need the guys talking about it."

"Your secret is safe with me, but I do think you need to tell Winnie."

"Yeah, I know," I answer, even though telling Winnie about Josh is the last thing I want to do, especially after how we just ended things with awkward uncertainty. "Thanks for the chat," I say as I head down the hallway to my room.

She dated Josh.

Fucking Josh.

Out of all the people in the world, the one person who treated her like hell, it has to be Josh.

Makes me hate the fuck even more.

As I close in on Winnie's room, I consider checking on her to make sure she's okay. We were in an intimate position, a position I would fucking love to repeat, especially if I'm able to repeat the shock in her eyes and the heady feel of her increased breath. But then I think better of it. She's probably embarrassed. Embarrassed by our conversation, her admission, and for being caught by Levi, even though he played it off as nothing.

But if she's embarrassed, it might be a smart idea to reassure her everything is good between us.

I pause and look over my shoulder at her door. Hell, should I knock?

She bolted pretty quickly.

Maybe she wants to be left alone.

Then again, she also trusted me with some private information. I want her to know whatever we talked about is between us.

Hell.

I spin on my heel and before I can stop myself, I knock on her door and call out her name. "Winnie?"

This time, I hear her footsteps against the hardwood floor. The door opens and her face peeks through the crack.

"Hi," she says, not showing her body, just her face.

Is she naked behind that door? *Wouldn't I like to know?*

"Hey, I just wanted to make sure you were okay."

"Fine," she answers casually.

"Okay, because you took off pretty fast and I'm sure that wasn't the kind of position you'd want one of the guys to find us in."

"Seemed as though Levi was good with it," she answers, more casual than I anticipated. She's brushing me off, and I don't know if it's because she's got something going on in her room and I'm disturbing her, or if it's because she's embarrassed by what happened. Either way, I need to let her know everything is cool between us.

"I don't want things to be awkward tomorrow."

"Why would they be awkward?" she asks.

"Uh, I don't know . . . because you're acting awkward right now."

"Oh." She glances down at herself. "I was just trying to be modest." She opens the door wider and her body comes into view. She's dressed in a thin, pink tank top, and it's obvious from how the shirt is clinging to her breasts that she's not wearing a bra. She's paired the top with a pair of dark purple silk shorts.

There's nothing overtly sexy about the pajama set, but the way the two articles of clothing cling to her body makes all the blood in my body rush to my dick.

Hell. She's so goddamn gorgeous. But she's not just gorgeous—she's fun, she's bubbly, she's interesting. *Josh let her go? How?* And then I think about her comment about the orgasms. What the fuck is wrong with Josh? How could he not spend his time worshipping this girl in bed? From her hot-as-hell tits to her curves, I would spend a decent time making it known just how hot I think she is.

"I wasn't trying to be weird . . . I mean, yeah, maybe I felt a little weird, but that's because of what I told you. I mean, who confesses something like that to someone they just met? So, that was embarrassing. I never should've told you that." She's rambling, but all I can focus on is the gloss on her lips and the bounce of her tits as she talks. "Anyway, I'm sorry for making things awkward. That's on me. I hope you're not weird with me." She places her hand to her forehead. "God, I told you that you were big in all places. That's just . . . inappropriate. I'm sorry. I seem to have lost my mind around you. Won't happen again. It's just—"

I move in close to her, and she audibly catches her breath as I slowly move my hand to her hip and pin her against her bedroom wall. Fuck, I want to know what those lips taste like.

I only keep one hand on her because I don't want her to feel as though she's trapped, and also, I know if I have two hands on her, one of them is going to go where it probably shouldn't, and that's up her tank top, to her tits. I'd roll those hard nipples of hers between my fingers.

"There was nothing weird or awkward that happened out there," I say, quietly.

I shouldn't be this close. I shouldn't even be touching her, but, Jesus, there's something about her innocence, about her rambling, about her sweet voice that draws me in. From the moment she stepped into this cabin, wet but full of life, I was drawn to her.

"I had fun," I add. "And I want you to know"—I lift her chin up so her eyes truly connect with mine. Once they do, I yank my hand away so it doesn't wander—"anything you said to me out there, it stays between us."

"Oh, I didn't even think about it." She nibbles her bottom lip, and my eyes fall to that beautiful mouth. What would those lips look like wrapped around my cock? Those eyes staring up at me as she sucks me off. Fucking perfection, probably. "Do you guys gossip much?"

Focusing on what she's asking, I say, "Only on occasion."

"I see." She sucks in a sharp breath when my thumb rubs up her hipbone.

Don't go any further, man. That's it. Any more and you'll lose control.

"Well, um, thank you for letting me know."

"You're welcome." Do her lips taste as sweet as her personality, as innocent as she says she is? Would she break me apart with one kiss? From the way she makes my body thrum with need simply from being this close, I'd say yes. But there's no way in hell I'm going to stick around to find out. The last thing she probably needs is some guy hanging all over her, let alone her ex-boyfriend's half-brother. Thunder erupts outside, signaling my cue to leave. I push off the wall and let go of her. As I take a step back, I keep my eyes trained on her, and that's when I notice her nipples, hard and pressing against her tight-fitting tank.

Fucking hell.

Her eyes track mine; she knows I'm staring at her tits. And I can't stop. I wet my lips. My body thrums with need—just one touch, one taste.

But it's complicated.

Everything about this situation is complicated.

Before I can get carried away, I drag my hand over my mouth and then turn away. "Have a good night, Winnie." I move to the doorway and look at her one more time. "Sweet dreams."

And then I shut the door and walk to my bedroom. When I'm inside, I shut the door and lock it, as if to prevent myself from leaving. Fuck, what is this? This . . . burning, explosive need I have all of a sudden? It's been a long time since I've been with a woman, but it's never felt like this. Like if I don't get a piece of her, I might combust.

I need a shower.

Now.

I hurry into my bathroom, turn on the water, and strip off my clothes. To my surprise, my cock juts up toward my stomach, hard as fuck. I grip it tightly as I close my eyes and wait for the shower to heat up. Fuck. It's been a while, I get that, but I don't think a girl has ever affected me the way Winnie did with that tiny tank and those rock-hard nipples.

Simple.

She didn't do anything but take quick intakes of breath when I moved in close.

But her reaction to me—the way she submitted so easily and didn't show an ounce of fear—made me want so much more than just those lips.

I slip into the shower, and instead of washing my body, I grab some soap, lather my hand, and then start moving it up and down my cock. With my other hand, I prop myself against the shower wall as the spray of the shower pelts my back. Legs braced, I pump while my mind goes to our time together tonight.

Her confession.

The honest look in her eyes.

The innocence in her expression, as if her own pleasure meant nothing.

The trust when she opened her legs for me without question.

When she let me touch her.

The hitch in her breath.

The headiness in her beautiful, deep blue eyes.

I stroke harder.

The way she smells like fresh soap and lavender.

Her melodic voice that captures me when she talks.

The feel of her within my arms as we hugged.

Her goddamn sexy figure in those short shorts.

Her tits . . .

"Fuck," I grunt as my legs start to go numb, all the pleasure pulsing at the base of my cock.

The way her nipples pressed hard against her shirt, almost begging for me to touch her.

And her submission to me. No fear. All trust.

"Ahh, shit," I mutter as my cock swells in my hand, and then I come.

I still, my cock pulsing, taking every last second of pleasure until I collapse against the tile with both hands.

I turn so my back is to the wall now and the water pelts my chest.

Holy shit.

I place both my hands on the tile over my head and take a few deep breaths.

I don't remember the last time I did that—the last time I came thinking about a woman. But not thinking about her naked, just thinking . . . about *her*. I'm not sure if I've ever done that.

Winnie seems to be pulling out a lot of firsts for me, and what scares me is I really don't know that much about her at all. I don't even know her last name or what she does, or why she's really here. But what I do know about her, I like a lot.

I move under the water and rinse off my body with some soap.

I have no idea how long she'll be here, when she plans on leaving, or if she plans on wanting to get to know me, but what I do know is for as long as she's here, I'm going to do my best to get to know her.

Despite knowing that she once belonged to Josh.

I FINISH TYING my running shoe and stand from my bed. The sun is barely filtering through my windows, since it's not even six in the morning yet, but I couldn't sleep.

Once again, Winnie was on my mind.

But this time, it was because of what she said about never experiencing an orgasm. It was all I could think about, how a man would let that happen. How could someone be that selfish and not attempt to make his partner come? How could Josh never let her come? What kind of tortured asshole is he? Yeah, they may have been together, but deeply in love? Nah, I don't believe it. I think they were just comfortable with each other. Because if they were deeply in love, then Josh would've tried to make her come. He would've given a shit.

And of course, at three in the morning, all I could think about was how *I* would make her come. It would be all about her, not me. I would spread her across my bed, strip her down, and then make her squirm with my tongue and lips and fingers until she couldn't take it anymore, and then I'd pull away, ensuring the feeling of teetering on the edge of bliss consumed her. And then, when she'd least expect it, I would make her come all over my tongue.

Hell, after I played it out in my head, I jacked off again.

And it's also the reason why I'm on my way to the gym to work off some of this pent-up energy. Normally, I'd go run outside, but given the storm we had last night, the roads won't be good for running, and I'm not looking for an off-season injury.

I slip out of my room and start down the hall just as Winnie's door opens, as well. Not expecting to see me this early in the morning, she jerks back and clutches her hands over her mouth, muffling her squeal of fright.

"Oh my God, Pacey. Were you standing there all night?"

I chuckle. "Yes, in fact I was. I went back to my room, but instead of sleeping, I chose to stand right here, in front of your door."

She lets out a deep breath and pushes at my shoulder. "Freak."

I take her in. Bike shorts and sports bra with some running shoes. Her hair is in one of those fluffy buns on the top of her head, and those sexy freckles are visible across her nose and cheeks. Damn, she looks good.

"Where you off to?"

"Thought I would go for a walk. Couldn't get much sleep last night so thought I would walk off some of this energy."

You and me both. But what I want to know is . . . was she thinking about me like I was thinking about her? Did she masturbate to the thought of me like I did of her? *No. She wouldn't have, because it sounds like she doesn't know how to get herself to orgasm.*

"Seems as though we had the same idea, but you're not going to want to walk outside unless you want to slide around everywhere."

"Ugh, I keep forgetting we're in the mountains with no regular roads. Where are you going, then?"

"The gym."

"Oh yeah, that makes sense." She turns back toward her room. "Well, I guess I'll just jump back into bed."

"Or . . . you can come to the gym with me?" I would love to see her work out in those short shorts and revealing sports bra.

She snorts. "Oh, okay. Yeah, let me get right on that."

"What's so funny? You can bench the bar."

"And you can bench me, plus some, so let's not pretend that I wouldn't be an embarrassment in the gym next to you. Plus, I'd rather you not hear me grunt."

I lick my lips and give her a smooth once-over. "You're wrong. I'd love to hear you grunt."

Her eyes widen. "Uh, oh . . . umm . . ."

Chuckling, I grab her hand and pull her along with me. "Come on, it'll be fun."

"Why do I feel as though it won't be?"

But I don't give her much chance to change her mind, because I lead her down to the basement to the state-of-the-art gym Taters put together for us. I flip on the lights, and the gym comes to life.

Free weights are off to the right, along with three benches and squatting racks. To the left is the cardio equipment, as well as jump ropes, bands, mats, medicine balls, and Bosu balls. It's everything we need for the off-season.

"Umm . . ." Her lips pop as she takes in the space. "This is incredibly nice."

"Taters went all out." I take my phone from my pocket and connect it to the Bluetooth speakers. "The gym is soundproof, so once that door is shut, we can crank up the music and the boys won't hear a thing. Do you have any music you prefer to listen to while working out?"

"You'd hate my music, I'm sure."

"Try me."

She cutely stretches her arms. "I like to listen to boy-band music."

"Why did I know you were going to say that?" Sighing, I go to Spotify and pull up a playlist made by someone, full of boy bands. I press play and the first song is "It's Gonna Be Me" by *NSYNC.

"Okay, now I really know you're flirting."

"What gave you that impression?" I ask, walking over to her and taking her hand in mine again. I bring her to one of the treadmills and then step up on the one next to her.

"Uh, what do you think you're doing?" she asks.

"Warming up, unless you have a better, more fun way to get our bodies worked up?" My voice drops when I ask her.

Adorably, she quickly shakes her head and says, "Treadmill works. So, what do you do, just start walking, or—"

I start with a solid jog, and she stares at me. "I'm going to say this right now," I tell her. "Comparison takes all the fun out of shit. Don't compare yourself to me, just enjoy yourself. Working out is supposed to be fun."

And I hope that because she's easygoing and seems to be up for anything, she's going to be okay with that.

Luckily, she is, because she cranks her treadmill up to a solid walk.

"Then show me some fun, Pacey."

Chapter Ten

WINNIE

Working out with a professional hockey player—not something I would set out to do on my own, but now that I'm here, ready to get sweaty with Pacey, well, I'm not regretting it. Especially since just seeing him run gives me all kinds of feels . . . as in, I'm *feeling* his body moving like that.

His strong, commanding body.

The same body that pinned me to the ground last night.

Sleep eluded me last night for a reason, because all I could think about was Pacey and how honest he is. How open he is about everything. There's no shame in what he does, in his actions. It's sexy.

"What's the plan?" I ask.

"Want to go through one of my workouts?"

"You mean do what you do?"

He nods.

"As long as I don't have to do the same weights, I'm in."

"Never expected you to." He turns up his speed and then adds some incline.

I do the same, but I keep my pace at a walk because, let's be honest, I don't tend to work out on the daily. I consider a jaunt through the woods a workout.

"Can't tell you the last time I was on a treadmill. Will you judge me?"

He glances over at me. "Never. I told you, I don't judge. Everyone has their own pace, their own level. I'm just glad you're hanging with me this morning."

See what I'm saying? He's adorable. Too good.

"Aren't you the charmer?"

"Nah, not really." He picks up the incline a few more notches. "You're just catching me on a good day."

"Seems like a good couple of days."

He doesn't say anything, but instead continues to jog. His thick, muscular arms pumping by his sides are almost hypnotic, so I tear my gaze away and turn my attention back to my treadmill. I attempt a jogging pace, something I know I could power-walk my way through, but adding that extra little bounce to my step makes me feel good about myself.

"Good pace," he says, while looking over at me. "Looking good, Winnie." And that genuine compliment makes me hold my head a little higher.

I don't do this. I don't work out, and I've always had an aversion to going to the gym. Probably because it's intimidating if you're not toned and muscled and know exactly what you're doing. And yet, I don't feel out of place next to Pacey as he's allowing me—*encouraging me*—to just go with the flow.

After another minute, Pacey slows his treadmill and then stops it completely. I do the same, and just as mine comes to a halt, he asks, "Are you ready?"

"Should I be nervous?"

"Nah, I got you." He reaches out and takes my hand, taking me to one of the benches. I shouldn't like it as much as I do, but

I really enjoy how small my hand feels in his large hand. "Let's work that impeccable chest of yours. Then we can get in some squats. Don't worry, we'll take it super easy."

"I'm ready for whatever you throw my way." And when he says work my impeccable chest, I'm hoping he means with my shirt off . . .

And . . . how about we keep those thoughts to myself? Best spare myself the embarrassment.

Pacey walks over to a triangular rack of fixed-weight barbells and selects a thirty-pound bar. "You said you can do the bar, right?" I nod. "Good, so we want to start lighter than that. Thirty pounds should be okay. Lie on the bench and I'll hand you the weight."

I lie on the bench and he goes to hand me the weight. I swear he could hand it to me with his pinkies and not strain a muscle. "You must think this is a joke weight."

"What did I say?" he asks sternly, holding the weight above me. "Comparison takes the fun out of it. Let me see those arms work."

He's right. *Enjoy the moment and stop putting yourself down.* That's something Mom used to say to me all the time.

Taking a deep breath, I grab the weight and test it a bit before lowering it to my chest and pressing it upward again. Pacey keeps his hand near the bar just in case it's too heavy, but I've got it with ease. I do ten reps and then he takes the weight from me.

"Atta girl," he says as I sit up. He offers me a high five, and I take it. The pride on his face is so damn sweet, and that smile, oof, I bet thousands of women would line up just to receive that smile from him.

He moves over to the next bench and starts putting some weight on the bar in the barbell catch.

"That's your warm-up weight?" I ask.

"Yeah. I've been at this for a long time."

I stand behind the rack like he did for me and watch as his

large hands wrap around the bar and lift it up with ease. He lowers the weight to his chest, then pushes it up. His breathing is in sync with his arm movements, and it's like a well-oiled machine working right in front of me. Before I know it, he's done with his ten and putting the weight back on the rack.

"I know I should be cool about it, but that was really impressive, Pacey."

He chuckles. "Thanks, Winnie. I'm glad I can impress you."

"Are we going to go all the way up to three hundred?"

"Nah, this is just to keep my muscles from getting stiff during the off-season. I'm not working on building or anything. Not yet, at least. Also, not that I don't like what we've got going on here, but if I'm going to push the weight, I would probably do that with one of the guys so they can actually spot me."

"Oh yeah, that's probably smart. Not sure I would be much help in the spotting department."

"You're good in other ways."

"Oh yeah, how's that?"

He smacks my bench with his hand, and I lie down while he grabs another straight bar. He comes over to me, hands it off, and then squats so he's more level with my body. "Well, one thing's for sure—you provide me an amazing view."

I glance down and notice my cleavage is on fire. Yup, that's a view, all right.

I chuckle and bring the weight down to my chest and back up. "Are you telling me Eli and Silas don't provide you the same kind of cleavage shot?"

"They refuse to take their shirts off for me. Prudes."

"Shame," I say as I count out ten reps. When I'm done, he takes the weight from me and puts it back on the rack with the others.

"You're killing it. Think we can get to the bar on the next one?"

I wiggle my arms. "Totally. I think there's more juice in these girls."

"That's the kind of attitude I like."

We do two more rounds and I max out at fifty pounds. Pacey gets super excited for me and offers a hug, which I gladly take, but I also know in the back of my head that Pacey benches my measly fifty with two hundred on top of that. I can't even imagine. He stopped at two hundred and said it felt good to have some easy reps.

Easy . . . sheesh.

"Have you done squats with a bar before?" he asks me.

"Yes. A while back, my friend Max decided to take me to the gym and forced me to do squats with the bar. I know I can handle that weight."

"You should be able to. We can always squat more than we can bench. But to be safe, let's start with the bar and move up from there." He reaches for a foam cylinder, which he slots over the bar. He explains, "For your shoulders."

I squat under the bar and get in position. I grab the bar with one hand on either side and then lift the weight off the rack.

"You good?" Pacey asks as he stands closely behind me, his hands close to the bar in case I need help.

"Yeah, it feels good."

"Okay." He doesn't back off, though, he stays close, and as I squat, he squats closely behind me. The attention he's giving me, the protection, actually makes me feel incredibly safe.

He makes me feel taken care of, and that's a feeling I haven't felt in a long time. I'm the one who's the caregiver; I look out for my loved ones and for myself. No one looks out for me. *Well, except for one exceptionally wonderful, psychotic friend. And Max.*

But Pacey just stepped right in and took that role, without even blinking, without knowing much about me. It seems to be just who he is, his personality—honorable.

I finish up my squats and then set the weight back on the rack. When I duck out from under it,

Pacey grips the bar and leans forward. "How did that feel?"

Like I'm a Ninja.

"It felt good," I say. *I'm so not a Ninja.* But the smile I get from that answer is worth being up this early, especially after I spent all night thinking about him and how I felt so . . . connected to him. He's so freaking adorable.

"Think we can add some weights next round?"

"For sure."

He goes to the other squat rack, adds some large, round weights, and then with ease—and without the foam padding—he lifts the bar and counts out his squats.

Ooh, look at those legs and that ass. No wonder it's so nice and round, popping out those athletic shorts of his. It's from hours in the gym doing exactly this.

When he sets the weight on the rack, I say, "You get down pretty far."

"Years of stretching and making sure I'm as flexible as can be."

"Wait, you're a goalie, which means . . . can you do the splits?"

He moves over to my rack and puts fives on each side. "What do you think?"

"Uhh, I'm thinking you can."

"Maybe if you tell me a little something about yourself, I'll show you."

"Seriously?" I feel as though my eyes nearly pop out of my sockets. "What do you want to know?"

He taps the bar and I get into position.

"Right now? The basics—why you're here, the real reason. What you do. Maybe a last name."

"That's quite a list." I start squatting, and even though the weight is heavier, I can still handle it.

"Just like that?" Pacey says, coming up behind me again, but this time his hands connect with my sides as I squat. When I put the weight back, he says, "I'm not sure which I like better." He scratches the side of his jaw.

"What do you mean?"

"Do I like watching you bench or squat more? The view on the bench is hard to beat, but having you stick your ass out so close is nice too."

I push my hand against his chest. "Don't be a perv in the gym. Let a girl work out in peace."

He captures my hand in his and pulls me close so the bar is the only thing between us. "I wasn't prepared to be working out with you this morning, so give me a break. It's new. It's exciting. It's better than watching Taters strut around the gym, chest puffed out like a moron."

I chuckle. "I can totally picture that."

He doesn't let go of my hand, but instead pulls me a little closer. "Are you enjoying this?"

"I am, actually, but I also have a good weightlifting partner. Not sure it would be the same with anyone else."

"Better not be." He releases my hand and then goes over to his rack. He adds more weight and balances the bar on his shoulders.

"So where are we at with the splits?"

"It's all on you. I get three questions and I'm going to need three solid answers in order for me to perform some acrobatics for you."

"How do I know it's worth it?"

He glances over at me. "Trust me, it's worth it."

I smirk and nibble on the corner of my mouth. "Hmm, I'm going to have to think on it."

"Think all you want. I've got time. I'll just keep getting to know you in a roundabout way." He sets the bar on the rack and turns toward me. He rubs his hands together and asks, "What's on your list of things to do today? Hide away in your bedroom some more?"

"No. I was thinking about asking one of you guys to take me into town."

"You plan on asking one of the guys?" He walks toward me

and reaches around me for a weight, his chest brushing against my shoulder. "Not me?"

"Well, I've taken up a lot of your time already. Wasn't sure if Eli would be willing. I know Silas is out of the question. Levi was my second option. I just need transportation into town."

He places the weight on the bar and then faces me, his body so close I can feel the heat coming off him. "I'll take you."

"You don't have to, Pacey."

His finger falls under my chin and pushes my gaze up to his. "I know I don't have to. I want to."

My stomach twists with a flurry of butterflies, not just from his declaration but from the way he insists on intimately touching me. His handholding, his grip on my waist as I squat, the way he tilts up my chin . . . or pins me against my bedroom wall. *With no hesitation.*

He taps the bar. "Let's go, Winnie."

"That's that?" I ask. "No conversation about it? You're just going to take me?"

"Yup."

Holding back my smile, I go under the bar and lift it up, feeling the weight difference he added.

"This weight okay?" he asks.

"Yeah."

He gets in right behind me, and right before I squat, I look in the mirror, catching the sight of both of us, him almost a foot taller than me. I have no idea why this man feels as though he needs to be here for me, help me out, get to know me, but I've a feeling I'm not going to be able to shake him, not that I really want to. I enjoy his company—hell, I more than enjoy it, I woke up this morning craving it.

His hands slide to my waist carefully, his palms connecting with my exposed skin. "Ready?"

I nod. And I begin squatting, him right there with me. In rhythm we sink down together and then back up.

"Give me eight," he says into my ear, sending a bout of chills down my spine. "That's it, Winnie, great job."

I finish up the last rep and he helps me rack the weight. I turn toward him and lean against the bar with both arms crossed over it. "I think if I do more, I'm going to rupture a muscle from overuse."

He places one hand on the bar, and then with the other pushes some stray hair behind my ear. "You did good."

"Thank you," I say shyly.

"I'm going to finish up here. You can stay if you want, keep me company." He leans in closer. "I'm playing your favorite music, after all; not sure it would make sense if it was just me in here."

"I planned on staying."

"Good."

As I slip under the bar and pass by him, his hand snags my waist and he stops me. I look over my shoulder at him and he doesn't say anything; instead, he just smiles and, yup . . . my entire body heats up from that one look. *Max will love this story.*

I have no idea what's happening between us, but whatever it is, I really like it. I also think it's probably time I start opening up a little more. Today might be a good time for that. *Even though Katherine won't approve one bit.* Luckily she's not here.

Chapter Eleven

PACEY

I can't seem to keep my hands off her. No matter what I try, I'm drawn to her. My hands need to stroke her. I need that connection.

And while we were in the gym, there was a hell of a lot more I wanted to do with her, and it didn't involve lifting weights. I wanted to lie down across the bench and pin her there while I found out what her lips tasted like. Push her up against the mirror and watch her face as I slowly peeled down her bike shorts to expose that beautiful ass of hers. I wanted to make her know what it feels like to be with a real man. A man who would take care of her.

My will is slipping with her. I can feel it, especially the frustration I felt when she suggested asking one of the other guys to take her into town.

Fuck that.

I would've been pissed.

She thinks she's taking up too much of my time, when really,

I want more of hers. And I want to be the one who shows her the town of Banff. I want to see her face light up when she takes in the picturesque views. Not Eli . . . because I know that's who would probably take her if she asked.

Dressed in a pair of navy-blue chino shorts and a simple white T-shirt, I head down the hallway, slipping past her door and into the main living space. The boys are gathered at the table, plates of eggs in front of them, Stephan at the helm in the kitchen.

The chatter at the table slowly dies out as I walk by them, and I know I'm about to get shit because normally I wouldn't be dressed like this. If Winnie weren't here, we'd all be in a pair of athletic shorts and no shirt, but that's not the case.

"Going somewhere?" Taters is the first to ask.

Stephan hands me a plate and I thank him.

"I offered Winnie something a little earlier, but she told me she has a protein bar," he says in reply. I smile. He knew I'd want to know that. *Good man.*

"Thanks, man."

I take a seat at the head of the dining table, knowing it'll be easier to address all the prying eyes. Even Holmes seems interested.

"Winnie needs to go into town," I answer while spearing a bunch of eggs and some roasted veggies with my fork.

"And you decided to dress up for that?"

"Figured I'd walk around town. I was considering bringing back some fudge for you guys."

"Oh fuck, get the Neapolitan," Posey says.

"Is there any other kind?" I ask with a smile.

Taters waves his fork at me. "You're in a really good mood. What's happening?"

"I'll tell you what's happening," Hornsby says. He sips his water and then continues, "Our boy likes a girl. I think this is the first time since we've known him that he actually *likes* a girl, is truly interested in her."

I'm not going to deny it. What's the point? They're going to notice the way I act around her, and what if I end up holding her hand in front of them at some point? I don't need them making a scene about it.

What I don't want them to know is who Winnie used to date. I don't need the lecture about Bro Code, because even though Josh is my brother, he really isn't. We don't talk. We don't see each other. He's just another human in this world with whom I happen to share some DNA.

Nor do I want them to know that when I saw pictures of Winnie on my dad's Facebook, how hot I thought she was. How jealous I was that Josh could land a girl like her. Yeah, fucking jealous, and before you start thinking this is some play to one-up my brother, that's not the case at all.

I truly like Winnie. I think . . . hell, I think she's cool as shit, and the more time I spend with her, the more I want to spend time with her. Her laugh, her teasing, her smile, her easygoing attitude. It works for me. And I could not give two shits what the guys think.

So, I keep it casual and say, "Yeah, I like her."

"Oh damn." Hornsby brings his fist to his mouth. "I didn't think you'd admit it."

"Yeah, I didn't see that coming," Posey says, but then winks at me. Jesus Christ, I knew he was the wrong one to confide in. The dude is a giant ditz.

"You like her?" Taters asks with skepticism. "You barely know her."

"So?" I take a bite of my food. "If you take a girl on one date, you get to know her on that singular date, and you can make a general assessment if you like her or not. It can take one night to decide if you like someone. How is this any different?"

"I don't know—maybe because she came out of nowhere," Taters says, and I truly believe he's still reeling from his own feelings, so this is not going to be easy for him. If he's suffering, he wants all of us to suffer.

"Doesn't matter where she came from, all that matters is she's here now and I'm going to take advantage of the time I have with her."

"Look at our boy," Posey says with pride. "Taking what you want. Good for you, man."

"She seems nice," Holmes says, adding his two cents. I'll take it.

"I like her," Hornsby says. "If she weren't digging you so much, I would've taken a crack at her, but I knew the first night she was here, there was no chance."

I smile inwardly at that, because normally girls gravitate toward Hornsby. It's easy for him, he doesn't have to work for it. But not with Winnie. She found me. She picked me. Yes, I know I'm good-looking, but like I told her, I've never found it easy to know what to talk to women about. Small talk. Girl shit. I'm not smooth like Hornsby.

"Glad we're having a guys' trip," Taters says with animosity.

"Dude, you need to calm down about that. It's not as if we party every night with strippers knocking on the door. We relax here."

"Yeah, and look at me, wearing a goddamn shirt at breakfast out of respect." He plucks at his black Agitators shirt. "This is my own goddamn house; I should do what I want."

"Then take your shirt off. Who gives a fuck, Taters?" I ask.

"I feel as though I'm walking on eggshells around here, and now I'm going to have to listen to you two giggle and flounce around in my own house while you get to know each other?"

Growing irritated, I ask, "Do you want me to leave? Want me to find another house to rent? Because I will. If you're going to be a dick about this, I'll leave."

"I think we'd all appreciate that," Taters says.

"Shut the fuck up," Hornsby yells. "Jesus, Taters, you're not kicking Lawes out of the house."

"Nah, it's cool. I can look for a place." I shovel some more eggs into my mouth.

"Don't, Lawes," Posey says. "Because that would leave us with Taters, and you're the best at calming him down."

"Clearly not." I finish my eggs, eating faster than I ever have before, and stand from the table. Looking Taters, who has guilt written all over him, in the eyes, I say, "I'll be out of here by tomorrow."

I take my plate to Stephan, and just as I turn to walk away, Taters calls out, "Fuck, I didn't mean it. Don't leave."

That's what I thought, but I'll make him sweat it out. Instead of acknowledging him, I walk down the hallway and knock on Winnie's door.

"One second," she calls out. The door opens and I hear someone ask, "Is that him?"

I peek through the door to see Winnie is on FaceTime with someone.

"Ah, shit, sorry. I'm out here when you're done."

"No, come back," the male voice on the phone says. "I want to meet him."

In an annoyed voice, Winnie says, "Pacey, come here."

Must be a prying friend or sibling . . . or father, maybe?

Either way, I step into her room. But instead of focusing on the phone, I take in the sight of Winnie.

She's wearing a cute red sundress that clings to her chest but flows out around her waist. Her hair is pulled back into two thick French braids, and she's wearing some makeup. She looks so fucking good.

I walk up to her and say, "This dress looks really good on you."

"Oh God, did he compliment you? Does he always do that? Turn the phone, I want to see him."

Instead of complying, Winnie puts the phone against her chest and says, "Thank you, but I need to apologize in advance for whatever comes out of Max's mouth."

I chuckle. "Bring it."

With a sigh, she lifts the phone up and points it in my direction. A man, probably in his mid-twenties, stares at me from the screen with wide eyes. He runs a hand over his perfectly coifed pompadour before resting his hand against his clean-shaven cheek. He clears his throat. "Jesus, you're hot."

I pull on the back of my neck. "Thank you." I wave. "I'm Pacey."

"I know who you are. I'm Max, one of Winnie's best friends. Katherine is currently in the bathroom, therefore, unable to be hear us at the moment. She's suffering from high anxiety and stress-belly from Winnie's choices."

"She's dramatic," Winnie adds.

Getting close to the screen, Max says, "I need you to know you're currently my second favorite Agitator."

"*Second?*" I ask. "Who's your first? If you say Eli Hornsby, we're going to have problems."

"Pretty face, but not for me. Ian Rivers." Max nods. "Ian is a goddamn snack."

I move my hand over my jaw. "Ian is a fucking hell of a guy. That's a good choice. If I'm going to fall second, I'm good with falling second to him."

"Is he as cool in person like I think he is?"

"Probably cooler. He's legit."

Max grins. "Can I have his number?"

"Max," Winnie chastises, pulling the phone away. "Don't give Max his number."

"Don't tell him what to do," Max shouts. "If he thinks I need Ian's number, let him give it to me."

Chuckling, I stick my hands in my pockets and say, "How about this, Max. Get your girl to open up more to me and I'll see what I can do about Ian."

"Jesus fuck, Winnie, open up to the man, if not for me, then for yourself. You need this." Shouting to me, Max says, "She's been through a lot, Pacey. This girl needs a man like you."

She's been through a lot?

Fuck, it bothers me that I didn't know that.

"And I think that's enough, Max. Say goodbye." Winnie holds the phone up to me and I wave. He goes to say something, but she hangs up before he can get it out. "God, I'm so sorry about that."

"Why? Max seems fun."

"He can be really obnoxious and overstep boundaries." She tucks her phone away in her purse, which she loops over her body so the strap nestles between her breasts. "I hope he didn't make you uncomfortable."

"Not in the slightest. He made me curious, though."

"I'm sure." She sighs and then looks me over. "Did you dress up for me?"

"Nope," I say while I walk over to the door. "Dressed for myself. I think it's good to flirt with yourself on occasion."

She pauses and gives me a twisted look. "Are you serious about that?"

"Does it look as though I'm a guy who would flirt with myself?"

"I wouldn't be surprised, at this point."

"Come on." I laugh. "I'm not that kind of guy." I lead her down the hallway, away from the main living space.

"Where are you taking me?"

"This is the back way to the garage. You know, where the cars are."

"Just making sure." We walk past my bedroom and she stops to poke her head in the door. "This is where you slumber?"

"That's a way to put it. But, yes, this is my bedroom."

"Not as tidy as I expected it to be," she huffs.

"Uh, it's tidier than your room. My bed is even made."

"Ooh, look at you, you little Monica Geller."

I roll my eyes and take her by the hand, pulling her toward the garage. There's a key hook next to the door and I grab the key fob to my Tesla Model X. When I open the garage door, Winnie lets out a low "whoa" as she takes in the fleet.

"Um, do you all drive the same model car?"

I chuckle. "I want it to be known, I was the first one to get the Model X. Taters followed after me, then Posey. Hornsby plans on trading in shortly, and Holmes—well, I think he still drives his car from college. He carpooled with Posey."

"Which one is yours?"

"The black in the middle," I answer. We make our way to my car and my driver's side door pops open, but I walk over to her side and press the handle to open her door.

"Fancy," she says as she climbs in.

"Comfortable?" I ask.

"Very. Thanks."

I shut her door and round the car to get in. I enter my key code into the touchscreen and buckle up.

"This is some sort of futuristic vehicle. There are no buttons. How do you drive it?"

"Like a normal car." I open the garage door and pull out. "Everything is just on the touchscreen."

"Fascinating. Still doesn't give Minnie a run for her money."

"This car would not have gotten stuck in the mud."

"Oh, is that right?" she asks. "Does it have rocket engines I'm unaware of?"

"No, because that would defeat the purpose of an all-electric vehicle."

"I guess you're right about that." She chuckles. "Okay, so if you drop me off, I think I'll only be an hour or so. Hmm, I don't have your phone number to contact you when I'm done. Not sure you want to hand that out. Maybe if—"

"First of all, you can have my phone number. Secondly, do you plan on ditching me when we get into town?"

I pull out of the driveway and then start heading down the hill.

"Are you planning on staying?"

"You think I'm going to just let you walk around town by yourself?"

"I thought that's what was happening."

I shake my head. "No fucking way. Not because you're not capable—although, you do seem to have problems with directions—but because I want to show you around."

"Show me around, as in, my own personal tour guide? Don't you have anything to do today?"

"Other than fuck around? No, not really. Got my workout in, and I'm free for the rest of the day. If you planned on ditching me, you're going to have a hard time doing that. I have plans for us."

"Plans?" she asks, surprised.

"Yeah, plans."

"Do these plans involve window shopping? Because even though I'm not much of a buyer, I really like looking, and I was hoping to find something for the guys. You know, a peace offering."

I smile to myself. "I have just the thing you can get them."

━━━

"WOW, JUST . . . WOW." Winnie stands at the edge of town, looking past the strips of shops and straight to the magnificence of Cascade Mountain, the backdrop for downtown. "I don't think I've ever seen anything like this. Sure, Mount Rainier is beautiful, but in Seattle, it's off in the distance. This is . . . this feels as if you're at the base of something spectacular."

"It's a sight I don't think I'll ever get tired of. I always feel awe when I come down here. When we're staying here, Posey and I like to venture into town often."

"I can see why. It's so gorgeous."

Standing at 9,836 feet, Cascade Mountain is a jagged but spectacular snow-covered peak that's set against a backdrop of the Rocky Mountains. It's hard not to fall in love with the picturesque views when in town. And it's hard not to just take a moment to stare in awe.

Winnie smiles up at me. "Thank you for bringing me into

town. I really appreciate it."

"No thanks needed." I look at my watch. "What do you want to do first?"

"Well, what are your plans?"

"I was thinking we could ride the Banff Gondola. It takes you up to a summit house where you can take in a 360-degree view of the Rockies. There are some shops around here I know you're going to want to look at, and for lunch, I was thinking we could go to the cidery that's here in town."

"Sounds amazing. Where is the gondola?"

"We can take a bus to it, or we could save that for last and drive. Up to you."

"Save that for last. I'm going to be hungry in an hour, I can feel it, so why don't we look around at some shops, you help me pick some things out for the boys, and then we head to lunch."

"That works."

Together, we walk down Banff Avenue.

"Do you think you're going to get recognized?" Winnie asks, her shoulder brushing against mine.

"Strong possibility," I answer. "It's common knowledge that we hang out here during the summer. For the most part, everyone is pretty cool, but we'll get a person here or there asking us to take a picture with them."

"Do you?"

"Always," I say. "My parents always said, it might be my tenth picture I take that day, but it's the first for that person, and you always need to make sure to remember that."

"That sounds . . . tiring. I couldn't imagine."

"Comes with the territory," I answer and then point to a store. "Posey is obsessed with the fudge in this store. Not that you need to win over any of the guys, but Posey would love you forever if you got him some of the Neapolitan fudge."

"Oh, I would love to be loved forever." She opens the door for me and the aroma of sugary confections assaults me. So good.

"Oh no," she says.

"What?" I ask, concerned.

"This is not good." She shakes her head. "Not good at all. It smells too good in here, Pacey. I don't have a strong willpower to resist buying everything, and my wallet can't handle that kind of binge."

"Do you have a sweet tooth, Winnie?"

She nods. "Oh, big time."

"Then get what you want. It's on me."

She glances up at me. "You're sweet, but that's not happening. You've done enough for me already." She moves over to the fudge counter and I hear her order some Neapolitan fudge. "How much would he like? I ordered a quarter of a pound. Should I get more?"

"Nah, I'm going to get some for the house as well. But if Posey has his own stash, he'll be grateful."

"Are you sure?"

I nod. "Yeah, positive." While the fudge is being wrapped up, I watch her carefully to see if she gives anything away as to what she'd want, but she doesn't stray far. I hate that I don't know what she'd like. I hate that I can't just get her something for the hell of it.

So, instead, I decide on something for the both of us.

"Ever had a caramel apple?"

She pensively taps her chin. "I don't believe I have."

"Want to share one with me? We can save it for after lunch, maybe when we're riding in the gondola."

"That sounds like fun. Sure."

"Do you have a flavor choice?" I ask, bringing her over to the display case where all the apples are. "They have tons of flavors."

"Oh, wow, they do." She studies them. "Although I'm obsessed with anything that has chocolate and peanut butter, I would say, let's go with the original."

Peanut butter and chocolate, good to know. That was easier

than I thought. And apparently, she likes caramel, too, if she's up for a caramel apple.

I order us an original apple, and while she pays for the fudge, I work with a lady behind the counter, who helps me fill up a small box with candies that I think Winnie might like. Once I pay for everything and thank the workers, I place my hand on Winnie's lower back and guide her out of the store.

"The boys must love their chocolate," she says as I take her bag from her. She doesn't need to carry that.

"They do, but I picked some stuff out for you, too."

"Pacey, you didn't."

"I did." I drape my arm over her shoulders and bring her in close. "I have to win you over somehow so you start talking to me."

"You can just ask; you don't have to bribe me with chocolate."

"Will you give me the real-deal answers, though?"

She moves her arm around my waist and says, "I think I'm comfortable enough at this point to give you the truth."

I gather two things from that: She doesn't trust easily, and when she does trust, she's willing to open up. That's really good to know.

I point to a shop up ahead. "That has a bunch of souvenirs in it. Shirts and whatnot. Hornsby collects souvenir hats. He gets at least one every time we come here, and I can help you pick one out if you like."

"That's perfect. Eli has been so kind to me. A hat would be perfect."

I let go of her and reach for the door, holding it open for her. She walks in past me, her hand grazing my arm in the process, and I can fucking feel it—the electricity bouncing between us. She's growing increasingly more comfortable with me.

We head back to the hats and I ask her, "So what do you do?"

She picks up a pink trucker hat and plops it on her head. She makes a cute face at me and asks, "Think Eli would like this one?"

"I think you need to keep looking."

She chuckles and says, "Maybe so. And as to what I do for a living . . . well, currently, I guess I still hold the title of student."

That wasn't what I was expecting.

"Oh, shit, how old are you?"

She pats my chest. "Don't worry, Pacey. I'm an old student. Twenty-five."

Hmm, okay, two years younger than me.

She glances up at me. "Seems as though I lean toward older men."

My brow shoots up. "Memorize that Internet search on me?"

"Just a few details." She leans in. "For the record, twenty-seven looks really good on you."

I like those kinds of compliments. Clearing my throat, I ask, "Since you're still a student, does that mean you're earning your masters?"

She picks up another hat and tests it out. This one is brown with a Banff label stitched across the front. "Bachelor's, actually, in business. What about this one for Eli?"

"He has it," I answer. "I never would've guessed that. You don't seem like the type of person who would be interested in business."

"I'm not," she answers. "Not in the slightest. Josh convinced me to pick that major. I was undecided for a decent amount of time and he came in with his pragmatism and said it would benefit my mom if I did."

That pisses me off. Who the fuck is Josh to convince her to go that route, when after spending only a few days with her I can tell that's not the major for her? "My mom owned a small used bookstore in Seattle. She adored literature and the pathways reading brought to every individual, but business wasn't really her strong suit. Josh thought it would help the store grow. I guess I did, too."

Holding back my angry tongue, I ask, "It didn't?"

She picks up a red hat. "We never got a chance to see. Mom was diagnosed with a brain tumor. I took a long break from college to help her run the store, and then, when she passed, I had a hard time keeping the store alive alone. Josh and I had split at that point. He couldn't quite handle the attention I was giving the store, I guess. And then I lost the store anyway. Honestly, it was a nightmare. Now I'm not sure I want to go back to school." She shrugs. "I'm not sure what I want to do at all."

Josh broke up with her . . . while she was struggling? What a fucking piece of shit. And from the tone of her voice, I can tell it wasn't easy on her. None of this has been easy on her—losing her mom, losing her mom's store. No wonder she doesn't know what she wants to do, a dark cloud has settled over her. I never would've known, though, because she puts on a happy, grateful front. And maybe she is happy and grateful, maybe it's not a front at all. But underneath her positive façade, there's a deep cut of insecurity, of pain.

"I'm so sorry," I say. "I can't imagine what it's like to lose your mom."

"Not fun." She holds up the hat, moving forward with the conversation. "What about this one?"

My stomach twists, wanting to comfort her but not sure how to do that. I didn't think my first question would dig up something so dark for her, something I'm sure she's still trying to work through. Maybe it's the reason she's here.

I grip the back of my neck and say, "He'd like that one."

"Wonderful." She moves past me with confidence and heads to the cash register, where she begins to check out, leaving me in the back with the hats while I figure out what to say to her.

I don't know anyone who has lost a parent before; I'm not quite sure what she's feeling or how to make that feeling go away, if only just temporarily. I don't like hearing the sadness in her voice, or knowing that despite trying her best, she failed. That can't sit easy on her heart, either.

I need to be there for her. That's the only thing I can do. Listen, be there, be supportive—the kind of support she didn't get from Josh. I move toward the cashier, but just then, someone taps me on the shoulder. I turn around to see a mom with a teenage boy whose eyes are lit up, star-struck.

"Mr. Lawes, would we be able to get a picture with you?" the mom asks, her hands trembling.

Turning on a smile, I say, "Of course." I drape my arms over both of their shoulders and bend down to get in the picture. The mom takes a selfie and then thanks me.

"We're huge fans."

"Thank you," I say. "Sorry we couldn't bring home the Stanley Cup for you this year."

"It was quite a run in the playoffs," the boy says.

From the corner of my eye, I spot Winnie moving closer with a bag in her hand.

"How is your head? Doing okay?" the mom asks.

"Fully recovered," I say with a wink. "If you'll excuse me, got some more shopping to do."

"Sure. Thank you so much," they say, and I turn toward Winnie and move through the store until we're outside.

I go to ask her more about her mom, but someone else comes up to us. "Mr. Lawes, could we get a picture?" I glance apologetically at Winnie, who seems to find it humorous as a crowd gathers just outside the souvenir shop.

Word has spread—there's an Agitator in town.

I spend the next ten minutes taking pictures and signing autographs. At one point, I lose Winnie and start to panic that she wandered off somewhere, but then I see her exit one of the alleys. She has more bags in hand and doesn't look upset, more entertained than anything.

I take my last picture, thank the fans, and then walk toward her.

"Hey, Mr. Popular." She grins up at me.

"Shit, I'm so sorry, Winnie. That was . . . not great timing."

"I thought it was rather lovely to see. All those adoring fans trying to get a small piece of Pacey Lawes. Reminds me just how lucky I am."

How could I not like this girl? Especially when she answers like that. I've seen some of my teammates deal with angry, jealous girlfriends, and although it's far too early for me to make a comparison, I wonder if Winnie would always . . . get it. Appreciate the responsibility I have toward the people who support me. She seemed to agree with my parents' sentiment earlier. Who knows?

I take her hand and entwine our fingers. "I really want to talk; think we can grab lunch?"

"That sounds nice." Completely unfazed, she bumps my shoulder with hers and says, "You're really great with your fans. Your parents should be proud."

"Thank you." Feeling awkward, I take her bags off her hands and say, "Get something else?"

"I found a book in an old bookstore I thought Halsey might like. The store was quite quaint. The smell of the old pages reminded me of my mom's store. So, I spent a few minutes just . . . letting it soak in. And then I ran into this woodcarving shop. They make wooden pint glasses. I found one that says 'Hostess with the Mostest'." She shrugs. "I thought it was stupid, funny, and right on par with something Silas might enjoy."

"Because it boosts his ego. You were right. Well, I'm sorry you had to shop alone."

"Stop apologizing. It's fine." She glances up and down the street. "Now, where is this cidery? I need something in my stomach other than a protein bar."

Chapter Twelve

WINNIE

Note to self—when traveling around with a professional hockey player, he's not only swarmed by adoring fans, but he also gets the best seats at the restaurant.

Because . . . oh my God.

We're seated on the second floor of the brewery, on the deck with the perfect view of Cascade Mountain. There's a light breeze to distract from the heat of the sun, and even though we're outside, we're tucked under a large umbrella, which provides enough shade for the both of us.

Since I've never been here before, Pacey ordered us a flight of cider to split and some shareable entrees, one of them being tacos, which I can't wait to get my hands on.

"Did you know tacos are my favorite food?" I ask him as I set my napkin on my lap. Food hasn't been delivered yet, but I'm prepared for when it is.

"Now I do. Any kind of taco?"

"Yup. I'm not picky. I'll take a taco any way I can get it.

There's a food truck in Seattle that specializes in tacos. Every week, they come out with a new taco of the week. I follow them on Instagram because every Sunday they announce the new addition. And then Max, Katherine, and I all grab the taco of the week and measure it up to the others they've had. It's a Thursday tradition." I lean forward and say, "The main reason why this girl has thighs—tacos."

"Curves are hot," he says.

Does that mean he thinks my curves are hot? From the longing in his eyes, I'm going to guess that maybe he does. And that makes me feel all warm and fuzzy inside.

The waitress brings our flight and sets it between us, along with a menu of each of the ciders we got so we know exactly what we'll be tasting.

"This is so cool," I say. "I've never had a flight of cider before. You always see beer flights, and although great for the beer lovers, what about the people who love cider?"

"You have a valid point."

"I usually do." I grin and then pick up the original, unfla-vored cider to try first.

"I'm sensing a theme here," he says as he picks up the blue-berry lavender. We already established we were okay with sharing glasses, something that made me smile inside. It shows how comfortable he is with me already.

"What theme?" I ask while taking a sip. "Ooh, that's crisp. Really good."

"You like to try the original of things rather than skip to a fancy flavor."

"You have to have a good baseline first, and then you jump from there. Just makes sense."

"Well, any cider you like, we can get cans to-go to take up to the cabin. I know Posey is going to want some, as well."

"Maybe I'll get you some cider for your trouble." I need to get him something. I'm pleased with the little gifts I got the boys, but Pacey, he needs something special.

He sets the blueberry cider down and looks me directly in the eyes. "This is no trouble, so stop acting like you're a burden. I enjoy your company. I want to be around you, Winnie."

Can't hear that enough, especially from someone as enchanting as Pacey Lawes.

The corner of my lips tilt as I set down my cider. "I enjoy your company, too, Pacey." Then I lean back in my chair and say, "I honestly don't know how this all happened."

"What?" he asks.

"This." I wave my hand between us and then around in the air. "I was expecting to find some cheap hotel to stay in, venture out a bit, maybe get lost in the mountains for a hot afternoon. But here I am, not alone, but rather, with wonderful company while I try to embark on this new chapter of my life."

"And what exactly is that new chapter?" he asks. "We touched upon something at the souvenir shop but I wasn't able to ask any questions. I feel as though I didn't handle it well, and I'm feeling pretty guilty over it. You opened up and you were shoved to the side for some fans."

"Oh my gosh, Pacey, no need to feel guilty. I felt as though there wasn't much to talk about."

"Yes, there is. Your mom passed away. That's life-changing, especially for your age. You lost her and the family business. You put your life on hold. Were you her caregiver, too?"

I nod, thinking back to those dreary days, her last breaths. "Yeah. Toward the end, I was there with her every second of the day, holding her hand, making sure she knew she wasn't alone." I feel my smile become watery. "A part of me thinks she was the one who made me take the wrong turn, that led to me ending up at the cabin. Like she's had a hand in this weird coincidence." My eyes meet his. "She'd think this is so funny, me lodging with five hunky hockey players. She was always a sucker for a romance. This would've been right up her alley."

"What was she like?" he asks.

Wistfully, I sigh. "She was loving. Adventurous. A storyteller.

She loved with her entire heart and always made you feel as though you were more than the person you thought you were. She could identify attributes about a person that they never saw as positives and twist them so they'd appreciate those attributes. Kind of like you."

I tilt my head.

"I complain about my thighs, you say they're sexy. I put myself down in the gym, you lift me up. She was the same way."

"I guess that puts me in good company, then."

"Very good company." Mom would've adored Pacey. She was so kind and thoughtful, and I think she'd see those traits in this endearing man before me. *How on earth did you make this happen, Mom?*

I lift up the blueberry lavender cider, sniff it, and then take a sip. Oh my God. My eyes widen and I bring the glass to my chest, claiming it. "This one is mine."

"Have all you want," he says, leaning back in his chair, humor written all over his face. He's a very easygoing man. He doesn't act as if much bothers him. He seems like someone who loves life and goes with the flow.

"Is this your favorite? Is this why you tried it first?"

"It is," he answers. "It's subtle but also packs a punch. Kind of like you."

"You think I'm subtle?"

He picks up the Pina Colada flavor and says, "Yes. You're polite, kind, don't want to step on toes, but when you feel comfortable with someone, boy, do you pack a punch. You can easily knock a guy off his feet."

I don't know what to do when he says things like that other than blush. My initial reaction is to tell him he's wrong, that I really don't knock a guy off his feet, just ask my ex. But I know he'd get angry if I put myself down . . . again—something I'm only just noticing I do quite often because Pacey has pointed it out. The last few years haven't given me time for much self-reflection, but I can see now that Josh had never been one to validate me. Which makes me wonder how I stayed with him as long as I did.

The man you love should always be your champion, Win. Always encouraging. Never settle for less.

And yet, for so many years, it seems as though I did settle. But I refuse to focus on that now, because I'm enjoying this far too much. The sun is warming my skin, and Pacey is warming my heart.

Joking around, I ask, "Are you saying I've knocked you off your feet, Pacey?"

He smooths his hand over his jaw as he studies me. "Yeah, you have."

The feeling is completely mutual.

"ARE you going to have that last taco?" I ask, showing no shame.

"I'll let you have the last taco if you let me have the last potato skin."

"Ooh, you know how much I enjoyed the crispy cheese on those, but tacos are the first love of my life. Deal."

We pick up the last shareables and both take a bite at the same time. It's cute how effortless this entire meal has been. Conversation has flowed easily, we've shared like civil adults, despite me wanting to swat his hand away when he reached for the tacos, and I've had a really good time. I think it's safe to say I like Pacey.

I like him a lot.

Probably more than I should, given the circumstances, but God, what's not to like? Yes, he makes my inner girl want to scream with how hot he is, but beyond the surface-level stuff and all those rippling muscles in his forearms, there's a man who's thoughtful, sweet, funny, and protective. He's a gentle-man, a helper, and someone I could easily imagine relying on.

And I shouldn't rely on him, because who knows how long

I'll be here? I already feel as if I'm overstaying my welcome, and at some point, I have to face reality and make it back to Seattle. I can't forget about Minnie, either. Once she's pulled from the bowels of the forest, she'll no longer be able to provide me with an excuse to stay at the cabin, and I'll no longer be dependent on the guys. That ought to make me happy, but I've enjoyed these stolen moments with Pacey.

Pacey picks up the water he's been drinking and takes a sip. He hasn't had much to drink at all, just sips here and there, allowing me to take down most of the flight. And yes, I'm feeling quite fine, hence slamming down this taco right now.

"So, you told me about your mom and how you've put school on hold, but you haven't told me why you're here exactly."

"That's a fun story," I say just as the waitress brings us the check. I reach for it but Pacey nearly snarls at me as he swipes it out from under my hand. Got it, he's paying. Doesn't seem there's any point to me putting up a fight; I know I'm not going to win.

He slips some cash into the billfold and sets it on the end of the table.

"Are you willing to share that story?" he asks.

I wipe my face with my napkin and nod. "I'm still confused by it all. My mom was actually born here, in Banff."

"Really?" he asks, surprised.

"Yeah, and then she was raised in Calgary. On a trip to the Pacific Northwest with her brother, she met my dad. Took them about five days to fall in love. It was quick." I lean my chin on my hand and recall how she spoke about my father. "She loved him so much. They were infatuated with each other. They were married within a month. My mom's family wasn't happy, because she left Canada and started a life with my dad in Seattle. They started the bookstore and lived a quiet little life, just the two of them. Neither of their families were pleased with how fast things moved. They always thought it was a mistake to get married that fast. But my parents both said, if you know, you know. At least, that's what Mom told me. I never really knew Dad. I have very few memories of him."

"Love moves quick. It should never have a timeline placed on it," Pacey says, making my romantic heart beat faster. I couldn't agree more with that statement. "What happened to your dad?" he asks.

"After 9/11, Dad wanted to serve our country, but unfortunately he lost his life to a roadside bombing during his first deployment. I think a piece of Mom died with him. She never dated again, didn't even consider the idea of it. Instead, she invested all her time in me. Things were strained with her family, so it was just us. It's why when she was diagnosed with the tumor, I was by her side every step of the way. She'd dedicated her time to me, so I thought it was the least I could do for her, despite having to put my life on hold." There was never any other option. Looking back on those two years, it was the exhausting, silent grief that consumed me mostly. The hardest years of my life. Thank God I had Katherine and Max.

Pacey runs his tongue over his teeth and looks away. Quietly, he says, "You're something else, Winnie. I don't think I've ever met anyone like you before. I'm not sure I know a lot of people who would put their life on hold to be a caregiver."

"There was no question. I wanted to be there for her."

He slowly nods and then stands from his chair. "Let's get out of here."

I stand from my chair as well and reach for my bags but he takes them from me.

Then he asks, "Can I hold your hand?"

Be still my heart.

He wants to hold my hand, not just to guide me somewhere, but actually hold my hand. What on earth is this reality?

And as if he even needs to ask.

"I would like that," I answer.

He gives me a sincere smile as he takes my hand in his.

Together, we walk out of the restaurant and toward the parking lot where we left his car. As we fall in step together, I can't help but notice how perfect my hand feels in his, how perfect this moment feels.

"Okay, so you told me about your parents, but not why you're here."

I snuggle in closer to him and say, "A few months before Mom died, we were talking about her childhood, and she told me some stories about her brother. Apparently, they used to share this trophy growing up that they won in a bowling league. One day, he just decided he was done sharing it and he was going to keep it, even though she was the one with the game-winning bowl. When she asked for her turn with it, he told her it was his, and he was going to keep it forever. Childish, if you ask me. After she was . . . gone, I was going through her things and found a box with his name on it. I opened it and found a bunch of notes and random things in it, pictures of them, ticket stubs —you know, random crap. One of the pictures was of them with the trophy. It was one of those old-fashioned things. An actual cup, not like a guy bowling or anything like that."

"I know exactly what you're talking about," Pacey says, humor in his voice.

"My mom was a lot like me, never really excelled at anything. And I'm not saying that to look for a compliment. Just average Janes, and that's totally okay, because as my mom always said, our talents may be average, but our personalities are extraordinary."

"I can very much agree with that statement. You are quite extraordinary, Winnie."

I squeeze his hand and lean my head briefly against his shoulder in gratitude. "Anyway, this trophy meant the world to her because it was the one thing that proved she'd won some-thing. Uncle RJ was always good at everything when it came to sports, so it shouldn't have mattered to him. But because it mattered to my mom, he was clearly a dick about it."

"Typical sibling animosity. My sister and I had a lot of animosity toward each other growing up, always vying for our parents' attention. Bickering. We're close now, though."

"Precisely. Anyway, after Mom passed, Uncle RJ sent me a letter with his condolences. It was weird, because I never spoke to him, but I accepted his condolences and sent him a thank-you note in return. Then he sent me an update on his life . . . not sure why? Maybe he felt the need to be connected. Who knows? But . . . he sent a newspaper clipping of his engagement announcement, a picture of him and his fiancée."

"Okay," Pacey says, sounding skeptical.

"And do you know what I saw?"

"What?"

"That trophy. Right there, in his living room, on the mantle, plain as day. He still has it."

"Seriously?" Pacey laughs.

"Yup, and after I saw that, I thought I had no other choice than to pack up, head to Banff . . . and steal it."

Pacey pauses his wide stride on the sidewalk and turns toward me, humor written all over his face. "Wait, you drove over eleven hours, to a foreign country—"

"It's Canada."

"Doesn't matter, you drove to a foreign country—to steal a trophy from your estranged uncle?"

"Yup." I smile widely. "My mom deserves that trophy. It's hers. And I'm going to get it for her."

"Wow," Pacey says and then chuckles. "That . . . Jesus, that makes me like you so much fucking more."

"My crazy makes you like me more?"

"Yeah, in fact it does."

I laugh and add, "For a brief moment, when Katherine was telling me all the things that could happen to a single girl on a trip by herself, I debated coming, but I just felt as though I couldn't move forward with saying goodbye to my mom without giving her the justice she deserves, you know?"

He nods. "Yeah, I would probably feel the same way." He squeezes my hand. "You're a good person, Winnie."

"Even if it means bamboozling my uncle?"

"Yeah, because you know it would mean something to your mom."

"It would. Thank you for the validation," I say as we get to his car.

He opens the door for me and helps me in, but he doesn't shut the door. Instead, he lifts my chin and looks me in the eyes. "Thanks for sharing that with me."

"It was easy to share with you, Pacey."

His eyes fall to my lips, and my breath catches in my chest as I wait with anticipation for him to lean in and claim my lips like I wish he would.

His tongue swipes his bottom lip and I mirror the action. He leans in and I still my breath, waiting.

I want him to kiss me. I want to see if this electricity bouncing between us is real. I want to see if he'd claim me like I think he would with those powerfully strong hands.

My heart beats in my throat, anticipation rolling through my stomach.

Just a little farther, just close that space . . . that's all it would take.

I mentally urge myself to reach out for him, to make the move he seems hesitant about, but before I can, he pulls back and closes the door. Disappointment washes over me, but then again, if Pacey were to kiss me, I doubt it would be in a parking lot. Would he pick somewhere else to make it more of a memorable moment? *Something special?* Is that what I want after so many years without romance in my life?

Something special.

He places our bags in the frunk—front trunk—and then settles into the driver's seat. He punches in his code and then pulls forward through the parking spot in front of us while placing his hand on my thigh.

A thrilling chill races up my leg and settles in the pit of my stomach as I glance down at his hand resting on my leg. It might not be a kiss, but I'll take it. Josh never did anything like this, not even when we were younger. He'd hold my hand in the car, but possessively hold me like this? Not so much.

This is why I feel so much around Pacey. It's the little things. Him listening. Him teasing. Him choosing the exact right moment to show his claim. Surprisingly, and I don't know whether it's just the passage of time, but he makes me feel more alive than Josh ever did. Pacey thrills me, and that scares me, because what's going to happen when I leave? Will he want to see me again? Will he want to exchange phone numbers? Or will he just want to go our separate ways?

"So, when are you going to go see your uncle?"

"I need to get my car towed out of the ditch first. Once that happens, I'll figure out my plan of attack."

His brow creases. "Can you do me a favor?"

"You've done so much for me. Of course I would do you a favor."

"Good." He shifts in his seat but keeps his hand on my thigh. "Can you take out your phone and send a text?"

"Uh . . . okay," I say, confused. I retrieve my phone from my purse and open a new text message. "Who am I sending this to?" He rattles off a phone number and I type it in. "Now what?"

"Type 'hello' and send it."

Unsure where he's going with this, I do as I'm told. Almost instantly, his phone lights up on the center console, where it's charging.

"Did you just give me your phone number?" I ask like a giddy girl.

"I did. Now if you try to ditch me, I at least have a way to stalk you."

"Ditch you, like . . . at the gondola?" I ask with a laugh.

But he doesn't laugh. Instead, he grows more serious. "No,

when your car is free. I don't trust that you won't just take off. Hell, I don't even know your last name. I feel as though you're blowing in the wind, ready to be freed, and I have no way of catching you when you're released."

"I would never leave without saying bye. Never, Pacey."

"Good." He squeezes my thigh and then rubs my skin with his thumb. "Now save me as a contact."

"Okay. Should I save you as Pacey Lawes, or something like" —my cheeks burn up—"Hot Ass?"

His brows skyrocket to his hairline and his lips turn up. "Hot Ass, for sure." I chuckle and then he asks, "Should I save you as Sexy Thighs, you know, since I still don't know your last name?"

"It's Berlin. Winnie Berlin."

He nods. "Think I'm still going to save you as Sexy Thighs."

"I would hope so."

Chapter Thirteen

PACEY

Winnie clutches her seat and says, "Soooo . . . this is terrifying."

We didn't have to wait in line very long for a gondola ride, and because we were talking so much while waiting for our turn, I don't think she really gave much thought to how we'd be in a little "cage" as she likes to call it, being held up by a cable above the mountains.

Leaning casually in my seat, arm draped over the back of the bench, I say, "You're more than welcome to join me over here."

"If I move, I think the gondola will fall off the cable."

I chuckle and lean forward, offering her my hand. She takes it and then squeaks with alarm as I tug her to my side of the gondola. She curls against me on the bench, and her hand lands on my chest. I drape my arm over her shoulders and hold her tightly.

"I swear this isn't a move," she says.

"A move?" I ask.

"You know, like how you're in the movie theater and you yawn just so you can drape your arm over your date. I'm not faking how terrified I am so I can get close to you."

"Are you considering this a date?"

She stiffens beneath my hold and says, "Oh, no, I wasn't saying it like that. I don't think this is a date. I fully understand the circumstances of this day."

Enjoying her discomfort too much, I ask, "And what are the circumstances?"

"Just two friends—"

"We're friends?"

The wind blows and the gondola slightly sways to the side. She clutches me tighter. "I would like to think we bonded after you dropped me into the mud while we were trying to get Minnie out."

"I didn't drop you into the mud."

She ignores my comment, which makes me secretly smile even harder. "But you know, two new friends going out on the town, learning about each other and buying things, sharing drinks, debating over potato skins and tacos, and then snuggling with each other because we're both terrified of heights."

"I never said I was terrified of heights."

She smooths her hand over my chest. "Shh, Pacey, it's going to be okay. This cable won't snap, we won't fall to our deaths. You have plenty of years left playing your ice sport."

"Ice sport?" I laugh. "You mean hockey?"

"God, I'm so terrified, I forgot what it was called."

Sighing, I wrap my arm completely around her and lean my cheek against the top of her head. "These are really safe. I promise we're going to be okay, and then it's all going to be worth it when we get to the top."

"And how long will it take to get to the top?"

"Let's not focus on that."

"Okay, what do you want to focus on?" she asks. "And be quick with it, because I'm going to need a distraction."

"I'm guessing you don't want the caramel apple right now."

She shakes her head.

"We'll save it for the top." I smooth my hand over her arm reassuringly and ask, "How long are you going to be in Banff?"

"Not really sure. I have to muster the courage to see my uncle, and then after that, I guess I'll head home."

"What are you going to do when you get home?"

"Figure out my life. Not sure I want to continue going to school for business. It didn't interest me. But I don't know *what* interests me. Isn't that pathetic?"

"No. There are plenty of people in the same shoes as you," I say. "Just because it takes you a little longer to find yourself doesn't make you pathetic. Remember, we all have our own timelines."

"And comparison takes the fun out of everything."

I smile against her hair. "Exactly. But let's see if we can dive into this a bit. What did you like about working at your mom's bookstore?"

"I loved the children's section. That's where I spent most of my time. I actually started children's programs at the store."

"What kind of programs?" I ask as I feel her body start to ease under my touch. Not as stiff as before.

"We had a generously sized children's book area, but it was in the far back of the bookstore, which always made me laugh, because back in the day, all the dirty novels used to be in the back. But after some older woman chastised Mom for carrying such 'filth', Mom decided to rearrange the shelves and brought the 'filth' to the front of the store. She started highlighting one of the dirty books every week and called it Filthy Friday. Bosoms were heaving all over covers, and shirtless men claimed their woman with a hand to the back of their neck. It was Mom's favorite part of the store."

"I think your mom and I would've gotten along very well."

"I can easily agree with that. She'd have really liked you." Winnie pauses for a second and then she continues, "So while

Mom was dressing up the front of the store with dirty books, I was taking care of the back with all the children's books. Our neighbor was good with woodworking, so he helped me cut some trees out of wood, and I spent a good portion of my weekend making wooden trees from recycled materials and scattering them throughout the space until it felt like a jungle. In the middle of the jungle, I made a circle-time area, and I would have a theme for the week for story time. I figured out what time worked best for the moms around the neighborhood, and before I knew it, we had a full story time, every day, twice a day. After story time, we did a craft that corresponded with the story. It was . . . it was a lot of fun, and there was something about seeing the connection between the parent and the child enjoying something that felt satisfying. My mom and I loved each other so much, and I saw the same love reflected in others."

"I can see how that would be very satisfying; bringing joy to others always feels good."

"I'm sure you have lots of experience with that."

I move my hand to her waist, easing up on my hold since she seems to be more relaxed now. "There's a tradition I have, where I toss a practice puck over the wall before every game. While we warm up, I scan the crowd for a kid who I think deserves it, and then I skate over to them and toss it over."

"How do you pick them out?"

"Depends. Sometimes it's because of a sign they worked hard on. Sometimes it's just a feeling I get, that maybe they need this puck to help them believe in something. Sometimes it's because I can see a sense of failure in a parent, as if they don't have as much pride as they should, and tossing a puck to their kid would make things that much better. Remember, I'm good at reading people."

"Yes, I do know that. You're also good at handling people. I feel very at ease with you, which is so strange, because I felt it right away, as though I knew I was going to be safe with you around."

"That's a pretty big compliment," I say while moving my hand over the scruff of my jaw. "Thank you. That means a lot to me."

"No, thank you." She lifts up so our eyes connect, and I get lost in the deep blue of her irises. "This has been a lovely day, and I don't think I thanked you for lunch. God." She shakes her head. "I'm so unappreciative."

"You're not. I can see that you're grateful. You don't have to say thank you."

"But I should. So, thank you, Pacey. I'm not sure you know how much I needed this, this help. I was really scared to come here, but I did it on a whim anyway. When Minnie got stuck, I was horrified that I had ended up in a really bad situation. But now, I don't feel quite as alone as I did when I first left Seattle."

"I'm glad you stumbled into our cabin."

She leans her head back on my shoulder. We stay like that for the rest of the trip up the mountain, embracing one another, and I feel a deep level of appreciation for her. I've not really had many girlfriends over the years. Not had the time. So, I can't recall the last time I just hung out with a woman like this. Care-free. Relaxed. *Content.*

And as I pull her a little closer, I realize that I'm not going to want to let go of this girl right away. I know it's way too early to say anything to her and she's going through a lot with her mom and her uncle, but Seattle isn't that far from Vancouver. I would want to see her whenever she decides to leave. We could make something work, that is, if she wants to make something work.

Who knows?

This could be a blip in the road for her, whereas I don't see it that way. I see it as a fork in the road, and I can either move on once she leaves, or I can follow the path that attempts to date this girl.

It's an easy choice for me. *But will her heart want someone like me?*

═══

"THIS ISN'T GOOD," Winnie says as she attempts to rise from the bench where we chose to sit and share our caramel apple.

"What isn't good?" I ask.

She slowly stands and then looks me in the eyes. "I'm already starting to get very sore from our workout this morning."

I can't help it, I chuckle. "It's a good sore. Shows that you put in the time."

"Don't say that to me tomorrow when I can't get out of bed." She picks up our trash and throws it away before coming back to where I'm still sitting on the bench. "What are you doing?"

"Enjoying the view," I answer.

She turns around toward the mountains and says, "Yeah, I think I filled my phone with pictures."

"I wasn't talking about that view."

She glances back at me and then throws her head back and laughs. "Oh, Pacey, I didn't peg you for being corny."

I stand from the bench and take her hand in mine. "And what did you peg me as?"

"You know what I thought you were—the ladies' man of the team."

"Yeah, and that could not be further from the truth."

"Oh? Please do elaborate on that."

Ever since we made it to the top, her spirit has picked up . . . along with her teasing. I like it, a lot.

"You want to know about my sex life?"

"Well, I was referring to dating life, but do those go hand in hand for you?"

"Not much time to date."

"Oh, right, duh. You're probably really busy."

"I meant, to be out on the dating circuit, trying to find someone I match with. If I were already matched up with someone, I'd dedicate time to that relationship." I just want to make that clear to her. "But going on blind dates and spending time on dating apps? Yeah, I don't have the energy for that, not after a long-as-fuck travel schedule."

"So, then, during the season, are you celibate?" she asks.

I chuckle. "This last season I was." I drive my hand over my head. "Some of the guys will go out to the bar, flash their professional hockey player card, and then take a girl back to the hotel, Posey and Hornsby being at the forefront of that endeavor."

"Posey?" she asks, surprised. "I never would've guessed he does that. Not that there's anything wrong with going to the bar and bringing someone home, but I just didn't expect him to even know what sex is. He seems innocent."

That makes me full-on belly laugh. "Oh, he's not fucking innocent. Last year he got caught getting a blow job on the bus before we left the hotel."

"What?" Winnie nearly shouts. "No way. Not Levi." She shakes her head. "No man who lives and dies for a certain flavor of fudge gets blow jobs on team busses."

"Think again. He might put on a certain façade, but the dude gets around."

"And Eli? Does he break hearts?"

We make our way past the sidewalk and to the edge of the summit house. I bring her to the fence. We both lean against it and look out at the expanse of mountains. It's incredible, a view I'll never get sick of, seeing peak after peak reaching up to the deep-blue sky.

"Eli might break ideas, but he doesn't break hearts. He doesn't ever let anyone get close enough to have their heart broken. But when it comes to the women he's going to fuck, he lets them know that's all it'll ever be. He's upfront. He's never lied about his intentions, and you have to appreciate that, because at least he's not leading anyone on."

"Yeah, if I were into him, I'd probably appreciate that."

"So, you're not into Hornsby?"

She looks over at me and smirks. "No, I like the silent, broody type." She pauses. "Think Halsey will go out with me?"

My jaw tightens as I look away. "He's gay, sorry."

Winnie laughs and pushes at my shoulder. "No, he's not."

"In this situation, he is."

"Okay . . . so what do you think about me and Silas?"

"You trying to get on my nerves?"

Her smile stretches across her face, and even though she's making me feel like a jealous fuck, I still get lost in the beauty of that smile. "Am I doing a good job?" she asks.

"An excellent job."

I take her hand and pull her in close so her back is to my chest, we're both looking out toward the mountains, and I have her pinned between me and the fence. Her head leans back against my shoulder and she says, "I could spend some serious time here."

"In my arms?" I ask.

She chuckles. "Fishing for compliments, Pacey? I was talking about the summit house."

"Sure you were. You're just too shy to admit it."

"Admit what?" she asks with a teasing tone in her voice.

"That you like me. That's okay—no need to admit anything. I can see it in your eyes."

"That sure of yourself?"

"Always." I lean against her body and say quietly near her ear, "And when I don't see it in your eyes, I feel it in your body language."

"And how do I show you with my body language? Because it seems to me that you're the one who's been all about the touching and handholding, which leads me to believe you're the one who likes me."

"Yeah, I do," I answer honestly, which seems to stun her, because she doesn't have a witty comeback. Instead, she turns in my embrace so we're facing each other.

"Just like that—you're going to claim it? That you like me?" She studies me. "I have a hard time believing that."

My brow draws forward. "Why do you have a hard time believing that?"

"Because you're . . . well, you're Pacey Lawes. We're on different levels. I'm lost, have absolutely no future, a dwindling bank account, and a car stuck in a ditch in the mountains. I don't see what I could possibly offer that you don't already have or could get from someone in a better position than me."

"Do you really think that little of yourself?" I ask. "Do you really not see what you offer?"

"I don't see what I offer to *you*," she says. "Trust me, I realize I've been living in a little fantasy world the last couple of days and I understand it'll come to an end quicker than it started. I know I'm fun and interesting right now, but that will wear off." She frees herself from my embrace and starts to walk toward the gondola. "I don't even know what I was thinking, allowing myself to spend this day with you. Seems ridiculous, if you actually think about it."

"What are you talking about? Hey, hold up," I say while grabbing her hand and stopping her before she gets in line for the gondola to head back down the mountain. "What's happening?"

"Realized I'm acting like a fool." She lets out a deep breath. "Yes, Pacey, I like you. It's obvious, I can't hide it, but there's no point in doing anything past today. I'll be leaving soon. My car could be towed tomorrow if it doesn't rain tonight."

"But you don't have to leave right away. You can stay longer."

"It's not your house. You can't decide that. It's already awkward with Silas. I don't want to make it even more awkward by staying when I don't have to."

"But where are you going to go? You don't have any lodging." Panic starts to consume me. She's a flight risk. Once she gets her car back, I have a feeling she'll up and leave, because she'll feel as if it's the right time for her to go. And, yes, she said she wouldn't leave without saying goodbye, but I don't want her to think she needs to leave, not yet.

"I'll figure it out." She heads toward the short line for the gondola again, and I follow her. Even though I want to pull her out of line and stay on the mountain longer, people have begun to recognize me and are pointing me out to their companions, and I don't want to cause a scene.

Instead, once our turn comes, we get into a gondola. After the door closes and we're on our way, I turn to face her head-on and ask, "Why don't you let me help you?"

"Help me with what?"

"Find out what you should be doing, what your next chapter is."

"Why would you do that?" she asks, her hands gripping the bench tightly as the gondola rocks. I want to pull her into my embrace again, but I also want to talk to her, see her facial reactions, let her see how serious I am.

"Because . . ." I say, the words on the tip of my tongue, but my nerves are shaking from the abrupt one-eighty of our conversation.

"Because why?" she asks.

I pull on the back of my neck. "Because I'm not ready to say goodbye." I look her in the eyes. "I like you, Winnie. I like hanging out with you. You have nothing pressing to get back to, and you're trying to figure out what you're going to do now. Instead of running back home, why don't you find yourself in the place your mom was born? And let me help you, because despite what you might think, I'm invested now, and I'm not going to let you just walk away as if the last few days haven't been special." I scoot forward on the bench and reach for her hand. "I'm telling you right now—I don't feel this kind of connection with people, but the moment I saw you, I knew there was something special about you and I needed to find out what it is." When she looks down, I force her to look at me again.

"I'm not ready to say goodbye, and I hope you're not ready either."

Her teeth roll over her bottom lip as she shakes her head. "I'm not."

Relief floods me. I can't be sure why this girl seems so special to me, so important, or why our connection is so strong, but what I do know is that I need more time to figure it all out.

"So, then you'll stay?"

"Silas—"

"Let me worry about him, okay?" She stays silent, so I add, "He's going through a rough time. Who knows—maybe you can help him."

She perks up. "Could you imagine? Wouldn't that be a turn of events?"

"One I'd be interested in watching."

"How much longer are you here for?" Winnie asks.

"I was set for a month, but I can come and go as I please. Taters really doesn't care, even though he likes to act like he does."

"I think Katherine and Max would kill me if I was gone that long."

"I'm not saying you have to stay for a month, just . . . stay a little longer. From what you've said, it sounds as though you've been carrying a heavy heart for a long time. Maybe you take this time to just breathe. To take a second for yourself. We all need those breaks. It's why we come up here, to just step away and recharge."

She nods. "I like that. Recharge."

"Recharge in the place where your mom was born. Reconnect. And who knows?" I smirk. "Maybe you hang out with a hot hockey player while you do it."

"I do enjoy Eli's company." She can't hold back her smile as her eyes meet mine.

"Such a fucking ball-buster."

She laughs and I pull her over to my bench. I drape my arm

over her shoulder and keep her close. She rests her head against my chest and we travel down the mountain together like this.

I have no idea what's going to happen, but at least I have the knowledge that this girl isn't going anywhere any time soon. And for the first time in a week, I don't feel the same pressing pain at being knocked out of the playoffs. I feel a purpose. Because maybe Winnie Berlin needs someone to help her not only recharge, but move toward her final destination. *And maybe that destination will include me.*

Chapter Fourteen

WINNIE

"Don't laugh at me," I say while pointing my finger at Pacey, who's carrying our bags.

"I'm not laughing at you. I saw a funny bird fly by."

"You're such a bad liar." I place my hand on one of the cars in the garage and take a deep breath. "Oh God, my legs. Why are they seizing on me?"

"You need to take a bath, or better yet, sit in the hot tub for a bit."

"There's a hot tub here?" I ask.

"Yes, in the pool room."

"Ah, yes, the pool room," I say in a hoity-toity voice. "Why didn't I think to check there? Silly me."

"Come on, smart-ass." Pacey opens the door for me and I hobble in, every muscle in my legs on fire. Working out with a professional athlete when you don't normally work out isn't recommended. I didn't even do that much, but just what we did do is killing me. "Want to give the boys their gifts and then hit up the hot tub?"

"Yes, Jesus Christ, yes."

Pacey lets out a hearty laugh as we pass his room, then mine, and then go to the main living area. Stephan is cooking. Halsey is lying across the couch reading, as usual. Eli is playing cards with Levi at the table, some sort of speed game that keeps their attention on the table in front of them, and Silas is nowhere to be seen.

"Hey," Pacey says.

Halsey looks up from his book and asks, "What's up? Have fun?"

Surprised he spoke, I say, "We did have fun. Got some presents for you guys."

"Presents?" Levi asks, slapping his arm across the cards on the table. "Pause, man. I want presents."

Chuckling, I take the bags from Pacey to the dining room table. I open the first one and hand Levi his fudge.

"You're an angel." He tears open the box and takes a bite of it faster than I can explain why I got them something. Moaning, he sinks back in his chair and clutches the fudge to his chest.

"Glad you like it." I chuckle. "I wanted to get you all something for being cool about me staying here with you. I know I'm crimping your bachelor style, but I truly appreciate it."

"You're not crimping anything," Eli says while looking past my shoulder to Pacey. "Just glad you're able to have a place to stay while you're here."

"Thank you." I reach into the bag and pull out the red hat I got for Eli. I hand it to him and watch his face genuinely light up when he sees it. "Pacey told me you collect them."

"I do," Eli says, fitting it on his head. "I love it. I don't have a red one yet. This is awesome. Thank you." He adjusts the bill, and I have to admit, not only is he a pretty man, but he looks damn good in a baseball hat, too. Just one of those people who looks good no matter what.

Turning toward Halsey, I say, "And since you love to read, I found an old bookstore in town and they happened to have my favorite Lee Child book. Not sure if you've read it, but I figured I'd get it for you anyway." I hand him the book and the smallest of smirks appears on his face.

"I actually haven't read this one yet, but it's on my list. Thank you."

"You're welcome." I move over to the kitchen where Stephan is tossing a salad, and I pull out the apron I found for him as we were walking back to the car after the gondola ride. I made Pacey stop so I could grab it.

I hand Stephan the apron and say, "I noticed you tend to get food all over your clothes and thought this would be helpful. It's classy, none of that 'kiss the chef' crap."

He laughs and puts it on. He ties it around his waist and says, "Thank you, Winnie. You didn't have to get me anything, but I do appreciate it. And for reference, I wouldn't have minded a 'kiss the chef' apron. Wouldn't kill these guys to kiss me every once in a while."

"I didn't know you take make-out sessions over money," Silas says, walking in with an empty beer bottle in his hand. "Dude, I would've puckered up a long time ago."

"I prefer your money." Stephan goes back to his salad while Silas sets his empty bottle near the sink and then turns toward us.

"You've been gone all day. What did you do?"

For some reason, Silas makes me feel really nervous, so I let Pacey tell him.

"Went into town, did some shopping, stopped at the cidery and picked up some cider. It's in the car."

"On it," Levi says as he heads down the hallway toward the garage. Pacey wasn't kidding—Levi really does like the cider.

"Then we took the Banff Gondola up the mountain."

"Cool," Silas says while folding his arms over his chest. "Did I hear something about gifts?"

"Yes," I say, feeling shaky. Instead of reaching into his bag and handing him his cup, I just give him the bag and then take a step back. I feel like if I'm too close to him, I might get burned, so I keep my distance.

"Thanks," he says awkwardly while opening the bag. He pulls out the wooden pint glass with "Hostess with the Mostest" and I wince, waiting to see if he's going to like it. He snorts and then nods while examining the cup. "This is far too kind, not quite accurate given how I've been a dick lately, but I appreciate it."

"Well, I appreciate you letting me be here. I know it's not how you envisioned your time off, so I want you all to know I appreciate it."

"You really didn't have to do this," Silas says. "You're not bothering anyone by being here. If anything, you've made Pacey forget about the season, which he was harping on every two goddamn seconds. You're doing us a favor." Silas goes to the fridge, pulls out a beer, cracks it open, and pours it into his new cup. He smacks his lips together and says, "Now that's a good beer. Thanks, Winnie."

"You're welcome."

Silas sits on the counter while Stephan lays out plates. "Seriously, though, I'm glad we don't have to watch Pacey study his game videos over and over again. It's a relief."

"All right, settle down," Pacey says while setting his bags on the console table near the couch. He then turns to me and asks, "Do you want to eat first and then sit in the hot tub?"

"Uh . . . yeah," I say as I feel every pair of eyes in this room on me.

"Are we hopping into the hot tub after this?" Eli asks, wiggling his eyebrows. "I'm game."

"Just me and Winnie," Pacey says—and thank God for that, because I'm already self-conscious enough about joining just Pacey. There's no way I'd be able to do it with the rest of the guys.

"Such a shame. I was hoping to sit close to you, man. I miss you." Eli holds out his arms. "Come give me a hug."

"Fuck off." Pacey laughs and then grabs us each a bottle of water from the fridge.

Levi comes bustling down the hall, arms full of cider and mouth full of fudge. "This is the best day of my life."

"There's no way," I mutter.

"No way what?" Pacey asks.

Quietly I turn toward him and say, "That he got blown on the team bus. He's such a goof."

"Don't judge a book by its cover, Winnie. You should know that."

———

TWO THINGS I didn't think through when Pacey said we should hang out in the hot tub.

I didn't pack my bathing suit, even though Max told me to because he said you never know when you're going to spontaneously jump into a lake. I thought he was an idiot and skipped the bathing suit. Little did I know the lake was going to be a hot tub.

And the second thing—I'm going to be in a hot tub with Pacey Lawes, the man currently walking toward me in nothing but a pair of navy-blue swim trunks, which hang low enough to catch the deep V in his hips. But besides his obviously built chest and defined abdomen, his hair is pulled up into a topknot, and he's carrying a box of chocolate, as well as two cans of cider.

Talk about feeling like a queen.

I have a robe wrapped around my body—provided by my room, of course; it truly has everything, except a swimsuit—and my nerves are eating me alive, because I know what I have under this robe will soon be exposed to Pacey.

"Why do you have a frightened look on your face?" Pacey asks.

"I forgot I didn't bring a bathing suit with me."

"Then what, uh . . . what are you wearing under your robe?" he asks, his voice growing deeper.

And then it hits me. "Oh, I'm not naked. I have clothes on. Well, not clothes per se, more like undergarments. I didn't think naked was an option—I mean, not that I would want to be naked. That would be weird, wouldn't it? 'Oh hey, I'm naked in here, move along, boys.'" I have no idea what I'm saying. "Can we just ignore everything I just said and finish this off with I'm not naked, I'm wearing a bra and underwear?"

"What color?" His eyes grow dark.

I clutch at my robe and try to hide my grin. "You'll soon find out."

And just like that, the feelings of being self-conscious fly away as Pacey takes my hand, even though his are full, and walks me through the house to the pool room. The boys are watching a movie in the theater room, you can hear the bass of the speakers booming as we make our way through the house. I'm just glad it's only going to be Pacey catching me in this getup, and not all of the guys.

"What are they watching?" I ask Pacey.

"Uh, one of the Star Wars movies, I think. One of the new ones."

"*Solo*?" I ask.

Pacey scoffs. "No, that movie is trash. All the boys hate it."

"Really? I didn't think it was that bad."

Pacey pauses in the hallway and turns toward me. "If you plan on staying here, I suggest you don't repeat that, but just keep it to yourself."

"They hate it that much?"

"Yes. That much."

"Good to know." We continue walking. "Anything else I need to know that they hate?"

"The movie *Annie*."

"What?" I laugh.

Pacey pushes open the pool door for me, and I'm instantly transported into another world. Large sliding glass doors are propped open, bringing the beauty of outside indoors. The vaulted ceilings resemble the ones in my guest room, but they're covered in pine shiplap and white bulb lights that twinkle in the dark night, offering the only light in the room.

It's incredibly romantic.

"They have something against *Annie*, not quite sure what. Maybe it's the music, the premise? Can't be sure. It's just not allowed to be watched when they're around, ever."

"Noted. I mean, I don't have a passion for *Annie*, but I'll be sure to never bring it up. I don't want to upset anyone."

"Smart."

I take in the in-ground hot tub, which is surrounded by teak wood decking and illuminated by purple and blue lights beneath the water. It's positively gorgeous.

"This is so beautiful. I don't think I've ever seen a house like this."

"Yeah, we all have an agreement that the house will stay with us no matter what. So, if Taters wants to sell, I'm next in line to purchase, then Hornsby, then Holmes, and last would be Posey."

"Why would Silas ever want to sell?"

"Not sure, but we're contractually bound to each other and this house."

"Very smart." I stand at the edge of the hot tub, my hands still clutching at my robe, while Pacey sets everything down and pulls two towels from a shelf. He sets them on a lounger and turns toward me.

"Are you going to get in?"

"Yes," I answer while dipping my toe in the water. "You know, just trying to find the best way to take off this robe."

"I don't think there is a best way. I think you just take it off," he says with a smirk.

I sigh and look off to the side. "Just feeling self-conscious is all. It comes in waves. Give me a second and I'm sure I'll be okay."

Pacey's lips twist to the side and then he walks behind me. He places his hands on my hips and moves in close. Without saying anything, he very slowly moves his hands to the knot of my robe and undoes it, letting the ends of the belt fall to the side.

"You're really fucking sexy, Winnie," Pacey whispers. "There's nothing you should be self-conscious about." The smooth, evening breeze caresses my heated skin exposed by the gap in the robe. "And I'm not the only guy in this house who notices how fine you are." His breath tickles over the back of my neck. "In fact, Eli had all the wrong intentions where you were concerned."

"Wh-what?" I stutter as he pushes one of the sleeves off my body, exposing my right shoulder.

"You heard me. I just seem to be the lucky one who gets to hang with you, who gets to share this moment with you." He pushes my other sleeve down, exposing my other shoulder. "Fuck, Winnie. When I was thinking of what color you were wearing, I was hoping it was pink."

A burst of heat sears through me as his finger draws a lazy circle on my back, right above the clasp of my bra. I envision him snapping it open and letting it slowly fall down my arms just like this robe, which is only being held up by my ass now.

"I didn't consider light pink, though. I like it. Does your underwear match?" He pushes the robe down and sucks in a sharp breath as my thong is revealed. "Ah, hell, Winnie." The robe pools at my feet and I quickly turn around so he's not staring at my bare ass. His hands fall to my hips, though, and he shows no shame checking me out. He wets his lips and says, "You're going to have to sit on the other side of the hot tub. Got it? Because there's no way I'm going to be able to share space with you and not touch you." His hands smooth up my ribs and then back down to my hips, where his fingers glide under the string of my thong.

"I didn't have any clean underwear that isn't a thong," I say, not sure what I should be talking about in this moment.

"I'm glad," he says, moving his hands to my back but keeping them in neutral territory, despite me wanting to feel them all over my body. "Now get in the hot tub, before I do something I shouldn't." I look up into his eyes, and the question I've been wanting to ask is on the tip of my tongue. He must notice because he asks, "What's on that mind of yours?"

Unable to stop myself, I ask, "You truly, honestly, find me attractive?"

He grips my chin and asks, "Who the hell fucked with your head? Who made you think you weren't attractive? Who put those ideas into this gorgeous, beautiful mind of yours?"

I look away and tears fill my eyes. Flashbacks to the night Josh and I broke it off flood through me. The pain just as hurtful now as it was back then.

"Tell me," Pacey says.

Swallowing hard, I say, "Uh, when Josh and I broke up, he said that— God, this is so embarrassing."

"What the fuck did he say to you?" Pacey asks, his voice sounding angry.

"He told me . . ." I bite my bottom lip and look toward the sky. "He said I had gained weight and that he didn't really find me attractive anymore. He told me it was one of the reasons why he stopped trying in bed."

"You have got to be fucking kidding me," Pacey says in a low, menacing tone. The level of malice in his voice is quite startling as he stares me down. Then he grips my chin and forces my eyes up to his. "You listen to me, Winnie, and you listen to me good. The only reason a man would ever say something like that to a woman is because he's insecure with his own self. He was trying to put you down to make up for his insecurities."

"That's what Max and Katherine said too—well, something

along those lines—and even though I've tried to lose the weight that my mom's health issues brought on, it's been hard. It's why I'm so self-conscious around you, because, I mean, look at you."

Pacey smooths his hands over my waist and then back up. His hands glide under my thong, and then up to the underwire of my bra. His jaw is tight, his eyes angry, and then he's taking my hand in his. "I don't want to be fucking crude with you, but I think this is the only way I can prove my point." He brings my hand to right above his crotch, but doesn't force me to touch him as he says, "If you cupped me right now, you'd see how goddamn hard I am . . . just from being near you. You'd feel how much my cock strains for you. You'd understand why I want to be around you all the time, because I think you're hella gorgeous, Winnie. You're all kinds of my type, Eli's too. I'm just the lucky bastard who stole you away from everyone else first." My hand hovers but doesn't touch— I'm too nervous, too scared. "Just having your hand right there, knowing how close you are . . ." He squeezes his eyes shut. "Fuck, Winnie, it makes me think of that second night we hung out, Jenga night, when I had to jack off in the shower thinking about you after we recreated your favorite position."

"You . . . you did?"

He nods, his teeth rolling over his lip as the muscles in his neck strain.

It's sexy.

It's tempting.

And before I know what I'm doing, my hand is connecting with his length, and oh my God, he isn't lying. He *is* hard as stone.

And so big.

God, is he big.

My fingers explore the outline of his length until they reach the head. He sucks in a sharp breath and I consider undoing his trunks and dropping to my knees, but that would require me to use my leg muscles and, right now, they need the warm water of the hot tub.

I pull my hand away and feel my face blush as I take a step back. His eyes shamelessly travel down my body and then back up again, lingering on my breasts before they rest on my face.

"So, yes, after careful observation, you are in fact hard." I pretend to tip an imaginary hat at him for some reason—God knows I can't act chill for one second. "That's quite the erection, dear sir." I pump my fist as if to say "good job, old chap" in an old-timey voice.

The corners of his lips tilt up. Glad he has a sense of humor, because this could be really humiliating if he didn't.

"So, I think I'm going to get into the hot tub now. You know, since I can barely walk and all."

He still doesn't say anything; instead, he takes my hand and helps me step into the tub.

"Ooh, that's nice," I say, letting my body sink into the warm, jet-propelled water. "This is just what I needed."

"Sit here," he says, helping me into a seat that's right up against a jet. "But don't groan like that again. Please."

He lets go of my hand and then takes the seat across from me. There could be an entire man's body between us, that's how big this tub is.

"Is it really necessary to sit all the way over there?" I ask, raising my voice to be heard over the loud rumble from the jets. "It'll be hard to carry on a conversation."

"I don't trust myself near you."

"Well, I trust you. Please, Pacey. Just a little closer. I don't want to be shouting."

Sighing, he moves closer, not directly next to me, but close enough.

"Thank you. Isn't that better?"

"It would be better if you sank a little lower in the water."

I glance down and see that my breasts are floating right at the edge of the water, and because my bra is not made to contain buoyant breasts, I'm practically giving Pacey a peek-aboo show.

"Oops, sorry." I sink deeper into the water and smile over at him. "This is fun."

"It would be more fun if you were sitting on my lap."

My eyes widen at his brazenness. Not sure anyone has ever talked to me like that. "That's upfront."

He shifts and says, "Tired of skirting around the truth, so I'm going to tell you like it is, because I feel like you need the truth."

"And, um, what . . . uh, would be the truth?" I ask, twisting my hands together in the water, my nerves getting the better of me.

"The truth is plain and simple: I want you."

Oh.

I want to full-on grin and fan myself, but I hold back. "That's a nice thing to say to someone. Thank you."

He raises one brow in my direction. "That's all you're going to say? 'That's a nice thing to say'? 'Thank you'? No reciprocation of feelings or anything?"

Wanting to bring back some of the fun, I decide to tease him a bit. "Well, I can't quite make that kind of statement, because I don't know much about you other than you enjoy cider, you apparently have a thing for curvy girls, and you play hockey."

"And those three things don't guarantee me an 'I want you, too'?" His voice is so cute, so perplexed and confused.

"Well, the second thing makes my heart beat a little faster, the first thing makes me believe we could have some fun visiting different cideries, and the third one . . . well, I know nothing about hockey, so it doesn't really affect me much. But I still want to know more about you."

"Ask your questions, then."

"Okay, so any siblings besides your sister you told me about before?"

"Just her," he answers, looking to the side. "She actually interns with the team."

"Oh, that's fun. So, you see her often?"

"No, but I try to get her to go out to dinner with me maybe once a month. She tries to act as though she doesn't know me because she's afraid people will scream nepotism when, in fact, she's worked her ass off to be where she is right now."

"I can understand that."

"She's actually your age and, oddly, I think you two would be good friends."

"Would we drive you nuts?"

He nods. "The ball-busting would be painful."

"That does sound fun. How long have you been playing hockey?"

"Growing up in Minnesota means the moment you can wear hockey skates and stand, you're playing hockey."

"So . . . young, I take it."

He winks. "That would be correct."

"Do your parents go to your games?"

"They catch a few throughout the year in person, and they watch every other game on TV. It pains them that I play for the Agitators, actually, because they're diehard Polar Freeze fans."

"Are they rivals or something?"

He chuckles and nods. "Yeah, they are. So, whenever we play Polar Freeze, Mom and Dad say they root for me, but cheer for the Freeze."

"Ooh, that can't be easy."

"Nah, it's all good. I take joy in blocking every shot that comes my way from their favorite team. Quite comical, actually."

I play with the bubbles at the surface of the water. "So, I take it you have a good relationship with them?"

"Yeah, pretty good. I call them every so often. They brag about me, and they put me in my place. I see them for the holi-days when I'm available, and they come to Vancouver over the summer for a few days just to visit. They love going on whale-watching tours."

"How fun. Okay, what's your favorite color?"

"That's one of your hard-hitting questions?" He chuckles. "Black, like my soul."

I tilt my head to the side in disbelief. "Your soul isn't black. I might not know if you wear boxers or briefs—"

"Briefs."

"Uh . . ." I clear my throat, trying not to think about him in briefs. "But I can tell you this—your soul is not black."

"Sure about that?" he asks in a challenging voice.

"Positive. And do you know how I know?"

"Enlighten me."

"Well, you see, not many guys would go out of their way to help me like you have. They'd be expecting something from all of that, like they were wooing me to get me into their bed, and even though you told me you want me, you're not pressuring me. Instead, you're sitting as far away from me as I'll allow while keeping your eyes trained on me. If your soul was black, you'd take what you want."

"Maybe you're right . . . maybe my favorite color is blue, like my eyes."

I push water at him, causing him to laugh. "You're an idiot. You tricked me into saying nice things about you."

"Wouldn't kill you to say a few nice things, you know, after you got all the boys a present except me." He bats his eyelashes at me.

"I've been waiting for you to point that out."

"To save you the embarrassment, I thought bringing it up without company around would be best." He rubs his hands together. "So, do I get a present?"

"No." I rest my head against the back of the hot tub.

"Brutal."

"SERIOUSLY, DON'T LOOK," I say. "I'm afraid things might fall off when I get out of the water."

"And that would be a bad thing because . . ." Pacey drawls out while holding up a towel.

"Because it's not a good time to show off the goods. I'm all wrinkly from the water."

He chuckles and turns his head away while holding out a towel. I slip out of the hot tub and then wrap the towel around my body.

"Thank you," I say softly as he picks up a towel for himself and dries off his chest.

"Do you feel better?" he asks.

"Yeah, I do. This was a good idea."

"I'd say so." He wiggles his brows and then picks up his phone. "Shit, I didn't realize it was midnight."

"What? Seriously?" I ask.

"Nah, it's just ten thirty."

"Dear God. I was going to say, that can't be good for a human, you could scramble your loins."

"Fuck." He cringes. "Winnie, the visual on that."

"Well, you need to be careful. Like Johnny Rose says, we need to be careful with our hearts . . . and our parts."

He shakes his head at me. "You're something else." He holds up my robe, and I slip into that as well, going for double coverage, and then he takes my hand again and walks me through the house. The movie is still playing and it must be some epic battle scene because the bass is pumping.

"They keep the movie loud," I say.

"And I would bet twenty bucks that they're all asleep. They always say if they keep the movie loud, they won't fall asleep, but they do every time. Taters is always the first to nod off."

"You must spend a lot of time with each other if you know such intimate details."

"Too much time. Hence why I'm spending my time with you."

"And here I thought it was because you couldn't get enough of my winning personality."

He squeezes my hand. "That too, along with the fact that you're much nicer to look at than the guys."

"I don't know. Eli is very nice to look at."

Leaning into my ear, Pacey whispers, "Watch it."

I let out a laugh as we stop. I turn toward Pacey and then lean against my bedroom door. "I had a lot of fun today. Probably the most fun I've had in a long time." I look him in the eyes. "I love my friends dearly, but they were there with me when my mom was sick, when she passed. Because of that, I think they treat me a little differently. With caution, you know? They have the image of me at my mom's funeral in their heads and things just haven't been the same." Will it ever be the same? I know it's only been a few months, but . . . "They're cautious and that hinders our fun. You don't look at me the way they do. You just let me have fun."

"I can understand that." He leans in closer and says, "I think we're the same way with Holmes. He's grieving too, and we don't really know what to do with him. We're often too nervous to push him to do something fun, but unlike you, we've watched him become more and more withdrawn. So, we just let him read, we let him escape."

"I noticed," I say quietly, and although I was curious, it wasn't my place to know Halsey's life story. "But you guys are there for him. I'm sure he'll come around. At least, I hope he does."

"Me too. Any plans for tomorrow?"

"Given it didn't rain today, I'm thinking about calling the tow truck and seeing if they'll get Minnie for me. And I don't know, maybe go for a hike."

"Let me join you."

I smirk. "I mean, if you want to."

"You know I want to."

I yawn and cover it up quickly, but Pacey catches it and chuckles.

He gives my hand another squeeze and then says, "I'll let you get to bed. See you in the morning."

That's it? Just a "see you in the morning"? After the day we had, I would've assumed there would be an epic end to it. But it's falling flat, and I'm not sure I'm okay with that.

He releases my hand and heads toward his bedroom but I call out to him before he gets too far.

"Pacey?"

He looks over his shoulder. "Yeah?"

Oh God, am I really going to do this?

Someone has to. Someone has to put the cherry on top of this wonderful day, and I know if I let him go back to his room without getting what I want, I'm going to regret it. I don't take charge like this; whenever I tried to do something spontaneous, Josh hated it. But Pacey isn't Josh. Pacey is completely different.

Nerves bloom in the pit of my stomach, and before I can chicken out, I walk up to him and place my hand on his bare chest.

"Don't you want your present?" My voice wavers, my nerves show, but I go for it anyway. Before he can answer, I bring my hand around the back of his neck, pull him closer to me, and then press my lips to his.

With the three first kisses I've received in my lifetime, I've always sat back and waited for the guy to make the move, but I don't want to wait with Pacey. I was hoping he'd kiss me as we were saying good night, but maybe it's time I take a chance and see if I'm wanted. *Take what I want.*

And I'm glad I did, because he groans and moves his lips across mine. His hand slides around my waist, pulling me in tighter against his rock-hard chest. Carefully, he backs me up against the wall and braces one hand next to my head as he holds my jaw with the other. With his thumb, he angles my chin up for better access to my mouth, and then he swipes his tongue across my lips. I open up and our tongues collide in demanding need.

There's nothing frantic about our kiss despite how desperately my body wants to get closer to him. Our kiss feels smooth, easy, meant to be as he moves his tongue deeper against mine. My hands fall to his chest and then back up to his neck. I allow myself to feel him, to take in the strength of his chest, the short-clipped hair sprinkled on his pecs, and the thick column of his neck.

And his lips are magic, not thin in the least, but not too thick either—a perfect medium. I feel like I'm being consumed by his mouth.

His mouth slows and then he lets out a sigh as he draws back an inch. He rests his forehead on mine and quietly says, "That was the best present I could've received." His eyes open and meet mine. "Have a good night, Winnie."

He pushes off the wall and grips the back of his neck as he stares at me with a goofy grin. His body language says he doesn't want to leave, but I think his brain is winning out because he takes another step back.

Hands behind me, leaning against the wall, I say, "Good night, Pacey."

He winces as if he's in pain, and says, "Fuck, you're gorgeous." And then he spins on his heel and heads into his bedroom, shutting the door behind him.

This is what giddy feels like, this consumption of happiness pulsing through your veins. I've met—*I've kissed*—the perfect man. And. He. Kissed. Me. Back.

Before I do something stupid like knock on his door and strip his trunks right off his legs to reveal that prominent bulge, I go to my room, shut the door, lock it, and then grab my phone, which is on my nightstand. Beaming with excitement, I text Max.

Winnie: *I kissed him.*

My face heats up just thinking about how assertive I was just now. I can't believe I did that. I wanted to kiss him all day and I was waiting for the perfect moment. In the hallway before bed wasn't picturesque, but it was everything I could've asked for.

My phone beeps with a text. Smiling, I read it.

Max: *WHATOHMYGOD!!!!YOUKISSED!!!!*

I laugh out loud. I knew Max would be the perfect person to tell because he'd cheer in excitement with me, whereas Katherine might ask if I used some sort of kissing guard to make sure we didn't transfer diseases.

Max: *Wait . . . we're talking about Pacey, right?*

Winnie: *Yes, I kissed Pacey.*

Max: *Wait . . . wait . . . you kissed him? As in you initiated the kiss?*

Winnie: *Correct.*

Max: *Damn, Winnie. Look at you taking charge. How did it happen? Was it good? Of course it was good. He probably pressed you against a wall, didn't he?*

Winnie: *He did. We were saying good night, and he was being a gentleman and took off toward his room. I called him back and reached up and kissed him. He then proceeded to push me against the wall and hold me in place.*

Max: *That's so hot. Does he win the best kiss award?*

Winnie: *Easily. There's no competition. I also took that moment to feel his chest a bit.*

Max: *Rightfully so, you have him in place, take advantage of it. Does he have a hairy chest?*

Winnie: *Clipped.*

Max: *Did he make out with tongue?*

Winnie: *Totally . . . I also might have felt his erection.*

Max: **Blinks* Excuse me? If you felt his erection, why are you texting me?*

Winnie: *I felt it earlier before we got in the hot tub.*

Max: *You were in the hot tub? But I know you didn't bring your swimsuit. Were you . . . naked?*

Winnie: *I knew you were going to throw that in my face. I wore my underwear and bra but those get flimsy in the water. Either way, I was self-*

conscious getting into the hot tub with him because he's this Adonis, and you know I've had some self-esteem issues. But he was proving to me that I shouldn't, because when he saw me in my underwear, he was completely turned on.

Max: *To be a fly on the wall for that moment. Was he big?*

Winnie: *God, Max . . . huge.*

Max: *You're one lucky bitch, but you deserve it. So, I'm guessing nothing happened other than a kiss?*

Winnie: *Yeah, just a kiss, but he told me he wants me. And it's taking a lot of my energy to actually believe what he says. I didn't realize the emotional job Josh did on me until another man showed interest in me.*

Max: *I've said it before, and I'll say it again—I wish chronic hemorrhoids on Josh. Teach him a goddamn lesson to mess with my girl. You're beautiful, and you don't need someone who doesn't know how to give a woman an orgasm bringing you down.*

Winnie: *I know. I need to keep reminding myself of that.*

I yawn again and stand to get ready for bed.

Winnie: *I'm exhausted. I'm going to head to bed.*

Max: *Okay. I'm happy for you, Winnie. You deserve this, you need this. Have fun and make the most of this strange but perfect adventure.*

Winnie: *Love you, Max.*

Max: *Love you, Win.*

Chapter Fifteen

PACEY

I'm fucking reeling.

After a long-ass workout that I started at four in the morning —I couldn't seem to calm my racing mind because of that fucking delicious kiss last night—I grab a towel from the shelf in the gym and head upstairs to the main level, where Posey and Hornsby are talking to Stephan in the kitchen as he makes egg sandwiches.

"Smells good, man," I call out.

"Thanks. I have a yogurt parfait in the fridge for your girl."

I don't even bother correcting him—because that's what Winnie feels like at this point, my girl—and I give him a nod as I head down our hallway. I consider going straight to Winnie's room, but think better of it, and instead, I jog to my room and take the quickest shower of my life. I dry off, throw on some deodorant, cologne, a pair of athletic shorts, and an Agitators shirt. I already brushed my teeth, because I hate working out with morning breath.

I head for Winnie's room and knock on her door.

"Come in," she says in a husky voice.

When I pop the door open, I spot Winnie still in bed, the comforter pulled up over her shoulder. The braids in her hair have come partly undone.

She looks adorable.

"Good morning, Pacey," she says in a sleepy voice.

I shut the door behind me and walk toward the bed. "Good morning."

Her eyes scan me. "I can smell you from here."

I chuckle. "I hope that's a good smell."

"A very good smell." She yawns and then says, "Let me guess—you've already worked out this morning, taken a shower, and had breakfast."

"Waited on breakfast, but the rest is correct."

She looks so damn comfortable; I need to lose myself in that comfort. I round her bed, draw back the covers, and slip into bed with her. I scoot in behind her and spoon her against my chest, letting my arm fall over her stomach as I hold her close. From what I can feel, she's wearing shorts and a tank top, and from the way her breasts skim the top of my forearm, I'm guessing no bra.

"Mmm, you smell really good."

I kiss her bare shoulder. "If you want, I can lie flat on my back and you can sniff me up and down."

She chuckles and snuggles in closer. "Let me guess—you're naked in this scenario."

"You can have me any way you want me."

"Just like this," she murmurs. "I want you just like this."

I allow my thumb to barely skim the underside of her breast as I ask, "Dream about me last night?"

"Yes," she breathes out heavily. "Mmm, that feels good."

"Yeah?" I continue to move my thumb just below her nipple.

She wiggles against me. "You're turning me on, Pacey."

My thumb pauses as my dick twitches in my shorts.

She rolls to her back and smiles up at me. My hand rests flat on her stomach, but I'm tempted to slip it under her shirt, to feel her bare breasts, to lift her shirt up and over her head, and to suck her nipples into my mouth until she comes.

"Not going to apologize for that. You've done your fair share of making me hard."

She chuckles and sighs. Her head rolls to the side so it's pressed against my arm that's propping me up. "I'm not ready to be a human just yet. I think you exhausted me yesterday, and then I kept thinking about . . . that kiss."

"Tell me about it. I woke up at four this morning and worked out because I couldn't stop thinking about it."

"It was good, wasn't it? Felt special."

I smile down at her. "Really fucking special."

Giggling, she presses her hands over her face and scissors her legs under the covers while quietly screaming. *God, she's cute.*

I laugh at her response and say, "I'll take that as good excitement."

"I am so embarrassing." She stills in bed and peeks through her hands. "You realize that, right? I'm just a goof, a dork. I get giddy over the idea of a first kiss."

My smile feels as if it stretches a mile long. "It's endearing. And I would be lying if I said I didn't get a little 'giddy' over that first kiss, as well."

She curls to her side, stuffing her hands under her pillow as she faces me. "Yeah? I've only had three first kisses in my entire life, and that one was easily the most memorable."

"Same." I move my hand over her face and gently stroke her cheek.

Her eyes soften and she says, "I was thinking about going on a hike this morning, maybe a picnic out in the woods. Care to join me?"

"Not really."

Her face falls. "Oh, yeah, of course. You're probably going to hang out with the boys."

I chuckle and lift off from the bed. I go to her window to pull open the curtains and reveal a steady downpour of rain. "Not really into hiking in the rain, and soggy picnic sandwiches doesn't sound appealing either."

She sits up in bed, and I allow my eyes to scan her beautiful body as she takes in the view outside. "Oh." She laughs. "Yeah, that doesn't seem ideal hiking weather."

I move back over to her and take a seat on the bed. "I would like to spend the day with you, just not outside."

"You would?" She gestures to her body. "You want to spend the day with this old bag of bones?"

"Yeah, I would."

"Okay." She sits up on her knees. "How about this—we play rock paper scissors to decide who gets to pick the activities. Every new activity means a new game, and whoever wins gets to pick."

I move my hand over my jaw. "I'm really good at rock paper scissors."

"How can you be good at a game of chance?"

I tap the side of my head. "Mind reader."

"Okay, we'll see about that. Do you have any rules for the day?"

"We're both naked."

She laughs a good, hearty laugh. "Not happening, but I will tell you a rule—nothing X-rated. Clothes shall stay on, hands will not fall under any garments, and kissing is allowed, but that's it."

"Way to take the fun out of everything."

She waggles her finger at me. "I want to have fun with you. Genuine fun, get to know you more. Just because I kissed you last night doesn't mean it's an open invitation to other things."

"That's fair." I'm actually surprised she let me hop into bed with her to cuddle, so I'm happy with whatever she'll allow today.

"Really?" she asks, surprised.

"Yeah, really. I like you, Winnie. Whatever you want, you get."

"Ooh, don't say things like that because I will take advantage."

"You would never," I say. "You barely take advantage of being here in this house."

"True." She stretches her arms over her head, and once again, my eyes land on her body, on the sliver of skin that shows from the lift of her shirt, on the way her tank top barely cups her breasts. "You're staring."

"I know," I answer just as I lift my eyes to hers. "You didn't say anything about not staring. That should be my right. Especially if I let you stare."

"That's fair." She hops out of bed and pads across the floor to the bathroom. "I'm going to get ready for the day. Think you can wait for me out in the living room?"

"I'd rather watch you get ready. I'm truly interested in the process."

She chuckles and points to her bedroom door. "Out, Pacey."

Capitulating, I stand from her bed and walk to the door just as my phone buzzes in my pocket. "Hurry up, there's a yogurt parfait in the fridge waiting for you, and then after that, the game is on."

"Can't wait."

I shut her door behind me and pull my phone out. My eyes nearly bug out of their sockets when I read who the text is from.

Josh.

He has some fucking nerve.

Josh: *Hey Pacey, it's Josh. I know Dad spoke with you. He told me you're in Banff. Wondering if you can carve some time out to talk to me on the phone. I have some things to tell you.*

I blink a few times, reading the text over.

Some things to tell me?

What could he possibly want to share with me, especially since he wanted nothing to do with me? All of a sudden, he wants to talk to me?

Fuck that.

I exit out of the text thread and stuff my phone back in my pocket. I have better things to worry about other than patching things up with a guy who dissed me thirteen years ago.

⸻

WATCHING Winnie eat her yogurt parfait was torture. I swear she was licking the spoon seductively on purpose. She claimed it was so good that she wanted every last morsel, but I don't believe her for a second. She was taunting me with her tongue. And it worked.

All I could think about was my dick in place of the spoon and her tongue running up and down it.

Yup. Torture.

"That was amazing. Thank you, Stephan," Winnie says as she puts her parfait dish in the sink. She returns to her barstool next to mine. She places her hands on my knees and gives them a little shake. "Are you ready?"

I clear my throat and shift on my stool, not wanting her to see just how affected I was. "Ready." I hold my hand out and so does she. "Best out of one?"

She nods. "Yup."

"All right."

Together, we pump our hands and say rock paper scissors. I throw down a rock and she shows up with scissors. Our eyes connect and I feel a smile pass over my face.

"Don't get cocky. It was one win."

"Just getting started. You looked like a scissors girl for your first throwdown."

"Stop it." She playfully pushes at my chest. "You did not know I was going to do scissors."

"Whatever helps you sleep at night." I rub my hands together and ask, "How good are you at golf?"

"Uh, never played it. But I've played mini golf. Does that count?"

"Not really. This will be more fun." I hop off the stool and take her hand in mine. "Let's go."

The boys are scattered throughout the house. Last I heard, Taters was in his room. Hornsby and Posey are playing chess upstairs and Holmes is reading in the library. No surprise there. Which means, the golf simulator is open.

I take her to the basement and she stops when we reach the bottom of the stairs.

"We're not working out, are we? I know I said we could do anything, but please, my legs are still recovering."

I chuckle. "Nah, I already got my workout in this morning, remember?"

"Oh, right. You were super productive this morning, unlike me, who slept in."

"Trust me, if I could sleep in, I would." I lead her down the hallway and into a room off to the side, then flip on the light, revealing the golf simulator. A large black screen is at the end of the room, a fake tee and greens are set up in front of it, and all different-sized golf clubs are on the right, along with a bucket of balls.

"Oh, this looks entertaining." She heads over to the golf clubs and picks one up. "Are we going to drive balls into the wall?"

I take the club from her and say, "For one, that's a putter, and secondly, we aren't just driving them into the wall." I flip the switch and the simulator comes to life. "We're going to play a round of golf."

She takes in the screen and her face lights up. "Wow . . . you boys really do know how to have a good time, don't you?"

"This was Hornsby's idea, and it was a very well-received idea. He spends the most time down here, but we all like to challenge each other. I'm not terribly good, but I can do a pretty good job. I thought we could take turns hitting. So, I would drive, you'd set up on the green, and then I putt. Then you drive, and so on and so forth."

"We'd work together."

I nod.

She smiles at me. "I like that idea, because I think we know that you'd destroy me if we played against each other."

"Uh, yeah, I figured that out the minute you picked up the putter and started talking about driving."

I go over to the screen and set it up for one player and a course of all par three holes. I figure that would be easier for Winnie.

When it's all set up, I turn to her and catch her staring at me with a smirk. She's in a pair of black leggings and a hot-pink top. Her hair is still drying from her shower but she put it half up, half down. She looks adorable.

"What's that smirk for?" I ask her.

"Are you going to be that guy who leans in behind me and teaches me how to hit the ball?"

"I thought about it."

"I knew it." She shakes her head and walks up to me, placing her hand on my chest. "Is your plan to get super handsy today?"

"Isn't that always the plan?" I ask, resting my hand on her hip.

"As long as I'm able to reciprocate, then I'm good with it."

"Babe, feel free to touch anything you want, at any time."

She tilts her head to the side. "You called me babe."

"Yeah, got a problem with that?"

She shakes her head. "Just never been called babe before, that's all. I like it."

Not that I want to bring the fucker up, but I ask, "Josh never called you babe?"

"No. He thought it was asinine—his words not mine. Why call me a nickname when I have a real name?"

"What a tool," I mutter as I go to the clubs and pick out a driver. "Do you want to drive first?"

"No, I want to watch you first and then you can teach me."

"Works for me." I step up to the tee, place a ball on it, and then I set up in front of it. I explain while I get into position. "Feet should be shoulder distance apart. And your arms aren't really driving through the ball, but rather your hips and shoulders are doing the work. It'll feel awkward at first, but you'll get the hang of it."

I set up, and then I bring the club back and swing forward. The ball shoots off the tee and smacks into the screen, rolling off across the floor while the simulator takes over, showing my ball onscreen as it soars down the fairway.

"Okay, that's really cool." She comes up next to me. "So, the simulator just knows how hard you've hit it?"

"Yup, and then it places you on the hole based on how you've hit the ball. It gets pretty addictive."

"I can see that." She walks up to the clubs. "Okay, what should I pick up?"

I select a club for her and say, "This would work. We're pretty close to the hole because of my superior drive, so you're going to have to chip it to the green."

"Is that like a half swing or something?"

"Pretty much," I answer. "Now get into position."

She stands in front of the starting position, I place the ball in front of her, and then I move behind her.

I smooth my hands down her arms to where her hands grip the club.

"Mmm, I knew you were going to straddle me like this. You can move your pelvis closer to my butt, though. Don't be shy." She wiggles her butt and I chuckle.

"Trying to be respectful."

"Forget respect. Make me feel good with your golf skills."

"If that's the case . . ." I move in closer and press my dick right up against her ass.

"Yup, just like that." She wiggles against my cock.

"Hey," I say in a stern voice. I'm actually surprised. She's way more comfortable, flirty, than I thought she'd be. *I'm glad, though.* "Unless you want this to turn into naked golf, watch what you do with that sexy ass of yours." I smack her ass and she lets out a little yelp, which makes me smile. "Now, focus. This is how you want to grip the club." I show her and she mimics my position. "Now you're going to want to bring the club back to about this height and then drive forward."

I give her a few practice swings with me and then pull away.

"So, just hit it?"

"Yup, just hit it."

"Okay." She takes a deep breath, shifts her feet, and then she pulls the club back and swings. "Where did it go?" she asks. "The screen isn't moving."

Holding back my chuckle is next to impossible. "You—you missed the ball."

"What?" She looks down and sees the ball at her feet. "Oh." She lets out a hearty laugh. "Well, that's not productive."

"We'll call it a practice swing. Try again. This time, keep your eye on the ball as you swing."

"Right, okay." She takes another deep breath, brings the club back, and then swings forward, this time connecting with the ball and sending it onto the green, just a few feet from the hole.

"Winnie, holy shit."

"Was that good?" she asks, looking for confirmation.

"Really fucking good."

She tosses the club in the air and then runs and jumps up on me, cinching her legs around my waist. I catch her with ease and then stare at her as she cups the back of my head.

She stares down at me and says, "I don't precisely know what I'm doing, but the celebration seemed necessary."

I laugh. "You could kiss me. That's what usually happens when a human jumps into another human's arms."

"A celebratory kiss." She leans down and presses the lightest of kisses across my mouth. It's so brief that I barely have time to open my eyes before she's back on the ground and picking up the club she tossed.

"Hey, that wasn't a very long kiss."

She claps her hands together. "We have a game to play, Pacey. We're not here to make out on the green. We're here to win."

I sigh and walk over to the clubs to select a putter. "Why do I feel as if I just created a monster?"

"You have. Now get it together, Lawes, and focus on this putt. I set you up, now you take us home."

Chuckling, I get ready for seventeen more holes with an intense Winnie at the helm.

"YOU DO REMEMBER THE RULES, RIGHT?" Winnie asks as I lie across the blankets in the loft, our lunch between us.

After a grueling eighteen holes with Winnie chastising and cheering, we played another game of rock paper scissors, and I ended up winning again with paper. I chose lunch in the loft, picnic-style. There are plenty of other places where we could eat lunch, but I wanted something intimate, something where we could be alone.

The loft is a transformed attic space. Holmes will come up here on occasion to read, but thankfully, he's stuck to the library today. But it's a small, pitched-ceilinged space no bigger than sixteen by sixteen. The room is filled with blankets and pillows to lie on, as well as a few adult-sized beanbag chairs. The room is lit only by bulb string lights, and there are two windows that can be propped open too. Taters never comes up here anymore because Sarah actually designed the room. It's hella romantic and exactly where I wanted to have lunch with Winnie after a competitive morning with the golf simulator.

"What rules?" I ask.

"The no-sex and naked rules." She lifts a brow at me.

"What makes you think I'm going to break the rules?" I prop the windows open, letting the sound and fresh smell of rain filter in.

She gestures to the room. "This is what girly dreams are made of. The lights, the pillows and blankets, the hot guy, the finger foods we can easily feed each other. I can see this getting incredibly romantic incredibly quickly."

"It's already romantic, Winnie. Deal with it." I take out the glasses I had Stephan pack for us and I pop open one of the blueberry lavender ciders I know she loves so much.

Sitting across from me, her legs are crossed and she's watching my every move as I prepare our picnic with drinks, a wooden charcuterie platter, and the chocolates I got from the candy store yesterday. Once everything is ready, I glance at her and I see the question in her eyes.

"What?" I ask her.

"Just thinking."

"What are you thinking about?"

She motions to the set up. "Have you, you know, done this before?"

"A picnic?"

She shakes her head. "No, have you set up such a romantic meal before, for someone special?"

"No." My eyes meet hers. "You're the first."

"But you're so good at it."

I shrug. "Just trying to make it nice for you. No experience necessary."

"Well, thank you. This is more than you needed to do."

I hand her a glass of cider. "Do you remember the second half of this lunch?"

She sips her drink and briefly closes her eyes, pleased with the flavor. "I do. You get to ask me anything, and I can ask you anything in return."

"Exactly. Since I won rock paper scissors, I get to ask first." I motion to the food. "Feel free to eat." I pick up a piece of cheese and a cracker and I pop them in my mouth. Winnie does the same and waits patiently while I think of a good question for her. "Tell me one thing you wish Josh did for you but never did."

She has her glass midway to her lips when she pauses. "Coming in hot with the hard-hitting questions. I wasn't expecting that. In fact, I wasn't expecting you to want to know anything about Josh, to be honest."

I'm not completely sure why I'm asking, either. "I don't really want to know anything about Josh, but I'm curious, I guess, about where you felt let down. Maybe I don't want to be another one of those people. That said, you didn't think I was going to toss you some softballs, did you?"

"That's very sweet, Pacey. And . . . I appreciate that. *You.* But, yeah, I thought maybe it was going to be something like 'what's your favorite dinner?' My answer would've been chicken parmesan with garlic bread."

"Noted, now answer my question."

"Hmm." She picks up another piece of cheese and takes a small bite from it. "I don't want you thinking Josh was entirely bad. He was really good at the beginning of our relationship, but then he just . . . stopped caring. Stopped trying, and that's when we grew distant. During the time we were growing apart, he always relied on me to cook him dinner, which was fine. We were living together at the time—"

"You lived together?" I ask, slightly shocked. I wouldn't have guessed that.

"Yeah, for a year until I moved back in with my mom to take care of her. He wasn't happy about that choice. He'd stay with me on occasion, but those visits became shorter and shorter. But when we lived together, I kind of wished that every once in a while, he'd surprise me by making dinner. It was challenging working all day at the bookstore and then being expected to make something for him for dinner."

I try not to show my anger too much, but seriously, what a fucking tool. I don't know that much about Josh, but from what my dad has told me, he's very self-righteous. He believes everyone owes him something. My dad thinks it stems from growing up without a dad. The bitter attitude. The anger he carries heavily on his chest. And the worst part is Josh blames my dad, when my dad had no idea he even had another son. If Josh needs to be mad at anyone, it's his mom.

"Did you ever make dinner together?"

She shakes her head. "No, I always thought it would be fun to take one of those dinner classes together, but he said it was stupid, and why take a class when I already knew how to cook? I tried to explain to him that it was about doing something fun with the person you love. He didn't get it; he had already pulled away by then." She looks off to the side. "At the end of our relationship, we barely kissed. I asked him if he ever cheated on me and he said no. He might have distanced himself, but he never cheated."

"What a hero," I mutter.

"What's that?"

I shake my head. "Nothing. Your turn to ask a question."

"Have you ever had a girlfriend?"

"No, not really. I mean, nothing serious. I've dated a few girls here and there, but I wouldn't say I ever had someone I would call a girlfriend. And it's not because I have a fear of commitment, just haven't found anyone I really want to call mine, you know?"

"So, you're not opposed to commitment?" she asks.

"That's two questions." I smirk.

"Hey, I answered more about Josh."

I nudge her knee. "Just teasing. And I would actually prefer to be in a relationship at this point. I know twenty-seven isn't old, but it's old enough for me to realize that picking up random girls at bars and having one-night stands really isn't for me anymore. I want the companionship, the feeling of not being alone. I want to be able to call my girl after a shit game and just listen to her tell me about her day to make me feel better. I want to come home from an away game to a smile and open arms, not a cold, sterile apartment. Just haven't been able to put the time into finding that special someone." I glance at her.

"I can understand that. After this last year, I can completely commiserate with being alone. It's not fun. Yes, I have Max and Katherine—"

"But it's different," I say.

She nods. "Very different. They're friends. Yes, they listen and they keep me company, but there's something different when you're with someone. The human touch is something special, something I crave. Having someone hold my hand, or just look at me differently than as a friend, it matters."

"I'm starting to see the importance of that."

She smirks and her cheeks blush. "You talking about me?"

"Yeah, I am." I pop a piece of cheese in my mouth, followed by a few pistachios.

"I appreciate the honesty." She picks up some pistachios, as well, and says, "Your turn to ask a question."

"Dream life—if you could paint it, where would you be, in this exact moment?"

Instead of answering right away, she gives it some thought, and when she's ready to talk, her eyes land on her lap and she speaks softly. "I'd probably be taking some homemade lemonade out to my cute backyard that I share with my husband. We'd live in a bungalow, because I think they're absolutely adorable. The backyard would be full of greenery that I've spent hours pruning and weeding. We'd have a firepit in the backyard with cedar Adirondack chairs. Sitting in one of them would be my mom. Sitting in another would be my husband. They would be talking, laughing, and reminding me how lucky I am to have them in my life." Her eyes meet mine. "I know it's simple, but it's the one thing I wish I could still have, the opportunity for my husband and my mom to talk. I know that will never happen and it makes me sad. My mom will never know who I end up with, she'll never meet my children. It's just . . . sad."

"I think that's the perfect dream," I say as I reach out and take her hand in mine.

"And I know she's looking down on me, watching over me, but it's not the same."

"I get it."

The smallest of smiles pulls at her lips. "I do think she had something to do with me getting lost, though, the first night. Or at least brought me here."

"Yeah?" I ask, forgetting about the food now, completely transfixed by Winnie. "How so?"

"She was never a super fan of Josh. I mean, she was in the beginning, when he was attentive, but toward the end, she saw the mental toll the relationship took on me—you've experienced it as well—and she told me I deserved better. One of her biggest fears was that I was going to be alone, since my dad passed when I was young and I don't have any siblings." Winnie shrugs. "I don't know, it's just convenient, is all, that I end up in a house with a bunch of guys that she'd drool over. It's her ideal meet-cute. She was really into that."

"Do you think out of the five guys in the house, she'd have picked me for you?"

Winnie smirks. "I want to say yes, but I've a feeling she'd have gravitated to someone else."

I sit taller. "Who?"

"You can't hold it against him."

"I'll do as I please. Now, tell me, who would your mom think is better than me?"

"Not better, per se, but I think she'd have just pictured me with someone more like my dad."

"Uh-huh, and who would that be? If you say Taters, I'm throwing this cheese platter into the wall."

She laughs out loud and shakes her head. "Silas would be my mom's last choice. She'd give me the troubled, quiet Halsey before she picked Silas." She rubs her thumb over my knuckles. "I really think she'd have liked Levi."

"Lev—" I calm myself and give it some thought. "Because he's just a happy-go-lucky guy, right?"

Winnie nods. "Yeah. He just has that air about him, you know?"

"I get it." I look toward the ceiling at the strings of bulbs. I'm not entirely convinced that Winnie's not spinning one of her tales here. After all, I was convinced she knew a lot about Mars just the other day . . . But I still need to know. "I would've been her second option, right?"

"Easily," she answers with humor.

"Then I'll take it."

———

"WHO ON EARTH came up with this game?" Winnie asks as Hornsby finishes filling the last of the water balloons.

"Posey. He used to play it when he was a kid, but instead of water balloons, they used eggs. He didn't think wasting eggs would be appropriate, so we use water balloons."

After we finished our lunch, Winnie and I lay on our stomachs, on top of beanbag chairs, and stared out at the falling rain until the clouds dried up and parted, allowing the sun to lift the moisture from the grass.

It was calm, serene, nothing compared to what we're about to do.

Winnie won the next round of rock paper scissors and, oddly, since she stated she had no clue what to do, she said she wanted Posey to decide. Which is why we're outside, standing in a circle with Taters, Posey, Hornsby, and even Holmes, who Winnie pleaded with to play, hovering over a flat rock with a water bottle on top.

"You promise this isn't a kissing game?" Winnie asks, looking concerned.

"Do you really think five guys would want to play a kissing game with each other?"

She chuckles. "I guess not."

Stepping in, Posey says, "Okay, Winnie. The name of the game is spin and peg."

"That sounds violent." Winnie moves in close to me.

"It's not. It's fun." Posey picks up the water bottle from the flat rock. "We each are going to take a turn spinning the bottle. When it stops spinning and lands on someone, that person is the chosen pegger."

"These are technical terms," I whisper into Winnie's ear. "Try to keep up."

She chuckles quietly as Posey continues, "The peggies—"

"See, technical."

"Dude," Posey says with annoyance. "You're ruining this experience for me."

"Sorry." I hold up my hand in apology.

"Anyway, the peggies must run in the opposite direction once they're not chosen. It's the pegger's job to run to the water balloon bucket, grab a balloon, and then peg one of the peggies. You get pegged twice and you're out."

"I fear I'm at an extreme disadvantage here," Winnie says.

"Nah, I got you," I whisper in her ear.

Posey claps his hands together. "Everyone ready?"

"Yup," we say as we gather around the flat rock. I put Winnie on the side furthest away from the balloons so she can leave the vicinity the quickest.

Posey leans down and spins the bottle. I get into position. It slows to a stop and lands on Hornsby.

"Run," I shout as I scoop Winnie up and over my shoulder and run with her as fast as I can, her laughing and screaming the whole time.

"He's coming for us," she shouts. "Duck."

As carefully as I can, I hit the ground, making sure to protect her along the way. The balloon breaks just to the right of me.

"What the actual fuck," Hornsby protests. "They can't double-team like that."

Water from the ground seeps into our clothes as I help Winnie up to her feet. "There's nothing in the rules that states it's illegal to carry a partner," I defend.

"It doesn't state that in the rules, but we all know this is an individual game," Posey says while jogging back. "Which means, peggies are supposed to use their own two feet."

In defense, Winnie says, "I had no idea he was going to do that."

"Throwing me under the bus? I see how it is."

We all make it back to the flat rock, and this time, Hornsby spins the bottle. It slows and then lands on me.

Winnie screams, I leap over the rock, grab a water balloon, and peg her right in the back, the water exploding all over her.

"Oh my God," Winnie says while spinning around to look at me, humor in her eyes. "You just hit me."

"Uh-oh," Hornsby says. "Looks as though there's going to be a fight on Lover's Lane."

"You threw me under the bus when I was helping you," I say while she pokes my sides, making me laugh. "I have to show you who's boss."

"Is that so?" she asks.

"Don't worry," Taters says to Winnie while draping his arm over her shoulder. "We got your six. Lawes is going down."

Winnie looks positively thrilled that Taters is interacting with her. "Are you telling me Pacey Lawes is enemy target number one?"

"Yup," Hornsby says. "He doesn't mess with our girl and get away with it."

"Our girl?" I ask, brows raised.

"Yeah, our girl," Hornsby says while leading Winnie back to the rock.

Ah, hell.

———

"I WANT to hear all of the embarrassing stories about Pacey," Winnie says over the roar of the fire.

After the boys ganged up on me and had me down after three rounds, I sat out and watched them all peg each other, leaving Winnie the winner in the end. It was rather comical, watching her scream and run in a zigzag motion—her classic move—as the other guys booked it for the woods.

Stephan called us in to dinner and we all quickly changed out of our wet clothes and enjoyed some homemade pizza. It was fucking delicious. I found out Winnie really likes meat, which confuses me, because I keep thinking she's a vegan because of her egg allergy. But no, she very much enjoys the meat. Once dinner was done, Taters brought out s'mores ingredients and we all headed to the firepit and roasted some homemade marshmallows. Our stomachs are absolutely full now, Winnie is curled against me, wearing one of my Agitators sweatshirts, which looks fucking amazing on her, and we're all enjoying some fireside conversation while the stars overhead are sporadically blocked by rolling clouds.

"We don't have to talk about me," I suggest, squeezing Winnie tightly.

"No, I like that idea," Posey says as he takes down one last marshmallow. I'll never know how that man has a six-pack with the amount of crap he consumes. He has to be one of those lucky fucks with the good genes.

"Where do we even begin?" Taters asks, while tapping his chin.

From behind his book, Holmes says, "The skates interview."

What the hell, Holmes?

"Nah, we're good with that story," I say, waving him off. "We don't need to recount what happened."

"Ooh, sounds good if Pacey doesn't want it told," Winnie says.

Taters and Hornsby are laughing behind their hands.

"Oh, it's good," Posey says. "Really freaking good."

"Let's hear it."

"You know"—I yawn—"I'm getting tired and, wow, Winnie, you really need some sleep. It's best that we leave right now."

Ignoring this, Posey leans toward Winnie and says, "Last year, before the first home game of the season, they were awarding Lawes with the Vezina Trophy."

"What's that?" Winnie asks.

"An award for best goaltender of the season," Hornsby answers. "Your boy has received it five times."

Winnie turns to me in surprise. "Wow, seriously?"

I lean in and whisper, "Don't look so surprised. I'm really fucking good at what I do." At least I was before I got hit in the head.

"Anyway," Posey continues, "it's this big ceremony in front of tons of fans, and there was this guy on the team, Igor Novikov. He hated Lawes, because according to Novi, Lawes stole his girl one night."

"Oh, is that right?" Winnie asks.

"No, he thought I did, but I didn't. Dude was delusional, and he also was psychotic."

"Facts," Taters says. "He knew Pacey was getting his award out on the ice, so he put clear tape on the bottom of Pacey's skates."

"What does that do?" Winnie asks.

Hornsby chuckles. "Makes it impossible to skate on the ice.

They called out his name to receive his award and Pacey comes flying off the bench and totally eats it in front of tens of thousands of people."

Winnie covers her mouth and laughs.

"And because he's a prideful man, he kept attempting to get up. After his third fall, he caught on and instead of skating, he tiptoed his way to the award ceremony, where he tripped one more time and landed face-first into the commissioner's wife's boobs."

"Stop it." Winnie laughs out loud. "He did not."

Being the silent but deadly one—apparently—Holmes hands his phone over to Winnie, cued up and ready to show the award ceremony.

"Dude, what the hell?"

Holmes doesn't say anything, just goes back to his book as Winnie presses play. Together, we watch as I crash and fall to the ice. Her hand goes to her mouth again as she silently chuckles. I tippy-toe across the ice, and then at the last minute, plummet straight into a set of breasts.

"Oh . . . my . . . God, that's just—that has to be the best thing I've ever seen."

"Seeing it in real life was particularly special," Taters says. "I like to show it on the TV screens in the locker room every once in a while, you know, when we need a pick-me-up."

Winnie watches it again, and because she's having such a good time, I allow it, despite the laugh being had at my expense. "Is this Novi guy still on the team?" she asks.

"Nah, traded last season. He's playing in New York now."

"I might have to start following him on social media, if he has an account."

"He does," Taters says with a laugh. "And it's a serious thirst trap. Dude only posts pictures of himself with his shirt off."

"Ooh, my kind of account to follow, then."

I squeeze her side and she laughs while handing Holmes

back his phone. This time she really does yawn and then curls farther into me.

"Tired?" I ask her.

She nods.

So, I take that moment—before the boys can tell more stories, because there are more—to stand from my chair. "I'm exhausted," I announce, and pull Winnie up with me. "Out of fear of what you might say to Winnie, I'm taking her with me."

"Sure," Taters says, "That's why you're taking her with you."

Ignoring him, I say good night and so does Winnie, and with my arm draped over her shoulder, we head into the house and down the hallway to our rooms.

"I had an awesome day today," Winnie says. "You're a great time, Pacey."

"I'm surprised it's taken you this long to recognize that."

"So full of yourself."

"All hockey players are," I say as we reach her door. She turns toward me and leans against her door.

"Are you going to kiss me good night, Pacey? Or am I going to have to make the first move again?"

"Can't a man play hard to get?"

"Is that what you were doing?" she asks, tugging on my shirt and pulling me closer.

"I'm not going to give away my secrets."

She chuckles and smooths her hand up my chest, and I take that moment to prop my hand against her door, next to her head, and then reach up and grip her cheek. It hasn't been just a good day. It's been one of the best I've had in a long time. Part of me feels like shit for getting information about Josh, but I did genuinely want to know how to please her. *For her.* And watching her get along with my boys . . . Nothing beats that, really. They've accepted her, can see her worth. Her quirky mischievousness. *They like her, too.*

"You're awesome to hang with too, Winnie."

"Yeah?" She tugs me closer. "Prove it."

Smiling, I use my thumb to angle her chin up right before my mouth descends on hers. Sweet, full lips meet mine and I immediately get lost in the taste of her. We really did keep everything PG today. Besides the occasional handholding or snuggling, we didn't kiss and all hands stayed above clothes. It made the day that much better, because instead of letting the sexual attraction we have for each other take over, we got to know each other on another level.

It was the perfect day.

And now has the perfect ending as I push my body up against hers. She gasps when I slip my tongue inside her mouth and demand more. Her hands grip the fabric of my shirt and one of her legs curls around mine. She clings to me, wanting more, needing more, and it makes me feel so goddamn amazing. This beautiful, fun, witty girl wants me.

But she doesn't want me because I'm a famous athlete. She couldn't care less that I play hockey—I'm not even sure that part of my life registers much with her. No, she wants me on a deeper level. She wants me because of the man I am, the true man.

Our tongues twirl together, twist, and because I can't keep my hands off her, I slip one hand under her sweatshirt to her bare skin. She gasps as my thumb swipes across her stomach before I guide my hand to her back. My fingers play danger-ously with the waistband of her pants. I'm tempted to slip them in, to grab hold of this sumptuous ass, but I also know I don't want to ruin today with a quick grab, a quick feel.

This kiss is where it stops. I pull away despite her protests and press a small kiss to her nose. I push off the wall and take a step back. I watch as her eyes slowly open, her chest rising and falling at a rapid rate.

"You're mean," she says, making me laugh.

"I'm mean?" I point to my chest. "How am I mean?"

"Kissing me back and then pulling away. It's not fair."

"What's not fair is how damn good you look in my sweatshirt."

She smiles and clutches at the sweatshirt. "Do you want it back?"

I shake my head. "Nah, it looks better on you."

I take another step back so I don't feel tempted to peel that sweatshirt off her myself.

Sensing my retreat, Winnie says, "Thank you for today, Pacey. Thank you for making the day . . . well, unique. It was good to laugh again."

"Anytime, Winnie." I give her a quick wave. "Sweet dreams."

"You too."

And with that, she slips into her bedroom and shuts the door. Once I hear it click, I move down the hallway to my bedroom, where I shut my door and flop back on my bed. I drape my arm over my eyes and take a deep breath.

Holy fuck.

I like a girl.

This was the last thing I was expecting after that nightmare ending to the postseason, but life has a funny way of happening. Instead of focusing on my flaws, my fears, I've completely forgotten about them, and I've been distracted by a girl who has imprinted her laugh and those eyes on my brain.

I've never had this feeling before. As if I'm itching all over while my stomach tumbles over and over again. The only way for the itching and tumbling to stop is to see her.

It's all new to me. And if she loved today because she was able to laugh, to forget that her loss is still so recent, so heart-breaking, then I'm glad to be the man giving her that. *And want to give it to her again tomorrow.*

I wasn't kidding when I said I'd never found anyone I cared enough about to call my girlfriend, but with Winnie, I could easily see her claiming that title.

Who am I kidding? I want her claiming that title.

My phone buzzes and I quickly snag it from my pocket hoping it's Winnie, but when I see that it's my dad, my hope falls.

Dad: *Has Josh reached out?*

Even more annoyed now, I text back.

Pacey: *Yeah.*

Dad: *Did you talk to him?*

Pacey: *Not yet.*

Dad: *Promise that you will talk to him.*

What a shitty promise to have to make, because the last thing I want to do is talk to Josh. Not after the way he treated me, my dad . . . and now Winnie. He doesn't deserve my time, nor my attention.

Tempted to text Dad back and let him know my true feelings, I instead let his request go unanswered.

I don't have time for Josh.

Chapter Sixteen

WINNIE

I check myself in the mirror one more time, something I don't do often, but when I know Pacey Lawes is just down the hall, I'm making sure not a hair is out of place. I'm not sure what today will bring, but I at least want to be comfortable while doing it. I chose a pair of navy-blue leggings and paired it with a white crop top. I kept my hair in a messy bun and dabbed on a little mascara.

Subtle, but cute. Doesn't look as if I'm trying too hard, thank God.

I have to call the tow truck company this morning because it seems as though it didn't rain last night, but it's supposed to possibly rain tonight. I want to see if he'll come up today, even though it rained yesterday. I hate knowing Minnie is stuck in a ditch, out in the woods by herself.

Unsure of how to greet Pacey, especially in front of the guys, I prepare for a smile and a wave while I get my coffee. Seems like the proper thing to do.

I head out of my bedroom, thankful the ache in my muscles has settled and I'm able to walk without looking as if I need a cane.

The chatter of the boys is the first thing I hear, and then when the main living space comes into view, I catch them all standing around the kitchen island, chatting it up with Stephan, who's hard at work. Even Halsey has his head out of a book this morning. I rove my eyes over the handsome faces but quickly notice one face in particular is missing.

"Good morning," Eli says, "want some coffee?" He's wearing the hat I got him, which is endearing. I feel like a child who painted their mom a mug and she uses it despite it being the ugliest mug in the cabinet.

"Oh, I can get it," I say, waving him off. I'm tempted to ask where Pacey is, but I don't want to be that girl. Instead, I move to the coffeemaker, grab myself a mug, and pour some coffee. I add some milk and sugar and then turn around to find all the guys staring at me. "Uh, everything okay?" I ask.

"Everything is great," Silas says as he scratches his chest. "Just wondering where your friend is."

"Pacey?"

"Yeah, usually he's up by now. Didn't know if you tired him out." Silas wiggles his brows, making my cheeks flame with embarrassment. I want to shout "we only kissed, that's it. Just a kiss."

"Dude, don't ask her that shit," Eli says while pushing Silas in the chest. "That's none of your business."

"That's not very hostess-like," Levi says with a nod toward Silas's cup that I got him.

"I'm just curious. Pacey is always busting our balls at this hour," Silas says.

"Even mine," Stephan adds as he hovers over the stove, making what smells like some miracle French toast.

"He's in bed," Halsey says from the side.

"And you know this because . . ." Silas asks, humor in his voice. "Wait, did you spend the night with him?"

Finding no humor in the situation, Halsey says, "Stopped by his room this morning to see if he wanted to work out. He has a migraine again."

The boys' jovial faces turn serious and the mood in the room shifts as an eerie feeling soaks up all the energy.

Migraine?

Again?

What are they talking about?

A far distant memory from our day in Banff strikes me. Some fan asked if Pacey's head was okay. Is that what they're talking about?

"Did you take him anything?" Eli asks, going into dad mode.

Halsey nods. "Yeah, gave him four Ibuprofen and forced him to drink a protein shake, too."

"Did he throw up this time?" Levi asks.

"Yeah, he admitted he threw up a few times this morning."

Okay, fear starts to travel up the back of my neck as I listen in. Throwing up, too? Migraine? This is serious. I want to ask what's going on, if he's going to be okay, but I also know Pacey probably kept this information from me for a reason.

"Shit," Silas says. "Should we call Doc?"

"I asked if he wanted me to call," Halsey says. "He said no, that it would pass."

"When was the last time you checked on him?" Eli asks.

"Five this morning," Halsey answers.

Eli glances at the clock and says, "We should check on him again."

"I can," I say, stepping in. I might not know what's going on, but I also don't want to sit by the sidelines, feeling helpless.

"Okay," Eli says. "Should we send her with some food?"

Halsey shakes his head. "You know he doesn't do well with food. He'll let you know when he's hungry."

"Do you have any electrolyte tablets?" I ask. "I can try to get him to drink one."

"Good idea," Eli says while going to a drawer near the coffeemaker. He fills up a glass of water and then drops a tablet inside. The tablet fizzes in the water and he hands it to me. "Let us know if he needs anything else."

"Okay, yeah," I say, feeling as if I probably shouldn't have volunteered, since the guys are the ones that have been with Pacey through previous migraines and probably know exactly what he needs. But it's too late now, so with water in hand, I head toward Pacey's room, wishing I did more background research on him. I was so caught up by his interviews that I didn't bother looking at anything else. But if I put the comment from a fan together with this recurring migraine, I'm going to assume something happened to him while he was on the ice.

Was he skating without a helmet and fell, slamming his head on the ice?

Did he get in a fight, take a punch to the head?

Possible scenarios stampede through my head until I reach his door. I swallow my nerves and carefully knock on his door, not wanting to make too much noise. When he doesn't answer, I test the knob and when it's unlocked, I let myself in.

The blackout curtains and blinds are drawn, making the room fall to an almost complete darkness. His room smells like his cologne, fresh with a hint of leather, and the eerie silence sets my nerves on fire as I take in the still lump on his bed.

Quietly, I walk over to the bed and set the water on his nightstand. Unsure of what to do, I whisper, "Pacey, it's Winnie. How are you doing?"

"Winnie?" he asks in a groggy voice, and then at a snail's pace, he turns in his bed to face me. He doesn't have a shirt on and his hair is all mussed up from sleep and probably the pain he's going through. Eyes closed, he reaches out, and I take his hand in mine. He sighs, as if this was all the comfort he needed.

I press my other hand against his back and trace small circles against his skin. "How are you doing?"

"Not great," he mutters.

"I can see that." I speak softly because I know the kind of pain a migraine can cause someone. I helped my mom through quite a few. I wonder if Pacey would let me help him. "I brought a Nuun tablet—it has caffeine in it too. Do you think you can drink a little bit of it for me?"

"Maybe," he whispers and then attempts to sit up. I help him and arrange his pillow so he's propped up more.

"Just take it slow." I hold out the drink to him and his shaky hand reaches for it. "Let me help you." I assist him in bringing the glass to his mouth and he takes short sips, a few at a time. "How's your stomach?"

"That's . . . that's it," he says, letting me take the drink.

"Okay, that's fine for now." I stand from the bed and say, "Let me help you lie back down." I help him move his large body down the bed and then I bring the comforter up to his shoulder. I gently rub my hand over his head and say, "I'm going to get you a cold compress to help. I'll be right back."

He doesn't say anything, but instead curls into a ball and keeps his eyes shut.

I move out of the room, trying not to let the light in, and then shut his door quietly.

That was—wow, that was way worse than I expected. Strong, protective Pacey was so feeble, weak, barely able to speak a sentence. I don't like it. Frankly, it scares me.

I hurry down the hall to the main room, where the boys are now sitting at the dining room table eating breakfast.

"How is he?" Eli asks.

"Not great. He looks incredibly weak. Is that normal?"

The boys nod and Eli says, "Yeah, these migraines take every last ounce of energy from him."

That's exactly how he seemed, as if he were drained.

Twisting my hands together, I ask, "Do you have any ice packs? A dish towel?"

"Yup," Stephan says moving around the kitchen to get me what I need.

"It's only been, what, three to four hours, but this sounds like a bad one," Silas says, concern in his voice. "I think we should call the doc, at least let him know. Didn't he suggest Pacey get in contact with him if he had another one postseason?"

"I was thinking the same thing," Halsey says. "He could barely walk when I helped him back to bed earlier after the vomiting. That was eerily similar to when he was first injured."

"I'll make the call," Eli says, standing from the table with his phone and going outside, where I see him scrolling through his phone and then bringing it to his ear.

What on earth happened?

What kind of injury are we dealing with?

Concerned and curious, I ask, "Um . . . can I ask what happened?"

"He didn't tell you?" Silas asks. "Figures. The man tries to act as though nothing bad ever happens to him, this injury especially."

"Too proud," Halsey says before taking a bite of his breakfast. "He doesn't want to show weakness."

"Yeah, well, pride isn't helping him," Silas says, and then he glances at me. "At the beginning of the season, Pacey was struck in the head by a ninety-four-mile-per-hour slap shot."

My stomach plummets, that scenario never even having crossed my mind.

"Even though he was wearing a helmet, he was knocked out. Severe concussion, some short-term memory loss, and since then, he's suffered from recurring migraines."

What?

I nearly swallow my tongue as I think about the kind of head injury that could occur from taking such a hit to the head.

And to mask it, as if nothing happened? That's so dangerous, neglectful.

"He hasn't been the same on the ice since," Silas continues. "He flinches, second-guesses, and isn't as strong in front of the net."

"He's still the best in the league," Levi defends.

"He is," Silas agrees. "But he's lacking the intensity he used to carry, and it's from the head injury. He missed several games because of migraines. The boy would never miss a game, even if his arm was dangling off."

"Here you go," Stephan says, handing me an ice pack and a thin dish towel.

"Thank you," I say, my mouth feeling dry all of a sudden as worry builds in the pit of my stomach.

Eli comes into the dining room and pockets his phone. "Doc wants to see him." He sits back down in his chair. "I told him that was going to be a monumental feat, to try to get him to leave here and go back to Vancouver. But Doc let it slip that right before we left, Pacey saw him with radiating pain in his head. Doc said he told him to keep an eye on it."

Silas scratches his jaw. "There's no way he's going to leave here."

"I can talk to him," I say. My voice comes out scratchy, scared, because this all feels too familiar. Way too familiar.

The headaches.

The throwing up.

The pain.

That's how it was when my mom first became sick.

The boys all look at each other and then shrug.

"Wouldn't hurt," Eli says. "Not sure how much pull you might have—"

"My mom died of a brain tumor." The boys fall silent, sympathy evident in their eyes. "I'm not saying Pacey has a brain tumor, by any means, but it's something that he should get checked, you know? Especially if he's in this much pain."

"I agree," Silas says. "But I think we give him a second before we bombard him. He probably won't like that Winnie knows . . . no offense," he says to me. "And he loves being here for the off-season, so taking that away from him might be hard as well."

"We don't have to make any decisions now," Eli says. "Let's focus on getting him better, and then we can have a group talk, go over his options, see where his head is at."

"Good idea," Silas says and then he turns to me. "We can handle this, Winnie, if you don't want to—"

"I want to," I say quickly. "I want to help." I need to help. I need to make sure he's going to be okay.

"Just wanted to make sure you were, you know, emotionally okay. Not sure if this would bring up any difficult feelings for you."

It's the first time I've noticed Silas be sensitive toward my feelings. It's new and surprising, but I appreciate it.

"I'm fine. I just want to make sure he's okay. I've dealt with many migraines; I think I can help him."

"Let us know if you need anything," Eli says.

"I will."

"Do you want any breakfast?" Stephan asks.

I shake my head. "I'm going to make sure Pacey is okay and maybe I'll come eat something after, but don't worry about me. Thank you."

With that, I head toward Pacey's room, my stomach churning with nausea as I try to process everything the boys told me.

Injury.

Missed games.

Migraines.

Memory loss . . .

When out of sight, I lean against the wall of the hallway and bring my phone into view. I quickly type *Pacey Lawes puck to head* into my browser and then click on the first video I see.

I clutch the ice pack as the video starts to play. Announcers call out the play in the background, but I don't pay attention to their babbling nonsense; instead, I watch as the man with the puck—whatever you call him—brings his stick back and slaps the puck forward. In the blink of an eye, Pacey falls backward into the goal and his defenders gather the puck and push it up the ice. The referees blow their whistles and medical staff rush onto the ice to care for a seemingly lifeless Pacey.

Pacey . . . oh my God.

Bile rises to the top of my throat as I quickly exit out of the video, unable to watch the rest. I lift my eyes to his door and my entire body shakes, thinking about how he could be seriously hurt. How something really bad could've happened to him.

And in that moment, it hits me . . .

I care about him.

Honestly care about him.

I'm—God, I think I'm falling for him.

But how? I've only known him for a few days. How could I possibly care about someone that quickly? How could I fall for someone that quickly?

Love doesn't have a timeline.

It should. Because this isn't normal. Having these strong, all-consuming feelings about someone shouldn't happen this fast. Don't people scoff at that? *You met this man a few days ago and now you're not only invested in his well-being, but you have this overwhelming desire to be near him?*

It doesn't work like that.

It's not supposed to work like that.

Isn't that how it worked for my mom, though?

Didn't it only take a few days for Mom and Dad to build a never-ending love? A love so strong that my mom never even considered another man after Dad died?

It's possible.

But . . . no, not for me. I shake my head, clearing that thought away. I'm just invested. This encounter isn't like my mom and dad, despite the bond I feel with Pacey. What they had was different, right?

I bite down on the side of my cheek and take a deep breath.

Wow, the emotions and thoughts that are taking over are far too heavy. It's . . . startling, staggering, something I don't want to think about right now.

I should be thinking about how I can help Pacey. How I can help him feel better.

Get it together, Winnie.

I move into his room again, quietly shut his door behind me, and then walk up to his bed. I gently place my hand on his arm. "It's me," I say softly. "I have a cold compress for your head. Are you open to trying that?"

"Yes," he whispers.

"Can you roll onto your back for me? I know it's not the ideal position, but it'll help with the cold compress."

As he starts to shift, I set the compress down and help him. I move the blankets with him and then make sure he's situated before I do anything else.

"I'm going to put this under your neck, okay?"

"Yeah," he says as his arms fall outside of the comforter, his strong, broad chest prominently displayed.

I place the cold compress under his neck and ask, "How's that?"

"Good."

"Think you can take a few more sips of your drink for me?"

"Sure," he answers, using one-worded answers, and I know it's because if he says much more, he'll probably regret it.

I lift the glass to his lips and he swallows a few sips before I set it back down on the nightstand and ask, "That enough?"

"Mm-hmm," he answers, his eyes closed.

"Okay, well, if you don't need anything else, I'm going to let you get some rest." I squeeze his hand. "I'll check on you—"

"No," he says. "Stay." He takes a deep breath. "Lie with me."

"Oh, I don't want to make it worse."

"Please." He winces.

Don't argue with him, Winnie. Just do what he says.

"Sure, of course."

I move around to the other side of his bed and slowly he pushes the covers back so I can join him. I slip between the cool sheets and turn toward him as I lie on the pillow next to him.

"No," he says. "Lie on my chest."

"Are you sure?" I ask, questioning if I'm going to make this worse.

"Please, Winnie." When he asks like that, pain lacing his every breath, his every word, I can't deny him.

Slowly, so I don't rock the mattress too much and disturb him, I close the space between us and then carefully rest my head on his warm chest. His arm pulls me in close, and when I place my hand on the space between his pecs, he lets out a deep, sated sigh.

"Thank you," he says.

Those two little words pack such a heavy punch, and before I know it, my eyes fill with tears and a bout of emotions lift to the top of my throat, cinching it tight.

I'm scared.

For many reasons.

Scared because I know how serious head injuries are.

Scared because I don't want anything bad to happen to Pacey.

Scared because these feelings I'm carrying for a man I just met shouldn't be this strong.

But they are.

I care for him.

I want him to be okay.

And as I rest my head on his chest, his arm wrapped around me, I realize that this, right here, is the most I've cared about someone since my mom died. And this is the first time I've cared about a man this much, more than I ever cared for Josh.

And that's probably the most terrifying revelation of them all.

———

A LIGHT, steady caress moves across my back, pulling me from my deep slumber.

"Hey." Pacey's voice wakes me up even further.

Oh shit, I fell asleep when I should've been making sure he was okay.

I sit up quickly and wipe at my eyes. "Oh my gosh, I'm so sorry." I blink a few times and realize there's some light in the room as well. How long was I out? I bring my hand to his cheek and ask, "How are you feeling?"

The smallest of smiles crosses his lips. "I have a dull thud in my head, but feeling much better." His hand smooths over my arm. "Easily the quickest I've ever gotten over a migraine. I'm usually out for the entire day and night."

"Really? Was it the cold compress?"

That smirk grows wider. "Pretty sure it was the beautiful girl clinging to me."

My cheeks flame once again. I'm not sure that will ever stop when he compliments me. "We both know that's not the truth."

"Trust me, I think it is." He shifts so he's facing me a little more. His eyes are more alert, and even though he looks slightly wrecked, there's so much more life in his movements, and that makes me breathe a sigh of relief. Not the feeble man he was hours ago. His strength is coming back.

"I'm just glad you're feeling better." I sit up even more so I have a better view. I want to be able to take in every inch of him.

"Come here," he says, pulling on my hip. "Why are you trying to get away from me?"

"I'm not." I chuckle. "Just trying to give you space since I was just wrapped around you like a koala."

His hand lands on my thigh and his thumb caresses my leg.

"I liked it. I want you near me." His grateful eyes connect with mine. "Thank you for taking care of me. Seriously, it might seem stupid, but having you next to me really helped."

"I don't see how." I try to laugh it off, but he grows serious.

"It was the comfort. That human connection. It helps, especially for someone who's alone so often."

I place my hand on his chest and move my fingers over the short-clipped hair. "I know the feeling . . . of feeling alone."

Knock. Knock.

The door opens and Eli pokes his head through the crack. "You're awake," he says, moving into the room now with a tray of food for two and fresh waters. "How are you, man?"

He sets the tray on the nightstand, carefully moving the drink I brought earlier.

"Better," Pacey says, keeping his hand possessively on my thigh. He looks at the tray and smiles. "You added a bud vase and flower?"

Eli glances at the tray and then back at us. "Stephan did that bullshit. You know that's not my style."

"Yeah, your style is more of a dildo centerpiece." Pacey cracks a joke, offering a smile. He really is feeling better. That should put my chest at ease, but it still feels tight. Worried.

A laugh bubbles out of Eli. "Yeah, you're right about that." He scans Pacey and adds, "Just from that little joke, I can tell you're feeling better. Maybe get some food in your system. I put some medicine on the tray. I'm sure you need more."

"Thanks, man."

"Sure. When you're ready, Silas has the pool doors open and the breeze is really nice. Might be good to get some fresh air."

"That would be great. Thanks."

Eli gives us a smile, and then he leaves, shutting the door behind him.

"Well, I'll let you eat and—"

Pacey's hand clamps down on my leg. "It's cute that you

think you're leaving," Pacey says with humor in his voice. "Nah, you're sticking by my side today."

"I don't want to be too . . . clingy."

"I would appreciate it if you were clingier, actually." He reaches for the tray but I lean over him and grab it before he can.

"Take it easy, big guy. We just got you talking again. Don't need you pulling a shoulder muscle." I place the tray on his lap.

"I doubt lifting a tray would pull a shoulder muscle, but I do like you leaning over me like that."

I smile softly while I hand him a glass of water. "I see how it is. You start feeling better and now you're flirtatious again?"

"Got to let you know I'm always interested."

I meet his eyes. "Oh, I know, just from the way you clung to me this morning."

He takes a sip of his water. "I think the feeling is mutual, since you passed out on me and I was the one who needed to wake you up."

"Maybe stronger," I admit, the words slipping off my tongue before I can stop them.

"Is that so?"

I shake my head. "I don't know why I said that."

"Because you mean it." He tips my chin up. "No shame in showing how you're feeling."

It is when the feelings absolutely terrify me.

"Why don't we focus on replenishing you." I busy myself with handing him a sandwich. "I do have to make a quick call to the tow company. I think the roads are ready and I don't want Minnie thinking I forgot about her."

"You do? It rained yesterday."

"Yes, but it's supposed to be sunny all day today. Worth a shot."

"You're going to have her towed here, right?" he asks.

"Yeah, I am."

"Good." He takes a bite of his sandwich and I reach for my phone.

I slide off the bed and say, "Be right back."

"You can make the phone call in here, you know," he says before taking a bite of his sandwich.

"I know I can, but I don't need you distracting me. This is important business."

Before he can bounce back with a retort, I exit the room and head for mine. I shut the door behind me and take a deep breath.

My body is heated, my heart is racing, and confusion consumes my brain as I slide down against my door until my butt is on the floor. *What just happened?* It's not a panic attack, I know that much. But it does feel a lot like when Mom came home from her first Gamma Knife surgery. That moment when I had no idea what just happened and how it would affect my future.

But in this situation with Pacey . . .

Why is my body heated?

Because of Pacey's touches, which showed me I was wanted.

Why is my heart racing?

Because of Pacey's words, which offered encouragement and thankfulness.

And why am I consumed with confusion?

Because I really like this guy and I have no idea what that means for the future.

Chapter Seventeen

PACEY

The breeze picks up, blowing through the open doors of the pool room and pushing past the doublewide lounger I'm sharing with Winnie. My migraine has subsided for the most part, I have some lingering pain in my shoulders from the tension, and my neck is stiff, but that's nothing compared to the violent, blackout pain I felt earlier. This is manageable.

After Winnie's car was delivered—yes, she sweet-talked the towing guy into trying—and the boys paid for the service before Winnie could even get her credit card out, they all went for a hike together—even Halsey—since the trails are pretty dry and it's a gorgeous day out. That left me alone to lie around with Winnie.

We're lying flat on the lounger and I have my body curled against hers, my arm around her waist, holding her close. We've been talking on occasion, but also allowing nature to do the talking.

I hear Winnie tapping away on her phone, which buzzes

with incoming text messages. Most likely Max and Katherine checking on her. I'm glad Winnie has them.

When we headed out to the pool area, Winnie changed into shorts but kept her crop top on, something I've appreciated because I've been able to graze her bare skin every chance I get. Now I smooth my thumb over her stomach and enjoy the simple human touch, having her near me like this.

Noticing I'm awake, she tucks her phone away and asks, "How's your head?"

"Good."

She glances at her phone again, picks it up, and holds it so the screen is out of my eyesight. She types a text in return, then shifts in the chair, twisting so she's facing me. Her eyes are still sleepy, but fucking dreamy as shit with their dark, mysterious blue color. And those lips—they're plump, full, and calling to me. Every time I glance at them, I remember how bold they were in claiming that first kiss. Nothing has been sexier to me than that moment, when she was the one who made the first move.

"So, are we going to talk about it?" she asks.

"Talk about what?" I ask, slightly confused.

"Your migraine." Her hand falls to my bare chest, where she draws tiny circles along my skin.

"Nothing to really talk about."

She looks away, but continues her circles. "I saw the video, Pacey," she says quietly. And just from the tone of her voice, I know exactly what she's talking about. She must have spoken with the boys, which led her to look up the clip of me getting struck in the head. It's not a great clip. The sound of the puck hitting my helmet is deafening. Watching me fall flat on my back, even worse. I was actually lucky I managed to flick my legs forward rather than tearing ligaments and muscles in my knees and groin. *Thank fuck.* But I don't want to make a big deal about it. Not with Winnie.

"You worried about me?" I ask in a teasing tone, but the

look she gives me says it all.

She is.

"I know I have no room to say anything, but . . . that was a hard hit, Pacey."

"Yeah, I know." I sigh.

"Aren't you concerned, you know, about the migraines?"

"It's fine. They come and go," I say casually, even though I know in the back of my mind that Doc would be up my ass right now if he heard I'd had another one.

"My, uh, my mom had migraines." Her voice is so feeble that it strikes a chord inside me.

Fuck. I didn't even think about her mom or how Winnie might relate to this.

"They were really bad," Winnie continues. "I helped her through them, but there were some days when they would never go away, where they were constant. She lost weight because she was so nauseated all the time. And I know I don't have a leg to stand on when it comes to saying anything about your life, but I just want you to think about being careful, you know? Your head isn't something to mess with."

Her phone buzzes on the side table, but she doesn't reach for it this time.

I capture her hand and bring the backs of her knuckles to my lips for a soft kiss. "I appreciate your concern, Winnie."

And I leave it at that, because frankly, I'm not ready to have this conversation with anyone. Not the doctor, not the boys, not my own family. Because I know what the result of that conversation will probably be, and there's no way in hell I'm even close to being ready to hang up my skates.

She takes that moment to glance at her phone and then set it back down again. She closes her eyes and I notice her eyelashes start to brim with moisture, so I squeeze her hand and ask, "Are you okay?"

She nods, but a tear falls down her cheek. I wipe it away before she can.

"Sorry," she says. "Rough day, and this just brought up a lot of emotions for me, lots of memories, and I've been trying to process them, but obviously not doing a good job."

"Then talk to me about them. What are you feeling?"

She shakes her head. "No, I'm good. Really."

"It doesn't look as if you're good. You're crying, Winnie."

"It's fine, seriously." She takes a deep breath and plasters on a fake smile. "Since I got Minnie back, she's currently flirting with the Teslas—"

"Better be mine," I add to keep things lighthearted.

"Pretty sure it is. But I think I'm going to go see Uncle RJ tomorrow. I've been here for almost a week and it's time that I do the thing I came here to do."

"I thought part of being here was relaxing."

"It is, and I have . . ."

I lift her chin up. "Don't fucking tell me you plan on leaving again. I thought we talked about this."

"I'm not sure what I'm going to do, but I'd tell you. I promise—no sneaking off."

That alleviates some of the pressure, but I still don't like that she's considering leaving.

"Anyway, I think I just want to go see him and complete my mission. I don't like having it hanging over my head."

"Okay, so when do we leave?" I ask, inviting myself along for the trophy theft, because I know she'd never ask me to go. She seems to be opposed to help.

"We?" she asks. "Oh, you don't—"

"I want to go," I say, moving my hand to her cheek and rubbing my thumb against her soft face.

"I appreciate that, but I think this is something I need to do on my own."

Even though I don't like it, I can understand her need for privacy. "I respect that. But if you get cold feet or want someone to sit in the car and wait for you, or have the getaway vehicle ready, I'm your guy."

"Thank you." She sits up a little taller and glances at her phone. Who's she talking to that's so important? "Do you actually mind if I head to my room? I want to go over an action plan and make sure my outfit will fit a stolen trophy."

"Uh, sure, go ahead," I answer, feeling confused by her abrupt need to leave. Was it something I said? Is it because of the person she's been texting?

"Okay." She goes to stand but I tug on her hand and she looks over her shoulder at me.

"Everything good?"

She nods. "Yup. Everything is good." She offers me a smile that barely lifts her lips and then she heads into the house.

Hell . . . what was that about? She completely shut down on me. Was it because of the head injury? I know today was a lot for her emotionally. Maybe she just needs some breathing room.

In the distance, I hear the guys laughing, and I lift up from the lounger to see them walking into the backyard from one of the many trail accesses we have here. I'm jealous they got to go on a hike. Being out here, in nature, away from it all, is one of my favorite parts of the off-season, and we swore to each other if any of us are traded at any point in time, we'll still come here together.

As they draw closer, I raise my lounger into a sitting position and place my hands behind my head.

"Look at that hunk of meat," Taters says, walking into the pool area. "Where's your lady friend?"

"Went to her room to work on some things," I say casually, even though I still have worry in the pit of my stomach about it.

"Good," Hornsby says, as he takes a seat on the lounger next to me. "We need to talk to you."

I know exactly what this is going to be. It's the same conversation they had with me after the injury when I was trying to get back on the ice quicker than I should have. And it's the same conversation they had with me after the sixth game I missed because of a migraine.

"Before you even start, I'm fine, okay? It was a short migraine—"

"We called Doc," Hornsby says.

I sit up. "What the actual fuck?"

"We have a responsibility," Taters says. "And that's making sure that our All-Star goalie is okay."

"I *am* okay. It was one fucking migraine—"

Calmly, Posey steps in and asks, "If it was one migraine, then why are you freaking out about it?"

I go to answer, but Hornsby says, "Doc let it slip that you saw him before you left, that you've been having head pain. Dude, this is serious."

"I know," I shout. "Do you really think I would fuck around with this?"

"I think you have too much pride to admit when you need help," Taters shoots back. "I think you're worried that if you dive deep into this issue, you're going to find out something you don't want to know."

"And what the fuck do you think that is, since you seem to know everything about me?" I ask.

"That they're going to tell you your time on the ice is over," Posey says.

And, yup, he nailed it on the head. That's my biggest fear, being told I can't play anymore. Life without hockey? Fuck, I can't even think about it. I don't know what life is without hockey. Without feeling the ice beneath my skates. Without strapping on my pads to protect my body. Without tracking the puck with my laser focus, daring anyone to try to score on me. Without watching the game play out, sending signals and words to help protect my team. It's not physically possible to leave that. To hit "stop."

I haven't known anything else my entire life other than this sport that I live and breathe, and to have it stripped from me without a goodbye, without closure? No fucking way.

I look away, my jaw clenched tight.

"I know that's not what you want to hear," Posey says in his soft tone. He's always the guy in the group trying to moderate the arguments. "But don't you think it's important to find out? What if something serious happened and you're ignoring it? What if you really shouldn't be on the ice? It's not worth it, man."

"Would you be able to accept that?" I shoot back to the boys. "Would you be able to just . . . throw it all away, give it all up?"

Posey stands with his hands in his pockets, looking down at the ground.

Holmes is leaning against the pool room wall, not saying a damn word, even though I know he's the one who told the guys what's going on.

And Hornsby and Taters—they avoid eye contact as they stare at their hands.

"That's what I fucking thought," I say. "So unless you put yourself in my goddamn shoes, you can't have an opinion on what I do."

"We sure as hell can have an opinion," Taters says, his voice rising. "You're our brother, and I'm not going to sit back and watch you make a mistake because you're too scared of the consequences. And I would expect any one of you to treat me the same damn way." He pushes his finger into my chest, his eyes lit with anger. "There's something wrong with your head. You need to get it checked out. Fully checked out. And whatever the end result is, we'll be there for you, but I refuse to stand by and not say a goddamn thing."

"Same," Hornsby says. "This is serious, man. This isn't a choice; this is a requirement. It's not as if you have a bad knee and some rehab will get you through it. This is your head, man. Your brain. They need to make sure that everything is okay."

"He's right," Holmes says from the sidelines.

"It would make us all feel better if you went back home and checked on things," Posey adds.

"I'm not going back to Vancouver. This is my break, my time off. The last place I want to spend it is in Vancouver, where it's crawling with fans. It's bad enough I've had people ask me how I am while being here. Vancouver would be even worse."

"We're not saying stay there the whole time," Hornsby says in a convincing voice. "Just go talk to Doc, get things checked out one more time, see a neurologist if Doc says to, and then go from there. We'll extend our time here. It's not as though we have anyone to answer to." Hornsby looks at Taters and says, "Not to rub salt in the wound."

"Thanks, bro."

"Please, Doc wants to see you," Posey says.

"What about Winnie?" I ask in a whisper. "I'm not about to just leave her here with you four."

"Afraid she'll fall for one of us?" Taters asks in a teasing tone.

"No chance," I answer. "But it'll be awkward for her."

"No offense," Hornsby says, "but you just met the girl. This is your head we're talking about. That's more important. She lives in Seattle—that's two and a half hours from Vancouver. If you really like her, try some long-distance shit."

"I don't know." I grimace, my head starting to get fuzzy from this conversation. "I should go lie down."

"Just think on it," Hornsby says. "We'll help you any way we can. Chartering a plane would be the fastest and easiest, and Doc can pick you up from the airport. Who knows? Maybe it won't be anything."

Or it'll be everything that stops me from going on the ice.

"I'll give it some thought," I say, knowing damn well I'm not going anywhere. When I stand, my body sways to the side, and I grip the back of the lounger to regain my balance. Fuck. I squeeze my eyes shut, my head spinning. *Deep breaths.*

It's just because of this conversation, because it was a tiresome day with the migraine. That's all.

But, of course, the boys notice. How could they not? I probably look like an old person trying to gather themselves before they start walking.

They exchange worried glances, and I try not to growl in frustration.

"I'm fine," I say as I move toward the door.

Just as I reach for it, Holmes says, "You either go see Doc, or I tell Coach."

And there it is—the ultimatum. I'm just surprised it came from Holmes and not Taters.

I pause, my fingers gripping the handle of the sliding glass door. Slowly I turn around and look Holmes in the eyes. "Excuse me?"

"You heard me," he says, his voice completely unapologetic, not faltering. "You either go see Doc, or I tell Coach. I'm not fucking around. These three might not go to that level, but I will." Intensely, he looks me dead in the eye and says, "I already lost one brother, I'll be damned if I lose another." Then he pushes off the wall and heads in the opposite direction.

Fuck.

If Coach finds out, he is not only going to force me to come home, but he's going to get the front office involved, and that's the last thing I want to have happen. They don't need to know their star goalie is having issues. That opens the door for trades, for rookies to take my spot.

And Holmes knows that. He knows the card he just threw on the table.

I don't have a fucking choice.

I have to go see Doc.

⌑

JOSH: *Hey, have a second to talk on the phone?*

I stare down at the phone, my grip growing tighter and tighter. Dude has the worst fucking timing. I'm in no mood to deal with this bullshit.

Pacey: *Rather not talk. Unlike Dad, I know how to hold a grudge.*

I'm feeling ripe, ready to take my anger out on someone, anyone who steps in my way. The last thing I want to do is leave Banff, especially because of something correlating to my injury. I don't want to be reminded of what happened to me. I don't want to be reminded of the fear. I don't want to be reminded of the possibility that my career might very well be over.

Josh: *So that's where we're at?*

Pacey: *You put us there.*

Josh: *So is that why I've seen your picture on the Internet . . . with Winnie? Is that so you can get back at me?*

How the fuck . . .

Jesus Christ, I should have known people were taking pictures of me and Winnie when we were out on the town, exploring.

Pacey: *You really don't know me at all.*

Josh: *You're right, I don't. But you realize, you're with my Winnie, right?*

Pacey: *She's not yours anymore. You gave up the best thing that's ever happened to you. You were an asshole to her. You can't claim her.*

Josh: *So you're not doing this out of spite?*

Pacey: *I have better things to do with my life than figure out ways to spite my half-brother. You act as if I spend time thinking about you.*

My fingers are flying.

My mind is shooting off with angry fireworks.

I can't seem to control this mad, pulsing beat through my veins that's propelling me to stoop to Josh's level.

Level asshole.

Is that why he's reaching out? After all these years? Is that why Dad is forcing me to speak to him? Because of Winnie? Does Dad know about her too? *Fuck.*

Josh: *It's just convenient . . .*

Pacey: *You can take your ellipses and shove them up your ass. Our meeting is purely coincidental. She doesn't even know you're my half-brother and I plan on keeping it that way.*

Josh: *Want some advice about Winnie? Never keep a secret from her.*

Pacey: *Pretty sure I'm not going to take advice from the piece of shit who left her alone when her mom was sick.*

Josh: *Watch it. You have no idea what you're talking about.*

Pacey: *She's told me everything, you prick. I know exactly what I'm talking about.*

Josh: *I see.*

Pacey: *Good. Now fucking be gone.*

I set my phone down and take a deep breath.

Fuck.

AFTER EATING dinner alone out on the patio and booking a private plane to Vancouver for tomorrow, I take my dishes into the kitchen, where Stephan is cleaning up. Winnie has been in her room since she left me on the lounger, and I decided to give her space, because it seemed as though she needed it.

I needed it too. I needed time on my own to think, to weigh the consequences of my decisions. Being bombarded by my teammates about my head and my future wasn't what I was expecting to happen today. Nor was I expecting Josh to talk to me about Winnie. It's been a rough night, to say the least.

When I turn to face the living room, I notice Hornsby and Taters playing chess, while Holmes and Posey are both reading. Looks as if Holmes started Winnie's book that she got him. I would be excited to see that if I wasn't ready to take him out with a right hook. All of them—I have a consuming urge to take them all out. I get that they're being protective, but they have no idea what their *good intentions* are putting me in. They don't know . . . fuck, they don't know how scared I am. I'm too goddamn young to retire, I have plenty of time left in my skates.

When I start to move past them, they all look up.

Instead of ignoring them, I say, "Booked my plane. I suggest you leave me the fuck alone until I contact you."

"Can't be mad at us for caring," Taters says.

"I can be mad all I want."

"Not if you need me to drive you to the airport," Hornsby says, moving his rook up the board. He flashes me a smile. "See you in the morning, sweetheart."

Not bothering to comment back, I head to Winnie's room and knock on the door gently.

"Come in," she calls out.

I open the door and quickly shut it behind me, blocking out the guys. Anger sears through me, but the minute I see Winnie, that anger begins to dissipate.

I lean against the closed door and study Winnie, who's sitting cross-legged on her bed, notebook in one hand, pen in the other. She's wearing her pajamas—silk shorts and a tank top—and her blonde hair is braided into two French braids. She looks so goddamn adorable.

"Hey, how are you?" I ask her.

She smiles at me, and this time it reaches her lips. "Good. Spent some time reading over my mom's old diary. Felt good to reconnect with her. How are you feeling?"

"Much better," I answer honestly—another reason why I didn't want to see Doc, because I am feeling better. This migraine didn't last as long as the other ones, which could take up to twenty-four hours, sometimes longer, to fade. And that knowledge irritates me, because it's not something the boys took into consideration before throwing down their threats.

"Good." She sets her notebook and pen on her nightstand and pats her bed, inviting me over. She looks so happy, I feel as though I'm going to steal that joy from her with the news of my departure.

Knowing I have to say something to her, that I can't just leave and hope for the best, I take a seat on her bed. "I have to talk to you about something."

Her brow pulls together. "What's up?"

I pull on the back of my neck. "I have to fly to Vancouver tomorrow."

"Oh . . . why?"

"The boys were really concerned about my migraine. They told our team doctor, and he wants me to come in so he can check me out, run some tests. I didn't want to, but Holmes threatened to tell our coach, so . . . I booked a private jet to get me there tomorrow. I don't plan on being gone for long, but I do have to leave."

Winnie takes my hand in hers. "I think that's probably smart, Pacey. You don't want to mess around with a head injury. Trust me. My mom didn't go to the doctor for a long time and I always wondered what it would've been like if she did. Would they have been able to help her if she'd gone sooner."

"Yeah, the guys are adamant about it even though I'm less than thrilled. This migraine wasn't nearly as bad as some of the others."

"They're looking out for you. No need to be angry about it."

"I'm worried about what you're going to do," I say, speaking my truth.

"Well, I've been doing some thinking, and even though I've enjoyed my time here, I think it's going to be hard for me to stick around after I talk to Uncle RJ. Don't worry, I was going to tell you, not just leave, but I think I'm going to drive back to Seattle afterward."

"What?" I ask, panic setting in. "What happened to wanting to find yourself while you're here, feeling a connection with your mom, figuring out your future?"

"Although I think the idea has merit, I just . . ." She doesn't look me in the eyes. "I don't feel her here."

"So, you're going back to Seattle? You said you set out to go on an adventure. I wouldn't say a week is an adventure."

"Hey." She removes her hand from mine. "You don't get to put a timeline on adventure."

"I'm allowed to mention something when you cut your timeline short. If this is about me leaving, I'm coming right back."

"I decided this before I knew you were leaving," she says.

"I don't get it." I look to the side. "What happened between yesterday and today?"

She doesn't answer right away. I hear her phone buzz on the comforter and when I glance at it, she flips the screen over.

"Honestly?" she asks.

"Yeah, honestly."

She scoots back against the headboard of her bed and crosses her legs, but then pulls them up to her chest. She puts enough space between us to let me know where this is going.

"I'm going to speak what's on my heart, because that's what adults do, but for your information, this is hard on me and not something I would normally do."

"Okay . . ." Why do I have so many nerves bubbling up inside of me?

She clears her throat and lifts her chin. "Since I arrived here, I feel as though I've been thrown through a gauntlet of emotions. I've been so grateful that I stumbled into your house. I'm grateful for the friendships I developed here and the experiences we've shared. I'm worried about my future, what the hell I'm going to do and how I'm going to recover from the devastation of losing my mom. With your injury, I've been reminded of the fears I lived with on a daily basis with my mom's brain tumor, which brings me to my last part—I'm terrified."

"Because of my migraine?" I ask, confused.

"Partially, but more importantly"—her eyes divert away from mine—"I'm terrified because in a short amount of time, I've grown to care about someone I probably shouldn't care that much about."

She cares about me? I go to reply, but she raises her hand to stop me.

"I like you, Pacey. I like you a lot, and that terrifies me because I've never felt this strongly toward someone. And certainly not this quickly. Watching you go through the pain of a migraine was scary. Seeing you get hit in the head with the puck made me physically feel ill. And it's all because I really, really like you. I don't know how to handle those feelings, how to process them."

My mouth goes dry as I say, "I can understand that."

"So, even though it pains me, I think it would be best if I went home and sorted things out, you know?"

"No, I think you're running away instead of facing your feelings head-on."

Her eyes snap to mine. "You have no right to say that."

"I have every right to say that," I reply in a harsh tone, harsher than I expected. "Look, Winnie, I understand you must be scared, because I'm scared, too. I feel the same way about you. This strong connection, this bond we have—it's special and I don't want to lose it."

"It's too quick." She shakes her head.

"Maybe it's supposed to be quick. Ever think about that? Remember what I said? There's no timeline when it comes to relationships. Everyone is different."

She sighs and looks off to the side. "Pacey, I'm so grateful—"

"I'm going to stop you right there," I say before she can start with whatever bullshit goodbye she's ready to give me. Because that's not happening. Not when I just found this girl. "This isn't the end, Winnie."

"What?" she asks, her face registering complete shock. "Pacey, we're going our separate ways."

"You live in Seattle, Winnie. That's two and a half hours from Vancouver. Do you really think that's too much of a distance to consider dating?"

"Dating?" Her eyes nearly jump out of her sockets. In disbelief, she shakes her head. "You want to date me?"

"Yeah." I take her hand in mine. "I want to fucking date you. I want to take you out, rest my hand on the small of your back while everyone wonders who the hell the gorgeous girl is walking next to me. I want to spoil you, take care of you, give you what you deserve—a man who you can count on, even when things seem tough."

"I'm not . . . I'm not good enough for you."

I grip her chin and force her to look at me. "You're more than enough for me. Understand that?" When she doesn't say anything, I lean in closer, my eyes connecting with hers. "You're more than enough, Winnie." Her lip trembles, and she closes her eyes as a lone tear falls down her cheek. I wipe it away and say, "I will fucking wait. I'll wait as long as I need to in order for you to come to terms with that."

"Terms with what?" she asks.

"With the fact that you're right where you're supposed to be —in this cabin, holding my hand."

More tears.

"And you can take all the time you want to come to that realization, as long as you still talk to me. I'll be waiting."

"You're going to wait for me?" She shakes her head. "I don't get why."

"Simple, Winnie." I bring her knuckles to my lips and press a soft kiss to them. "You're worth the wait."

Her cheeks blush cutely as she stares at our joined hands. "No one has ever talked to me like that before, the way you talk to me."

"Good. I'd be pissed if someone else did."

She lets out a deep sigh. "Thank you for everything, Pacey."

I force her to meet my eyes. "That sounds like a goodbye."

She shakes her head. "No, it's not. Just letting you know how much I appreciate you."

"So, what does that mean for tomorrow?" I ask.

"I still need to leave. I have some things to take care of and you need to see the doctor."

"Then meet me in Vancouver, spend the summer with me. Date me." I'm grasping for anything at this point, because I'm not ready to say goodbye.

She stands from the bed and leads me to her door. Hand on my chest, she looks up at me and says, "I like you a lot, Pacey. Even though I have this feeling like I need to let you go, I know my heart won't allow it."

Confused, I ask, "Why would you need to let me go?"

She shakes her head, not getting into it. "If you want to try to date me, then we'll have to take it slow."

She's opening a window and I will fucking take it. But I hate not knowing what's holding her back.

"I told you, Winnie, I'll wait. Okay?"

She nods. "Okay."

Her hands smooth up my chest and to the back of my neck as she lifts her head and kisses the underside of my jaw. She attempts to pull away, but now that she opened that box, I keep her close and lift her chin, my mouth descending on hers. The moment our lips touch, her body melts against mine and her grip tightens.

Clinging to her, my hand travels up the back of her neck and I hold her tight, only allowing her to angle her mouth better, not pull away.

She tastes good.

Really fucking good.

Soft lips, gentle swipes of her tongue. Nothing too aggressive, but also not tentative. She knows what she wants, and that's me.

Parting her lips, she raises herself onto her toes and swipes her tongue against mine. I match the touch, and then our tongues tangle in a sensual exploration. Fire ignites in my very soul as her fingers thread through my hair. My other hand falls to the small of her back, and I pull her in just an inch more. She moans against my mouth and then releases me, her head falling back.

When my eyes connect with hers, I find disbelief.

She reaches up and presses her fingers gently to her lips, seeming shocked.

"Wow." She pats my chest. "I should, uh, I should just take a step back here."

"You're telling me you're going to let that go? That electricity—you felt it, didn't you?"

She nods and moves backward another step. "Yeah, I felt it. I felt it all the way down to my toes, which is why I'm going to put some distance between that heat developing between us." God, she's so fucking cute. "And then I'm just going to stick these"—she waves her hands at me—"in my pockets so they don't do any exploring. And with a gentle but courteous nod, I shall say, good night, dear sir."

I chuckle. "My body wouldn't mind those hands doing some exploring."

"Good to know." She nods. "Very good to know." She takes another step back. "Well, glad we covered that. So, yeah, I'll, uh, I'll just sit back on my bed and offer you a safe flight for tomorrow."

I wish she'd offer a hell of a lot more.

"Thank you." I reach for her doorknob and open her door. I want to tell her that I've never met anyone like her before, that she's worth the wait because I'm not sure I'll ever want anyone else. But she's not ready to hear that. Partway out the door, I ask, "Are you sure you're okay going alone to see your uncle tomorrow?"

"Yeah, I'll be fine. Keeping my hands to myself tonight, now that will be the true test of strength and courage."

If she gave me the okay, I would be all over her right now, but even though I can sense her need for me, I can see in her eyes that maybe she's just not completely ready.

Doesn't mean I can't tease her, though.

"Well, you know where my room is if you change your mind." With a wink, I head out of her room and straight to mine. I don't even bother to stop by my bed, but go straight to the shower.

Chapter Eighteen

WINNIE

I can't sleep. No matter what I do, I can't seem to shut my brain off.

The last forty-eight hours have been an absolute roller coaster.

I spent the day with Pacey.

I kissed him—me, I kissed him, I made the first move.

I spent another day with him and his friends and fell for the man over and over with every word that came out of his mouth.

Then I slept with him curled around me for a good portion of the day and it was . . . the best feeling I've ever felt.

Then I freaked out because I shouldn't be feeling things like that about a man I just met.

Then . . . hell . . . then Josh texted me.

Yeah, Josh.

Apparently, he needs to talk to me about something. *And he kept texting back after my replies.* I'm finally in a healthy state of mind and completely over him, so why is he texting now? Why is he trying to throw me for a loop?

And on top of that were my emotions—dredged up, I know, because of Pacey's migraine—about my mom.

Things have gotten complicated.

Then Pacey said he was leaving. And I said I was leaving.

Then Pacey said he wants to date me. I think he's insane for wanting to hitch his wagon to this hot-mess express.

Then I kissed him again because apparently, I have no willpower.

And now I'm lying here, alone, in my bed at one thirty in the morning, with nothing better to do than stare at the ceiling because my mind won't stop racing, thinking about a man I can't seem to forget. And it's also racing, thinking about a man I'd rather forget.

I roll to my side and pick up my phone, pulling up the text thread with Josh. The last thing I ever expected was to receive a text from him, from the man who left me feeling empty and alone at the most devastating moment of my life.

I read our exchange, still trying to wrap my head around it all.

Josh: *Hey, Winnie, it's Josh. Not sure if you deleted my number after everything we went through. I wanted to reach out and see how you were doing.*

I didn't respond to him right away, because what was I really supposed to say to that? I decided to ignore him because I didn't think he deserved my attention. But then he texted again.

Josh: *I probably deserve your silence. I didn't handle things very well with you and it's one of the biggest regrets I have. I've been doing some work on myself and I really need to see you. I need to talk to you, in person. Please tell me you're open to at least seeing me.*

I'm not sure if it's because I was in a weak state of mind, or if it's my personality to be nice to people even when they're assholes to me, but I texted him back.

Winnie: *Hey, Josh. I still have your number, even though I probably should've deleted it.*

It's all I could stomach writing, but it opened the lines of communication.

Josh: *That's really fair. I'm grateful that you didn't. How are you?*

Winnie: *Doing okay.*

Josh: *I heard about your mom and the bookstore. I went by the old storefront the other day and a pang of sorrow blasted through me. I fucked up, Winnie, big time, and I need to see you.*

Winnie: *I don't think that's a good idea.*

Josh: *I can understand your reservations. I wasn't very kind to you toward the end of our relationship.*

Winnie: *You made me feel less than I am, Josh. You left me when I needed you most. You made me second-guess my beauty and put a dent in my self-esteem.*

Josh: *There's no excuse for how I treated you, none at all. Despite what I was going through, there's no reason for me to have treated you the way I did, and I'm really sorry, Winnie.*

Winnie: *Going through? You were going through something?*

Josh: *It's why I want to talk to you, in person. It's important, Winnie. I can meet you wherever you want to meet. I'm in Vancouver now, but I can drive down to wherever you are now. Just let me know when and where, and I'll be there.*

I haven't responded to him yet.

I honestly don't know what to say to him, because if he was truly going through something and I wasn't there for him, that would make me feel even worse than I already do. But what would Pacey think if I met with him? I know Pacey lays no claim to me, at least that's what I'm assuming—not sure after the conversation we just had—but Pacey thinks very lowly of Josh. I know he'd despise me talking to him because of the damage he knows Josh caused me.

This is all such a mess, and one of the reasons why I just need to leave, to clear my head, to start fresh.

And the worst part of this all is I feel as though my mom has taken a backseat to this entire mess. It's why I decided to pay Uncle RJ a visit tomorrow. Because despite Pacey and Josh floating around in my head, I know one thing for sure—I'm getting that trophy, even if I have to peel out of his driveway, unbuckled, hair whipping in the wind. I'm getting that trophy.

As for Pacey, I have no idea what the future is going to bring, if he's really going to want to date me, like he said. He's going to have a lot on his plate with whatever is going on with his head and the upcoming season. Sure, two and a half hours seems doable now, but what about when the season starts? It's all just so up in the air.

But that kiss . . .

"God," I mutter while snagging my pillow and putting it over my face, preparing for the scream of frustration that wants to pop out of me.

Ding.

I still.

Was that my phone?

I lift the corner of the pillow and glance toward the lit-up screen on my bed.

That *was* my phone.

God, please don't be Josh. Please don't be Josh.

I move my pillow to the side, reach for my phone, and see there's a text . . . from Pacey.

Thank God.

I quickly unlock my phone and read his text.

Pacey: *You up?*

Oh yes . . . I . . . am.

I flip onto my stomach, prop my pillow under my chest, and text him back.

Winnie: *Yup. Can't seem to sleep. I'd ask if you're up, but I'm pretty sure you are, unless you're really good at sleep texting.*

Pacey: *Nah, I'm up. I think all my daytime sleeping fucked me up.*

Winnie: *Yeah, it was that long nap that killed me too.*

Lies. All lies, but he doesn't need to know that.

Pacey: *Then talk to me. Tell me something. Anything.*

Anything? Hmm, well, my ex-boyfriend, who you like to often call a tool, texted me today, asking if he could talk to me, that it's important, and a crazy part of me is actually thinking about meeting up with him.

Clearly, that's not what I'm going to say.

Winnie: *Anything?*

Pacey: *Yes, anything. Hold nothing back.*

I give it some thought. I push Josh to the back of my mind, because he doesn't deserve any space in my head, not right now. And because I can't stop thinking about that kiss, I say . . .

Winnie: *Not to boost your already inflated ego, but you're easily, hands down, the best kiss I've ever had.*

And that's the scary truth, why being with Pacey is so terrifying. I know he's special. I know he could possibly be what I've been looking for, what my mom would want for me.

Pacey: *What made it the best?*

Winnie: *It was the way you made me feel.*

Pacey: *And how did I make you feel?*

I think on it, bringing the kiss to the forefront of my mind, letting myself get lost in the moment all over again.

His strong body gripping me tightly, not allowing an inch between us. The controlling way he claims my lips so I can't focus on anything except him. The softness of his lips, the light strokes of his tongue, the deeply masculine scent of his cologne. He's intoxicating.

Winnie: *Claimed. Owned. It was how you gripped me. How your lips roamed mine. How you put your body into the kiss, your entire body. You made me drown in need.*

Pacey: *Confession—you're easily the best kiss I've ever had, as well. Hands down, no competition. I can't stop thinking about your lips, the soft moans from the back of your throat. Fuck, Winnie.*

I feel a smile lifting the corners of my mouth. And just like that, I get lost in Pacey, in his words, in the bond we share.

In his honesty.

Winnie: *What made it the best?*

Pacey: *You weren't putting on a show for me.*

Winnie: *What do you mean, exactly?*

Pacey: *Given my profession and celebrity status, in the past, women have just been extravagant in their kissing. Trying too hard. Acting overzealous, trying to prove something with their mouths. Not with you. It was genuine. There was passion, there was need, but you also captured me with a hint of innocence in your touch. Everything about it turned me on.*

Winnie: *Me too.*

Pacey: *If you were in my bed right now, would you be saying this to my face?*

Winnie: *Probably not. Text messaging gives you an ounce of anonymity. More confident behind the keyboard.*

Pacey: *Okay, if that's true, then tell me, if you were in my bed right now, what would you be doing? Would you just want to snuggle?*

Winnie: *Knowing me, I probably would snuggle, but be burning inside to do more.*

Pacey: *Like what?*

Winnie: *Draw circles down your abdomen.*

Pacey: *How far would you go?*

My face heats up. I'm sexting Pacey Lawes right now, actually sexting him. I've dreamed of sending naughty texts before and I did once with Josh, but he never went along with it. So, I've never tried again. But from Pacey's response, from his questioning, I can tell he's open to it. At this point, what do I have to lose? I need to get lost in the moment and just . . . enjoy.

Winnie: *To just above the waistline of your briefs. And then I would pull back up.*

Pacey: *Fucking tease.*

Winnie: *I would circle around your nipple and then slowly rotate my finger across every one of your abs until I hit the waistline again . . .*

Pacey: *Fuck. I can feel it. Would you slip your finger past the elastic?*

Winnie: *For a second, but then pull away.*

Pacey: *I would be hard as stone, begging for you to go farther.*

Winnie: *I wouldn't, not until I repeat the process as least three more times.*

Pacey: *Three? Fuck. Then what?*

Winnie: *When I finally reach your waistline, I would push your briefs down just enough to expose your cock.*

Good God, I wrote cock. I bury my head in my mattress, my cheeks burning from embarrassment. But then he texts back.

Pacey: *And then?*

Winnie: *With my index finger, trace your length to the very tip and then pull away again.*

Pacey: *Goddamn it, I'm hard. Right now, fucking hard. I want your finger on my cock, Winnie. Your whole goddamn hand. Your mouth.*

He's so dirty. I love it. I shift to my side as I feel a dull pulse start to throb between my legs. I'm just as turned on from the mere thought of doing something so salacious to Pacey and him letting me.

Winnie: *I would make circles up your abs again, but this time, I would smooth my leg over your legs while doing it, drawing closer to your body so you could feel how hard my nipples were.*

Pacey: *Would you be naked?*

Winnie: *No, but at your request, I'd take off my shirt.*

Pacey: *I would DEMAND you take off your shirt.*

Winnie: *I wouldn't want to disappoint you, so I'd sit up, look you in the eyes, and take off my shirt, exposing my bare tits to you. I would revel in the way you took me all in.*

Because I'm feeling extra spicy and because Pacey instills such bold confidence in me, I turn on my nightstand light, flip my phone to camera mode and drag down my tank top so my breasts are almost entirely exposed, leaving just my nipples covered. Leaving my face out of the picture, I send it to him.

Pacey: *Holy fuck . . . Winnie.*

Winnie: *I'd climb on top of your legs, loving the way you reach out and slowly roll my nipple between your fingers, and I'd pull your cock out to rest it on your stomach.*

Pacey: *I'm so goddamn hard. It's painful.*

Winnie: *Bracing my hands on either side of your hips, I'd lower my head, and starting at the base of your cock, I'd drag my tongue up your length until I reached the tip. Then I would suck on the head.*

Pacey: *Winnie . . .*

Winnie: *Jesus, Pacey, I'm so turned on right now. I'm throbbing.*

Pacey: *Are you touching yourself? Like, I'm gripping my cock right now.*

Winnie: *No. But I need the relief. What would you do to ease the ache between my legs?*

Pacey: *Why don't you come here and find out?*

Winnie: *Why don't you tell me?*

Pacey: *I'd start with demanding you strip for me. And then stand in front of me, naked, so I can see just how goddamn sexy you are. You'd twirl for me, and then I'd spread you across the bed.*

Winnie: *Would you force me down?*

Pacey: *Only because you let me.*

Winnie: *Would you spread my legs?*

Pacey: *I wouldn't be able to stop myself.*

Winnie: *Would you want to taste me on your tongue?*

Pacey: *Fuck.*

Pacey: *Yes.*

Pacey: *Your pussy would be my goddamn feast.*

I moan out loud as my hand inches down to my pajama shorts. I don't really know what I'm aiming for, but I just know I need something. A touch. Something to stop this terrible aching.

Winnie: *Would you*

God, this is embarrassing. I don't even know if I can orgasm. How do I ask for something when—

Pacey: *Would I what?*

Winnie: *Would you help me orgasm?*

Now I feel stupid. I'm sure he's ready to turn off his phone and bolt. I bet no other woman has ever asked him that because they don't even know if they've orgasmed before.

He doesn't respond right away, and because I'm way out of my comfort zone, I think about retracting that last text, but then my door opens and Pacey pushes through, shutting the door behind him.

Standing in the barely lit room, Pacey is wearing nothing but a pair of athletic shorts that prominently display how aroused he is. His chest rises and falls and his hair drapes over one eye as he stares me down. There's no mistaking what he wants.

He wants me.

The image in front of me is carnal.

The man before me is everything I want. Everything I need.

I set my phone on the nightstand and sit up in bed, letting the comforter slide down my body, exposing the way my nipples are pebbled against my shirt.

"Stand up," he says.

The deep, demanding tone of his voice has me lifting from the bed, ready to listen for his next direction.

"Take your shirt off."

Adrenaline pumps through me and as I reach for the hem of my tank top, my hands shake. I grip the hemline tightly and, with one smooth pull, bring it up and over my head, allowing the fabric to slip out of my hand and drop to the floor. When I find the courage to look Pacey in the eyes, he doesn't meet my gaze; instead, he's dragging his hand over his mouth, taking in my chest.

"Shorts. Off. Now."

I slip my thumbs into the waistband of my shorts and push them down. When they hit my ankles, I toe them away and stand in front of Pacey with nothing but my hair in two braids.

He deliberately gives me a once-over, starting with my legs, moving up my abdomen, to my breasts, and then connecting with my face. He takes a step forward and I feel a bout of chills roll up my spine.

Another step and my mouth goes dry.

One more and I watch him push down his shorts, as well. I take a deep breath and allow myself to take in the beautifully sculpted man in front of me. A powerful chest pushes and pulls with his deep, turned-on breaths. His abs contract as my eyes land on them, and his erection sits thick between his two powerful thighs, enticing me. Begging for my touch.

With two more steps, he closes the distance between us. My skin tingles with excitement as he moves one hand to my hip and slowly drags it up to my waistline and then to the underside of my breast. I suck in a sharp breath when his thumb drags over my hard nipple. A wave of arousal pulses through me and pools between my legs, thumping, spiking every sensation inside me.

I can feel my heartbeat in the base of my throat.

I can taste my need on the tip of my tongue.

And I can hear my needy breath with every rise and fall of my chest.

"This body deserves to be worshipped," Pacey says as he rolls my nipple between his fingers. "Tell me what you want, Winnie."

"You," I answer, so quickly that it's almost embarrassing.

His other hand falls to my inner leg and drags upward until his finger glides along my slit, feeling my arousal.

"That's evident," he says right before bringing his finger to his mouth and sucking on the long digit.

Fuck. Me.

"But what do you want me to do?"

Insecurity fills me as I shake my head. "I . . . I really don't know. I haven't done much."

His eyes soften and he moves in even closer. "Where do you need me the most right now?" He brings both hands to my breasts and plays with my nipples, rolling them, teasing them. My legs tremble beneath me. I let out a moan from the depth of my throat. "Do you want me to pay attention to your tits, make you come by just playing with them?"

He can do that?

"Oh God," I say as, at that moment, he pinches my nipples, sending a bolt of pleasure through me.

Letting go, he brings his hands to my cheeks and lowers his mouth to mine. Right before his lips meet mine, he whispers, "Or do you want me to fuck your mouth with my tongue until you feel your arousal drip down your legs?"

His mouth descends upon me and I grip him as he lowers me to the bed so my body is completely splayed out on the mattress. His large body hovers over mine, his erection rubbing against my bare skin.

When he pulls his mouth away, he moves down my body, dragging his fingers over my breasts, my stomach, and to the top of my pubic bone. "Or do you want me to play with your clit?"

I barely have enough time to suck in a sharp breath before he parts me with two fingers, and with the other hand, he moves his thumb over my clit.

"Oh fuck," I say, draping my hand over my eyes. "That's . . . oh God."

"Mmm . . . I think you want me right here, don't you, Winnie?" His mouth descends and pulls at my nipples, then travels up my neck to my mouth, where his tongue demands entry, and then drags his seductive tongue down the column of my neck and to my breasts once again. "That feels good, but you want my attention on your clit, don't you?"

"Y-yes," I breathe out as my legs part even wider for him.

"Mmm, I like that," he says. "Greedy with wanting more. Can you spread even wider for me? Can you pull your knees against your chest?"

"S-sure," I answer, feeling more exposed than I ever have before. I grip my knees, and when I look at Pacey, he's wetting his lips as he stares down at me.

"So fucking beautiful." And then he's lowering his head between my legs.

"Pacey, I never . . . this is—"

"Shh." He brings his mouth to my clit and hovers there for a moment. "Fucking amazing." His tongue peeks out and connects with my clit.

All at once, it feels as though every muscle in my body pulls to the center between my legs. A sensation so wildly erotic that I forget to breathe as he strokes again.

And again.

And again.

"Oh my God, Pacey," I moan.

"You taste phenomenal," he whispers before lapping his tongue against my clit, again and again. "I could spend all fucking day here."

He pushes at my legs, helping me hold them where they are as he moves his mouth over me. Twisting, turning, dancing his tongue. My muscles pull, my nerves bundle.

A sensation builds inside me, blooming in the pit of my stomach and then hammering out over my limbs. This tingling, floating, effortless sensation that I can't quite explain other than it's pulling all the focus away from everything around me and zeroing in on what Pacey is doing.

The walls start to close in, the room fades to black, and my pelvis begs—screams for more as the pleasure builds and builds.

Rolling through me.

Pulsing.

Throbbing.

Drumming.

His tongue pulls more and more.

My body goes numb.

"Pacey, oh my God. Oh . . . oh my God!" I scream. I'm loud, my moans reverberating off the walls, but it's too powerful, it's too consuming.

His tongue.

Oh . . . fuck.

White-hot pleasure rips through me, forcing my back to arch. My legs slip from my hands, but Pacey keeps them still as I come.

I come hard.

My pussy pounds against his lapping tongue as he draws out

my orgasm.

"Pacey . . . oh my . . . God," I say breathlessly as the roar of my climax subsides.

He kisses my clit and then slowly and carefully lowers my legs to the mattress.

I bring both my arms over my head as I try to catch my breath. Oh. My. God. I've never . . . felt that before. I've clearly *never* had an orgasm. All these years . . . Oh dear God. That was the most incredible feeling of my life. I feel so sensitive everywhere. I feel so . . . incredible.

Hoarse. Feverish.

And a little angry that Josh never gave me that.

His lips press kisses along my heated skin, up my stomach, to my breasts, and then he hovers at my mouth. Intimately, he leans down and presses a kiss to my lips.

"See how good you taste?" he asks. "So fucking good." He moves his lips to my jaw, and down my neck, and then to my breasts. "These tits belong in my mouth." He grips my right breast and sucks in my nipple. My chest arches off the bed as my hand falls to his hair. My fingers sift through the long, wavy locks as he teases and plays with my breasts.

His rock-hard length rubs against my leg as he continues to focus on my pleasure. He must be painfully hard, but instead of taking care of his own needs, he's focusing on me. He's making me feel like a queen. He's allowing me to seek out my pleasure rather than chasing after his own orgasm, his own needs.

"Pacey," I sigh, my body melting into the mattress as he moves to my other breast. "You make me feel so good." I drag my free hand down his chest and past his abdomen, until my fingers connect with the tip of his erection. A deep hiss escapes his lips and he drops his head to my chest for a second.

"Winnie, you can't do that."

I smooth my fingers over the head. It's the lightest of touches, but it seems to carry a heavy impact, because his hips thrust into my hand, his cock a stone, his skin like velvet.

"Winnie . . . hell." He thrusts again and I quickly become addicted to the feel of his cock in my hand, seeking out his own climax.

"I want you, Pacey."

He lifts up so he can look me in the eyes. "I want to fuck you, bad, but I want to make sure you get what you need first."

"You did. I have. And now, all I need is you, inside me."

And that seems to be all he needs to hear, because he pulls away, reaches for his shorts on the floor, and pulls out a strip of condoms.

I raise a playful brow at his assumption.

He smirks at me. "Don't plan on getting fucked only once tonight, Winnie. I know once I'm inside that sweet pussy, I won't be able to stop." He rips open one of the packages and, as he maintains eye contact, he slides the condom over his length, his teeth biting into his lip. He rests his hand at the base and squeezes. His chest contracts as his abdomen hollows. His body strains—the muscles in his arms, the veins in his neck, the need in his cock. I've never seen anything so sexy.

"On your beautiful stomach, now."

It takes me a second to register what he's saying, but when it does, I flip to my stomach, and I feel him come up behind me.

"That's it." He smooths his hand over my ass. "So fucking fine, Winnie. Do you know that? You're so goddamn fine. I crave your body, your shape, your curves. You're so my fucking type and it's painful I've waited this long to get inside of you." He moves his hand up my back and gently pushes my head down into the mattress. "Just like that." He guides my ass into the air and stuffs some pillows under my stomach. "Are you comfortable?"

"Yes," I breathe out heavily, anticipation rocking me.

"Good." He brings his hands to my ass cheeks and spreads them. "This perfect little hole." His thumb passes over it. "Fuck, do I want to have fun with it." Arousal beats through me. "But that's for another day." His hand must go to his cock because the next thing I feel is his girth rubbing against my slick pussy. "God, you're so fucking wet, Winnie. Tell me I turn you on."

"So much, Pacey. I want you. Inside me. More than anything."

"That's what I want to hear, but I need you to beg for it."

"Pacey."

His hand connects with my ass, and I let out a muffled scream as my pelvis tilts higher and arousal pools between my legs.

"Holy. Shit." I brace my hands on the mattress.

He tests my pussy again with his cock, and I hear a satisfied sound come out of him. "You like it dirty, Winnie." He slaps my ass again and a long, tortured moan falls past my lips. "That's it, baby. I can feel you throbbing against my cock. How close are you?"

I swallow hard, unable to answer.

He slaps my ass again.

Pleasure vibrates through my bones.

"Fuck, Pacey." I grip the comforter. "Close."

His hand smooths over the sting and I mentally beg him to do it again. When have I ever mentally begged for a man to spank me? Never. This is new. It's thrilling. And I want so much more.

"I need this pussy," Pacey says as his thumb glides over my entrance. "I need it really fucking bad."

"Then take it," I say as his cock glides up and down my slit.

He groans and then pushes himself in an inch.

"Oh, Jesus," I say, while taking in a big breath. His hand connects with my ass again, catching me off guard, and he slips in deeper at the same time. I let out a feral moan. I clench around him and he lets out a moan as well. "Pacey, I'm going to come. I'm right there."

"Not yet. Do you understand me?" He moves in another inch. "You don't fucking come until I tell you." His thumb rubs over my asshole and I clench around him again.

"You fucking like that. You want my cock there, don't you?"

I swallow hard, because just the thought of his finger there turns me on.

"We got time for that, babe."

He smooths his hand over my left ass cheek and then pulls back and lays down another slap.

"Oh, fuck," I groan, my pussy clenching tightly around him.

"Yes, Winnie."

"Pacey," I cry. "It's too good. I can't hold on."

He stills behind me. "Winnie. I'll pull out right fucking now. Do not come. Do you hear me?"

I bite on the side of my cheek and squeeze my eyes shut, trying to not think about how delicious Pacey feels sliding inside of me. Long, thick, commanding. He has my ass in his hands, guiding himself inside, taking what he wants, but also giving me everything I need.

"Fuck, I can't hold out," he says, and drives his cock all the way inside me, hitting me in a spot I didn't know existed. Spasms erupt deep within me and I try to take deep breaths to ward them off, but it doesn't work.

"Pacey . . ."

"I know, baby," he says soothingly right before he pumps his hips against me. He's not slow about it. He's demanding. His thrusts rock me forward, sending a jolt through my pelvis.

Relentless.

Powerful.

Consuming.

He pumps into me, thrust after thrust, pushing me further and further to the edge, where I teeter but never fall.

"Your cunt is so tight, so perfect. Shit, Winnie."

His fingers dig into my skin. His breath matches mine, seeking air. The sound of his legs, slapping into mine, over and over—it's so erotic, so electrically charging.

"Fuck, I'm close," he groans.

"I'm right there," I say.

And then the crack of his hand against my ass has me coming violently all over his cock.

"Oh God, Pacey," I yell as my body contracts. My insides all pull to the center, and I black out completely. I hear him groan. His cock swells, I contract around him, and then his chest presses against my back as he holds on to me and comes.

"Fuck . . . fuck," he yells as he grips my sides tightly. "Oh shit, Winnie." He stills and then slowly sinks against me as his breathing slows, and we both lie there, unmoving, as our bodies recover.

His lips land on my back as he presses small kisses across my shoulder.

"Are you . . . okay?" he asks, still breathless.

I smile into the mattress. "More than okay."

He presses another kiss to my shoulder and lightly against my cheek. "Let me clean up. I'll be right back." As he lifts off me, he drags his hand down my back, across my ass, and he gives it a very, very light swat.

I chuckle against the comforter and then just lie there, completely satisfied.

So that's sex.

No. That's what sex is supposed to feel like. *With two orgasms.* Two. Orgasms. Now I *know* what I've missed out on. For years. With and without Josh.

After a few moments, Pacey comes back. He helps me off the bed and I quickly go to the bathroom to take care of business, not bothering with turning the light on. Instead, I tiptoe back into the bedroom, nervous to see if Pacey is getting dressed to leave, but when I find him lying in bed, the comforter pulled back, waiting for me, I bubble with giddiness.

"Get that sweet ass over here."

Normally, I'm not one to walk around naked. After sex, I'd normally slink out of bed and cover up before heading to the bathroom. I would change into pajamas and call it a night. Strutting across the room wearing nothing is new for me, but

I've never felt more confident. And it's all because of the man waiting for me in bed.

I slide in under the covers next to him. His arm goes around my shoulders and his hand lands on my bare ass as he pulls me in closer. I tilt my head up, and he looks down at me at just the right time. He leans in and presses a sweet, gentle kiss to my lips. When I go to pull away, he presses his hand to my jaw and, with his thumb, tilts my chin up, granting him more access. I melt into his touch, in the dominant way he handles my body.

His kisses slow down until he presses a kiss to my nose, and I cuddle against his chest.

"I need more time with those lips."

"Have them whenever you want," I answer.

His finger draws small circles on my backside as he says, "I cancelled my flight for tomorrow."

"What?" I ask, sitting up to look him in the eyes. "Pacey, you need to see the doctor."

"I will." He chastely kisses me. "But I figured I could drive to Vancouver with you, after you visit your uncle."

"Pacey—"

"Hear me out." He shifts so I can look him in the eyes. "It doesn't matter if I see the doctor first thing in the morning or the next day, so long as I get there. And I want to be there for you after you see your uncle, even if you don't think you need the company. I know it's not going to be easy and would rather be there to hold your hand, than know that you're alone, by yourself, sad or upset." He shakes his head. "I wouldn't be able to stomach that."

"So, you want me to drive to Vancouver with you after?"

"Yeah, and if you're up for it, maybe stay with me for a few days." The hope in his eyes cripples me. "I can show you around." His voice is vulnerable, as if he's nervous of my answer.

"That's kind of a big ask. Are you sure you want me to stay with you?"

He chuckles. "I wanted you to stay with me before I showed up in your room. After what we just did, I'm not sure you have much of a choice."

My body is thinking the same thing—not sure I've much choice after the two orgasms he just gave me.

I drag the tip of my finger over his lips. "You know, I didn't think sex could ever be like that. So consuming and carnal. I didn't think I could get enough of you."

"I sure as hell didn't get enough." He kisses my lips softly. "And I don't think I've ever come that hard, Winnie."

Shyly, I ask, "You're not just saying that? I mean, I know you probably have more experience than me, so I wasn't sure—"

"I wouldn't lie about shit like that. Your pussy is fucking magic."

I laugh. "Maybe it was all that spanking . . . my pussy needed a good lesson on sex etiquette."

"Nah, you knew exactly what you were doing and you had me coming a lot sooner than I wanted."

"You wanted to last longer than that?" I ask in surprise.

"Fuck yeah. Babe"—he looks at me, and God, I love that little nickname—"the longer I could keep driving into your tight cunt, the better. You have no idea how it felt being inside you, as if your pussy was made for me."

My cheeks flame.

"But since it was that good, I had no chance at lasting." He scratches the side of his face. "Kind of embarrassing."

"Maybe you can try harder next time, then," I tease. And I am teasing. I've only ever been with Josh, and he never lasted as long as Pacey just did. And Pacey thought *that* was embarrassing.

"When I get feeling back in my legs, I fucking will." He settles back down on the pillow and hugs me close. "Damn, Winnie, you've fucking rocked my world."

I could say the same exact thing about him.

Chapter Nineteen

PACEY

"Hey, gorgeous," I say, as the shower water sprays off my back.

Naked and fresh from bed, Winnie steps into the shower with me and presses her hands to my chest. Her hair is a complete mess. Sometime during the night, she took her braids out, and I ended up driving my fingers through her hair and pulling on it as I fucked her from behind again.

My new favorite position of all time, now.

She has the perfect ass, and all I want to do is stare at it while I drive into her over and over again.

Fuck, and the way she moans when she's almost ready to come drives me crazy. Don't even get me started on her pussy. I wasn't lying when I said it was magic. Whatever Josh was doing, he needs to learn a goddamn lesson about appreciating what he has when he has it. Now that I have Winnie, there's no way in hell I'm losing her.

She leans in and kisses my chest without saying a word as her fingers play with my chest hair.

I had her three times last night, and it wasn't enough. And seeing her in the shower with me, drops of water cascading down her naked tits . . . yup, I'm already fucking hard and she knows it. She smirks at me and her hand falls to my cock.

"Jesus, yes," I mumble as she strokes my length.

"How can you be hard again?"

"How can I not be when you walk into my shower?" I suck in a hiss as she drops to her knees and places her hands on my thighs. "Fuck, or when you're naked."

She moves her hands inward, and then she pushes her hair to the side as she presses the flat of her tongue against the underside of my cock.

This is one thing we haven't done yet and one thing I'm totally interested in. She kept saying she wanted to taste me, she wanted me in her mouth, but I couldn't allow myself that pleasure when I needed her pussy over and over again. More than that, I wanted to pleasure her. I'm not and never have been a selfish lover, but I wanted Winnie to know how much she deserves to be satisfied during sex. *She has to come first*, in every way, as far as I'm concerned. So, that's what I made sure happened.

Seems as though she has different plans right now.

I brace one hand against the tiled wall as she brings her mouth all the way to my tip and then sucks in the rim, and that's where she stays, twisting, sucking, lapping with her tongue. Her movements are making me as hard as stone, and the way she looks up at me with those mysterious eyes makes me want to come violently in her mouth so I can watch her swallow every last drop of my cum.

"So fucking good," I mumble as I attempt to thrust my cock farther in her mouth, but she doesn't let me. Instead, she removes her mouth and snakes her hand between my legs, where she cups my balls and rolls them in her palm.

"Hell . . . " My head drops forward and I spread my legs

wider, giving her more access. Her hand plays with my balls gently, moving back and forth, farther . . . and farther.

My cock bobs as she plays dangerously close to my backside. I spread my legs even wider, encouraging her.

I'm frustrated when she brings her mouth back to my cock, sucking me in deeper this time, but her hand never releases my balls. Her mouth drives deeper until I hit the back of her throat.

"Yes, baby."

She opens wider, and takes me deeper still until I'm continuously hitting the back of her throat. She doesn't gag, she's doesn't even flinch, so I thrust inside and she takes me.

I'm a goner.

There's no way I'm going to be able to—

"Ahh, fu-uck," I shout as her hand slips to my backside and her finger presses into my tight hole. I slam my fist against the wall as my balls tighten.

She presses the finger in farther and I lose all sense of what the hell is going on. Her finger doesn't stop until I'm panting, begging, and heaving.

Then, she takes me all the way to the back of her throat again, sucking hard.

She presses her finger in . . .

"Fuck! Fuck me," I yell as my cock swells and I come in her mouth, down her throat. I come so fucking hard that I have to brace against both walls of the shower so I don't fall. My cock pulses in her mouth, my cum still spilling as she pulls every last drop from me.

When my cock finally stops, I lean against the wall. She stands up and presses a kiss to my chest, then rinses off quickly and hops out of the shower. Unable to stand, I switch off the water and slowly sink to the floor as I catch my breath, my cock heavy across my leg.

A satisfied smile on my face, I look up at her as she towels off.

"What the ever-loving fuck was that?" I ask.

She smirks. "The best blow job you'll ever receive." She winks and then leaves the bathroom, a sway to her hips.

Yup, she's right. Hands down, the best blow job I'll ever receive. I think the only person who'll be able to top that . . . is her.

———

THE TABLE IS silent as I take a seat with my breakfast plate in hand. I can feel all sets of eyes on me as I scoot in my chair and pick up my fork.

Winnie is packing her things and, uh, taking a moment to herself. Apparently, she needs one after I tossed her up on the bathroom counter and went down on her. I had her lean against the mirror, her legs pulled to her chest again, and I teased and played with her clit until she was thrashing from her climax. I can still hear her moan and taste her arousal on my tongue.

There's no mistaking we've been loud.

And there's no mistaking that the boys heard us, even on opposite ends of the house. The pounding of my fist on the tile wall alone was evidence enough.

But I choose to ignore their stares as I stab a piece of egg and put it in my mouth.

"You know, I heard this weird sound this morning," Taters says, breaking the silence.

Yup, here it goes.

"Sort of like . . . a donkey in heat," he continues.

"Yeah, I heard that too," Posey adds. "Like a *heeeeee-haaaaawww, hehehe-hahaha.*"

I did not fucking sound like that.

"You know, I thought it was more like a duck who got his bill stuck in a door." Hornsby does a horrible impression of a duck while slapping the table.

The boys point at him and nod.

"Yes, that's more accurate," Posey says. "The duck is spot-on."

I glance over at Holmes, who has his head down but a smirk on his face. No doubt he got the brunt of the noise since he's in the same wing as us.

"I checked the backyard for a duck," Hornsby continues, "but couldn't find anything. Say . . . Lawes, did you happen to hear a duck this morning?"

Keeping my eyes on my plate, I shake my head. "Nope."

"Funny, because the noises seemed to be coming from your end of the house. Holmes, any ducks in your room?"

"No, but I recall a donkey at one point."

No, not Holmes, too.

"I remember the time I heard a donkey-duck in the hotel once. Two years ago. Do you guys remember that?" Taters asks.

Hornsby snaps his fingers. "I do remember that. Pounding on the walls. Hotel security was called." Apparently, I like to pound on walls. Didn't really know that about myself until now.

"Hey, didn't that donkey-duck turn out to be"—all their eyes land on me—"our friend Pacey Lawes?" Posey asks.

Knowing this isn't going to end, I lean back in my chair and say, "I'm not going to talk about it. Winnie deserves more respect than that."

"Uh-huh," Hornsby says. "Getting in a goodbye before you leave?"

"I cancelled my flight."

All kidding flies out the window as the boys focus on me.

"What?" Taters asks. "Doc is expecting you. Why the fuck would you cancel? If you say it's for the girl, I'm going to murder you."

"It is for Winnie," I say and try to continue, but Taters slams his fork on the table.

"You've known her for a week. A fucking week. And you're going to—"

"I'm still going," I say in a stern tone. "But today Winnie is going to confront an uncle she's never met, and then she's driving back home. I wanted to be there for her. Asked her to drive me to Vancouver."

The tension in the room eases, but only slightly.

"When are you leaving for Vancouver?" Hornsby asks.

"Right after we're done at her uncle's." I fork some eggs and say, "I promise, I'm going to get checked out."

"When?" Taters asks, still looking pissed.

"Tomorrow. I already set it up with Doc. I have an appointment with him at three tomorrow afternoon."

"Can we call and ask him?" Posey asks.

"Have at it. Want me to make you my point of contact, as well?"

"That would be appreciated," Hornsby says. "We'd like copies of all medical records, too."

"Fine," I say easily. "Whatever you want to get you off my back."

The boys exchange glances and Posey says, "I don't like how agreeable he is to all of this. It's making me feel uneasy."

"Me too," Hornsby agrees. "Do you think it's because he got some last night?"

"And this morning," Holmes says before taking a sip of his orange juice.

"I think the orgasms have helped him relax." Posey speaks more quietly. "Blink twice if the orgasms helped. Blink once if you're in some sort of sexual trance you don't know how to get out of."

"Jesus Christ," I mutter.

Pointing his finger at me, Hornsby says, "He blinked once."

I stuff the rest of my eggs in my mouth just as Winnie walks into the main living space. She's freshly showered, her hair is braided, and she looks fucking hot in a yellow sundress. Silence fills the room as she slows to a stop, noticing all eyes on her.

Immediately, her cheeks turn pink. Fuck, she's embarrassed.

"So, Pacey told you what happened?" she asks.

"No," I nearly shout. Shit, I don't want her thinking she's part of some classless locker-room talk. "They——"

"He told us jack shit," Taters says, stepping in. "Said he respects you too much to say a goddamn thing. But we knew from the starry look in his eyes." Taters pats me on the back and lifts up from his chair. "This boy likes you . . . a lot." He takes his plate to the kitchen and sets it in the sink. Before walking off to his room, Taters adds, "I expect updates tomorrow." And then he leaves.

"We also heard Pacey. His orgasm wheeze is unmistakable," Hornsby says, standing from the table with his plate, as well. "Just glad it wasn't his hand giving it to him this time."

Such a dickhead.

He drops his plate in the sink and heads for his room.

"Got some vegan waffles for you," Stephan says to Winnie, sliding a plate across the island for her.

"Thank you," she answers shyly. She brings the plate to the table with her, taking a seat next to me. When she sits down, I reach under the table and place my hand on her thigh, letting her know everything is fine.

"You're headed out today?" Posey asks.

"Yeah. I figured it's time," Winnie says while cutting into her waffle.

"Are we going to see you again?"

Winnie looks up, but before she can answer, I squeeze her leg and say, "Yeah, dude. Winnie's my girl now. You're going to be seeing a lot of her."

A surprised look crosses Posey's face before he says, "Cool. So we'll see you in Vancouver."

"Yup," I answer, hopefully not jumping the gun for her.

"Good," Posey says. Then he and Holmes clear their places at the table, discarding their breakfast dishes in the sink. They thank Stephan, and before they leave the room, Posey turns back and tells Winnie, "Don't leave without saying bye."

Now alone with Winnie, I direct my attention to my plate,

but Winnie turns to me, crossing one leg over the other, which knocks my hand from her leg. She props her elbow on the table and leans in.

"That was an interesting conversation."

"How so?" I ask, acting casual.

"You told them they would see me in Vancouver."

"Was that inaccurate information?" I ask her, finishing my bacon.

"Who says I'll be in Vancouver by the time they come back?"

"If I have anything to do with it, you will be." I lower my voice and say, "And after I just ate that delicious cunt of yours, I'd assume you'd want the same thing."

Her eyes widen as she looks over her shoulder. Stephan is now wearing earbuds, listening to music and cleaning the kitchen. "Pacey."

I chuckle. "He can't hear a damn thing." I smooth my hand over her thigh again, and she sucks in a subtle breath as I move my hand north. "And sorry to say, but I'm going to make sure I work my ass off to make you happy, to keep you happy, and to make sure you don't go anywhere." I move my hand up to her chin. "You're mine now, Winnie." When she doesn't say anything, I ask, "Does that scare you?"

"A little," she answers. "I don't want to disappoint you. I might be shiny and new now, but who knows what I'll be like two months from now?"

"Still fucking beautiful and taking my breath away, that's what you will be." I absolutely hate that Winnie doesn't see what an amazing woman she is. That she doubts that I'll still be interested in her. I'm the fucking lucky one that she's giving me the time of day. *How do I help her see that she has this all the wrong way around?* I was so scared I'd lost her before I left her room last night. I lean in and press a kiss to her lips. "Trust me when I say I'm invested, and I'll prove it to you."

"You're crazy." She shakes her head and turns to her waffles.

"Why?" I ask. "Because I know what I want?"

She side-eyes me. "Because I sucked your cock and now you're sporting heart eyes."

I throw my head back and laugh before closing the distance between us and kissing her on the cheek. "Babe, I was sporting heart eyes before your delectable mouth sucked my cock, you just didn't see them yet because you were still guarded. It wasn't until I nibbled on your clit that you finally lifted the veil and saw what was right in front of you—a man infatuated with you." I stand from the table and say, "I'm going to finish packing. Are your bags ready to go?"

She blinks a few times and then nods. "Yeah, they're by my door."

"I'll put them in Minnie. Is there anything you need before we leave?"

"I don't believe so." Her head tilts to the side as she studies me.

"What?" I ask.

She smiles and tugs on my shirt. "You're a good guy, Pacey Lawes."

"Remember that when I do something stupid, which most likely will happen."

She chuckles. "I'll plug it away for when that moment comes, because being a woman, I know it will come. Just a matter of time."

I place a chaste kiss on her lips and take my plate to Stephan, who gives me a nod. I head to my room to finish packing my suitcase. I'm not taking everything I brought with me, just a small bag, and if for some unpredictable reason I don't come back to the cabin, I'll have the boys pack up the rest for me, and I'll have one of the guys drive my car back to Vancouver.

As I finish packing my toiletries, there's a knock on my door. Before I can say "come in", the door opens and Holmes peeks his head in. "Can I come in?"

"Sure," I answer.

He shuts the door behind him and leans against it, crossing his arms over his chest.

When he doesn't say anything, I ask, "What's up, man?"

He looks toward the window as he says, "I wanted to make sure we're cool." He stuffs his hands in his pockets. "I don't regret my threat, because I'm glad that you're going to see Doc, but I also know it was overstepping. I don't want there to be any bad blood."

"Was I pissed when you said you'd tell Coach? Fuck yeah, I was, but I also understand where you're coming from, and I can't hold that against you, Holmes."

He wets his lips and keeps his eyes on the ground as he says, "I can't stop thinking about what I could've done differently with Holden. If I'd seen the signs earlier of his depression, if I'd looked for help, if I'd set aside my skates for a goddamn second and helped him, would he still be here?"

"Dude, you couldn't have controlled anything about that night, about Holden's behavior. That was on him."

"But I can't help but wonder." His eyes meet mine. "It's why I threw down the threat with you, because I knew that it would make you leave, make you get checked out. It was all I had left in my arsenal."

"You don't have to explain to me, Halsey," I say, seeing the weight of the world on his shoulders.

He toes the ground and quietly says, "You're my brother, Pacey." His eyes connect with mine. "I can't lose another."

"I know." Guilt consumes me that my actions would worry Holmes so much. "I'm going to get it sorted, I promise. I'm just scared, is all. I'm not sure what they're going to say, and I can't stop playing yet."

"But you're not one hundred percent. Maybe that fear is there for a reason. Maybe it's protecting you."

"It's hindering me." I step up to him and say, "Just like your fear of losing someone else is hindering your ability to get close to anyone besides us."

"There isn't enough room in my goddamn soul to worry about anyone else," Holmes says, his voice cracking. He drags his hand over his mouth as he avoids eye contact. "Look, I just wanted to make sure we're cool."

"You know we are. I don't hold grudges against my boys."

"Cool."

He pushes off the door and reaches for the handle when I say, "Hey, Halsey."

He looks over his shoulder. "Yeah?"

"You can't let your brother's death dictate your future. He wouldn't want that."

"If he cared about everyone in his life, he never would've driven that night." And with that, Holmes yanks open my door and vanishes into the hallway.

Sighing, I collapse on my bed. Fuck. Holmes needs some help, more than I expected. And, yeah, we might be enabling his reclusiveness, but we also don't know how to handle him either. We don't know how to help, because any time we talk to him about what happened, he becomes angry like he just did.

I drag my hand over my face.

One problem at a time. Once I figure out what's going on with my head, I'm going to pull the boys together and come up with a plan to help Holmes. We're not doctors or psychologists, but we have access to some of the best of both due to our jobs. And maybe it's time to utilize that to help a brother.

***

"MAKE sure he takes care of you," Hornsby says, giving Winnie a hug.

The boys are lined up in the driveway—including Holmes—and they're all saying bye to me and Winnie—but mainly Winnie, who they seem to care more about.

"I'll be sure to give him just as much shit as you would if he doesn't."

Hornsby laughs and squeezes her tight. "We've taught her well."

Posey steps up and opens his arms. Winnie gives him a hug and he says, "You were a welcome surprise to our little dick den. Next time, bring friends."

Winnie laughs hard, and so do I.

She pats him on the chest. "Katherine is available. I can hook you up."

"Is that the paranoid one?" Posey winces.

"Yes."

He shakes his head. "I have enough paranoia on my own, I don't need to feed into someone else's. But if you happen to have any other single friends, let me know. I think I'm ready to settle down."

"Lawes's sister is still single," Hornsby says with a wink.

I point my finger at him. "Off-fucking-limits and you know that."

Holmes keeps his distance and offers Winnie a wave. "Thanks for the book, really enjoying it."

It's awkward and uncomfortable watching him say goodbye, but Winnie handles it well. "You're welcome. I have some others you might like. I'll pull a list together for you."

"Sounds great." He steps back and then Taters takes a step forward.

He pulls Winnie into a hug and says, "Sorry I was such a dick to you at first. You're pretty cool."

Winnie squeezes him back. "Thank you for being the Hostess with the Mostest . . . attitude, Potato."

Taters laughs. "Someone had to put some challenge into the fairy tale you walked into. I don't mind being the villain."

She pats his cheek. "A gracious villain. But now that I know we can be friends, be prepared to be annoyed with me."

"Already am annoyed with you." He smirks. "Good luck, and give this guy hell."

"Oh, I will." She winks and then walks around to the driver's side of her car. Four days ago, I don't think Winnie would've felt that level of comfort around the boys. She'd seen us all as overgrown, potentially dangerous men when she first arrived. And yet, she's treating them like—like brothers now. *I like that. A lot.*

"Thank you for everything, guys. You really did save me. I couldn't have asked for a better group of guys to stumble across." Her eyes well up. "My mom would've been so jealous of me." They all laugh and then she waves to them. "Bye."

"Bye," the boys say in unison.

I exchange fist bumps with all of them. Taters reminds me to text them updates. Hornsby reminds me to stay hydrated— God knows for what reason. Posey gives me a bro hug and asks to be updated, as well. And Holmes—well, he gives me a nod and that's about it, but I know it's the best he can give right now. We had our talk; we know where we stand.

I open Winnie's car door and climb into the passenger side, only to fold up like an accordion, knees to my chest. The boys let out a roar of laughter as I struggle to find the lever to send the seat back. As I look back to give them the bird, I notice that every one of them has their phones out—probably videoing my humiliation. Assholes.

"Oh dear," Winnie says, laughing as well once she's sitting comfortably in her seat.

"Little help," I say.

Still laughing, she says, "The button is on the side of the seat. It's electronic."

My hand reaches to the side and I find it. I push back, and the seat slowly slides backward and then stops. My legs are still cramped. I glance at Winnie. "Is that how far it goes back?"

"Must be." Her hand covers her mouth as she laughs. "I didn't think about how big you are when we planned this out."

"We're taking my car." I start to get out, but Winnie grips my arm.

"How are we going to get Minnie back?"

I turn to the boys, who are all shaking their head. "None of you want to drive this back to Vancouver?"

"Hmm." Hornsby taps his chin. "Drive a comfortable Tesla back to Vancouver or a cramped Mini Cooper. Wow, what a tough decision." He waves at me. "Have a good trip."

I clutch my head. "You know, this cramped space is really hurting my head, I don't think it's good for me."

"Fuck off," Taters says while laughing. "Your head is fine, but nice try."

They all turn and go inside the house, leaving me with Winnie and her Mini Cooper.

Sighing, I say, "You're going to need to rethink your car choices." I shift and my shoulders bump into her. "And I hope you're okay with breaking the speed limit, because we're going to need to get to Vancouver fast."

She chuckles and puts her car in drive.

Chapter Twenty

WINNIE

"This is stupid, right? Like . . . this is a really stupid idea?" I ask, wringing my hands together. We're parked just around the corner from my uncle's house.

"It's not stupid," Pacey says, stretching his arm across the back of my seat. We haven't been in the car for more than twenty minutes and he's already incredibly uncomfortable. I feel bad for him. "This means something to your mom. Like you said, this trophy meant the world to her."

"It did. And she always said she wished she'd had it." I bite my bottom lip as I look out the window. "We didn't have a funeral for my mom. She wanted to be cremated and then turned into a tree. I thought that when I plant the tree, I could plant the trophy with her." I grip my head. "Wow, it really sounds crazy. I mean, what sane person decides to drive across North America to hopefully steal a fifty-year-old artifact from the house of an uncle they've never met?"

This is insane. If I was watching this play out for someone

else, I'd be thinking this is the most asinine thing I've ever heard of.

Pacey scratches the side of his jaw and a smile pulls at his lips. "It's kind of ridiculous, not going to lie about that. It's something you'd see play out in some low-budget comedy."

"Exactly. Something a D-list actor would star in. You'd watch it and think *this is dumb*, but then have a chuckle here and there, making your time spent watching it worthwhile. Is that what my life has come to, Pacey? A low-budget comedy that gains a few laughs?"

"I think temporarily it has, but it's going to be worth it, right? Because if you didn't go through with it, if we turned around right now, you'd regret it. Wouldn't you?"

I nod. "I would. I would always wonder if I would've been able to gain justice for my mom."

"Which is exactly why we're going to do this." He nudges my shoulder. "Told you, you would need me on this trip."

"You were right." I lean against his shoulder and rest my head in his strength. His hand falls to my hair and he gently runs his fingers through it.

"Do you have an action plan?"

"What do you mean?" I ask.

"Do you plan on just going in there, spotting the trophy, stealing it, and running? Or do you plan on having a conversation with him first?"

"Oh, huh. I didn't really think about it." I lift off Pacey's shoulder. "Oh God, I'm so not prepared for this." *What if he has me arrested? He'll know who I am. What was I thinking?*

Pacey links his hand with mine and brings my knuckles to his lips for a soft kiss. "It'll be okay. We'll work it out right now. Do you want to talk to him? To your uncle? Anything you have to say to him?"

I shake my head. "Not really. He's obviously a dick, but I have no desire to dive into that. Because—what's the point? It's not as if I want a relationship with this man."

"Okay, so this mission is purely an extraction. Grab the trophy and run."

"Yes."

"In and out."

"Yes." Excitement blooms inside me. "He'll have no idea what's happening." An idea comes to mind. "How about this—I ring the doorbell, they invite me in once I explain who I am, and then while I take a seat in their living room, I spot the trophy and then ask for a drink. While they're fetching a drink, I grab the trophy and then flee the premises." In all seriousness, I turn to Pacey and say, "I'm going to need you to drive the getaway car."

"You realize I'm going to look like a clown in a toy car, putt-putting the hell out of here?"

I laugh and say, "I do, but I think it's going to be necessary."

"You know I'm here for you, babe. Whatever you need."

I lean over the console, grip his cheek, and place a chaste kiss on his lips. "I appreciate you so much."

"And I appreciate your lips and your gratefulness. I wouldn't mind more affection."

Rolling my eyes, I push at him, but he grabs my hand and pulls me in close so his lips can capture mine. Instead of pulling away, I fall into his embrace and allow myself to revel in this small moment where I'm not alone. Where I have this strong, protective man at my side, helping me, guiding me.

"Mmm," I say when I lift away from him. "You're such a good kisser."

He wiggles his eyebrows. "What else am I good at?"

"Hopefully driving fast when you see me fleeing the crime scene."

He chuckles, the sound hearty and addicting. "I got you, babe. Your uncle will have no idea what happened."

"That's what I like to hear. We should exchange seats now, so you can pull up and wait in the car."

"Probably a good idea." He opens the door and unfolds out

of the car. He stretches his long body and then rounds the car toward me. We meet by the back and he slaps my ass as I pass him.

"Hey," I say, grabbing my butt. "Watch it, man."

"Oh, sorry." He holds his hands up. "I forgot spanking gets your sweet pussy wet."

My cheeks flame. "Pacey." My voice comes out embarrassed.

"Aww, Winnie, you shy talking about the things that turn you on?"

He gets into the car and adjusts the seat so his legs can barely fit. I slide into my seat as well. "I don't mind talking about the things that turn me on, I just don't want to talk about it in front of a house with a white picket fence and a sign that says 'Grandma Crossing' in the front yard."

Pacey looks out the window and then laughs. "Maybe we just spiced up the grandma's life. You never know."

"If that's the case, should I shout out the window that you like your balls played with while your cock is pulsing against my throat?"

Pacey's hands grip the steering wheel as he looks out the window. "Go ahead, make me hard, see where that gets you when it comes to fleeing the scene. My cock is going to bump into this steering wheel, making it impossible to get out of here properly."

"Your dick is big, Pacey, but not that big."

His eyes shoot to mine and I chuckle. "You don't think my dick could get in the way of this steering wheel?"

"That wasn't a challenge. Please don't attempt to get yourself hard outside my uncle's house to prove a point."

"I don't know . . . I think getting my dick up while you're stealing a trophy adds to the low-budget comedy we're starring in here. Everyone loves a good slapstick comedy, and that can easily be accomplished with a hard dick." He pretends to swat at his crotch. "Oh fuck, I'm too hard to steer. This dick is in the way."

I stare at him, wondering where this side of Pacey is coming from. "Starting to get more comfortable with me?" I ask and motion to him with one of my fingers. "Is that why you're acting like a fool?"

"You know, once you lick someone's asshole, there's no more holding back."

My eyes widen. "Pacey Lawes. Do not talk about that. Oh my God."

He laughs out loud. "I'm guessing you don't want to talk about how much you liked it either."

I pinch the bridge of my nose. "You realize the more you tease me, the more your chances of peeling off my clothes later are diminishing."

He chuckles lightly and leans in to press a soft kiss to my neck. "I'm confident in my ability to make it up to you." He kisses me again, and damn it, he's right. Just those two kisses and I'm already inclined to forget everything he said. "Shall we get on with this heist?"

"Yes." I place my hands in my lap. "I'm ready."

Pacey starts the car and puts it in drive. "Where am I going?"

I glance down at the directions I wrote out and say, "Turn right at Oak, and then it should be the third house on the right."

"Okay." He eases the car down the road. "Before you go in there, I want you to know that I think you're completely insane." He glances at me. "But you're also a fucking badass, and I think your mom would be really proud of you."

"Thank you." I reach over and grab his hand, looking for comfort. "Just be ready, because if I hightail it out of there, yelling and screaming, we have to fly."

"I got you, babe."

I GLANCE BACK AT PACEY, who's sitting in the car, encouraging me with a smile as he dips his head so I can see him. With a deep breath, I turn toward the front door of a modest, blue bungalow and without giving it a second thought, I ring the doorbell. Luckily, my uncle RJ hasn't graduated to the twenty-first century yet and doesn't have a camera in his door-bell. That bodes well for when I bolt out the door.

Also noted, no screen door to have to fumble with.

No stairs either.

Or cracks in the sidewalk.

It should be—*should be* being the key phrase—an easy exit.

Footsteps approach, and a bout of nerves hits me all at once, triggering my flight instincts. My feet itch to sprint back to the car, but then I think about my mom and what she would do. If she were in this situation, taking on this adventure, she'd see it through. Despite how awful she was at things, she always saw them through.

That's exactly what I'm going to do. I'm going to see it through.

The door opens and a man in his fifties stands on the other side. With long, gray hair and a matching beard, he looks as though he belongs in the mountains. The only resemblance to my mom is his blue eyes, the same color eyes I have as well.

He adjusts the glasses that rest on the tip of his nose and says, "No solicitors."

He goes to shut the door, but before panic can consume me, I put my hand out and stop the door, surprising him. "I'm not a solicitor," I say quickly. "I'm your niece, Winnie Berlin."

His eyes widen in shock before they soften. "Winnie." He clears his throat. "I, uh, I wasn't expecting you."

Duh.

"I know. I was in the area and thought I would just pop on by." I twist my hands together. "Think I could come in, maybe chat?"

He looks behind him and then back at me. "Uh, of course."

He steps to the side and lets me into the house. I stand in the entryway, not wanting to go too far in without an invitation, but I allow my eyes to roam the quaint dwelling. The entryway connects with the living room, which opens up to the kitchen and a small dining room off to the right. The house is stark white, sparsely decorated with a few pictures of mountains, and the furniture looks at least twenty years old. It isn't very homey nor welcoming.

When Uncle RJ shuts the door and moves into the living room, he scratches the back of his head, his brow knitted in confusion. "I'm sorry, I'm a little taken aback because I never in a million years expected you to show up at my door."

"Yeah, I know, because you didn't get along with my mom." There's a bout of confidence that surges through me the minute I step into this house and I don't know if it's from Pacey pumping me up, or if it's because I seem to have the upper hand over Uncle RJ, but I seem to be bypassing my filter.

"It wasn't, uh . . ." He clears his throat. "It wasn't that I didn't get along with her. She just made a choice I didn't agree with."

"Marrying my dad, I know. She told me. But she told me that she still sent you pictures and updates about me. That was kind of her, don't you think?"

"It was." He shakes his head. "I'm sorry. Why, uh, why are you here?"

"I was in the area. Thought I would say hello."

"Right, right." He nods and looks at the ground. My eyes wander to the fireplace and I spot the trophy. My mouth waters at the sight of it. "Marisol—my . . . new wife—she's not here right now."

"Oh, that's okay. It's just nice to see family, you know, after I lost both my mom and my dad."

He nods some more and then clears his throat. "Yes . . . uh, can I get you a drink?"

"That would be delightful," I say, happy that I didn't have to ask. Because, even from being here for just a few moments, I know one thing for sure—this guy doesn't deserve my time or energy. I considered talking with him, but there doesn't seem to be any sort of remorse in his eyes for how he treated my mom. Therefore, the heist is on.

He turns toward the kitchen and says, "Make yourself at home."

Don't mind if I do . . .

I step into the living room, and he says, "Oh, please take off your shoes. The carpets are new."

Crap. That's a bump in the road to my escape.

I kick off my flats and step into the living room. Now is the time, as he moves into the kitchen to get me something to drink. Run up to the trophy, grab it, and run.

It's right there.

Unpolished.

Old.

Something I'm surprised he still has, but then again, it seems as though he doesn't get rid of anything besides the carpet. That he can part with. I'm almost nervous to see what the old carpet looked like in order for him to get rid of it.

I move toward the fireplace and scan the trophy. Yup, that's the one.

I move in closer.

Closer.

"Do you want water or milk?" Uncle RJ asks, peeking his head in, startling me just as I was about to reach for the trophy.

"Both," I answer.

"Both?" he asks, confused.

"Uh, yeah. I like them to be mixed together." The thought of milk and water mixed together actually makes bile form in the back of my throat, but I'm not as quick on my feet as I would've hoped. *What host only has milk or water to offer a guest?*

"Oh, that's an, uh, an interesting combination."

"Tastes like breastmilk, watered down like that."

What on earth am I saying? Breastmilk? Why? Why is that what just came out of my mouth?

I'm nervous. I'm so close to capturing the trophy, but I'm choking, I can feel it. My muscles are seizing on me, my legs are turning into stone.

"Breastmilk?" Uncle RJ says.

"Yeah, nothing like a good cup of breastmilk," I say, wringing my hands together. I literally want to die from that answer.

"That's confusing," he says from the kitchen.

"Don't judge until you try it." I edge closer so I'm right next to the trophy. "Have any pickled beets? They go swimmingly with the breastmilk."

"I don't."

"Triscuits?" I move my hand up to the mantle.

"No, unfortunately."

"Corn nuts? Ranch flavor? Delectable with breastmilk."

"No, I don't."

I bring my hand to the base of the trophy, and I swear the moment I touch it the sun shines through the window and angels sing.

The Holy Grail.

It's in my grasp. I pull it off the mantle and hold it out as I stare down at the prized possession about which my mom would speak so fondly. This . . . trophy.

This piece of plastic.

It was so important to her.

Her crowning achievement.

"The best I can offer you is tortilla chips with your faux breastmilk." He steps into the living room with a tray of watered-down milk and a bowl of tortilla chips. "What are you doing with that?"

I look him in the eyes, then back down at the trophy. Then back at him.

Now or never.

I clutch the trophy to my chest like a football, hold my hand out for blocking, shout, "See you, sucker!" and I charge out of the living room, like a bull straight out of the gate, bypassing my shoes and going right for the door.

"Hey, come back," Uncle RJ shouts.

But I don't look back. I throw the door open and yell, "Start the car. Start the car!" Feeling like an absolute banshee, I sprint down the walkway in my bare feet, swatting at overgrown branches that attempt to stop me.

"Come back here," Uncle RJ says, hot on my tail.

"Never!" I shout back. "Vengeance will be mine."

I leap over a bush, push through the dried-out grass—it's called watering your lawn, Uncle RJ—and sprint to the car just as Pacey pops the door open for me.

"Thief. Thief," Uncle RJ shouts, his voice closing in.

"Drink my breastmilk, you old hag," I yell as I hop into the car and slam the door. Smacking the dashboard, I yell, "Go, go, go. Jesus, Mary, and Joseph, GO!"

Pacey slams down on the gas pedal and we fly down the street. I sink into the seat and catch my breath.

After we twist and turn through the neighborhood and reach the center of town, Pacey slows down and pulls off into a parking lot, in the far back, where he parks Minnie and then turns toward me, a huge smile on his face.

"Holy shit, Winnie. You actually did it."

I unravel the trophy from my clutches and hold it out. "I did it." A tear comes to my eye as I stare down at the trophy. "I freaking did it."

Pacey wraps his arm around my shoulder and brings me closer to his chest as he presses a kiss to my head. "This was the weirdest, craziest, probably stupidest thing I've ever been a part of, but holy shit, Winnie, you did it. I'm proud of you."

"Thank you." Silently, I stare down at the trophy and think, *This was for you, Mom.*

"Not to push this along, but not knowing your Uncle RJ, I

think it would be in our best interest to leave the area, just in case, you know, he calls the cops or something."

"Probably best."

"Care if I drive?" he asks.

"Not at all. My adrenaline is far too high for me to think straight and get us out of here at the moment."

"I prefer to drive, so this works." Pacey puts the car in drive and then places his hand on my thigh. "You're a badass, Winnie."

"I am," I say with pride. I place my hand on top of his. "Thank you for coming along with me. I know this is insane, but I appreciate you being here. I don't think I would've been able to do it alone."

"You would have, but I fear what you might have done when you got to the car. By the way, a few questions."

"Shoot away." I relax into my seat, letting my heart rate return to a normal rate.

"Your shoes. You realize you don't have any on."

"He made me take them off. It was a sacrifice I was willing to make."

"The sign of a true robber, willing to sacrifice footwear." I chuckle and he says, "And the whole 'drink my breastmilk' thing, care to comment on that?"

I smile to myself and rest my head on his shoulder. "Can't be sure."

———

"HOW ARE YOU DOING?" I ask Pacey after he extracts himself from Minnie and stretches against his shut door.

"I'm going to need a massage after this," he answers. He lifts his arms above his head and moves side to side. I catch his shirt lifting up, showing off the waistband of his boxer briefs and his taut stomach. "And from the lustful look in your eyes, you're in the running to give me that massage." He grabs my hand and laces our fingers together.

"I was staring. Sorry, hard not to."

"I know the feeling," he says, and places a kiss on the top of my head. "Three more hours and we're in Vancouver. Think you can make it?"

"I know I can," I say. "The question is—can you?"

"The only thing getting me through those three hours is knowing there's a jacuzzi tub in my apartment, calling my name." He leans in and whispers, "And it's big enough for two."

Chills run down my spine as he opens the restaurant door for me. We found a simple pizza joint to stop at for dinner. It looks like a dive bar, so I'm hoping we can get in and get out.

"How do you know it's big enough for two?" I ask.

There's a sign at the entrance that directs us to seat ourselves, so we find a table at the back where we'll be secluded and take a seat.

"Because that's what the listing said when I bought the place. Haven't tested it out with two people . . . yet." He pulls my chair out for me and helps me sit.

When he takes a seat across from me, I ask, "So you take baths on your own?"

"Fuck yeah," he answers. "When you train like I do, baths are your best friends, and Epsom salts."

I don't know why I find that so funny, but I do. A laugh escapes me and he quirks an eyebrow.

"Do you find it funny that I take baths?"

"I do."

"Why?" He opens the menu and asks, "You good with sharing a pepperoni pizza?"

I nod and then say, "I'm just picturing this six-foot-two—"

"Three," he corrects. "Six-foot-three."

"Sorry—six-foot-three, intimidating man stepping into a dainty tub and listening to Enya while soaking away."

He sets the menu down and says, "I listen to Harry Styles, not Enya, and I'm not intimidating."

I laugh out loud. "Not with a Harry Styles playlist."

"Hey, he has good music. I have no shame."

The waitress stops over, and Pacey orders for us—two Diet Cokes and a medium pepperoni pizza. He goes completely undetected, the waitress barely even lifts up her head to look at us, so this was the perfect place to go. I like having these quiet moments with Pacey. Just me and him. I don't know what the future has in store for us, or if these moments will be short-lived, but I'm going to soak it up as much as I can.

I reach across the table and move my finger over the top of his hand. "So, what you're saying is that when we get to your place, we're going to take a bath together?"

His eyes darken as he says, "That . . . and other things."

My lips quirk up. "Like what? Show me around?"

"Yeah, I'll show you around." He leans back in his chair and rubs his hand over his jaw. "I'll show you around my place by fucking you in every room."

Good God.

I wasn't aware men actually talk like this in real life, but here I am, sitting across from a dirty, dirty man. A sexy one, but dirty for sure. And I love it.

"That's quite the invitation. Are you sure you're not going to get sick of me?"

He lets out a sarcastic laugh and leans forward, placing both of his arms on the table. "Babe, after that blow job you gave me in the shower, pretty sure I'm addicted." I feel my cheeks blush as he takes my hand. "But putting the physical aspect to the side, after seeing you sprint out of your uncle's house with a trophy, shoeless, and telling him to suck your breastmilk, I'm pretty sure I won't ever be able to let you go."

I laugh and shake my head. "You should be scared, because who does that? Honestly, there's crazy in me and that should terrify you."

"Oddly, it excites me. Just tells me you're up for anything." He grips my hand and says, "Want to know something?"

"Always," I answer.

"I think, from the outside looking in, someone hearing you going to your uncle's house who you've never met only to take something your mom always wanted, might see it as juvenile, maybe even insane. But that's not how I see it at all."

"How do you see it?" I ask.

"I see someone who's brave. Someone who loves with all their heart. And someone who wants to make a wrong a right. Was it done in grand style? No, but it still was pretty awesome to watch. It's sexy, being with a confident woman like you, someone who's so courageous they don't care what other people think." He kisses the back of my hand. "I feel lucky that you stumbled into my life."

"Pacey," I say softly as tears form in my eyes. "I'm the lucky one."

He smirks. "Maybe we're both lucky. How about that?"

"I think that's a good compromise."

He winks and then smooths his thumb over the back of my knuckles. "Where do you plan on burying her with the trophy?"

"There's this hike we used to do when she needed some fresh air. It was an easy trail through Discovery Park, but it was one of her favorite things to do when she was up for it. We'd take our time, breathe in the fresh air, and admire all the beautiful foliage along the trail. Mom said she'd want her tree to be planted there." I glance up at Pacey. "Not sure really if you're allowed to plant anything there, but you know me—I'm a rebel now."

He chuckles. "That you are, babe. When do you plan on doing this?"

"When I get back to Seattle. I have what I need now."

He nods slowly. "Think I can go with you?"

Surprised, I ask, "You want to help me plant my mom's tree?"

"I want to be there for you, Winnie. I know you'll have Katherine and Max, but if you're okay with it, if you wouldn't mind me coming along, I'd just really like to be there supporting you."

Wow. Just wow. He's serious. He's respectful, kind, generous, and I think he actually wants to be mine. I blink a few times and then say, "Pacey, I don't know what to say. I'm—"

"Sorry, Winnie. I overstepped. I understand if you don't want me there, baby. That's fine."

"No, you don't understand. Pacey, that's one of the most thoughtful things anyone has ever offered me. Yes, you're right, Katherine and Max would be there by my side if I asked them to be. But I'm honestly so blown away by your offer. And yes, please. I'd really love that, if you come with me."

He lifts my hand to his lips and kisses my knuckles. I love how affectionate he is. *Something I also lost when Mom passed.*

"So, this"—I motion between us—"this is real, then? Like . . . really real."

"Yeah. It's fucking real."

And it feels like it. It feels real. More real than anything I had with Josh, and even though that was a three-year relationship, the connection I share with Pacey is more intense. There's pride in what he feels for me, and he treats me like my mom always wished for me to be treated. And as I sit here, staring at him across the table, I know, deep in my bones, my mom would not only approve of Pacey, she'd encourage me to put away my worry and live in the moment with him.

Even though this is all so quick, so terrifying, that's what I plan on doing. Living in the moment.

MAX: *Wait, you're going to stay with Pacey in Vancouver? For how long?*

We're an hour away from Pacey's apartment and he's quietly jamming to some Harry Styles, which makes me chuckle.

Apparently, "Golden" is his jam. He also confessed to enjoying some One Direction songs, but he's very particular about which ones. Not all of them, just the ones where Harry is front and center—which I tried to explain is almost all of them, but that didn't go over well.

Winnie: *Not sure. God, Max, I really like him. Is that crazy?*

Katherine: *Yes, it is crazy. What's even crazier is that you're driving across Canada with this man, and that you actually let him drive your car.*

Max: *You shouldn't have texted to group chat. What were you thinking?*

Winnie: *That maybe Katherine has taken a valium since we spoke.*

Max: *I wish.*

Katherine: *The irresponsibility and total disregard for personal safety during this entire trip is frankly disturbing. I'm not sure I can stand to be your friend anymore if you continue to make these kinds of decisions.*

Max: *She doesn't mean that. She was telling me this morning how much she misses you.*

Katherine: *I miss her muffins.*

Max: *She's putting on a brave face.*

I snort, and Pacey glances at me. "Everything okay over there?"

"Yes, sorry, was just texting with Max and Katherine. Max is obviously thrilled about my decision to stay in Vancouver for a few days—"

"More than a few days, but we won't argue about that right now."

I smile inwardly and continue, "But Katherine is putting up a front about wanting to divorce me as a friend for not looking out for my personal safety."

"She's the one who thought you were going to be abducted, right?" Pacey asks, his hand slipping from the steering wheel and back to my thigh. There's something about a man driving with one hand on the steering wheel and the other on his girl's thigh that's so . . . ugh, sexy. I can't take it.

I also can't take the way the lights from other cars flash through the windows, highlighting Pacey's carved jaw, or the way the muscles in his forearm flex when he's driving, or the scruff on his jaw from not shaving for a few days.

It makes my pulse pick up and my need for him reach crazy levels of begging. I've never experienced such lust. I'm insatiable and have no idea how that happened—*well, that's a lie because Pacey is a god in bed, clearly*—nor that I was capable of that level of sexual attraction. My libido is through the roof. How is this me?

"Yes, Katherine is the crazy one."

"Think she'll ever like me?"

"Want me to ask her?" I hold up my phone.

"Yeah, I do."

Smiling, I type away on my phone.

Winnie: *Pacey wants to know if you'll ever like him.*

My phone beeps with a response right away. "That was quick," Pacey says.

"It was from Max. He says—" I pause and laugh. "God, he's such a horndog. He says, 'Tell Pacey I liked him from day one and I'll like him even more if he follows through on the whole Ian Rivers thing.'"

"Text me a picture of Max. I'll send it over to Ian."

"No," I say with a shake to my head. "No way am I doing that. Max will ruin any sort of relationship you have with Ian."

"Ahh, I don't know. It sounds as if there could be something there."

"What does Ian even look like?" I ask as I pull up my browser and type in his name. The first picture that comes up takes my breath away. "Oh my God."

"He's gay," Pacey's quick to say.

"I know." I chuckle. "But, oh my God, I can understand Max's obsession. Ian has that whole dark, bad-boy look about him. Super hot."

"You're going to give me a complex."

I lean into him and press a kiss to his cheek. "Ian is hot, but you take my breath away," I whisper.

His hand grips my thigh more tightly and he rumbles with a low growl. "I like it when you stroke my ego like that."

"I'm sure you do." I laugh as my phone buzzes with a text. "Oh, Katherine wrote back."

"Give it to me. What does she have to say?"

"'How could I possibly like someone when I've only experienced their character secondhand? If I intend on making any sort of judgment on the man, I need to spend at least a combined total of thirty-six hours with him, making my own assessment, and even at that, he'll need to earn my trust through action.'"

Pacey chuckles. "Man, tough crowd. But since I seem to be falling for her best friend"—he looks at me—"then I'll put in the time."

I swallow hard.

Falling for . . .

Did he just say that?

I believe he did, and he said it so effortlessly. I'm pretty sure if I ever made such a confession, I would be stumbling over my words.

Not Pacey. He's so confident, as if he knows exactly why we met. I'm still trying to figure that out, but I know I'm not going to take our time together for granted.

My phone buzzes again. "Another text," I say, going to read it out loud. But then I see that it's not from Max or Katherine, but rather Josh.

Panic washes over me and a thin veil of sweat breaks out on the back of my neck. "Did Katherine up her restrictions?" Pacey asks with a laugh.

But I don't answer.

Instead, in a great panic, I read Josh's text silently to myself.

Josh: *Haven't heard from you in a bit. I know my recent texts have caught you off guard, but I really want a chance to explain things to you.*

Please, Winnie. I truly believe letting you go was one of the biggest mistakes I ever made. Let me prove it to you.

"Hey," Pacey says, squeezing my leg. "Everything okay?"

"What? Oh, yes, sorry." I awkwardly laugh. "Max just being an idiot." The lie feels dirty rolling off my tongue, and I'm disappointed in myself for lying to Pacey. But I know if I told Pacey it was a text from Josh, he wouldn't react well. He's made it quite clear how he feels about Josh.

"You sure? You look like you're a little shocked."

I smile and set my phone down while I rest my head on his shoulder. "Max can be outrageous. He never ceases to surprise me," I say as I stare out at the road, my throat growing tight.

Let me prove it to you.

Those six words make my stomach roll, because even though I don't want anything to do with Josh, not after how he treated me, after how much my mom despised him, I'm still curious. Curious what he has to say.

Chapter Twenty-One

PACEY

"Thank you for always carrying my bag," Winnie says as we ride the elevator up to my apartment. "It's really sweet."

"My mom taught me well," I say before I lean down and press a kiss to her lips.

Toward the end of our trip, Winnie went silent on me. She claims it was something Max said, but I don't fully believe that. There was a dramatic shift in her mood. I've seen her talk to Max before, and I doubt there's anything he could say that would make her shift that drastically. Or even Katherine, for that matter.

I think she got some news and she's not willing to share it just yet.

Yeah, that might fucking sting, knowing that she's not entirely comfortable in sharing things with me, but that's probably going to take time. I also wonder if that's to do with the fact that I'm from a largish family—hockey brothers included—

and she's used to only having her three people in her life. *It's going to take patience, Lawes.*

The elevator doors open and I nod toward the left. "Down here."

"You mean you don't own the entire floor?" she asks with humor.

"There are three apartments on this floor. Sorry to disappoint. But it's pricey as shit because of the views of the Burrard Inlet." I stop at my door and fish my keycard from my pocket.

"Keycard? That's fancy."

"It's kind of annoying, actually. Have to pull the damn thing out of my wallet every time." I unlock the door and hold it open for her. She steps inside and I switch on the lights for her.

"Oh, wow," she says as she looks straight ahead, to the entire expanse of windows with a view of the inlet. As she walks toward them, I set our bags down in the entryway and shut the door behind me. "Pacey, this is gorgeous."

"Best apartment in the building," I say, walking up behind her. "Great views, and I have a private rooftop. It might be a little smaller than some of my teammates' places, but I don't need anything big. I just want the views."

"It's spectacular." She turns toward me and takes in the rest of the apartment. "Did you decorate yourself?"

"My mom helped a bit," I admit. "She was adamant about me having a grown-up place, but I'm not much of a color guy so we compromised with blacks and whites and some *pops of green.*"

"It's extremely sophisticated." She smiles at me. "Makes you even hotter."

I chuckle and pull her into my grasp by her hips. "Is that so?"

She nods. "The white walls, white furniture, black fixtures, and black cabinets—I don't know, gives you a whole different vibe than I was expecting."

"A good one, I hope."

"A very good one." Her hands fall to my lower back. "Are you still stiff?"

"I'm always stiff around you."

She rolls her eyes. "I'm not referring to your penis, Pacey."

I laugh.

"But I know your back was bothering you in the car." She rubs it with her knuckles. "Are you okay?"

"I'd be better in a bathtub, with you naked, between my legs."

Her eyes turn soft as she says, "Then show me the way."

Fuck—this woman. She's going to be the death of me, I know it. So willing to do anything.

I take her hand and lead her to my bedroom, where she makes a few comments about the size of my bed, the comfortable linens, and the surprising throw pillows. I take her into my master bathroom and head straight to the tub, turning the taps to start the water.

"Lavender good with you?" I ask her.

"As in bath salts?"

"Yeah. That good?"

Her smile is so fucking sexy. "Yeah, that's perfect."

I sprinkle lavender bath salts in with the filling water, pull a few towels from my cabinet and set them to the side, and then stream some soft pop music from my phone to the Bluetooth speakers. When I turn to face her, she's stripped out of her dress, leaving her in a red bra and matching red thong.

"Fuck, warn a guy," I say, taking a step back to take her all in.

I'm a fucking sucker when it comes to Winnie's body. Curvy, sexy, and so goddamn beautiful. She really checks all my boxes when it comes to a girl, and I think she's starting to realize that as she gains more confidence around me.

I reach up and pull off my shirt, dragging it over my head and letting it fall to the ground. Her eyes roam my chest and then fall to my shorts as I undo them. Just her perusal with those sultry eyes has me hard. Keeping my eyes on her, I strip out of my shorts and push my boxer briefs down, revealing my hard-on.

Her lips quirk to the side as her eyes meet mine. She reaches behind her, undoes her bra, and allows it to fall. She brings her hands to her tits, which are more than a handful for me, and massages them a few times, making my dick jolt up. Still with that grin, she pushes her thong to the ground and steps toward me. She smooths her hand up my chest to my nipple, and slowly plays with it.

"I love that you're already hard," she whispers.

Fuck . . . that feels good. Who knew I liked my nipples played with?

"I told you, I'm always stiff around you." I suck in a sharp breath when she pinches my nipple. "Fuck, baby. That feels really good."

"I also like that you enjoy your nipples being played with. It's hot." And when I think she's going to reach up and kiss me, she moves past me to the full tub. She bends over, giving me an amazing view of that slappable ass, and she turns off the water. "Am I getting in first, or are you?"

"Me," I say, my voice cracking from the thought of being inside her body.

I slide past her, my hand dragging along her back as I get in the tub. I settle in and then hold out my hand to help her in. She settles between my legs, my erection pressing against her back, and then she leans against my chest. Her hands fall to my thighs and her head rests against my shoulder. I move my hands to around her waist and then I kiss her neck.

"Comfortable?" I ask her.

"Very," she coos as she smooths her hands up and down my thighs.

"Good," I say as I bring my hands to her breasts. She expels a long moan and sinks deeper against me as I carefully tweak her nipples between my fingers.

"Mmm, Pacey, you make me feel so good."

"Same, babe," I say into her ear before I kiss her neck again. She leans to the side, giving me better access, and I take advantage of it, sucking and nipping at her skin.

"You're going to leave marks," she says casually.

"Would it be bad if I claimed you?" I ask.

"No. I prefer it."

That pulls a growl from me as I pinch her nipples and then suck the bottom of her neck into my mouth.

"Yes," she moans as one of her hands falls to the back of my neck, keeping me in place. "Pacey, you make me so hot, so crazed, like if I don't have you right now, I might combust."

"You feel how hard my cock is?" I ask her. "You make me want to come before I'm ready."

"Touch me," she moans.

"I am." I squeeze her nipple and she hisses between her teeth.

"My clit," she breathes heavily. "Touch my clit."

"Ah, my girl is ready for my fingers."

"So ready, Pacey. I'm pulsing down there. I need relief."

"Then you'll have to stay that way." I move my mouth to her shoulder and continue to work her breasts, pinching, lightly pulling, rolling, teasing her.

"Pacey." She shifts against me, my cock painfully hard as her back rubs against it. "I'm going to touch myself."

I bite down on her shoulder and she groans.

"Don't even fucking think about it. Hands on my knees."

"But don't you want to watch me make myself come?"

Tempting, it's really fucking tempting.

"I do, but I prefer to watch your hand bring you to completion, your legs spread wide for me. I can't see anything under the water."

I roll her nipples, applying more pressure.

"Fuck, Pacey." She wiggles against me. "I want your dick."

Can't fucking hear that enough.

"And I want that tight cunt, but not yet," I whisper as I run my tongue up her neck and to the spot behind her ear. She shivers under my touch and grips my knees more tightly as I ease the pressure on her nipples and now just lightly stroke them.

"You're torturing me," she complains, unable to be still.

"I'm pleasuring you." I kiss back down her neck, nibbling along her skin, marking her as mine.

"I'm so close, Pacey."

"I know." I move one hand down toward her pussy. Her stomach hollows out, and when I reach the spot just below her belly button, her breasts arch and her pelvis seeks out my hand.

"Please."

"Patience, baby," I say, bringing my hand back up to circle my index finger around her breasts.

"I'm going to come. Just from your touch, I'm going to come."

"Then come." I grab her earlobe with my teeth and growl into her ear as her backside rubs against my cock again.

With my index finger and thumb, I grip her left nipple and playfully roll it, playing with the hard nub, loving how responsive she is as I move my hand back down. Her breathing picks up, her chest pushes against my hand, and she exposes the beautiful column of her neck as she begs, "Fuck me with your fingers, Pacey."

"Greedy tonight." I press my fingers just above her slit and then slide them back up. A feral moan flies out of her mouth right before she turns in my embrace. Her eyes are wild, her neck is red from my scruff and mouth, and her breasts are marred from my teasing.

Fucking gorgeous.

"I need your cock." She grips me and I nearly buckle over from relief. "You need me just as much as I need you."

"I need you more," I admit, falling victim to her hands as she strokes me under the water.

"I want you bare. I'm on birth control. Do you trust me?"

"Fuck . . . yes," I say, not even having to think about it. Even if she weren't on birth control, I'm not sure I'd be able to hold back.

"How do you . . . how do you want me?" she asks, all of a sudden acting awkward.

"Climb on top of me."

She shakes her head. "That position—"

"I'm not *him*," I say, silencing her with two fingers to her lips. "Trust me, I want to see you ride my cock. I need to see you take control. I want to look you in the eyes when you take me bare and then come all over my cock."

She bites down on the corner of her lip as she considers her options.

"I'll help you," I say, when I see how apprehensive she is. I grip her hips and say, "Sit up on your knees and move over my cock." She takes a second to respond, but when she does, I grow even more excited. "Now reach down and grip my cock between your legs." She does and then presses me against her entrance. "Fuck, yes, baby, right there. Now when you're ready, slowly sink on top of me. But keep those gorgeous eyes on me."

With a deep breath, she moves my erection right to her entrance, and then she slowly starts to sink down. The second I penetrate her with nothing between us, my eyes slowly start to roll to the back of my head.

Focus, look at her. Watch her.

When my eyes find hers, I see her take a huge breath as she sinks lower, her mouth drops open in awe, and then she grips my shoulders as she goes lower and lower.

"Pacey, this is . . . I'm so full."

"You're not done, Winnie. Keep going."

She bites her bottom lip. "I don't think I can."

"Look at me," I demand. When her eyes meet mine, I say, "Put your hands behind your back and lace your fingers together." When she gives me a confused look, I add, "Now."

At the snap of my voice, she laces her hands behind her back, and her chest puffs out right at my eye level. Perfect. I smooth my hand around her back, bring her closer, and then hold her in place as my mouth descends on her breast. I suck one of her nipples between my lips and pull on it gently. She moans and slides farther down my cock.

"That's it, baby. Relax." I play with her other breast until she relaxes some more and takes me all the way in. I know the minute I'm at the hilt, because her mouth falls open and her head falls back.

"Oh, God," she moans as her hips grind down on mine. "You hit me in a spot that no one ever has." She grinds down again, making little circles. "Yes, Pacey."

"Look at me."

She opens her eyes, but keeps her hands behind her back.

"That's it. Now, lift up and then slam back down." She does as I say, and when she pushes back down on my cock, a loud moan falls past my lips from how fucking good it feels.

My hands fall to her hips and I guide her, repeating the process over and over again. Her hands unlock and they land on my shoulders, where she holds on for balance.

"Pacey, this is too good. Oh my God, it feels too good."

"You're perfect for me," I say, unable to control what comes out of my mouth as her pussy tightens with spasms. "Fuck, you're so goddamn hot. So tight."

Her pace picks up, her tits bounce in front of my face, and her increasing moans light up the bathroom. "Yes, yes . . . yes," she pants.

"Faster, baby." I help pump her up and down. My balls grow tight as all the pressure in my body builds at the base of my cock. I'm ready to fucking explode, but I need her with me. "Where are you?"

"Fu-uck, Pacey," she yells as her pussy clenches around my length, and she climaxes ferociously.

"Jesus, fuck," I say. My cock swells and I come, hard, my

head falling forward as I still and hold on, my orgasm twitching deep inside of her. "Mother . . . fucker," I say, catching my breath.

Winnie loops her arms around me and then collapses against my chest, my dick still fully inside her, just where I fucking like it.

I rub my hand up and down her back as we both catch our breath. "Are you okay?" I ask her.

She nods against me but doesn't say a word.

"You sure?" I ask as I feel a hitch in her breathing.

She lifts up from my shoulder, revealing a tear streaking down her cheek. "I'm sorry," she says. "This is so stupid. I shouldn't be crying after sex. It's so embarrassing."

"It's not," I say. "Why are you crying?" When she tries to look away, I force her chin back so her eyes match up with mine.

"It's terrifying, how much you make me feel . . . how much I feel for you."

I rub my thumb over her cheek and smile up at her. "That's not something to cry about, baby. It's something to celebrate."

"These are happy tears," she says. "You make me feel like a queen, Pacey. I've never felt that way with someone before. I'm still trying to make sense of it all."

"No need to make sense of it," I say. "Just accept it. You are a queen. You're my fucking queen." No woman has ever made me feel this way, either. I've never said *those* words to anyone before. Never wanted to. But Winnie? I'm enraptured. I'm lost in her. *I'm hers. And only hers.* I bring her lips to mine and I allow myself to get lost as she sits on top of me.

—

"ARE YOU NERVOUS ABOUT TOMORROW?" Winnie asks.

Her back is to my chest, she's wearing one of my shirts and I'm wearing boxer briefs, and I'm spooning the hell out of this girl.

"A little," I answer honestly.

"What are you nervous about?"

I snuggle her in closer, finding comfort from the simplicity of having her in my arms.

"General nerves. If they find something, what would that mean?"

She's silent for a second and then says, "Would you tell me about it? About the day you were injured? Or is it too much of a sensitive topic for you? I understand if you don't want to talk about it."

I sigh and kiss her head. "I don't mind talking about it with you." She turns in my arms and faces me. Cutely, she tucks her hands under her pillow and waits for me to start talking. But I can't help but notice just how breathtaking she is. "You're beautiful," I say.

"Thank you," she answers.

Sighing, I think back to the day. "We were playing Oakland. It was a preseason game and I was feeling a little off. I couldn't tell you why, but for some reason, my head wasn't fully in the game. Oakland broke out and when defense was catching up, I blinked and lost sight of the puck. Next thing I know, I glance to my right and that was it. I was out cold after that. Next thing I remember, I'm in the training room with our doctor hovering over me, checking me out. When I was finally able to process what was happening, and realize I was in the hospital, they told me I had a severe concussion and that I would be out for a few weeks."

"Did someone stay with you that night?" she asks, her voice incredibly concerned.

"Taters did. He woke me up every hour to make sure I was okay. He can be a dick, but he's also one of the best guys I know."

"I can see that." Her finger glides over my chest. "How long did it take for the migraines to kick in?"

"Immediately," I answer. "But I didn't say anything."

"What?" she asks. "Why wouldn't you say anything?"

"I was at home, fucking pissed, sitting back and watching my team do all the work. I wanted to be back on the ice and I wasn't about to prolong that."

"Pacey, when did *they* find out about the migraines?"

"Two months in, after I didn't show up for a warm-up. I couldn't get out of my car after driving to the stadium. I still don't know how I made it there, how I drove through traffic while my head was hurting that bad."

"Did they do tests then?"

I shake my head. "No. I downplayed it a bit, said it's something I've experienced before but always tried to work through it. After my sixth missed game, they caught on. I told them I would take care of it after the season, but I wanted to make it through the playoff run. I saw Doc before we left for Banff, told him even though I had some migraines, I was fine and feeling good."

"But you weren't, were you?"

"At the time, yeah, I was fine. But the boys know me better and called me out. Hence why we're here and not in Banff, where I want to be."

"I'm glad they called you out."

"I'm glad you're here with me," I say, pressing a kiss to her lips.

"I think you're lucky you have *brothers* that care that much about you. You're an elite sportsman and have to be at peak condition. You're paid to be, so you have to put your health first. But you're also their friend and someone they obviously care about. Not everyone has that." She's right. And I ought to be more grateful.

"Yeah, you're right. Thank you for saying that . . . much more gently than said *brothers.*" She laughs.

"I was thinking—while you're getting checked out tomorrow, I'd make you dinner," she says while her fingers dance across my chest.

"Yeah? What were you thinking about making?"

"Any requests?"

I think about it. "Besides your pussy for dessert?"

"Oh my God, Pacey." I chuckle as she pushes at me. "Are you always such a horny man?"

"Never. You've done this to me."

She shakes her head and asks, "Seriously, anything you don't like? Anything you're allergic to?"

"I like pretty much anything and I'm sure I'll like whatever you make me." I press a kiss to her nose.

"Do you need me to drop you off?" she asks. "How do you plan on getting to your appointment since your car is in Banff?"

"Got a driver coming to get me tomorrow. No worries there."

"Oh, you're fancy," she playfully says and then asks, "It's not going to be weird, you know, me staying at your place for a few days, cooking you dinner? That doesn't freak you out?"

"Why would it freak me out?"

"Most guys would be freaked out," she says. "I think you're a different breed, because we're moving pretty fast, and I want to make sure you know you have an out. Don't think you need to—"

I press my fingers to her lips. "I'm going to stop you right there. Stop associating me with other men you've known. If I didn't want you here, I wouldn't have asked you to come back here. Things are moving fast because I want them to move fast, because I feel strongly about us. Okay?"

She nods as I reach out and tap the side of her head.

"Are you letting that sink in? Because I don't want to have to keep validating my decisions. I don't make choices just for the hell of it. Everything I do is for a reason. Understood?"

"Yes . . . Daddy."

My eyebrows nearly shoot to my hairline as a laugh erupts out of me. "Excuse me?"

She laughs too. "You heard me . . . Daddy."

Laughing some more, I push her to her back and move her shirt up her body, exposing her breasts. Her legs spread without me having to ask and she sinks against the mattress. "You realize I'm about to own your body, right?"

"That's what I was hoping for," she says with a glint in her eyes.

Hell, when she looks at me like that, I'm a goddamn goner.

━━━

TATERS: *From the lack of text messaging, I'm going to assume you made it to Vancouver last night, but instead of letting your friends know you were okay, you "showed" Winnie around the apartment.*

Hornsby: *They totally fucked.*

Posey: *What did you have for dinner?*

Taters: *That's what you're concerned about? His dinner?*

Posey: *[shrug emoji] It was a road trip. Didn't know if they got something we haven't tried yet.*

Hornsby: *I'm guessing he ate something else for dinner last night . . .*

Lawes: *Yes, we arrived in Vancouver last night. On my way to see Doc now. We had pizza at a dive bar. And yeah . . . I "showed" her around. And that's all I'll say on that matter.*

Taters: *Good.*

Hornsby: *Not to distract from seeing Doc, but . . . admit it, she's the best you've ever had.*

Posey: *I could see that for him.*

Taters: *Why would you assume that?*

Hornsby: *Did you see the way he looked at her? Dude is fucking sunk when it comes to this girl.*

Posey: **whispers* I think he's falling in love.*

Taters: *^^Are you insane? It's way too soon for that. Right? Lawes, are you falling in love?*

Hornsby: **taps watch* Waiting for an answer.*

Posey: *Would love an update on that status of your heart. Does she hold it in her dainty hands?*

Holmes: *Interested too.*

Taters: *Not you, Holmes. There's no fucking way.*

Lawes: *Easily, hands down, the best I've ever had. She makes me come so hard I black out every time Don't ask me again, I don't share details. And am I falling in love? Yup. Hard not to with this girl. She's had it tough, yet she's so real. Kind. She's genuine and supportive of me, not just me as a hockey player. She listens. Didn't know anyone like that existed, really. So, yeah. I'm falling hard. Now I need to figure out how to keep her.*

Hornsby: *Called it.*

Posey: *My nipples got hard reading that.*

Holmes: *Congrats, dude.*

Taters: *Umm . . . this is serious? You're really falling for her?*

Hornsby: *Are you not paying attention? He's already fallen.*

Posey: *On their way to the altar.*

Taters: *Whoa, don't get ahead of yourself.*

Hornsby: *Wait, important question. Who'll be your best man?*

Posey: *Ooh, great question. ^^^ Inquiring minds want to know.*

Holmes: *Bet I know who it is.*

Taters: *Not that I want to get involved in this ridiculous scenario, but . . . who is it?*

Hornsby: *Holmes, who's your guess?*

Posey: *It's me. Obviously. I'm the most chill with him.*

Taters: *We were roommates in our early days.*

Hornsby: *I've helped him put on his socks many times in the locker room.*

Holmes: *Best man = me.*

Taters: *^^ HA!*

Hornsby: *Laughable.*

Posey: *Not to be a dick but . . . fat chance.*

Taters: *Lawes, fucking jump in here. An answer would be great.*

Lawes: *Not that I'm getting married any time soon, but if I had to pick—hands down, no question, it would be Holmes.*

Hornsby: *BullSHIT!*

Taters: *What the absolute fuck?*

Posey: *Malarky!*

Holmes: *Told you.*

Taters: *I need an explanation.*

Posey: ^^^ *Please note the hostility.*

Hornsby: ^^^ *Don't listen to him. He's in the kitchen and I heard his outraged roar from the pool.*

Taters: *Posey is having a conniption over here. He threw his water bottle at Stephan.*

Posey: *They're fucking liars because they know I'm your number two.*

Holmes: ^^^ *Facts.*

Hornsby: *Go back to your GD book, Holmes.*

Taters: *Still waiting on an explanation.*

Lawes: *Not that I owe anyone an explanation, but Holmes doesn't give me shit about anything. He goes with the flow, does what he's told, and doesn't interject his asinine opinion.*

Taters: *Umm, am I the only one who remembers that Holmes was the one who dropped the Coach card?*

Hornsby: *That is, in fact, true.*

Posey: **Holds hands up* I didn't want to be the one who pointed it out.*

Holmes: *I speak up when it matters.*

Lawes: *Another reason why he'd make a good best man. Also . . . thanks for the distraction, you assholes. I appreciate it.*

Posey: *Does that mean we're all best men?*

Hornsby: *Valid question.*

Lawes: *We can talk about it when the time comes.*

Taters: *Which means, boys, there's still time to impact the decision on the best man role.*

Hornsby: *You weren't even a fan of a soon-to-be marriage.*

Taters: *Now that I know it's a competition for best man status . . . it's on. Also, keep us updated on what Doc says.*

Posey: *We're here for you.*

Hornsby: *Whatever happens, we got you.*

Holmes: *Good luck, man.*

⊐

"DO you think I'm going to have to hang up my skates?" I ask as I sit down in Doc's office.

He moves his hand over his mouth and leans back in his chair.

The last few hours have been hell. I've been through a gauntlet of exams, and I'm not only physically exhausted, but I'm mentally drained. So many goddamn questions, so many times that I worried something serious could be wrong. Now that it's all over and I'm sitting across from Doc, I want to know —what the fuck is going on?

"If I had a straight answer, I'd give it to you, Pacey." He pulls his leg up and crosses it over the opposite knee. "Do I wish we had done this earlier in the season? Yeah, I do. I think if we'd got to the root of the problem, we'd have been able to attack it sooner. Now given your migraines, I'm worried we might have exacerbated the injury."

"Yes, but I told you the last one wasn't as bad."

"Which is a good sign, but that doesn't mean this is getting better."

"So what now?" I ask, fear creeping up the back of my neck.

"Dr. Flannery, a neurologist, will examine the MRI and CT-scan results, looking for any abnormalities and soft tissue injuries." He looks off to the side and says, "We really won't know any more until those results come in."

"And?"

He rests his hand on his desk. "When or if we get there, I will let you know." His inability to look me in the eyes worries me.

"You're not telling me something."

He glances up.

"Just fucking say it or else I'm going to lose my shit."

He folds his hands on his desk and levels with me. "If there's a brain bleed or nerve fiber damage, Pacey, this past season was most likely your last."

My hands turn into angry fists as I tightly grip the armrests.

"I know that's not what you want to hear, but I figured I need to at least prepare you."

I shake my head, completely in denial. "This was not my last season."

"Pacey."

"It wasn't," I yell, slamming my fist down. "It fucking wasn't."

Slowly he leans back and nods. "Let's just take this one day at a time. Until then, try to relax."

Yeah, easy to say coming from someone who isn't about to lose everything they ever fucking worked for.

But instead of putting up a fight, I have the urge to get the hell out of here, so I nod solemnly. "And you're not going to tell Coach?"

I met Doc in his personal office today, rather than at the arena. I did that on purpose, because I didn't want to raise any red flags. It might be the off-season but word still travels.

"It's my duty as the team doctor to report anything I find out about a player. For now, though, I won't submit my report until I know the facts."

"Doc—"

"I can't lie, Pacey. This is my job too."

I lean back in my chair. "Fuck."

"I know this isn't what you want to hear, Pacey, but nothing good will come from worrying. What you can do is start a headache diary. I want you to note what you eat, what exercise you do and for how long, what other factors affected your behavior prior to each migraine. Also, what they're like. Write a description of each incident of visual disturbances or unusual sensations, including when they occurred, how long they lasted and what triggered them.

"If we can see a pattern of what precedes your migraines,

we can see if they're exercise related, diet, or even stress-related. The neurologist will need that too, so if you could try and note anything you can recall from the last few migraines you've suffered, we'll have more to give him. I'll provide him a list of vitamins or supplements you're taking, but if that changes, let me know to add that too. Stress doesn't help, so try to relax. Any of the boys come back with you? Maybe you can hang out with them tonight."

I shake my head. "They all stayed in Banff. I actually, uh"— I scratch the side of my cheek—"I came back with a girl."

"A girl?" Doc asks, surprised. "I don't think in all the years I've known you that you've ever shown interest in someone."

"Yeah, well, Winnie is different." My voice is terse, angry, as I speak about my girl, and it's all because of what's hanging above my head—possible forced retirement. "She's staying with me. Actually, she was heading to the market today to grab some food to make me dinner."

"Then I suggest you channel your energy there."

I stand from my chair. "You'll call me the minute you hear anything?"

"Yes." He offers me his hand and I give it a shake.

"Thank you."

I head out of his office and pull my phone from my pocket as I make my way to the car. I send a quick text to the boys.

Lawes: *All done with Doc. Waiting for scan results and to see the neurologist. Will keep you updated. He has no answers. I'll keep you updated.*

And then I send a text to Winnie.

Pacey: *Have to make a stop and then I'll be back home. I need to see your face.*

I pocket my phone and make my way through the building, taking a deep breath.

It'll be okay.

Everything will be okay.

Chapter Twenty-Two

WINNIE

I'm so behind. I should've been cooking already, but here I am, at the grocery store, wandering around as if I've never shopped before.

After Pacey left for his appointment, I cleaned up around the apartment, aka, picked up my discarded clothing, and then I spent way too much time looking up recipes. When I looked at the clock, it was an hour later and I still hadn't shopped for anything.

Giving up on making anything fancy, I decided to make tacos . . . well, because . . . I love tacos. But I decided on shrimp tacos with a lime sauce, homemade guacamole, and some microwave rice because I don't have much time. I hope he doesn't judge me.

"Where are the godforsaken tortillas?" I mutter to myself, rounding a corner and crashing right into another cart. I bounce back, bumping into a display of chips. I knock down a few bags, but thankfully don't take out the entire thing.

As I bend to pick up the chips, I hear, "Shit, sorry about that."

My back stiffens and my head whips to the side at the sound of that familiar voice.

I slowly stand, my eyes boring into, trained on, the man in front of me.

I swallow hard. "Josh?" I ask.

He also rises, and his eyes focus on me. "Winnie," he says breathlessly. "Wow, you're the last person I expected to run into."

Oh God, what are the chances of running into Josh, in Vancouver, at Pacey's neighborhood market?

Pretty slim.

But here I am, playing the statistics of the universe.

"Josh, wow, I, uh . . . I didn't know you live around here."

"Yeah, moved up here a few months ago for a job. Did you move up here too?" His voice has hope in it. Too much hope.

"No," I say. "I'm, uh, staying with my boy—I mean, my friend."

Josh's brows draw together. "Your boyfriend?"

Sweat breaks out on the back of my neck and, I don't know why I'm so nervous or why I'm hiding anything. Josh is the one who broke up with me. He's the one who left me when I needed him the most. He's the one who treated me like crap toward the end of our relationship. If anything, he should be the one squirming, not me.

Chest puffed out, I set one of the bags of chips back on the display and say, "Yes, my boyfriend."

"Oh, I wasn't sure you were—"

"Why would you? It's not as if we've kept in touch since you broke up with me," I say, bitterness rolling off my tongue.

"I deserve that." His shoulders slump as he says, "I'm guessing you never responded to my texts because of your boyfriend." I don't appreciate the tone of his voice when he says boyfriend. It's . . . snide. *What's up with that?*

"No, that's not it. I just didn't think it was appropriate. Nothing you could say would change my mind about how you treated me."

He nods. "I can understand that." His eyes lift to mine and the expression on his face nearly startles the breath right out of me. I've seen that expression before, but not on Josh . . . on someone else. "At least can I apologize?"

I'm so stunned, so taken aback by the look in his eyes, the set of his jaw, the shape of his nose. He almost—God, I must be losing it, because he almost looks like Pacey.

When I don't say anything, he takes that as an invitation to continue, right here in the middle of the grocery store. "I should've treated you better, Winnie. I was going through some things, and instead of talking to you about them, I pushed you away because I was scared it would be too much for you to handle. The only way I knew how to push you away was to be an asshole. So that's what I did."

I snap out of it for a brief second and ask, "What do you mean, I couldn't handle it? Handle what? As far as I knew, you were stressed because of your new job."

He shakes his head and quietly says, "I was stressed because they found a nodule on my prostate."

"What?" I nearly shout.

He pulls on the back of his neck. "I was diagnosed with prostate cancer. I found out just as your mom had to step away from the store. I thought it would be too much for you to handle and I didn't know what my status was when it came to survival. I thought it would be easier on you if I just . . . stepped aside."

"Easier?" I ask, my mind swirling. Josh had cancer. CANCER. And he didn't think he could tell me? "Josh, you made me feel like I was less of a woman than I am with the things you said. You emotionally battered me, telling me I gained weight, that you didn't think I was pretty anymore. You truly, from the depths of your soul, think that was better than telling me you had cancer?"

"Yes," he says right away. "At the time, I thought it would be better to sever all ties. I would rather you lose me by hating me, than lose me still loving me. At least hating me you could move on, which you have. What if something happened to me, and you lost both your mom and me? I'm not sure you would've—"

"But I lost you anyway," I nearly shout, my emotions getting the best of me. "I lost you anyway," I repeat. "And who the hell are you to tell me what I can or cannot handle?"

"You were barely surviving as it was," Josh shoots back. "I don't want to rub salt in the wound, but you were losing your-self, you were setting your life to the side, putting it on pause so you could help everyone else. And where are you now?" he asks, his voice growing stern. "What are you doing with your life, Winnie?"

"I—" I go to answer but my words fail me, because even though I hate him, I hate him so much—especially in this moment—he's right. He's right that I put everything on hold, that I would have dropped my entire life to not only help my mom—which I did—but to help him, as well. Because that's the person I am. I'm a helper, a lover, a caring individual. *And I shouldn't ever feel shamed because of that.*

Josh steps closer, and for some reason, I don't step away. "I know what I said to you and how I said it is inexcusable. At that moment, though, it was the only way I knew how to handle things. I see now that it was a huge mistake, because I could've used you going through treatments. I could've shared you with your mom, and I could've been there for you on my good days." He reaches out and takes my hand in his. "I was scared, and I reacted instead of sitting down and thinking about the best way to approach things. Losing you is my biggest regret."

"You—you broke me, Josh."

"I know." He takes a step even closer. Shoppers move around us, calls are made to the deli over the loudspeaker, and faint music plays in the background, but all of that fades into the background as I stare into Josh's eyes. "And I'll have to live with that forever, knowing the way I treated the love of my life." He lifts my chin up. "I'm sorry, Winnie. So fucking sorry, and if I could go back and change things, I would. Instead of telling you I didn't think you were pretty, I'd tell you that you're actually the most gorgeous woman I've ever laid eyes on. Instead of saying I wasn't attracted to you and that was the reason I couldn't . . . perform, I'd tell you I had prostate cancer and that was one of the side effects I was dealing with. And instead of telling you I didn't love you, I'd say you're the love of my life, and I can't imagine another minute knowing you're with someone else."

He can't be serious.

He can't possibly mean that.

Because if he does, if he speaks truthfully, then . . . then . . . everything I've ever known about the demise of my relationship with Josh are all falsehoods that hide the real truth. That he was sick, that he was hurting, that he didn't need distance. He'd actually needed someone holding his hand, just like I was holding my mom's hand. And yet, he chose to hurt the person he "loved" over and over again. For what? I truly cannot reconcile that he thought shattering me could be a good thing. And then he realized his error, but again, it was all about him. *I could've used you going through treatments*, he'd said.

"Josh, I . . . I don't know what to say." My mouth goes dry as I stare into his eyes.

"Then don't say anything," he answers. "I'm not looking for instant forgiveness. I know that's something I have to earn." He brings my hand up to his lips and presses a kiss to my knuckles. "I'm just grateful I was able to talk to you. To see you. And maybe in time, I'll gain your trust again. And after that, maybe I'll earn your forgiveness. Until then, I just hope to be able to text you on occasion, see how you're doing. Would that be okay?"

I'm so lost, so confused, so knocked down emotionally, that I nod.

"Thank you." He pulls me into a hug and presses a kiss to the top of my head. Before I can comment on his actions, he steps away and sticks his hands in his pockets. "I'm sorry I took up your shopping time." He glances at my cart and smiles. "Making tacos?"

"Yeah." I swallow hard, still in a daze.

"He's a lucky guy."

I smile, but don't say anything.

"Are you happy, here in Vancouver?"

I try to shake myself out of this haze. "Uh, I'm not here permanently, just . . . visiting."

"I take it you have to get back to work?" he asks.

"Not really. I don't have much to get back to. You were right —I did put my life on hold, and now I'm trying to figure out how to get it back on track."

He looks at me gently. "You're resilient, Winnie. There's no doubt in my mind that you'll figure out your next chapter in life, but if you ever need anyone to talk to, I'm here for you. I might not have been in the past, but I am now."

"Thank you," I say, my emotions starting to get the best of me. "Well, I should probably get back to finding the tortillas."

"You're close. If it wasn't for bumping into me, you'd have found them. Right around the corner."

"Great." I smile at him. "Okay, well . . ."

"Yeah." He steps to the side. "Thanks for the chat, Winnie. It was good seeing you."

"You too," I say as I move past him. His hand reaches out and his finger drags over my arm as I turn the corner. When I look over my shoulder, I catch that same look in his eyes, a familiar look, a look so eerily similar to one I've seen on Pacey that I feel bile rise in the back of my throat. *Why the heck would I think that?*

When I find the tortillas, I stare at them for a few moments, trying to collect my thoughts, but it feels impossible, because all I can think about is Josh's confession and how it makes me feel . . .

Like I wasn't adequate enough for him . . . all over again.

Chapter Twenty-Three

PACEY

I slam the door to my apartment and throw the flowers I got for Winnie onto the console table in my entryway.

I pause, hands on my hips, trying to catch my breath.

What the actual fuck?

I check my phone again to read Winnie's last text.

Winnie: *At the grocery store, running late. Be there soon.*

Yeah, I know exactly why she was fucking running late.

I storm to my fridge, whip open the door, and pull out a beer. I use the counter to knock off the top and then take a long pull from the bottle.

She was with fucking Josh.

I grip the bottle in my hand so goddamn tightly that I fear I'll snap the neck of the bottle right off.

Josh.

How in the actual fuck did that happen? Did she know he was in Vancouver? Is that why she came with me? So she could meet up with him the first chance she got?

Is that . . .

Holy fuck.

Is that who she's been texting?

I bring the beer to my lips again and chug. I chug the entire thing and then toss the bottle in my sink, where it shatters. I reach into my fridge and grab another. I pop off the top and pace the length of my kitchen as my mind spins with accusations, of scenarios, of the moment I caught them together—hugging, him kissing her on the goddamn head.

"Fuck," I shout as I grip the kitchen counter and gulp down some more of my beer. I pull my phone out and open up the text thread with Josh. Without thinking, I shoot him a text.

Pacey: *Stay the fuck away from her. Do you hear me? She's not fucking yours, stop trying to make it that way.*

There's no way she'd get back together with him. Right? The dude was a total asshole to her. He emotionally belittled her. He made her feel as if she wasn't good enough. He threw away the best thing to ever happen to him.

And yet, they were hugging.

My phone buzzes.

Josh: *Never thought I'd see the day when Pacey Lawes was jealous of me.*

Pacey: *I'm not fucking jealous. I just don't want you fucking with her head. You've done that enough.*

Josh: *I wouldn't do that to her.*

Pacey: *You already did.*

Josh: *If you'd actually let me fucking explain, maybe you'd have a better understanding.*

Ha . . . okay.

I tip my beer back, taking a giant gulp until it's completely done. I set the bottle on the counter this time and stare at the front door, waiting.

My headspace is foggy.

My fury over my future is terrifying me. I'm trying to act as if everything is okay, but in the back of my mind, I can feel it—

something *is* going to happen. Doc's going to call me into his office and deliver life-changing news. From his demeanor, I could fucking feel it.

Pair that with Winnie, standing there with Josh, as if they never skipped a beat. Watching her from afar, falling into his embrace, allowing him to touch her like I touch her.

I've never felt more . . . betrayed.

She's mine.

And I thought I had forever.

Pacey: *Just stay the fuck away. Got it?*

I reach into the fridge again, grabbing another beer. This one I open with my actual bottle opener, taking a small sip just as my front door opens. Winnie shuffles in, carrying two reusable bags, one in each hand. Her eyes immediately take in the tossed flowers splayed out of their packaging. She turns her head to find me, fuming in the kitchen.

"Pacey," she says, her voice startled. "Is everything okay?"

I push off the counter and back up until I hit the other side of the kitchen. I lean against that counter and bring the beer to my lips as I keep my eyes on her.

"Pacey?" she questions as she brings the groceries to the kitchen. She sets them on the counter and then turns toward me. "What's going on? Did you hear from the doctor?"

I take another sip of my beer, lick the residue off my lips, and then casually ask, "How was the grocery store?"

If it weren't for her eyes widening only slightly, I wouldn't have noticed any difference in her composure.

"It was—it was fine. Confusing. Not used to where they placed things." Her brow knits together and she comes up to me. She rests her hand on my chest. "Pacey, what's going on? You're heart—wow, it's racing."

I take a long pull from my beer this time. "What did you have trouble finding in the grocery store?"

She gives me a confused look. "Uh, the tortillas. Why aren't you answering me?"

I push away from her and say, "Just trying to understand why it took you so long, at the grocery store."

She wrings her hands together, a telltale sign of her nerves kicking in. "Are you hungry? Is that what this is about? Because I can quickly—"

"I'm not fucking hungry, Winnie," I snap at her, causing her to take a step back in surprise. "I want to know why it took you so long at the grocery store."

"Wh-what's happening?" She scans the room. "I don't understand."

I tip back my beer, finish it off, and then set the empty bottle on the dining room table. "I'll tell you what's happening." I close the space between us and point to the flowers. "I went to the store to get you some goddamn flowers because . . . well, fuck, because I'm infatuated with you, and, to my shock, I catch you embracing another man."

Her eyes widen with guilt as her lip trembles.

"Pacey . . ."

"But not just any man. I catch you with Josh. Fucking Josh, Winnie." I get in her face. "Is that who you've been texting? Is that who put you in a weird mood yesterday? Were you planning on meeting up with him this entire time?"

"No," she says quickly. "I mean, yes, he was—he was the one I was texting—"

"Un-fucking-believable," I shout before walking away from her, hands in my hair. My back tenses, the muscles in my shoulders firing off. "You were texting Josh, the fuckhead who belittled you." I face her. "He made you doubt your beauty, your sex appeal, your compassionate heart. And you just go and let him back into your life?"

"I wasn't." She shakes her head.

"And what about me?" I ask. "Am I nothing to you?"

"No, you are, Pacey. You're—"

I pull at my hair, unable to calm myself down. "Do you know what it felt like to turn the corner and see you there, with *him*? But you weren't just with him. He was holding you. He was kissing you."

"On the head, Pacey."

"Doesn't matter," I shoot back. "He was still kissing you. Imagine how that made me fucking feel, seeing you with Josh."

"I can't——" She pauses. Her head tilts to the side and then she takes a step back. "Wait . . . how did you know that was Josh? I've never showed you a picture of him."

Fuck.

When I don't say anything, she takes a step forward and asks, "Pacey, how did you know that was Josh?"

My teeth roll over my bottom lip and I look away.

"Pacey . . ." Her voice grows tight. "How do you know him?"

Throwing my arms out to the side, I shout, "He's my half-brother, okay?"

"What?" she asks, her eyes wide with shock. "Your half-brother? Did you know——" I can see the wheels turning in her head as she puts the pieces together. "Have you known this whole time? Every time I spoke of him, every time I mentioned the damage he'd done, you knew he was your brother. Didn't you?"

What's the point of lying? There isn't any, so I answer, "Yeah, I fucking knew you belonged to him."

"I don't belong to anyone," she says, her tone angry.

"Bullshit," I shout, taking a step forward. "You belong to me. Not him."

Her eyes grow angry. "Is this some sick competition between you and your brother? Am I just some pawn in your game?"

"Don't flatter yourself," I say, before I can stop myself. *Fuck, I didn't mean that.* From her shocked and furious reaction, I know she's not happy with that response, either.

"I see." She pushes past me and heads to my bedroom.

Growling in frustration, I walk after her. She goes straight to her suitcase, tosses it on the bed, and then starts putting her things in it.

Because I'm a masochist and can't seem to stop myself, I ask, "Packing up to go see him?"

She stops and looks over her shoulder. "You're something else, Pacey." She shakes her head in disappointment. "Let me ask you this—how did you know I was talking about your half-brother?"

"I recognized you," I admit. "From my dad's visit. You were in the pictures he showed me. I thought you were fucking gorgeous and I had no idea how my dickhead of a half-brother landed a girl like you. He's not the kind of man who deserves someone like you."

"So, this *was* a competition for you. You have some sort of beef with your brother—"

"Don't disparage my feelings about my relationship with my half-brother. You have no idea the kind of pain he put my father through. Josh fucked up so many summers because he was a bitter asshole who blamed our dad, when he should've been blaming his mom. He made my dad's life hell, even though my dad tried to have a relationship with him."

She slowly nods. "So this"—she motions between us—"this is some attempt to get back at him, then. Like a 'ha ha, I got your girl.'"

"Does it matter?" I ask. "Does it really matter, Winnie? Because you're missing the point."

"And what's the point? I thought it was you deceiving me this entire time."

"Me not telling you about Josh being my half-brother has zero impact on us."

She points her finger at me. "That's where you're wrong. You deceived me. How could I possibly believe anything you've said to me is genuine? How do I know it wasn't all a ploy to get the upper hand over Josh?"

"If you can't tell that I'm fucking genuine, then we have bigger problems."

"You're right, we do have big problems," she snaps while pushing past me to the bathroom. She comes back out, arms full of her toiletries. "The fact that you'd even question my loyalty to you is insulting."

"Yeah? Then why did you keep your texts a secret?"

"I'm sorry, when did you become my master and I had to answer to you about everything in my life?"

"Don't be sarcastic, Winnie. I'm trying to have a goddamn conversation."

"No, you're trying to push your anger and blame onto me when I'm not the one who did anything wrong."

Arms wide again, my voice rises as I say, "He kissed you on the goddamn head. That's pretty damning. Tell me you wouldn't lose your shit if you saw a girl kiss me on my jaw like you do." When she doesn't answer, I say, "So don't tell me you did nothing wrong. You let him touch you. After all he did to you—"

"He told me he had cancer," she yells back. "Okay?"

My mouth closes up and I stand taller. Cancer?

Josh had cancer?

My mind connects the dots.

The apologies.

Wanting to reconnect.

Needing to talk.

That's what he was going to tell me, that he had cancer?

Well . . . fuck.

"That's why he pushed me away, because he didn't want to put that burden on me when my mom was dying. Did he go about it the wrong way? Completely, but at least he was in a roundabout way looking out for me. Given the possessive behavior I'm witnessing tonight, I'm going to guess you wouldn't have done the same."

My jaw tightens from the comparison. "You're right, I wouldn't have done the same, because no fucking circumstance in my life would ever push me to the limit of telling you that you aren't beautiful. That you aren't the sexiest and most precious person on this earth. That I could live without you. You'd never hear me utter those words, because they just aren't true."

"But you are willing to withhold information from me, and instead of listening to my side of the story, you jump to conclusions, painting me in a disgusting light." She tosses her clothes from the dresser in her suitcase and zips it up. When she sets the suitcase on the ground and starts to wheel it out of my bedroom, panic ensues.

"Then what the fuck happened?" I ask her.

She shakes her head. "You missed the opportunity to receive that explanation."

"If you're not going to explain, then what the hell am I supposed to do?"

As she gathers her purse, she says, "You were supposed to trust me, Pacey. You were supposed to have my back. You were supposed to be honest with me."

"How can I be honest with you when you aren't honest with me?"

"Because I didn't tell you Josh texted me? Maybe I didn't tell you because I knew you were already dealing with a lot, and the last thing you needed was that extra stress. I was looking out for you, Pacey. And just so you know, I didn't meet up with Josh. I happened to run into him at the grocery store by some mad coincidence. And, yeah, he hugged me, but I didn't hug him back and, the only reason I allowed it to happen was because I was so shellshocked by what he told me. I've known him for so long, so excuse me for taking a freaking second to process."

She hoists her purse over her shoulder and snags her keys from the console table in the entryway, right next to the flowers I got her.

"Despite what you might think, Pacey, my intentions have always been pure with you. You were the first guy I ever considered being with after Josh broke me. And piece by piece, I felt you put me back together. But now, it all feels like a lie. It feels like a joke. Like I'm a pawn."

"You were never a pawn, Winnie."

"How can I ever trust that?" She gives me a once-over. "How can I trust *you?*"

I don't know how to answer that. I can feel words on the tip of my tongue, but everything is rushing at me all at once. The beer is kicking in and my ability to process is slowing down.

"That's what I thought." She reaches for the knob and I quickly place my hand on the door, stopping her from leaving.

"So that's it?" I ask her. "You're just going to leave? You're giving up on this?"

She lets out a long sigh and then looks at me. "I kept myself in a relationship longer than I should have. I clung to his every word and desperately needed his validation. I feel myself slipping into that same frame of mind with you, but this time it's worse."

"I'm not fucking worse than Josh; don't you dare put me on that level."

She shakes her head. "That's not what I mean. It's worse because the feelings I have for you, Pacey, are much stronger. Josh cracked me, but you, Pacey, I know you could break me. And if you broke me, I wouldn't have anyone to help me pick up the pieces."

She pulls the door open and more panic erupts inside me. "You're giving up on us, just like that? One fight and you're done?"

"This isn't just a fight, Pacey. This is a situation of distrust unfolding. And without trust in each other, what do we have? After everything I've said to you, you should know how hard it is for me to trust a man's word."

"Fuck, Winnie. I'm sorry I didn't say anything about Josh. I didn't think it was important. And I lost my cool. I'm going through a lot right now and, fuck, I can't control what's coming out of my mouth."

"You're right, you are going through a lot, and it's probably best that we break things off before we get in too deep."

"Too late," I shout as she crosses the threshold of my apartment. "I'm already in too deep. I'm already falling. I'm already there, Winnie. You'll break me if you leave this apartment."

Her eyes connect with mine and in a cold, detached tone, she says, "You broke me first, Pacey."

And then she rolls her bag down the hallway of my apartment building.

"Fuck," I shout before slamming my door and dropping to the floor. I clutch my head, fingers tightly gripping my hair. I draw my knees to my chest, and I feel a dull throb erupt behind my eye. This is where I spend the rest of the night, trying to comprehend how I just blew my chance of the best possible future—*one with Winnie Berlin by my side.* Even maybe forever.

⸺

TATERS: *How you doing, man?*

Hornsby: *Just checking in.*

Posey: *Do you need me to order you some dinner? What does Winnie like?*

Holmes: *You good?*

Taters: *Yo, I know you're probably wrapped up in Winnie, but we just want to know how you are.*

Hornsby: *It would be cool if you texted us back.*

Posey: *I'm going to assume that's a no on the dinner?*

Holmes: *Dude, you need to respond.*

Hornsby: *Taters is going nuts.*

Posey: *I tried giving him some fudge and he rejected it. He's really concerned. We all are.*

Lawes: *Winnie left. I fucked up.*

Taters: *What the hell happened?*
Hornsby: *Shit, man. I'm sorry.*
Posey: *She went back home?*
Holmes: *. . . Hello?*

Chapter Twenty-Four

WINNIE

My suitcase rolls behind me, echoing with empty promises of what it was supposed to represent.

Adventure.

Excitement.

Closure.

But instead, it's a reminder of how I can't seem to get it together.

Stopping at the door of the townhome I share with Max and Katherine, I fish for my key in my purse. I dig my hand in, searching, just as the door opens, revealing dearest Katherine in a robe, her hair perched on the top of her head in a bun, and her glasses pushed against her face, a disapproving look in her eyes.

"Did you lose your key?" She crosses her arms.

"I can't seem to find it."

She tosses her arms in the air and says, "I'll be calling a locksmith. We need a whole new set now."

She walks away and I sigh as I roll my suitcase into the entryway and leave it there. "How did you even know I was home?"

"The Ring camera," she says while scanning me up and down. "You seem sad. Did something happen?"

"Who are you talking to?" Max says, coming down the stairs. When his eyes meet mine, he comes barreling down the rest of the stairs and pulls me into a huge hug.

His familiar arms wrap around me.

My emotions erupt.

And before I know it, my tears come crashing down as I bury my head in his chest.

"Oh shit, Winnie, what's going on?"

"She lost her key," Katherine says. "Trust me, I'm upset about it too, but I'll call the locksmith and we'll have this all sorted out." She pats my shoulder coldly.

"I don't think it's about her key, Katherine." Max walks me down the hall and into the living room, where we take a seat on the couch. His hand smooths over the back of my head and he asks, "What's going on? Is everything okay with Pacey?"

I shake my head.

"Told you it wasn't about the stupid key," Max sneers at Katherine.

"Well, I'd be devastated if I lost a key."

"Hence why you're still single," Max shoots back.

"From the looks of it, we're all single, so not sure how you're proving your point."

I lift up my head and look between my two friends with blurry eyes. "What's going on here?"

Max leans in. "She's driving me crazy. I didn't realize how much you acted as a buffer until you were gone."

Katherine motions her hand at Max. "He has no regard for my needs."

"For the tenth time, we are not buying a twelve-pack of tasers. No one in their right mind needs that many."

"You don't know that."

Max pinches his nose and takes a deep breath. When he's done, he looks at me and with soft eyes, he asks, "What happened with Pacey?"

"Broke things off," I answer, more tears streaming down my face as I recall what happened.

Pacey was right—the drive between Seattle and Vancouver really isn't that bad, but what made it almost unbearable was replaying our fight over and over in my head.

I lie back on the sofa and stare up at the plaster ceiling. "I ran into Josh."

"What?" Max nearly shouts.

"Oh my God, has he been following you? I know someone down at the police department. We can get a restraining order filled out in a snap." Katherine snaps her fingers.

I shake my head. "It was an insane coincidence. When I was in Banff, Josh contacted me—"

"Hold up. Why are we only hearing about this now?" Max asks. "This is shit you need to tell us when it happens."

"I felt weird about it. I didn't know what to say, honestly. He was telling me he made a mistake and he really needed to talk to me. Since I was with Pacey, I really didn't want to get involved with anything to do with Josh. Pacey already hated him so much. I ignored him, but then when I was getting groceries to make Pacey dinner, I ran into Josh. He just moved to Vancouver."

"Wow, the universe really wanted you to talk to him," Max says.

"He had cancer."

"What?" Katherine says this time. "Pacey or Josh?"

"Josh." I look at my friends. "That's why he treated me the way he did. He didn't want to 'put me through his illness' when I was already helping my mom. He didn't think it was fair, so he pushed me away."

"What a way to fucking do it," Max says, anger in his voice. "The prick made you miserable."

"He apologized for the way he went about it."

"Hold on." Max forces me to look him directly in the eyes. "Are you trying to tell us that you're getting back together with Josh? Is that why you're here, why things ended with Pacey? Because you're getting back together with Josh? I'm telling you right now, that would be the biggest mistake of your life. Yeah, Josh was okay, but he wasn't the guy for you. But the way you talked about Pacey, the confidence I saw emerging in you, the way you interacted with him, it was amazing, Win."

"Not that I agree with the way you met Pacey," Katherine says, "but I do believe what Max is saying is you have seemed happier."

"I'm not getting back with Josh. That ship has sailed. I can see now that he wasn't the guy for me, and I'm sure he'll find the perfect person for himself, but that person isn't me."

"So then, what happened with Pacey?" Max asks, confused.

I'm confused as well. I'm not exactly sure what happened.

"I got home and he was pissed. Livid, actually. When I asked him what was going on, he accused me of taking a long time at the store." *Or rather, testing me to see if I'd tell him the truth.*

"Controlling. You don't want to be with anyone who's controlling," Katherine says. "They're the ones who flip a switch one day, and then all of a sudden, you're tied up in the basement."

"Jesus Christ, Katherine," Max groans. "You think everyone is going to lock you in the basement. Get a grip." Max turns to me. "That's where you ran into Josh?"

I nod. "Yeah, and Pacey was getting me flowers before he came home, so he saw me. Josh was embracing me. When I got back to his place, he lost it. He asked why I was meeting up with Josh."

"Oof, yeah, that couldn't have gone over well in his head. I get where he's coming from. He's slightly possessive, from what you've told us. Seeing you with someone else set him off."

"That's not what broke things apart."

"What did?" Katherine asks.

"Pacey knew exactly who Josh was even though I never showed him a picture."

"Google stalking—I approve," Katherine says.

I shake my head. "No, he knows who Josh is because Josh is actually Pacey's half-brother."

"What?" Max shouts, leaping to his feet. He glances around the room and then back at me. "Am I in some weird soap opera and don't know it?"

"I wish," I say, leaning back against the couch cushion. "Pacey has known for a while and never said anything to me. It turned into this fight about if he was using me to get back at his brother for being a dick to their dad. To him asking if I was still into Josh. To . . . God knows what. We blew up at each other, and before I knew what was happening, I was packing my bag and leaving."

"Wow," Max says while dropping back down on the couch. "That's insane. Okay, two things. Firstly—didn't you say there was something familiar about Pacey that you couldn't put your finger on? And secondly—why did you just pack up and leave? Why not try to at least resolve this?"

I nod. "Yes, I did see something. His facial expressions—they were familiar. They don't look alike, but there are little looks and glances that are eerily similar." I take a deep breath and ask, "Why didn't I stay?" It's a good question. I know how short life is, and that Pacey is one of a kind. *But* . . . "I just felt betrayed. Like that's something Pacey should've told me."

"If you knew, would you still have wanted to be with him?" Max asks.

I purse my lips. "Probably not. I would've thought it was weird."

"And Pacey really likes you, right?"

"I thought he did," I say, thinking back to the awful things we said to each other.

"Maybe he wanted a chance at winning your heart before you judged him for being Josh's half-brother."

"I hate to admit it, but Max is making sense," Katherine says.

"That doesn't negate the way he treated me. I've never seen him like that before. He was out of control—"

"Did he hit you?" Katherine interjects, now sitting in a chair across from us.

"No." I shake my head. "He'd never do that. But he was set off, angry—"

"Didn't he get his tests done today? Maybe the results weren't good."

For the first time since I left Pacey's apartment, I remember that's exactly where he'd come from. From visiting with his doctor. *Oh shit.*

"Did you not ask him?" Max asks.

"I didn't have time to ask. The minute I got back to his apartment, he bombarded me with questions and accusations. I've no clue how his appointment went."

"That could be the reason he flew off the deep end."

"I think we all know I have a hard time controlling my emotions," Katherine says. "I'd most likely displace my anger onto you if I were in that situation."

I bite on my lower lip. "Do you think they were bad results?"

Max shrugs. "Won't know unless you ask him."

I consider it, but then something inside me tells me it doesn't feel right. None of this feels right. My life hasn't felt right in a while.

"It doesn't matter," I say.

"What do you mean *it doesn't matter*? You broke things off over this fight. If there was a reason, then you should talk about it."

I shake my head. "It doesn't matter, because I don't think it would've lasted. I mean, look at me. I'm a mess. Everything about my life is a mess. My ex-boyfriend is trying to get back together with me, the guy who—God, who I thought was my soulmate just broke me, and I have nowhere to be tomorrow, on a Monday, because I don't have a job. I have nothing." I shake my head again. "I don't have it together."

"You've been through a rough patch," Max says, taking my hand in his. "You're allowed to take a moment."

"I think that moment is over." I stand and retrieve my suitcase from the hallway before heading upstairs to my room.

Once I'm settled in my bedroom, I shut the door. Then I fall onto my bed and clutch my pillow to my face, crying into it.

Why did Pacey have to hide that information from me?

Why did I have to fall for him so hard and so fast?

And why do I feel as though everything around me is falling apart, but when I was with Pacey, it felt put together?

Why, for the first time since losing my mom, did I not feel so utterly alone?

And why do I feel as though I've made a terrible mistake?

Chapter Twenty-Five

PACEY

The blackout curtains are drawn, with only an inch of light cutting into my rather dark apartment.

There's an empty six-pack in front of me.

And I haven't bothered with a shower or a shirt today.

What's the point?

I've been waiting on the call from Doc all goddamn day. I've run through my fight with Winnie far too many times. And I haven't had anything to eat since yesterday. I'm so fucking miserable, that instead of entertaining the idea of turning on the TV, I've just sat in solitude instead. No noise, no distractions, just my toxic thoughts on how I could've handled things differently.

As I sit on the couch and stare into space, there's a knock at my door.

Desperate hope blooms in the pit of my stomach as I sit up and look to the entryway. Could I be the luckiest son of a bitch in the world and have my girl come back?

I peel myself off the couch and go to open my door.

All hope fades as I see the four faces smiling at me from the other side of the door.

"What the fuck are you doing here?" I ask.

"Couldn't let our man suffer alone," Hornsby says, grabbing me by the shoulder and giving it a squeeze as he walks into my apartment.

One by one, they give me a pat on the back or a squeeze to my shoulder and then roll their suitcases into my place. I hope they don't think they're all staying here.

"Love the dark and moody vibe you have going on here," Taters says, right before he tears the curtains open, letting the sun scorch me with its brightness.

"Look at that. The sun is having some vampire-melting vibes on our friend," Posey says as I cover my eyes.

"Does it smell in here?" Hornsby asks, sniffing.

"There's a definite stink," Taters agrees.

Holmes just walks past me with a sympathetic look and then takes a seat in one of the chairs in my living room while the other boys start airing out my apartment and cleaning up my bottles.

"Look, he's drinking light beer." Posey tsk-tsks. "If you're going to mend a broken heart with alcohol, you have to throw calories out the window."

"Have you eaten anything?" Hornsby asks.

"From the lack of plates in his sink, I'm going to say no," Taters announces. "Order some pizza. I'm starving."

"On it," Posey says, taking charge in the food department like always. He pulls his phone from his pants and heads down the hallway. He most likely has our favorite pizza place as one of his ICE contacts in his phone.

"I'm going to grab some real beer from the store around the corner," Taters says.

"And I'm going to snag some ice cream." Hornsby rubs his stomach. "I know we could all use some after that car ride and listening to Posey drone on endlessly about the chocolatier guy he likes following on Instagram."

Taters and Hornsby take off, leaving me alone with Holmes, who just placed my car keys on the kitchen bench. *So he drove my car?* Good. His brow crinkles as he looks up at me. He doesn't have to say anything, it's all in that look.

You okay, dude?

Sighing heavily, I walk over to the couch and take a seat. "I'm such a fuck-up."

"So you've said."

I roll my head to the side to look Holmes in the eyes. "I'm fucking scared about the test results. Doc didn't seem optimistic. And I drove away the one person who could take away that worry."

Holmes scratches the side of his jaw. "Yeah, that's a bad fucking day."

"Tell me about it."

━━━

PIZZA BOXES ARE SCATTERED across my living room, two gallons of ice cream—one rocky road, because Hornsby thought it was appropriate, and the other cookies 'n cream—are almost entirely consumed, spoons just resting in the boxes now, and there are empty beer bottles all around the coffee table—not the light kind.

Posey is lying across the floor, a throw pillow under his head as he clutches his stomach. Hornsby is sitting next to me, licking his ice cream spoon, and Taters is pacing the living room, while Holmes hasn't moved since he sat down.

"Did you really think Winnie would go behind your back to be with Josh? Seriously, dude?" Taters asks.

I drag my hand over my face. "No," I groan. "But I didn't trust Josh, I still don't."

"You say this as if you know him," Taters says.

Posey glances at me, giving me a knowing look. Sighing, I say, "I do know him. He's my half-brother."

All the boys, besides Posey, turn toward me. Hornsby is the first to say something. "Your half-brother? Are you fucking serious with that shit?"

"Yes," I say. "I thought I recognized Winnie. I couldn't place her at first, but when I did, it was like everything clicked. The guy, who was a dick to her, who made her second-guess everything about herself. That was Josh."

"Holy shit," Hornsby mutters.

"Did you talk to him about it?" Holmes asks.

"He's been trying to get in touch with me for a few weeks now. I think to tell me he had cancer. I don't know, I've ignored his attempts. But we did share a text thread where he called me out for being with Winnie. He must have seen a picture on social media or something. Who fucking knows, but I told him he had no right to even talk about her after what he had done. He didn't take it well, I guess in my mind, I thought he was trying to steal her back."

"Jesus Christ," Taters mutters. "That's the stupidest piece of crap I've ever heard. Have you seen the way the girl looks at you? Nothing is going to change that, especially some lame attempt at a grocery store—if that is even what he was doing, which I doubt that it was."

"I know," I groan. "Fuck. I was in a shit headspace yesterday and when I saw them together, I just saw black, and no matter what, there was no way of getting me out of that headspace. Not until I watched Winnie walk out the door. By then, it was too late."

"Never too late to chase after the girl," Posey says, his voice pained from how much food he scarfed down.

"He's right. Chasing after her would've been ideal," Hornsby says. "Could've been like a movie." He holds his arm out and says in a dramatic fashion, "No, don't go. I—I love you."

"You're an asshole," I say.

"No, he's got a point," Taters says. "Chasing after her would've been a very smart move."

"Ideal," Posey says.

"Well, I didn't. So let's drop it." I reach for another beer but Hornsby swats my hand away.

"You've had enough. Plus, beer isn't going to fix your problem. What you need is an action plan."

"What?" I ask, completely exhausted from having to recount everything from yesterday and listening to the boys berate me for being a dumbass. I knew they liked Winnie, but I didn't think they liked her this much.

"Wait." Posey lifts his finger in the air. "We first need to ask him—does he want the girl back? That's how this goes. I've seen it many times. Boy meets girl, boy falls for girl, boy is a jackass and loses girl, boy confides in bros and tells them what a jackass he is, then boy CONFESSES his need for girl, and boy creates action plan with bros to get girl back. We need the confession before we can move on."

"Beautiful point," Hornsby says, turning toward me now, his hand draping over the back of the couch. "Do you want Winnie back?"

"He'd be an idiot not to want her back," Taters says, surprising us all. When he feels all eyes on him, he casually shrugs. "I might have been a dick at first, but she grew on me. And I'm not an idiot, I could see how happy she made Lawes."

"You make my nipples hard," Hornsby says.

"I think that's just because you haven't gotten any for over a month," Taters says. "Longest drought since I've known you."

"Over a month? Really?" Posey asks. "Are you ill?"

"Can we bring it back to me, please?" I ask.

"That's right. Hornsby might be . . . well, horny, but that's nothing compared to the DEFCON 1 situation we have going on with Lawes," Taters says. "So, like Posey was asking, are we dealing with a situation where you want the girl back?"

There's no need to think about it. The past twenty-four hours have been absolute hell. Winnie is the kindest person I know. Her bravery, even after losing her mom, astounds me. I've relived so many of our moments over the last day —playing Jenga, our day in Banff, eating together in the loft, our hilarious drive from Banff to Vancouver—and even though we've only known each other such a short time, my heart knows her. My soul knows her. She's quirky but sweet. *She stole her mom's trophy back.* Her sharp wit makes me laugh, and her body . . . I miss curling into her body at night and then exploring it with my tongue. Her trust in me sexually blew my mind. But I miss her trust *in* me. I miss hearing her say my name and watching her eyes grow soft whenever she sees me. How I fucked all of that up just makes me angry.

I just miss her. So fucking much.

"Yeah, I want the girl back," I say. "I want her back desperately."

"That's what I like to hear." Posey fist-pumps the air. "Now, Hornsby, we can form a plan."

"This is where I excel." Hornsby rubs his hands together.

"How do you excel at this?" Taters asks. "You've never been in a relationship."

"Doesn't mean I don't know how to get a girl back. I've seen enough shows and movies." Hornsby turns toward me. "First things first—deal with whatever Doc has to say. There's no way you can make up with Winnie if your mind is completely fucked from whatever news he has for you."

"True." Posey pumps his fist from the ground.

"Secondly, you need to talk to Josh and clear the air with him. It's evident you hate the guy, but you need a clean slate." The thought of talking to Josh physically makes me feel ill. "Once we deal with that, then we go in softly."

"Why does that bring up an image of a flaccid penis?" Taters asks.

"I thought of the same thing," Posey says. "Too ashamed to say it, though."

"I don't mean go in with your penis." Hornsby rolls his eyes. "I mean, you have to slowly woo this girl. Let's be honest, she's been freaked out with how fast her feelings for you grew, so why not take the time—and yes, it might be painful—but take the time to woo her? To get to know her better, on a deeper level. To just . . . talk. Become her friend. And from there, then you swoop in."

Taters nods his head. "This is a good plan."

"How is that a good plan?" I ask. "I want her back right fucking now."

Hornsby grips my shoulder. "The best things are worth waiting for. Didn't you tell her she's worth the wait?" Why do these assholes remember everything I tell them? And why the hell do I tell them everything?

"Yes," I grit out.

"Then, prove it. If she's worth the wait, then she's worth the time. If she's worth the time, then you need to take it. Make the most of it. Don't come barging in like a goddamn alpha asshole demanding she goes out with you again. Befriend her, woo her, sweep her off her feet, and then when the time comes, you win her back."

"My nipples are hard thinking about the end result." Posey rubs his nipples.

"Oddly, mine are too." Taters brings his fingers to his chest. "I'm concerned."

I turn to Holmes, who has been silent this whole time, looking for his opinion. "My nipples aren't hard," he says, then adds, "but it's a good plan."

Damn it.

I was hoping for something much faster, something that gets my girl back in my arms by tomorrow, but as much as I hate to admit it, I think they're right. Winnie was always freaked out about how fast things happened, so why not slow it down? Why not give her a chance to take a breath and realize that it wasn't just a whirlwind, that this—what we have—is real, and I'm hoping it's forever.

Buzz. Buzz.

My eyes go to my phone on the coffee table. Doc's name comes across the screen.

Fuck.

I reach down and pick it up. "Hey, Doc," I answer. All the boys sit up and stare at me.

"Hey, Pacey. Do you think you can come into my office tonight?"

Fuck . . .

I swallow hard. "Yeah. I can come in."

⸺

"I WASN'T aware I would be graced by all of you," Doc says as he takes a seat at his desk.

The boys file in behind me. Hornsby and Taters both sit next to me, while Holmes and Posey stand behind.

Hornsby reaches out to hold my hand and I swat him away.

"No," I say.

"Seemed like the thing to do." Hornsby shrugs.

"Can I conclude that you're comfortable with the boys hearing what I have to say to you?" Doc asks.

I would prefer to be alone, but they won't let that happen. They've been attached to my side ever since they arrived. Plus, it might be good to have an extra set of ears—or four extra sets of ears—to hear whatever Doc has to say.

"Yeah, I'm good with them knowing."

"Very well." Doc lets out a deep sigh, folds his hands on his desk, and looks me in the eyes. "The scans all came back negative."

I expel a sigh of relief as the boys all clap it up.

"That's right, our boy is a healthy motherfucker," Taters says.

"Dude, settle down," I say, even though I feel the same juvenile urge to yell at the top of my lungs. "Does that mean no tumors or anything like that?"

"Correct," Doc says, "but we did notice something on the X-rays."

"Fuck." Posey punches Taters in the arm. "You celebrated too early, you fuck."

Taters rubs his arm as he looks at me, concerned.

From his desk, Doc pulls out a skeleton's head and sets it on the desk.

"Is he missing part of his cranium?" Hornsby asks.

"His jaw is inverted," Taters throws out.

"A loose fragment in his brain," Posey shouts.

"Can you not guess?" I ask. "Just fucking listen to what Doc has to say."

"Thank you," Doc says, the corner of his lips tilted up. "Have you ever heard anyone talk about the atlas? The first bone in your neck. You might have heard it referred to as C1 before."

I shake my head. "No."

"The atlas is ring-shaped and has the important task of supporting the head. It's also responsible for facilitating movement in the head and neck. When you nod, that's the atlas at work. It serves as a pivot, and it allows your head to move forward and backward." He points to the skeleton and shows us the bone. "Right here—you see how the general curve of your neck looks like a banana facing out?" We all nod together, the boys leaning a little closer for a lesson in bones. "This is what we'd call a healthy spine. Now, over the course of time, our spines have their fair share of wear and tear, getting out of line, flattening, and in your case, curving in the opposite direction." Doc cranks the neck of the skeleton in the opposite direction and we all groan from the sound.

"Oh Jesus, that made me nauseous," Posey says from behind me.

"This is what your neck looks like."

I study the skeleton.

"It's farther forward than it should be. This is what I was wondering about yesterday. I believe you'd already developed poor spinal health from being a professional athlete. It's common, especially with all the heavy lifting you do and lack of spinal care. But your injury we believe worsened the abnormality. You suffered whiplash from how you fell on the ice, and it did more damage than we expected. And when your atlas and neck are misaligned, this can cause the debilitating migraines."

"That makes sense," I say. "So, there's nothing seriously wrong with me?"

"This is still serious. If we don't treat the problem, then your pain will increase and your days on the ice will be shorter."

"But there's a plan to take care of it?" Taters asks. "We need this guy in front of the net."

Doc nods. "Yes, we have the best medical staff in the league, and I've spoken with our exercise physiologist and physiotherapist to start you on a treatment that stabilizes the muscles in your neck. They've devised a physical therapy routine with the aim to have you ready for next season, but it means staying here and going through physical therapy."

"If it'll get me ready for the season, I'll do anything."

"That's what I like to hear." He places a piece of paper in front of me. "We want to start you off with an ART therapist."

"Art therapist?" I ask. "How the hell is that going to help?"

"Painting can be very soothing," Posey offers.

Doc laughs. "Not that kind of ART therapist. I'm talking about active release technique. All the teams in the league are starting to hire them and the Agitators just brought one on staff."

"What do they do?" I ask.

"They work on individual pain zones by releasing the

tension in the muscles while moving your body. It's extremely successful and there have been great results worldwide. We're going to start loosening the ligaments and muscles in your neck first so we can make the proper adjustments, then we're going to pair that with chiropractic work and physical therapy to strengthen you the proper way. We're very confident you'll no longer experience migraines and be feeling brand new by the beginning of the season."

"That's what we like to hear," Hornsby says while patting me on the back. "Our boy is going to be on fire this fall."

Relieved, I ask, "When can I get started?"

"Tomorrow. We'll set up a schedule."

"I DON'T WANT to fucking do this," I say, phone in hand.

"It's part of the plan," Hornsby says while driving his pen into his notepad. "The Plan" is written at the top. Underneath are three bullet points. Head. Josh. Girl. That's it. That's the immaculate plan Hornsby came up with.

"We can skip this part of the plan."

"No," the guys say in unison.

Then Taters steps in. "We're right on this. Clear things up with Josh, and then we can move on."

"Fine," I draw out before clicking on his name and letting the phone ring. Nerves drive up my spine as I wait and as time ticks by, I think he's not going to answer until . . .

"Hello?"

Fuck.

Eyes squeezed shut, I swallow hard and then say, "Josh. It's, uh, it's Pacey."

"Pacey, yeah, hey."

To the boys, I mouth, "Awkward. Fucking awkward."

Taters whirls his finger around, motioning for me to continue.

"So, uh, this is that phone call you've been asking for." Sweat drips down my back. Please, for the love of God, let this be over.

"Thanks. I appreciate it. I wasn't sure you'd ever call me."

"For reasons I'm sure you're aware of," I say in a snippy tone.

"Yeah, I am. Now. Not sure if Dad told you, but I was diagnosed with cancer a while back. It was pretty tough. I'm not looking for sympathy, it's just part of this journey I'm on. When I was going through treatment, I realized that if something happened to me, not a lot of people would care because of what a dick I'd been. That first night of chemo, I decided to make amends when I was done. I wanted people to know that I am a good guy."

"Makes sense."

"Which means I owe you a huge apology. I'm not looking for your acceptance or forgiveness, I know that has to be earned over time, but I want you to know I'm sorry for the way I treated you and Dad. If I should be mad at anyone, it was supposed to be my mom. But it seemed to be easier being mad at two people I didn't even know."

Hell, I hate that he's making sense, that I can feel his pain because it's softening me, weakening me.

"For what it's worth, Pacey, I'm sorry. And I'm sorry for the way I texted you about Winnie. It was a shock, seeing you with the girl I love, but I understand I lost her and that's all on me. But I took those bottled-up feelings out on you, and I'm sorry."

What the hell do I say to that? The guy has been an ass since I've known him, so I'm not going to automatically want anything to do with him. But I know what my dad would want. *Our dad. He'd* want me to extend an olive branch.

Even though I'm on the phone, I sit taller and then say, "Thank you for your apology, Josh. It does mean a lot to me. And who knows, maybe over time we can find out what being brothers means for us."

"I'd like that," Josh says.

"Just not anytime soon, I'm still fucking pissed by the way you treated Winnie. She deserved so much more."

"I know. I fucked up, big time." That makes two of us. "And even though I can't have her, I know she's in good hands with you."

"Thanks," I say, knowing good and well that I'm still in the doghouse with her.

"Sure." He sighs. "Think I can text you every once in a while, get to know you better?"

I roll my teeth over my bottom lip.

"It's hard, man. It's going to take me some time to have a different mindset where you're concerned."

"I can understand that—"

"But I'll give it a try."

"Yeah?" Josh asks, full of hope.

"Yeah."

Emotion heavy in his voice, Josh says, "Thank you, Pacey."

"Just take it slow."

He chuckles. "I will. Promise."

"Okay." I glance at Hornsby who is giving me the thumbs up. "I should get going."

"Yeah, sure. Don't want to take up too much of your time. Thanks again, Pacey, you're a real class act."

"Bye, Josh."

"Bye, man."

We both hang up and then I fall back into the couch, sweat streaming down my back.

"See? Was that so hard?" Hornsby asks.

"That was fucking torture." I take a second to gather myself. "But I'm glad I did it."

Hornsby taps his notepad. "Okay, boys, we're on to our third and final bullet point. Time to get the girl."

"Onward!" Posey shouts, pointing his hand in the air.

Jesus Christ, why did I get these guys involved?

———

"I'VE NEVER WANTED to jack off so much as I want to right now," Taters says as he flops down on my couch.

"What the fuck, man?" I ask.

He shrugs. "Dude, that was a stressful few hours. Doc calling you into his office, the fear of the unknown, all that atlas talk . . . I was ready to crawl inside my body and wish it all away. Then the phone call with Josh. Shit, that was awkward. And now that it's over, all that pent-up energy needs to be released."

"Well, go back to your fucking place. Jesus," I mutter as I take a seat on the other end of the couch, letting out a solid breath.

He's right, though—what a stressful few hours. I feel as though a huge burden has been lifted off my shoulders. Does it suck that I won't be going back to Banff this summer? Fuck yes, but in the grand scheme of things, maybe it's best. Getting my shit together before the beginning of the season is what I need, and that includes solving things with Winnie. The buzz of my phone makes me jump. *Surely Josh isn't texting me already.*

Dad: *Heard you spoke to Josh. How was it?*

Pacey: *Sucks about his cancer. And I don't know, better to have that stuff said, I guess. It will probably take me a while to forgive the way he treated you, but that's normal.*

Dad: *It is. Glad you reached out, Pacey. You're a good man and I'm proud of you.*

Pacey: *Thanks, Dad. Appreciate that. Call you and Mom soon, okay?*

Dad: *Sounds good. Love you.*

Pacey: *Love you too. Send my love to Mom.*

Posey is ordering us food and Hornsby and Holmes are both pouring beers in the kitchen for everyone as I put my phone away. I need to let Mom and Dad know about my neck at some point, but that's for another day.

"So now that we know what the hell is wrong with you, we have to focus on Winnie," Taters says.

"Yeah." I smooth my hand over my forehead. "Why does the physical therapy and schedule Doc will put me through feel like a walk in the park compared to what I'm going to have to do to win Winnie back?"

"Because that will be a breeze. Playing with emotions, convincing someone they're the one for you . . . trust me, that's not fucking easy." Taters directs his attention out the window, clearly struggling with the pain of losing his girl.

"Still nothing from Sarah?"

"Not sure I really want anything from her at this point. She's done with me and I think I have to accept that. I think I'm holding on to the past, when maybe she's right and we outgrew each other. And my mom, who's friends with her on social media, said she went away for the weekend with some guy."

"Shit, man. I'm sorry."

"I think it's what I needed. Her moving on. I've been in limbo, I think. For so many years, I've never looked at another girl. Never thought about sex with another woman, but now . . . suddenly I'm allowed to, and that's weird. It's as though I've been given permission, and I hadn't felt that it was real. But now it is. Now it is."

"Yeah, I can see that." *Is that what it was like for Winnie in some way? Despite being so hurt by Josh, was she also not quite sure she could pursue someone else?*

"But enough about me. What's your approach with Winnie?"

The boys all filter into the living room at the same time.

"We need to ease her into conversation," Hornsby says. "Let's be honest, she's not going to respond to phone calls at this point. Our best bet is text message. Also, do you have her address?"

I shake my head and then say, "But . . . I think I can get it. Her best friend Max might trade me info. He's dying to get Ian's phone number. I'm pretty sure he'd give up Winnie's address for that."

"Then do it," Hornsby says. "Because you're going to be sending her shit." He rubs his hands together. "Fuck, I'm excited. We're getting our girl back."

"My girl," I correct him. "We're getting my girl back."

"Whatever." He holds out his hand. "Let me see your phone."

"You're not texting her."

"No, you fuck, I'm going to draft a text. The first one has to be important."

"He's right," Posey says. "The initial contact after a break is the most important. We have to think on this."

I pull out my phone and open up a new text, but I don't put in her contact information just yet, in case of an accidental send. I hand the phone over to Hornsby, who holds it out and starts typing away.

"Share with the group," Taters says. "Read out loud."

"Okay." He clears his throat. "'Hey, sexy ass—'"

"I would never say that to her."

Hornsby looks over his shoulder. "Maybe that's the problem."

I grab the phone from him. "That's not the problem."

Taters takes the phone from me and starts typing. "'Hey, Winnie boo-boo—'"

"Or that," I yell. "What the hell is wrong with you two?"

Posey takes the phone this time and starts typing while saying, "'What's up, Winnie? Daddy misses you.'"

We all groan, and to my surprise, Holmes steps up and grabs the phone.

He spends a few silent seconds typing away and then he tosses the phone on the coffee table before reclaiming his seat in the chair.

As a collective, we all lean over the coffee table to read what he wrote.

I read it out loud. "'Hey, Winnie, I know I'm probably the last person you want to hear from, but I wanted to make sure you got back home safely. And I also wanted to apologize for what happened the other night. There's no excuse for my actions. All I can do is apologize, and I plan on doing that, over and over, until you feel comfortable enough to accept that apology.'" We all look up at Holmes and sit back.

"Wow." Hornsby starts to slow clap. "Who fucking knew?"

"And that's why he'll be my best man," I say.

"There's no way I can compete with that." Taters takes a sip of his beer. "That's perfection."

"Now, what if she doesn't respond?"

"Then it's a text a day until she does," Hornsby says. We all look to Holmes, who slowly nods.

"That's correct."

"Then we might want to draft some follow-up texts," Taters says.

We all turn to Holmes again, who smirks. "Might be a good idea."

Chapter Twenty-Six

WINNIE

"You know I love you," Max says as he walks into the living room from the kitchen, holding up his peanut butter jar. Well, empty peanut butter jar. "But I'll murder you if you do this again—finish off my peanut butter and then put the container back."

"Sorry," I say from where I lie on the couch. "I was too sad to clean it out and recycle it."

Max points at me. "You get that excuse once."

"Understood."

My phone buzzes on the coffee table and Max's eyes go to it. "Is that Pacey?"

"Why would you ask that? Of course it's not. Why would we be talking?"

"I don't know. A part of me thinks that maybe he'd come chasing."

I shake my head and grab my phone. "Trust me when I say that's not going to happen." *He didn't chase after me when I left his apartment and it's been days since I left.* I peek at the screen and see Pacey's name.

My mouth falls open, and Max must be watching my every move, because he hops over the couch with the empty peanut butter jar in hand and asks, "What did he say?"

I sit up now and unlock my phone. I pull up his text message and read it out loud. "'Hey, Winnie, I know I'm probably the last person you want to hear from, but I wanted to make sure you got back home safely. And I also wanted to apologize for what happened the other night. There's no excuse for my actions. All I can do is apologize, and I plan on doing that, over and over, until you feel comfortable enough to accept that apology.'"

Max grips my shoulder tightly and whispers, "Christ. Look at him coming in hot with the text message."

My pulse picks up as I read the text a few more times to myself. "I don't understand."

"What don't you understand?" he asks. "He's clearly trying to make up with you."

"But after everything we said to each other . . ."

"You know, people can say shit to each other and be apologetic about it. I know Josh fucked you in the head, but that's not how relationships usually go." He nudges me. "You should write him back."

"I don't know. I'm not even sure I should be thinking about him, pursuing this."

"Why the hell not? He makes you happy."

"He does."

"Then that's all the reason you need to text him back."

"But I'm not . . . ready for a relationship. I should really focus on myself," I say.

"You don't have to marry the guy, but a response won't kill you."

"I have no idea what to say."

"I have an idea." Max takes my phone and starts typing.

"Hey, Pacey, I forgive you with everything in my heart. Now please bring that cock over here."

I snatch the phone from him quicker than I can blink. "Oh my God, Max, no. What is wrong with you?"

"Trust me, any guy would appreciate that text."

Groaning, I turn away from him and study Pacey's text a few more times before beginning to formulate my own response. Something that doesn't involve the word *cock*.

PACEY

"HERE IT COMES—HE'S going to hit a homerun. I can feel it in my bones," Posey says.

"No way. Maddox Paige is going to strike him out," Taters says. "That fucker has a wicked changeup."

"You're talking about Knox Gentry. The dude is a goddamn legend. No way is he going to strike out under pressure."

My leg bounces up and down, and not because of the game on the TV between the Bobbies and Rebels, probably the biggest sports rivals in history. I sent my text an hour ago, and there's been no response, which means one thing—I'm going to have to reference the text message drafts we sat down and worked out for every situation.

"Look at the stare in Paige's eyes. Dude is fucking intimidating," Posey says as Paige winds up. He throws the ball, zipping it toward the catcher, only for Knox Gentry to make contact and knock it right over the shortstop's head.

"Ha, told you." Posey claps.

"Hey, idiot, you said he was going to get a homerun."

"Homerun, single, same thing."

My phone beeps and Taters mutes the TV as all the guys turn toward me. "Is that her?" Taters asks.

I flip my phone over and look at the screen. Seeing Winnie's name makes my heart trip in my chest.

"It's her," I say.

"Jesus Christ," Taters yells while motioning with his hands to calm everyone down. "Quiet. QUIET! It's her, everyone fucking keep it together."

"Idiot, you're the one who's being loud," Hornsby points out and then says to me, "Read it out loud."

"Please, Jesus, read it out loud," Taters says, far too invested in this.

I unlock my phone and with a shaky finger, open her text. "'Hey, Pacey. I made it back to my place safely. Thank you for asking. And no need to apologize. We said what we said.'"

"Ooh, not the response we were looking for." Hornsby winces.

"I feel like throwing up," Posey says as he stands and starts pacing. "How do we respond to that?"

Once again, we all look to Holmes who rolls his eyes and extends his hand. I place the phone in his palm, and we all rock back and forth as he types a response.

Maybe I should be doing the typing, but Jesus Christ, I'm right there with Posey—I feel as if I could puke, because I want her that bad. I want my girl back.

WINNIE

"WHAT'S GOING ON HERE?" Katherine says, walking into the living room as Max and I use our fingers to clean out any scraps from the peanut butter jar. "Fingers aren't spoons. Don't be a disgust." She moves past us and we just exchange glances, about to dip our fingers in again, when we're each slapped on the back of the neck with a wet paper towel. "Clean yourselves." She snatches the peanut butter from Max's hand as she walks away.

"Why does she hate us?" I whisper to Max.

"I think she just hates life in general, and that hate is directed toward us."

Ding.

Our eyes fall to my phone.

And then . . .

"He texted you back," Max whispers while wiping his fingers. "Oh my GOD." His voice rises. "He texted you back!" Max shakes my shoulder and then taps my phone. "Open it. Open it."

I wipe my fingers and then, with a hesitant heart, open my messages and read the text out loud. "'You didn't deserve what I said, or how I acted. I acted and spoke out of jealousy, out of fear that I was going to lose you. At the time, I didn't know I was going to lose you anyway. I want you to know just how sorry I am.'"

Max leans back and lets out a deep sigh. "You know it's not common for a man to admit when he's wrong. He's setting his pride aside and he's making it known that he was in the wrong. You need to acknowledge how important that is."

"I know it is," I say, while staring at his text. "Josh never would've done that. Even when he apologized to me, I'm not sure if he fully understood what he was apologizing for."

"Not Pacey." Max shakes his head. "The man is totally in tune with his fuck-up."

He is. Because even in Josh's apology, he was clear that his greatest regret was that I wasn't there when he *needed to use me.*

Max nudges me. "Text him back."

"Yeah, I should, right?"

"You really should."

___

PACEY

"DID you see Jason Orson's Tik Tok the other day?" Posey asks. "He did the cake check and his ass was like a brick blockade. He then proceeded to hump the floor in celebration. I almost peed myself from laughter."

"What's a cake check?" Holmes asks.

"When you lie on your stomach and someone rolls a barbell with twenty-fives on each side up over your legs to see if your butt stops it. If it does, that means you have cake in the trunk, if you don't . . . more leg days for you," Posey explains.

"That's idiotic," Holmes says.

"You only say that because you know you don't have any cake," Posey says.

"No one has cake like Orson," Taters says. "I've never seen an ass like his."

"And he's so proud of it," Hornsby adds. "I've seen many interviews where he thanks his backside for his superior skills."

"I don't blame him," I say just as my phone beeps.

"Quiet in the house," Taters yells while muting the TV again.

I unlock my phone, see Winnie's name, and say, "It's from her."

"Fuck yes," Hornsby says while kicking his leg in the air. "What does it say?"

Not sure how she'll respond, I tentatively open the text and then read it out loud. "'I really appreciate your apology, Pacey. It means a lot.'" I look up at the boys. "That's it. That's all she wrote. What the hell do I do now?"

With a satisfied smile, Hornsby places his feet on my coffee table and crosses his arms behind his head. "The line of communication has been opened. Now . . . we woo. Message the best friend on Instagram, get her address. Tomorrow, we go into a full-court press."

"I don't even know what that means."

"You will . . . you will."

Chapter Twenty-Seven

WINNIE

"What are you doing?" Max asks as he takes a seat next to me at the dining room table.

"Taking a quiz."

"What kind of quiz?"

I lean back in my chair and say, "A career quiz."

Max sighs heavily. "Why are you taking one of those stupid things? You know it's not going to tell you what you want to hear."

"And what is it exactly that I want to hear?"

He drums his fingers on the table. "You want a definitive answer about what you should do. That's going to give you a broad variety of things to try. You already know that."

The doorbell rings. "I got it," Katherine says as she hurries down the stairs, phone in hand, most likely checking the Ring camera.

"And what exactly is that?"

"Kids. You love working with them, reading to them, spending time with them. It's as simple as that."

"Who sent you?" Katherine shouts.

Max and I both crane our necks to see a poor deliveryman trying to drop off a box. "Uh, I'm not sure. I was just told to deliver this at this address."

Katherine pushes the package away. "You think I'm an idiot? I know that's a bomb. Get away with that ticking murder box."

"Jesus Christ," Max mutters as he gets up from the table and goes to the door. He moves Katherine to the side and takes the package. "Sorry, my friend is wasted. Excuse her insanity."

"I'm not—"

Max shuts the door and, instead of addressing Katherine, brings the package to the table and hands it to me.

"That guy was completely unmarked," Katherine says, barreling down the hallway. "Delivery people always wear some sort of logo, advertising who they belong to. He was unmarked. That package is death."

"I honestly can't handle you right now." Max holds his hand up to Katherine. "Please, go chew on a weed gummy or something. I need you to bring your insanity level down at least ten notches." Max pushes the box toward me and says, "This is for you."

"Me?" I ask, confused. "I didn't order anything."

"No, but I'm pretty sure I know who it's from." Max smiles.

"What did you do?" I ask.

He drags his finger over the box. "I just happened to get a message from a certain hockey player, looking for your address in exchange for a certain hockey player's phone number."

"He didn't," I say.

"Oh, he did, but I told him I would give him the address without the phone number. I don't want to look desperate. I'd rather shine in a one-on-one meeting, which Pacey promised would happen if you two get back together. So, you know I was already rooting for you two, but now I'm gung-ho about making it happen."

"You sold out."

He shakes his head and grows serious. "I would've given him the address even if he just asked, because I believe you two belong together."

"When did you become a hopeless romantic?" I ask him as I peel off the tape.

"Not a hopeless romantic. But I've known you ever since high school. I saw your relationship with Josh, and I've seen your brief time with Pacey. Trust me when I say there's a huge difference between the two. Pacey made you light up. Josh never did that."

Because Pacey was different. He cared. He was interested. He was protective. He was helpful. He thought I mattered. From the way he held my hand, to carrying my bags for me, to the way he intently listened to my stories with his eyes focused on mine—it was different.

I mattered to him, and that's the difference. In fact, I mattered so much that seeing me with Josh upset him instantly. Yes, I'm still angry that he didn't tell me they were related once he realized, but he was truly fearful that I'd planned to see Josh. He was so worried that I'd leave him for Josh. *I mattered to Pacey.* He'd stopped to buy me flowers, even though he was the one who'd had the doctor's appointment, something that would determine his future. Something I haven't even asked him about. *And yet, he bought me flowers.* Oh God . . .

I reach into the box and pull out a six-pack of blueberry lavender cider.

"Ooh, what's this?" Max asks, looking at the cans.

I smile to myself. "Cider we had in Banff. It was my favorite."

"Okay. I have no idea how he made that happen, but I do believe that deserves a text message."

I tip the box over to look inside. "Is there a note?"

"Does it need a note?" Max asks. "This is thoughtful. No note needed."

He's right. It is thoughtful. And I agree—I have no idea how Pacey pulled this off in such a short amount of time; I only messaged him yesterday. But I'm grateful.

"Can you put these in the fridge for me? We'll have one a little later."

"I'm holding you to that," Max says.

As he walks away, I pick up my phone and move to the couch, granting myself some privacy. I pull up the text thread with Pacey and start typing.

Winnie: *Just got some cider delivered to the house. Max confessed to giving away our address. Thank you, it was very thoughtful of you.*

There. Short, sweet, to the point.

I go to set my phone down, only for it to buzz in my hand.

Pacey: *I'm glad it arrived. Enjoy it. I got some delivered to my place as well. Have a good night.*

Oh . . . that was also short and sweet. To the point. For some reason, I expected more from him.

Confused, I text him back.

Winnie: *You too.*

"How is our main man?" Max asks, hopping over the couch and joining me.

I set my phone down, my thoughts running a mile a minute. "Good. He told me to have a good night."

"Huh?" Max says, looking as confused as I feel. "That's it?"

"Yeah. That's it."

"Well . . . I guess . . . we should toast to him tonight."

"I guess so."

———

"LOOK AT THIS," I say to Katherine as we take a walk through the park across from our townhome. "Ants are so fascinating, aren't they?"

"Are you asking me to look at an ant hill?"

"Yes, look. Do you think they all have their own apartments underground?"

"I know one thing." Katherine crosses her arms. "They sure as hell don't have a proper way of preventing assholes from destroying their homes."

I squat down and watch the little guys work in and out of their home.

"Is this what life has come to? Staring at ant hills?"

"You can go home if you want," I say. "I know too much fresh air can be toxic to your well-being."

"I'm glad you get me." Without another word, Katherine heads back toward the house as I decide to take a seat in the grass, right next to the sidewalk.

I stare up at the partially cloudy sky and take in the sun, welcoming the warm rays as they soak into my skin.

My phone buzzes in my pocket and I take it out to find a text from Pacey. I can't help my physical reaction as my pulse picks up and my stomach does a somersault from the sight of his name.

I open up his text message.

Pacey: *Hope you're having a good day.*

It's so simple, and yet, it feels . . . good. *He's thinking about me.* Going about his day, he makes time to see how I'm doing.

I text him back.

Winnie: *I am. Thank you. Sitting in a park right now, in the grass, looking up at the sky. What are you doing?*

I send the text before I can change my mind. I'm engaging in conversation, and even though that's scary, I think Max is right—no one has ever made me happier and maybe I should give this a chance. Pacey didn't get the chance to explain why he hid his relationship with Josh, but I have wondered if Max was right. And I never thought of Pacey as someone who'd lie to protect himself . . . so maybe I need to be willing to ask in this situation, rather than assume. He really isn't someone who'd use me as a pawn . . .

My phone buzzes and I still my breath as I peek down at it.

Pacey: *Sounds as if you're finding some peace. I'm headed home from the arena. Just got done with some PT.*

Guilt consumes me as I quickly text him back.

Winnie: *Oh my God, I never asked you what the doctor said. Is everything okay?*

I impatiently stare at my phone, waiting for a response. Thankfully, he texts back quickly, the little dots indicating I'm about to get a response.

Pacey: *Apparently my neck is fucked up from many years of abuse, and then the slap shot to the head tipped everything over the edge. Working with Doc on a solid therapy program. Won't be heading back to Banff this summer, hence the cider.*

I let out a sigh of relief and text him back.

Winnie: *That's really great to hear. I'm sure you're relieved.*

Pacey: *I am. Doc has been pretty easy on me so far, but that's because he's taking it slow, not wanting to spike a migraine. I know he's going to increase the therapy and it's going to be a bitch.*

Winnie: *I'm sure you can handle it. Are you missing the boys?*

Pacey: *They actually all came home. I think Taters and Hornsby are going to head back to the cabin, but Posey and Holmes are staying in town. Posey mentioned something about his fear of packing on the pounds with access to fudge and me not being there to stop him.*

Winnie: *I never would've guessed he'd be concerned about his figure.*

Pacey: *A new development. Have you had any of the cider?*

Winnie: *Max and I drank all of it the other night. It went down quick. You?*

Pacey: *Destroyed it. Posey of course helped me.*

Winnie: *I wouldn't think any less.*

Pacey: *Yeah . . . well, just wanted to make sure you were having a good day.*

Winnie: *Thank you. That was sweet.*

Pacey: *All right. Enjoy the sun, Winnie.*

Smiling, I set my phone down and lift my chin to the sky again, closing my eyes. This is something I miss doing with my mom. How often did we simply sit outside in the sun and appreciate its warmth?

Mom, did you have anything to do with this? You read all of those romance books, and I'm pretty sure you're orchestrating this entire thing for your pleasure.

━━━

DING–DONG.

"Katherine, don't even bother," Max says, going to the door before Katherine can fly down the stairs and fire off an obnoxious round of questions at the person on the other side of the door, questions that include: who sent you, who do you work for, how much are they paying you, and are you aware the Ring camera is recording everything you're saying?

"Thank you," Max says as I peek my head around the corner to see what it is. Max turns around with a bag in hand.

A very familiar bag.

A bag that makes my mouth water.

"Tacos," I whisper.

"Did you order?" Max asks.

"No . . . you didn't?"

He shakes his head and smiles. "Oh, let me guess—lover boy sent them. You better text him. While you do that, I'll be serving up these tacos on a platter."

I walk over to my phone and pull up a text thread that's given me so much joy over the past few days. *Something I wasn't sure I'd feel this close to losing Mom.*

Winnie: *Tacos? You really know how to cut me deep.*

His response is immediate.

Pacey: *My mouth was watering while ordering them. I'm jealous.*

Winnie: *Just the smell alone is giving me all the feels.*

Pacey: *Take a picture. I want to see what they look like.*

Max sets a serving plate on the dining room table and then goes back to the kitchen to grab drinks from the fridge.

"Katherine, lover boy sent tacos," Max shouts.

"Were they delivered by a stranger?"

"Yes," Max shouts.

"Enjoy your arsenic," Katherine shoots back.

"More for us," Max says with a smile.

I walk over to the table and take a picture for Pacey. I send it with a drooling emoji.

I sit down as my phone buzzes.

Pacey: *Damn, I'm really jealous now. Especially since I have some shit salad for dinner.*

I pick up a taco and take a bite while texting him back with the other hand.

Winnie: *Salad? That's boring. Why a salad? Don't tell me Doc has you on some special meal plan.*

Pacey: *Unfortunately, he does.*

Winnie: *Does he know about your cider consumption?*

Pacey: *No, and I would appreciate it if you didn't go shouting that around.*

Winnie: *Lol, so I'm going to retract my Sunday morning announcement from the paper, then.*

Pacey: *Do people even get the Sunday paper anymore?*

Winnie: *I don't think so.*

Max pokes my arm. "Look at you all giddy."

I take another bite of my taco. "I'm not giddy."

"Yes, you are. Your face is the definition of giddy."

Ignoring him, I go back to my texts.

Pacey: *I would say you're showing your age, but we both know that's not the truth.*

Winnie: *As an old man yourself, you would know.*

Pacey: *I found a gray hair this morning.*

Winnie: *No, you didn't.*

Pacey: *Right by my ear. I showed Posey, and he choked on his own saliva from laughter.*

Winnie: *Still don't believe you. It's probably just a really blond piece of hair.*

Pacey: *You know, that's exactly what I'm going to call it. My platinum strand.*

Winnie: *Lol! How incredibly fancy of you.*

Pacey: *That's me, a fancy fuck.*

I snort and then glance at Max, who sports a knowing look on his face. He doesn't have to say anything—he just needs to glance at me and I know exactly what he's thinking. *I really like this man. I forgive him, too.*

Pacey and I are supposed to be together.

PACEY: *Hey, how was your day?*

I roll to my side on my bed and text Pacey back. It's been a long day and I was starting to worry that I wasn't going to hear from him. That should tell me all I need to know.

Winnie: *Hey. It was long.*

Pacey: *Yeah? Anything you want to talk about?*

Winnie: *Nothing bad, just spent a very long time online with a recruiter.*

Pacey: *A recruiter, huh? That sounds interesting.*

Winnie: *It was. Apparently, even though I don't have a college degree, I have enough experience and proof of my work to possibly run a consulting business on building a proper reading and learning environment for kids.*

Pacey: *What? Seriously? Winnie, that's pretty damn cool.*

I smile proudly.

Winnie: *It is, actually. There's a company that's looking for someone like me with my experience and background. They're putting together packages of programs and environments to sell nationally to schools, libraries, and bookstores. The hope is to inspire interactive and creative play that's been designed around books, and that it'll encourage children to read. I have an interview tomorrow.*

Pacey: *Damn, girl, that's pretty badass. Are you excited?*

Winnie: *Sort of. I don't feel qualified, at all. Max thinks otherwise. I really don't want to get my hopes up, but the job is working remotely, not working with kids directly. It's about bettering their lives, which is nice, and it's mostly all online consulting. It seems pretty chill, but fun. Pay isn't superb, but I feel as if that doesn't matter when I love what I'm doing.*

Pacey: *Could not agree more. I'm proud of you, Winnie.*

Tears well up in my eyes.

Winnie: *Thank you.*

Pacey: *Well, good luck. I know you'll dominate.*

———

I SHUT my laptop and then reach into my shirt and pull off my bra, flinging it to the ground.

God, I've never sweated so much in my entire life.

"Are you done?" Max asks from the other side of my bedroom door.

"Yup."

He opens the door, and just like the good friend he is, he hands me an ice-cold margarita.

"Bless you," I say.

"Chips and salsa are downstairs, waiting. I'll let you get changed and then you can tell me all about the interview."

"Sounds great."

My phone buzzes and Max smirks.

"One guess who that is."

Rolling my eyes, I push at Max and he leaves me to my room as I look at my phone.

Yup, we both knew who it was.

Pacey: *The anticipation is killing me. How did it go?*

Winnie: *Just ended.*

My phone buzzes in my hand, but it isn't a text. Pacey is actually calling me.

Oh God, do I answer?

Texting is easy, you can think about your response, but a phone call?

I bite my bottom lip, trying to decide.

God, just answer it.

"Hello?"

"Hey." His deep baritone rings through the phone. "I hope this is okay, me calling."

"Oh, yeah, it's totally cool," I say awkwardly.

"Okay, because I really wanted to hear you tell me about the interview. You killed it, didn't you?"

I move out of my desk chair and go to my bed, where I lie on my stomach and kick up my heels. I feel like a teenager, talking to her crush for the first time on the phone . . . and if I think about it, this is the first time I'm talking to him on the phone.

"I wouldn't say killed it. I said something awkward but I think it came out more endearing."

"What did you say?"

I feel at ease talking to him on the phone, comfortable. "They asked those weird questions, you know, that big tech companies ask. They asked how much I would charge to walk every dog in Seattle."

"What?" He laughs, and it's such an addicting sound. I want to hear it more.

"That was my same reaction, but I held it together. I cleared my throat and asked, 'Am I in charge of picking up feces, as well?'"

"Great follow-up question."

"I thought so. And they said yes. So then I cringed and said, 'Well, that would be an upcharge,' and I left it at that. I didn't give them an exact answer, which I know they wanted, but that's all I could offer on the spot today."

"I think it's a great answer. It's endearing."

"Thank you. Luckily, I was brought to them highly recommended by their recruiter, so hopefully I have a leg up on the competition."

"I'm sure you do. You got it, Winnie. I really think you did."

"We shall see." Not wanting to get off the phone, I ask, "How's physical therapy going? Have you had any migraines?"

"Woke up with a headache today, but it was nothing compared to what I've experienced in the past. Doc said that initial PT will stir up the muscles and ligaments and to expect pain. But other than that, it's going pretty well. I've been seeing an ART therapist, and no, not the drawing kind."

"Active release, right?" I ask.

"You know about that?"

"Yeah, Max has been studying to become certified. He swears by it. He's practiced on me and Katherine and it really feels like magic. Although, if it were truly magic, he'd be able to find Katherine's chill button and release that."

He chuckles. "Let me guess, Katherine didn't partake in tacos?"

"Her direct quote was 'enjoy your arsenic.'"

"Arsenic—now that's pretty strong."

"That's what I thought. You'd think she'd choose something more subtle. But she just went for it."

"Ballsy going big like that, but she seems like a ballsy woman."

I chuckle. "That she is."

━━━

"MAX! KATHERINE!" I scream as I run down the stairs, tripping on the last one and flying into the front door with a crash.

"Jesus Christ," Max says, coming to the entryway to help me up. "What the hell are you doing?"

When I catch my breath, I look him in the eyes and whisper, "I got it."

"Got what?" His eyes widen. "Wait, the job? You got the job?"

I nod as tears start to form in my eyes.

Max lifts me up and over his broad shoulder and parades me down the hallway while shouting, "Our girl got the job."

"Really?" Katherine asks, standing from the couch.

Max sets me down and I look at both of them. "Yes, I got it. I got the freaking job."

We all look at each other, and then in unison we scream while dancing in circles.

"Holy shit, that's amazing," Max says. "We're celebrating. I'm getting tacos."

Katherine holds up her hand. "I'll go get them. You start on the margaritas."

Max groans. "I used the last of the tequila on the other ones."

Katherine points her finger at him. "This is exactly why you save tequila for big moments, not a random Tuesday. You get the booze, I'll get the tacos." She looks at me. "Are you going to want flan?" She waves her hand. "What am I saying? Of course you will, and some of those churros. We're on it. Come on, Max."

He winks at me. "Be right back. We love you."

I smile and wave as they head out the door. I sit back on the armrest of the couch and then stare at my phone.

Do I call him?

Too nervous, but wanting to tell him, I send him a text.

Winnie: *Hope I'm not bothering you, but I thought I'd just tell you that I got the job.*

I press send and clutch my phone, only for it to immediately buzz with a phone call.

Pacey.

Unable to control my smile, I answer the phone. "Hello?"

"A text? You're going to tell me that fucking fantastic news through a text? Winnie, holy shit, this is amazing."

And just like that, tears well in my eyes, because I can hear true excitement in his voice. Pride.

"Thank you. I'm really excited."

"As you should be. Please tell me Max and Katherine are celebrating with you tonight."

"Yes, they're currently on their way to get tacos, dessert, and tequila for margaritas."

"Good. Wow, this is incredible. I'm really happy for you, Winnie. Proud."

"Thank you, Pacey."

He sighs and I can tell he wants to say something but he stays silent.

"What is it?" I ask, curious as to what he's holding back.

"Nothing, just . . . hell. I just wish I was there to give you a hug. But I'm glad you have Katherine and Max. Have fun celebrating. You deserve it." His voice has a distinct sadness to it and it makes me think that he honestly wishes he was here. Who am I kidding? Of course he does. He's never led me to believe otherwise about his intentions. He's always been upfront, honest, which makes me feel like a fool for reacting the way I did.

Taking a giant leap in—well, whatever this is, I say, "I wish you were here too, Pacey."

Chapter Twenty-Eight

PACEY

"What the hell do you think you're doing?" Posey asks, walking into my bedroom.

Ever since they decided to stay in Vancouver with me, the boys have been rotating staying at my place. I prefer when Holmes is here because he doesn't say a goddamn thing—yes, he's taking in my every movement, but he stays silent and reads his books. Posey, on the other hand, he's in my goddamn business every second of every day.

At one point, when I went to the bathroom, he asked what I was doing, and I told him I was relieving myself and asked if he wanted to hold my dick for me while I did that.

Right now is no exception.

"What does it look like I'm doing?" I ask while packing a bag.

"Uh, it looks like you're going to go somewhere, and if I were to guess, you're going to Seattle."

Sighing, I turn to Posey and say, "She got a job, dude. I want to congratulate her."

Posey shakes his head. "That's not part of the plan. It's too soon."

"I'm just going to say congrats, give her a hug—"

"No." Posey rips the suitcase off the bed and throws it to the floor, scattering my things to the ground.

I point at the discarded bag. "Was that really necessary?"

"To prove a point, yes." He approaches me. "Listen, I know you're eager to see her, you want to congratulate her, but it's too soon still."

"Says who?" I ask, my patience wearing thin today.

"Do I need to FaceTime the guys?"

I shake my head. "No."

"Okay, then. Instead of driving down to see her, what can you do instead?"

"Send her something to congratulate her," I say in an annoyed voice.

"Precisely." Posey holds up his finger. "Remember, we're establishing a friendship, getting to know her again, taking it slow. Build up the anticipation, the need. Patience, Lawes, we need patience."

"Easy for you to say. You're not the one having to be patient." I flop back on my bed.

"Uh, pretty sure I have blue balls for a happily ever after, here. You're not the only one suffering. I need this to be over and done with as much as you. That's why we need to do it right the first time and not go through this shit again. Got it?"

I give him a once-over. "Where did the attitude come from?"

He places his hands on his hips and says, "Fudge withdrawals." Taking a deep breath, he points to my phone and says, "Start ordering something. Make it good."

Frustrated, even though he's right, I pick up my phone and get to work.

⊏⊐

"FEELING GOOD?" Doc asks.

"Feeling good," I answer as I lie on one of the training tables, icing my neck after an intense ART session.

"Glad to hear it. When the timer goes off, you're free to leave. Take it easy today, no lifting, and try to keep off devices unless you can hold them at eye level. I don't want you straining today."

"Got it," I say as he pats my table and heads to his office.

As I stare at the ceiling, I think about the upcoming season, wondering if all this therapy is going to help. Hell, I haven't had a migraine since I started therapy, which is good. Just minor headaches here and there from irritating the muscles and moving them around, loosening them up, which is a given. But a headache is a cakewalk compared to the migraines.

My phone buzzes next to me and I lift it up to eye level to see it's a text from Winnie.

Whenever I see her name cross my phone's screen, I get so fucking excited, because even though it's been painful to be patient, to wait this out, to grow this relationship like the boys have said, having these moments where she's talking to me makes it all worth it.

Unfortunately for me, it's just a text message. Might be best, though—don't feel like carrying on a conversation in the training room.

Winnie: *I just got a beautiful cookie bouquet delivered to the house. Max already shoved an entire cookie in his mouth. Thank you.*

I really think Max and I could be good friends. We've chatted a bit through Instagram. He's very openly stated that he's rooting for me and he'll help in any way he can. I've clearly taken him up on that.

Pacey: *I was going to send you some cupcakes, but I asked Max. I take it this might be HIS favorite cookie place, not yours.*

Winnie: *Oh no, I love these cookies, but I do think Max had ulterior motives.*

Pacey: *As long as you love them, that's all that matters. Did you have fun celebrating?*

Winnie: *I did. Katherine passed out on the couch and Max was wasted, so he pretended to ride Katherine like a horse while whipping his shirt over his head. I have damning evidence of such events that I'll use as blackmail when I need to.*

Pacey: *I have a whole folder on my phone of damning evidence on the boys. It's a smart tactic.*

Winnie: *Let me guess, you have the most on Silas?*

Pacey: *Yup. He's the guy who does stupid shit. Posey will end up doing some idiotic things, but nothing he's embarrassed about. Taters, on the other hand, he's given me a lot of gold.*

Winnie: *I can only imagine. So, as I sit here eating one of these deliciously soft cookies, what are you doing?*

Pacey: *Icing my neck. Just got done with an ART session. I'm supposed to take it easy for the rest of the day.*

Winnie: *Are you feeling better?*

Pacey: *Yeah, it's a slow process because they don't want to stress the muscles out or anything, but I can feel a difference. Haven't had a migraine since the one in Banff.*

Winnie: *That's great news.*

Pacey: *Yeah. Anyway, glad you like the cookies. Enjoy, and congratulations again, Winnie. I'm really fucking proud of you.*

Winnie: *Thank you. That means a lot, Pacey.*

Itching to do more, I set my phone down on my stomach and practice patience. This will pay off. It has to.

PACEY: *What are you doing?*

Holmes just left for the night, my stomach is full from the stupid-ass steak salads we had, and I'm bored.

It's been two days since Winnie received her cookies, and

with each passing minute, I'm growing more and more impatient.

I want to call her.

See her face.

Chat about everything and nothing.

Call her babe.

Hold her goddamn hand.

Kiss those perfect lips.

If anything, this time apart has solidified my feelings for her. I need her in my life. I want her in my life.

My phone buzzes, and like a rabid beast looking for his next meal, I quickly unlock my phone and read my text.

Posey: *I miss fudge.*

Fucking idiot. Jesus Christ. I ignore his text and set my phone down while laying my head back on the couch. *Full House* is on TV. It's the serious moment when the music turns inspirational and Danny Tanner gets eye to eye with his girls and teaches them a lesson. Normally, I'd be invested in the lesson, because we all have to learn and grow—right?—but right now, I wish Danny Tanner was giving a lesson on patience instead.

My phone buzzes again and I clutch it in my palm.

If it's Posey telling me to feed him fudge, I'm going to fucking lose it.

I quickly flash the screen in my direction, and relief floods me when I see Winnie's name on the screen.

Winnie: *Listening to Katherine review a PowerPoint she put together to tell us every reason why we need bars on all of our windows. She sees that I'm texting and she doesn't look happy.*

Pacey: *I would say slowly put the phone down and pay attention, but that would mean I don't get to talk to you.*

Winnie: *You want to talk to me? Anything important? I just left the room.*

Pacey: *In the middle of a safety presentation? Ballsy.*

Winnie: *I walk on the wild side. Everything okay?*

Pacey: *Everything is fine. Just bored out of my mind. Posey is driving me nuts. Need to talk to someone sane.*

Winnie: *I would hardly call me sane, but I do think I have a leg up on Levi.*

Pacey: *More than a leg. Since you walked out on Katherine, aren't you afraid she's going to hover over your bed and stare at you when you sleep?*

Winnie: *No, I'm used to that by now.*

Pacey: *LOL. Does she really do that?*

Winnie: *Just once, and it was the scariest thing of my life. I slapped her in the chest, which she ended up complaining about for days after.*

Pacey: *Why was she over your bed?*

Winnie: *Long story, but we'd had food delivered and she'd thought the delivery person was sketchy. She thought the food was poisoned, so she'd rotate between my room and Max's to make sure we were still breathing. She was being a good friend, but I could've done without waking up to her intently staring at me.*

Pacey: *Pretty sure I would do worse than a slap to the chest if that happened to me.*

Winnie: *Karate chop, maybe?*

Pacey: *Nah, this boy uses fists.*

Winnie: *Oh, how could I forget all of the fighting in hockey?*

Pacey: *It's one of the reasons hockey fans tune in.*

Winnie: *Was there a fight after you got injured?*

Pacey: *Not right after, but after I was taken off the ice and the game resumed, Hornsby crushed McAllister, the guy who did the slap shot, right into the boards. A cheap shot, and then that turned into a brawl.*

Winnie: *I can't see Eli fighting. He doesn't seem like that kind of guy.*

Pacey: *He's really good at not getting hit in the face. Not sure if it's height or what, but in all the years I've known him, I've seen him with one black eye. And don't let his easygoing attitude fool you, the man is a killer on the ice.*

Winnie: *I guess I'll just have to believe it when I see it.*

Pacey: *Plan on watching some games this fall?*

Winnie: *Won't hurt me to tune in.*

Pacey: *Who knows? Maybe you might find a favorite player.*
Winnie: *Maybe . . .*

———

PACEY: *Guess what?*

Winnie: *What?*

Pacey: *I found a four-leaf clover today.*

Winnie: *Send a picture.*

Pacey: *[picture]*

Winnie: *Wow, you really are good at finding them. Where are you?*

Pacey: *The park. Thought I'd take a walk.*

Winnie: *Risky since you're often recognized.*

Pacey: *Needed out of the house. Feeling restless today. I'm not used to being here over summer so I needed some fresh air. Luckily, only one person recognized me.*

Winnie: *Well, looks like luck is on your side today.*

Pacey: *You think so?*

Winnie: *I do.*

Pacey: *If that's the case, can I ask you something?*

Winnie: *Sure.*

Pacey: *Think I can FaceTime you tonight? Totally okay if you're not cool with that. Just thought it would be nice to see your face.*

Winnie: *I would like that.*

Pacey: *Cool. I'll call you later, then.*

———

"YOU'RE SWEATING," Hornsby says. He just got back from Banff and is in town for a few days. He has meetings with his agent about different sponsorships.

"Of course I'm fucking sweating." I wipe at my brow. "I'm seeing Winnie for the first time in over a month tonight. I'm nervous."

"What are you going to say to her?" Posey asks as he takes a bite of fudge. Hornsby spoils the guy.

"I don't know, regular things."

"What are regular things?" Hornsby asks.

"Like . . . how's the job, what's the weather like, those kinds of things."

"Oof, that's boring," Posey whispers. "Good luck, man."

I lift my eyes to him and point to my front door. "Out. Both of you."

"Touch-y," Hornsby says while he gathers Posey and they head to the front door. "Just remember, be cool and don't break the patience rule."

"Fuck your patience rule," I say as I sit down at my dining room table and prop the phone up. My dinner is in front of me and I'm ready for a conversation. Earlier, I asked her if it was okay if I called her around dinnertime. Told her I would be eating and she's more than welcome to eat with me.

She said that would be fun.

And that's when the sweating began.

My front door clicks shut, I take a few deep breaths, wipe my hands on my shorts, and then I call her up on FaceTime.

Be cool, man. Be cool.

After three rings, she answers, and my heart nearly beats out of my chest when she comes into view.

Fuck, she's so goddamn beautiful.

"Hey," she says shyly.

"Hey, you," I say, taking her all in. Her almost platinum hair is down and straight, she has mascara on, highlighting her eyes, and she's wearing a simple blue top that makes her eyes seem even bluer, if possible. In front of her is a plate of tacos. I'm not surprised. "Tacos?"

She nods. "I can't help myself. What about you?"

I tip the phone down. "Salad." I bring the phone back up. "It's a pretty lame dinner, but the diet Doc has me on has been helping, too."

"Are you going to be jealous watching me eat my tacos?"

Only because your tacos get to touch your mouth and I don't.

"Very jealous," I say.

"Well, you can live vicariously through me." She pushes her hair back and then lifts up one of her hard-shell tacos and takes a bite. The crunch makes my mouth water. "Mmm," she says in a teasing tone.

"Brutal," I say while I stick my fork in my lettuce and bring it to my mouth.

"That looks appetizing." Her voice drips with sarcasm.

"It's not."

She laughs and, fuck, I've missed that sound, that smile, the way she so easily meshes with me.

"So how is the new job?" I ask her.

"Hard. It's challenging, which is a good thing, but I feel like I'm doing a lot of studying right now, making sure I know what I'm doing. The materials are easy to understand, nothing new about creating enriching environments, but there's more information to remember than I was expecting."

"Ah, you know what you're doing, but I understand the need to reaffirm that. But you're liking it so far?"

"I am. I think it's just enough challenge in my life, keeps me busy during the day. Not a lot of time to think."

"Yeah? What would you be thinking about?"

She makes eye contact with me. "Just . . . you know . . . things."

She doesn't have to say it out loud for me to know what she's talking about. She's talking about me. Us. I wish I had the luxury of keeping busy, but when I'm not at therapy or lightly working out, I'm sitting at my apartment, thinking of her. Wishing I could be with her.

I pierce my fork through some lettuce and chicken. "I know what you mean. I've been thinking about *things* every day."

She smiles softly. "Let me guess—the things you're thinking about are what you'd take if you were stranded on an island, right?" She attempts to lighten the heavy tone and it works.

"Yeah, that's it," I answer. "I can't decide between a machete and a beach towel."

She chuckles. "Obviously the beach towel for me. I'm not a survivor, I think we know that after getting my car stuck in a ditch, so might as well lay out the beach towel and enjoy the deserted island, hoping some cabana boy stumbles over me."

"Just like you stumbled into five hockey players?"

She points at me. "Exactly. Hey, maybe I'm the one with all the luck, not you."

"Nah, I've been feeling pretty lucky," I say, lifting my eyes so she knows I'm talking about her. When she smiles, I know I've been really fucking lucky, that's for damn sure.

"HEY," Winnie says, answering FaceTime. She's lying on her bed, stomach against the mattress, and she has some sort of facial mask on her face.

"I like the look. Green is really your color."

She chuckles and then "vogues" her face. "It's gorgeous, isn't it?"

The other day, she gave me a tour of her bedroom while we were talking. It's subtle, sweet, and totally Winnie. The only thing missing in it is me. I wanted to tell her that, but it still felt too soon. Although, I think I'm getting closer. We've FaceTimed every day this week, and yesterday, we spoke twice. I can feel my hard work paying off, and that the bond we built is not only still there, but stronger than ever. This has been the right thing to do for us. We really did launch into our *relationship* very quickly. It felt right at the time, but this time of learning, of *listening*, has been so helpful.

"Beautiful," I say, meaning it. "Why the mask, though? Your face is stunning."

She grins. "Why, thank you, but it's all about upkeep, Pacey. Start when you're young is what I say."

"Think I need some upkeep?"

She shakes her head. "Wrinkles are stupidly dignified on a man."

My eyes widen. "You think I have wrinkles?"

She laughs, but her mouth barely opens from the restriction of her face mask. "You have laugh lines at the outer corners of your eyes. They're sexy."

"Sexy?" I ask. "Tell me more about that."

She rolls her eyes. "No, I don't need your ego getting any bigger than it is."

"Trust me, babe, the ego is barely inflated these days."

She slowly smiles and then looks away.

"What's that smile for?" I ask.

She shrugs and then fiddles with her comforter. "Nothing really. You just called me babe, is all." Her eyes flash to the screen and my pulse picks up. I'm so fucking close; I can feel it. I'm right there. I'm winning her back.

"Should I have called you fart face instead?"

"What?" She roars with laughter. "Oh my God, what is wrong with you?"

I sigh. "Been hanging out with guys way too much lately. I need a feminine touch in my life."

"Keep FaceTiming me. I'll help you out."

And that's exactly what I wanted to hear.

—

"YOU'RE CHEATING," Winnie says, looking at her game board.

"How am I cheating?"

She looks behind her and then back at the phone. "I don't know. Are you in cahoots with Max or something?"

"He's not even in your room."

"Is there a hidden camera in here?" She looks around her room.

"You've been hanging out with Katherine too much. Just admit it, I'm amazing at Guess Who."

"Never," she says, chin held high.

I sent her Guess Who in the mail so we could play together, each having our own play sets. Every night we've been playing, that and Battleship. It's simple, but fuck, it's been the best week of my life . . . since Banff, of course.

"Does your person have glasses?"

"No," I answer.

"Damn it."

"Is your person Anita?"

She flips her board and says, "I hate you."

I laugh out loud and then stretch my hands over my head. "It's nice to congratulate your opponent."

Arms crossed over her chest, she asks, "Oh yeah? Is that what you do when you lose? Congratulate your opponents on the ice?"

She's got me there. "No, because the congrats I'd offer would be a fist to the gut."

"I don't know why I find that hot. I really shouldn't."

"Hot?" I ask, wiggling my brows.

Over the last week, Winnie has become more and more . . . open. I've clung to every word she says, every compliment, every teasing jab. It's as though we're back in Banff, but in fact, we're two and a half hours apart. And that's killing me.

"Yeah . . . hot."

Hell.

I wet my lips and I'm about to open my mouth, when she yawns.

"Sorry." She covers her mouth. "Been waking up early to work off all the tacos I've been eating. I'm exhausted."

"You're working out without me?"

She tilts her head to the side. "It's not a Pacey Lawes workout. It's just some light jogging around the neighborhood, but it's better than nothing."

"Sounds like fun to me."

"Of course it does. Any physical activity sounds fun to you." She yawns again.

"You're tired. I'll let you go," I say, even though I could stay on the phone with her all night.

"Okay." She rolls back on her bed and then curls to the side. She stares at me for a few beats and then says, "I miss you, Pacey."

And that right there, that's what I've been waiting for. That's what all this time between us has been about, getting her to realize that I'm not the asshole who broke her heart. That I'm the guy she met in Banff, the guy who's addicted to her, who wants to be with her, who misses her so goddamn much.

"I miss you, too, Winnie." I give her a soft smile. "Get some sleep. I'll talk to you tomorrow, okay?"

"Okay. Good night, Pacey."

"Good night, babe."

We hang up and I quickly pull up my text thread with the boys.

Pacey: *It's time.*

That's all I have to say. They'll understand. And as the texts roll in, I know from their response that they agree.

Hornsby: *Fuck yes.*

Taters: *Jesus Christ, about time.*

Posey: *Goodbye, blue balls.*

Holmes: *Go get her, man.*

Chapter Twenty-Nine

WINNIE

"Aren't you having a dinner date with Pacey tonight on FaceTime?" Max asks.

"Yeah, why?"

"Uh, don't you think you should at least put on a shirt that doesn't have a hole in the collar?"

My fingers graze my old shirt from middle school. "Do you think I need to?"

"Uh, yes. Standards, woman. Weren't you the one telling me how much you miss him this morning? How you wish you could see him? Well, not saying you need to make an effort with makeup, but a little class with the outfit couldn't hurt."

I chuckle. "If he truly likes me, then he won't mind this outfit." I bite the corner of my lip and say, "I told him I missed him last night."

"What?" Max sits up. "You did?"

I nod. "It just came out. I couldn't hold it back anymore. I really miss him. I want to be with him but I don't know how to cross the bridge. How to tell him that."

"Uh . . . you just tell him. Trust me, I think the boy would do a backflip on the spot if he knew you wanted to get back together. He's infatuated with you."

"Did he say that to you?"

"Yup," Max says. He picks up his phone and scrolls through it. "We've been chatting, you know. We're friends now. He's head over heels for you."

"Then . . . why hasn't he said that?"

Max shakes his head. "I love you, but you can be so oblivious."

"What do you mean?"

"What was one of your biggest fears when it came to Pacey?" When I don't answer, he says, "That it all happened so fast. Therefore, he knew to take his time. Let you adjust to talking to him, to your feelings. It's why he slowly started talking to you, taking it one step at a time. He didn't want to scare you. Looks as though it worked, because you're now craving him."

Stunned, I think back to how we started talking. Short, quick text conversations. They weren't in-depth, but they did show me he was still around, that he wasn't going anywhere. And then they grew into full conversations. Those text conversations grew into phone calls, which then turned into FaceTime dates every night.

"You're right."

"I know I'm right," he says. "Trust me, it's pained him. All he's wanted to do is see you, be with you, but as he told me, he didn't want to screw it up this time."

"I don't think he could screw it up."

"You can, though," Max says, his face still buried in his phone.

"How?"

He glances up at me. "Josh."

"What about him?" I ask.

"Uh, isn't that a loose end? I thought he was all about seeing you again."

I shake my head. "He texted me about two weeks ago, asking if he could see me again, and I shut him down. Told him I appreciated his apology and that I would cherish the good times we had, but that . . ." I swallow hard and stare at my nervous, shaking hands. "I told him I was in love with someone else."

Max's lips stretch up and curl in a satisfied, Grinch-like grin. "About time you admitted it." He goes back to his phone and waves at my shirt. "Go change. I refuse to let you have a Face-Time date in that thing."

He's probably right. It's a comfortable shirt, but let's ease Pacey into my holey clothes. I spin on my heel and head up the stairs to my bedroom, just as I remember about our food. "I put money on the counter for dinner," I call down. "Don't forget to tip."

"I forgot once, so sue me."

"And then we had to hear Katherine bitch and moan about how that delivery person would come back and murder us."

"True," Katherine says from her bedroom.

I reach my room and open my closet. I riffle through my clothes. I really don't feel like dressing up. Pacey is always dressed casually on our calls. Yes, his shirts cling to his chest like paint, but he's not wearing holey shirts.

The doorbell rings just as I reach for an emerald-green shirt.

"I got it," Max shouts.

I switch out of my holey shirt and put on the emerald-green, and then turn to my mirror on the back of my closet door to take in my reflection. I'm wearing sweatpants, but like every other Zoom call or FaceTime, the person on the other end of the call only sees waist up, so this will have to do. My hair is in a messy bun and I wonder if I should've done something with it today. Pacey has always liked braids.

But he's calling in five minutes and I don't really have any time to fix it, so instead, I fluff some of my hair out and call it a day.

He's seen me worse than this. Max is just getting in my head.

Content with how I look, I head for the door so I can run downstairs and grab my food. Then I'll have just enough time to make it back up here for our date. I swing open the door and almost run face-first into a bouquet of beautiful purple flowers.

The bouquet lowers, and Pacey's handsome face comes into view.

My jaw drops, and my hand covers my mouth. "Pacey," I whisper.

"Hey, baby," he says and then holds the bouquet out to me. "I owe you some flowers, since the last ones I bought you I threw against a wall."

I let out a nervous chuckle as my shaky hands take the bouquet. "Th-thank you." I sniff them and then look back at him. Those glacial eyes sear me, his smile destroys me, and I itch to hold him, to have him hold me. "You're . . . here. In my house."

"I am." He sticks his hands in his jean pockets and says, "I hope that's okay." There's a hint of vulnerability in his voice, and I want nothing more than to wash away that vulnerability.

Taking a leap of faith, I step toward him and curl against his chest, my arm snaking around his waist. Automatically, his arms wrap around me, and he kisses the top of my head.

"Hey, you," he says quietly, and that sweet greeting destroys me. My eyes well with tears and I press myself into his embrace, listening to the rhythm of his heart, soaking in this moment.

He's here.

He's mine.

He's everything I need.

"I missed you," I say as a tear moves down my cheek. I don't bother wiping it away because I don't want to let go of him.

"I missed you, babe." He kisses the top of my head again.

I look up at him and I smile. "I'm sorry, Pacey. I'm sorry for everything."

His finger goes to my lips. "You don't need to apologize. I'm the one who should be sorry."

I shake my head. "I should've told you about Josh. I was nervous. I didn't know what to make of it, but I want you to know, he texted me two weeks ago and I told him that whatever we had was over because . . ." I swallow and look away.

"Because why?" Pacey asks, his fingers forcing my chin up so he can look me in the eyes.

I set the flowers on my bed and then take his hands in mine. "Because I quickly realized, once you were no longer in my life, that I was missing this huge puzzle piece that had made me feel whole again for the first time since my mom died, and that was you." My eyes stay locked on his as I say, "I told him I was in love with someone else."

I watch as Pacey's Adam's apple bobs up and down. His hand reaches up and grips my cheek. "I love you so fucking much, Winnie. I want to kiss you every goddamn minute of every day. I want to be able to hold your hand whenever I fucking want. I want to be able to hear your laugh in person, hold you at night, be the man you deserve."

"You are," I say. "You're everything I've ever wanted and so much more. I love you, Pacey, and I don't want there to be distance between us anymore."

He sighs and lowers his forehead until it presses against mine. "Fuck, I've missed you so much. I love you, Winnie. I want to make this work. I have to make this work. And I swear, I'll do everything in my power to make sure you're happy and that you never have to deal with a broken heart ever again."

More tears stream down my face. "I believe that you will." I tilt his head up just enough so that my lips meet his. His grip slides against the back of my head and intensifies as I smooth my hand up his chest.

He backs me up until I reach my bed and then, making sure

he doesn't crush my flowers, he lays me back and crawls over top of me, propping his body up with one hand as he stares down at me.

"You're mine, Winnie."

I rub my thumb over his cheek. "I'm yours."

Then his mouth descends on mine and I get lost in his lips, in his kisses, in the way he so commands me. *Loves* me.

I was searching for adventure, for justice when I took Minnie on a road trip, and I came back with the love of my life. There's no doubt in my mind that my mom was on that road trip as well, directing me, pushing me, pointing an arrow at where I needed to go. Because if anything, she believed in love, and more than anything, that's all she wanted for me.

To love.

Epilogue

WINNIE

"Are you sure you're okay?" I ask Pacey.

"Jesus, woman," Max says as he huffs behind me. "The man is made of muscle. He's fine."

"He shouldn't be lifting too much because of his neck."

"Babe, this tree is like thirty pounds. I can handle it," Pacey says with ease as he walks next to me.

"Winnie, where is the pocketknife I gave you?" Katherine asks as she turns around to look at me. The girl is not only wearing every reflective shield you could buy, but she also has a backpack full of wasp spray, bear spray, tasers, knives, and one of those crinkly blankets for God knows what reason. According to her, you never can be too sure who you'll run into in the middle of the park. When I told her it was the middle of the day, she told me people aren't safe during the day just because they believe they are. I honestly can't with her.

"It's in my pocket, and I wouldn't call the dagger you gave

me a pocketknife. Pocketknives usually have other tools on them. What you gave me is a switchblade."

"And you'll be glad I did when you're attacked. But you need to hold it in your hand."

"I'm not walking around a family-friendly park with a freaking switchblade in my hand."

"Katherine, please, you said you wouldn't ruin this experience with your neuroses," Max says.

"All I'm saying is we have to watch each other's sixes."

Leaning in toward me, Pacey says, "You should put a child lock on her Netflix account so she can't watch those crime shows anymore."

"And that's why I love you, for smart ideas like that."

"Ah, come on, you love me for more reasons than that," Pacey says with a wink.

And boy oh boy, is he right.

After he surprised me, we rented a hotel room for the weekend because there was no way I would've been able to keep quiet for Max and Katherine, not with the way Pacey worshipped my body. The man was bound and determined to make me come at least—in his words—twenty times. Not sure if he did or not, I lost count. But I've never been so satisfied. Nor have I been fucked in so many different ways. And then, to top it off, we made love as well, slow, passionate love. And it was . . . God, it was everything I could've asked for.

Now, while it's the off-season, we're splitting time between Vancouver and Seattle, spending more time with Max and Katherine, because once the season starts, I'll be moving to Vancouver to be with my man. Thank God for an online, remote job.

Max isn't thrilled, especially since he'll be stuck with Katherine, but I know a small part of him enjoys her crazy. It thrills him, gives him something to laugh about.

"Is this the spot?" Max asks, as he points to a concealed alcove in the trail.

"That's it," I say.

It's taken me longer than I preferred to plant my mom's tree, but I also didn't want to do it when I wasn't in the right headspace.

Now that I'm here with my people—including Pacey—this could not be more perfect.

This is how Mom would've wanted it, a day full of love. *Without the switchblades perhaps.*

"Right over here," I say, directing everyone. I find the rock Mom loved sitting on and place the trophy on it while Max sets down a shovel and Pacey gently puts the tree on the ground. Lucky for me, Uncle RJ never sent the cops after me for theft of the trophy, nor did he say anything. I think he knew . . . it was something I needed to do for Mom. And strangely, I appreciate that.

Pacey grips my hand in his and looks around. "This place is beautiful. I can see why your mom liked it so much."

Katherine swats at the bushes and then says, "All clear. No perverts lurking."

"I'm sure my mom would be grateful for that," I say with a laugh.

"You never know with the granolas out here in Seattle. People love walking around in the nude behind bushes."

Max presses his hand to his forehead. "Where the hell do you get your information from?"

Chuckling, Pacey presses a kiss to my head and asks, "Are you ready for this?"

"I am."

He picks up the shovel and asks, "Want to do it together?"

"I don't think Mom would want it any other way."

Printed in the USA
CPSIA information can be obtained
at www.ICGtesting.com
CBHW071001160724
11662CB00006B/67